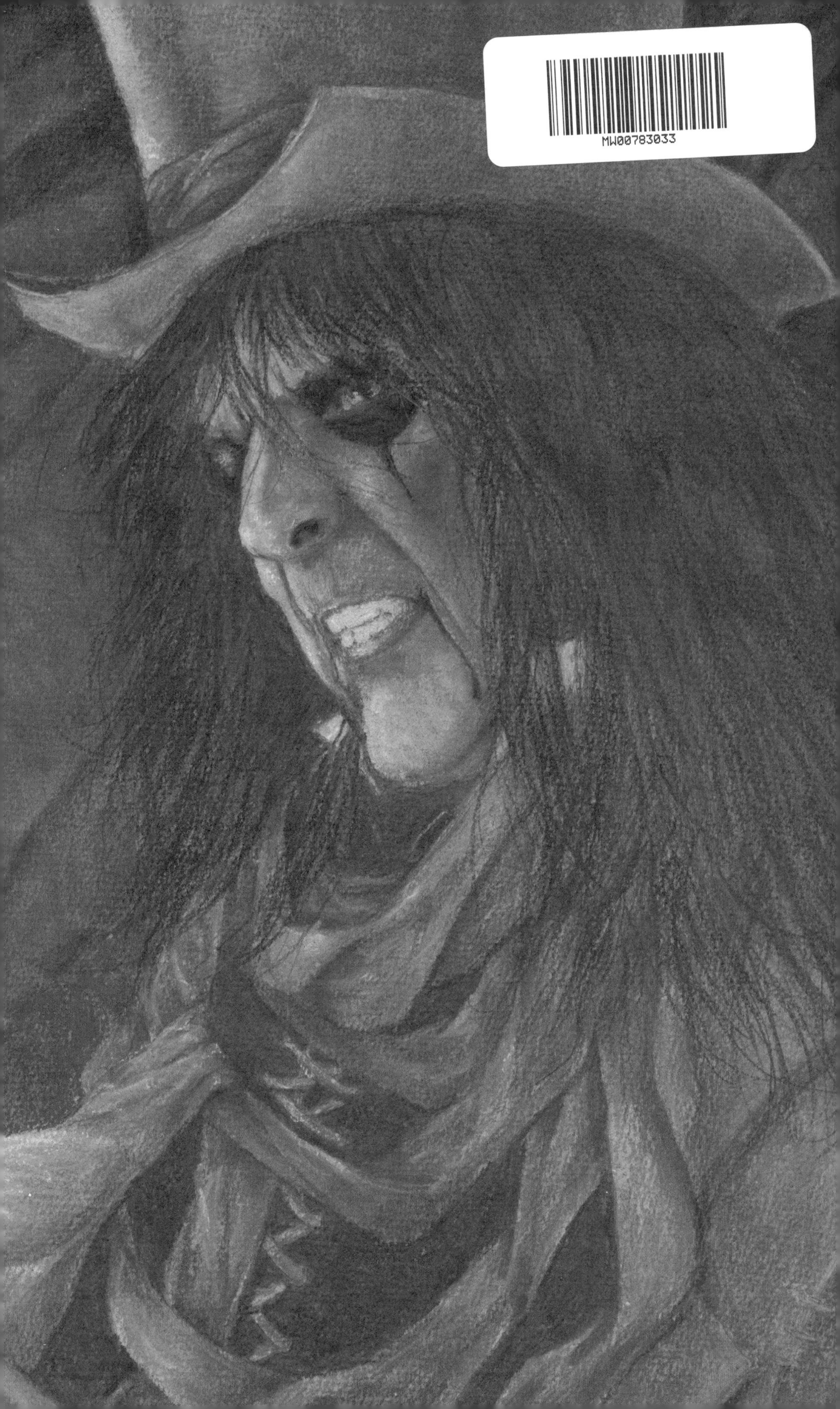

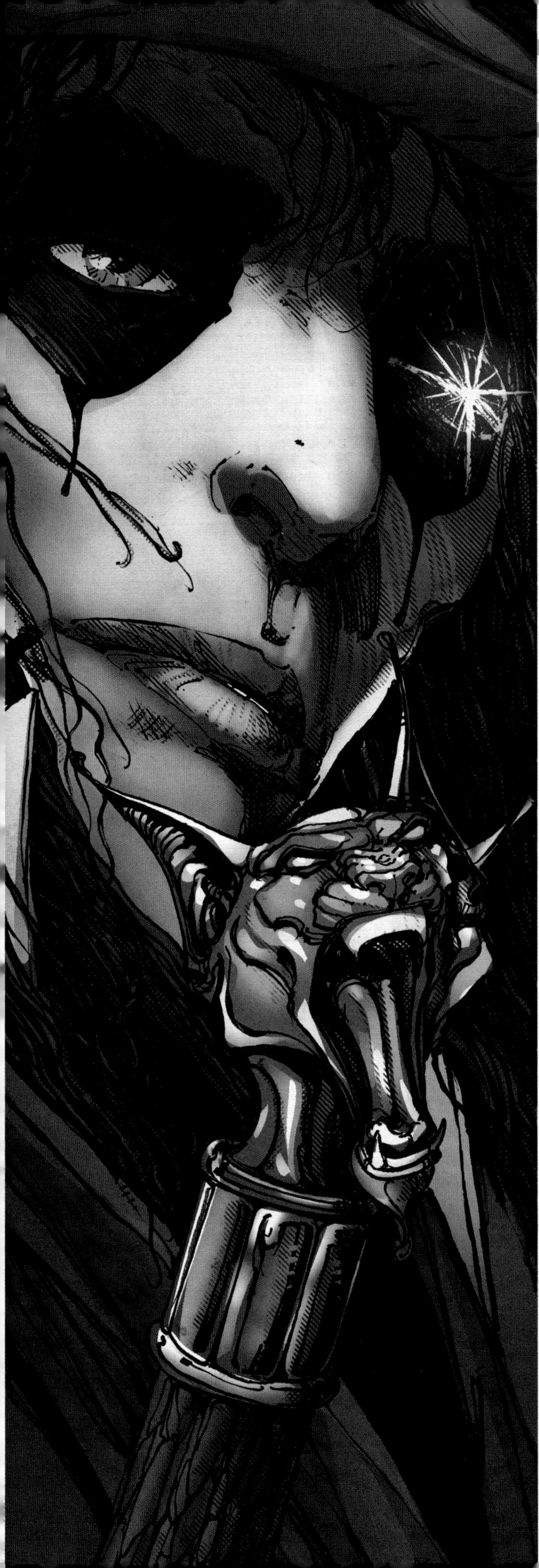

SUCH A FEAST OF MARVELS YOUR EYES SHALL BEHOLD

SUCH A TERPSICHOREAN ARRAY OF SHEER AND UNUTTERABLE DELIGHT

WHEN YOUVE BECOME THE THING THAT SCARES

editor **HANNAH ELDER**
original series editor **MORT TODD**
book cover **DAVE McKEAN**
book design **JASON ULLMEYER**

DYNAMITE®

Nick Barrucci, CEO / Publisher
Juan Collado, President / COO
Rich Young, Director Business Development
Keith Davidsen, Marketing Manager

Joe Rybandt, Senior Editor
Hannah Elder, Associate Editor
Molly Mahan, Associate Editor

Josh Johnson, Art Director
Jason Ullmeyer, Design Director
Katie Hidalgo, Graphic Designer
Chris Caniano, Production Assistant

Visit us online at **www.DYNAMITE.com**
Follow us on Twitter **@dynamitecomics**
Like us on Facebook **/Dynamitecomics**

Regular Edition: ISBN-10: 1-60690-536-8   ISBN-13: 978-1-60690-536-4
Signed Edition: ISBN-10: 1-60690-544-9   ISBN-13: 978-1-60690-544-9
First Printing 10 9 8 7 6 5 4 3 2 1

writer **NEIL GAIMAN**
artist **MICHAEL ZULLI**

letters **TODD KLEIN**
original colors **JOHN KALISZ** and **BERNIE MIREAULT**
remastered colors **DAVID CURIEL** of **INLIGHT STUDIOS**
based on a story by **NEIL GAIMAN** and **ALICE COOPER**

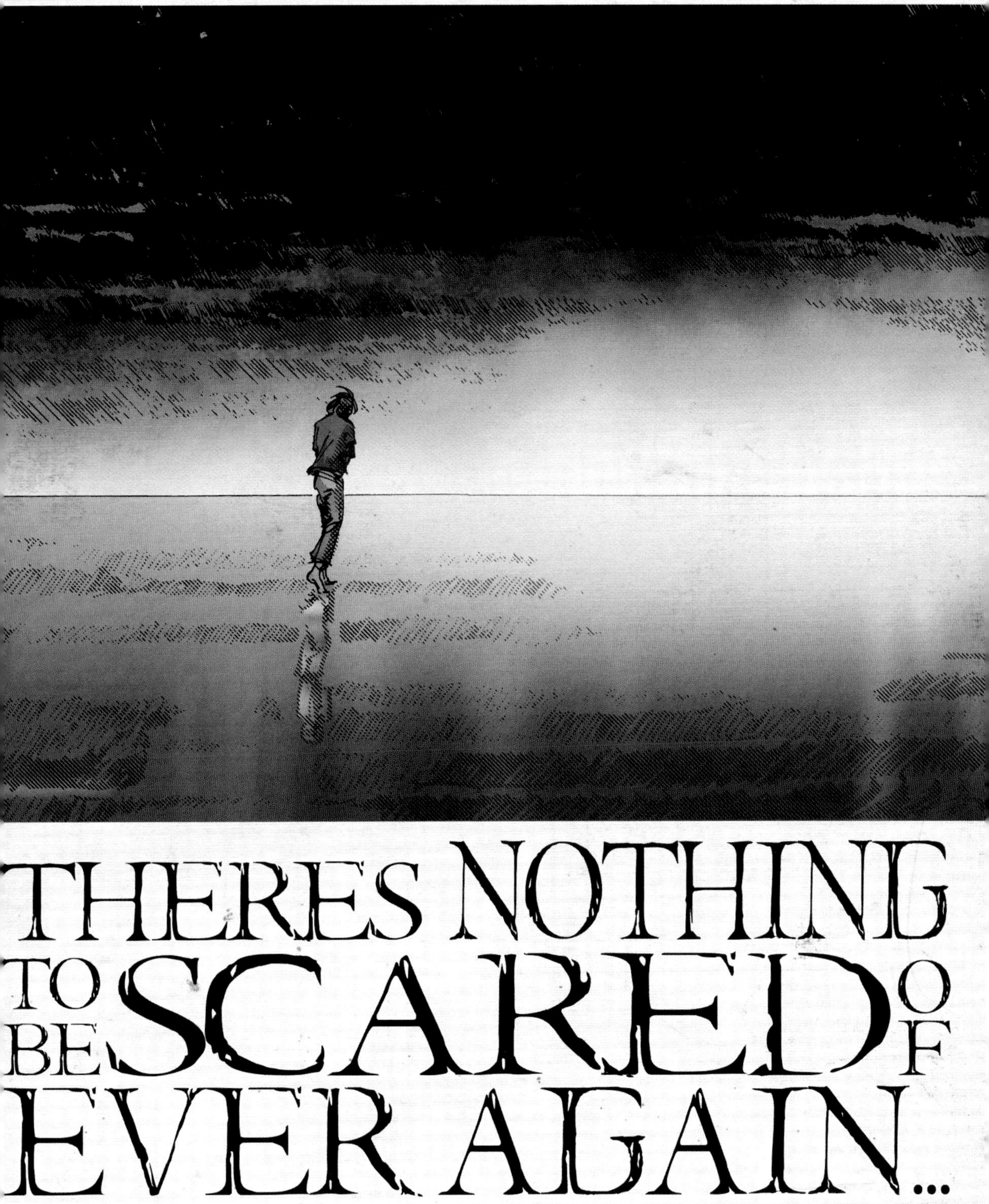

THERES NOTHING TO BE SCARED OF EVER AGAIN...

NEIL'S DEDICATION

This book is for the remarkable Cindy Shapiro, who worked hard and long, and over and above, on the project, all those years ago, and for Jack Wall, and for Grace, who is more than old enough.

MICHAEL'S DEDICATION

To Big Steve K. and to Alice, who have walked the walk. And to all the little Stevens out there ... there is no Mercy.

TABLE OF CONTENTS

INTRODUCTION
BY NEL GAIMAN

It seems only natural that the House of Wax is next to the graveyard.

It's cold and dark, and a low mist smudges the light of the gas lamps that flicker unreliably outside the House of Wax. You walk though the graveyard, thick clay sticking to your bools, weighing you down.

The House of Wax is a huge tent, made of thin brown leather which hangs lifelessly in the windless mist. You walk through the entrance, muddy boots rustling through dead leaves.

The mist curls and writhes in the corner of the tent. You step back, nervously.

"You've come to see the sideshow," says a voice from behind you.

"I have?"

"Of course you have."

You turn and look at the man. His clothes were once elegant, but are now shiny and frayed at the edges. His hair is long and black, his face thin, his eyes set deep in his head. He raises his top hat to you, and grins like a wolf.

He gestures with his stick. A hundred candles burst into flame, illuminating a bad place.

Wax statues stand in the tent, each on its own raised pedestal.

The Showman walks you over to a statue. He runs a finger down its spangled side.

The life-sized wax figure is clasping a microphone. It is a rock-and-roll star, black make-up outlining its eyes and mouth. The sign next to it reads ALICE COOPER.

"He looks like you," you tell the Showman.

"There's a certain family resemblance," he admits.

You walk past a wax statue of an artist, a tall man with mustachios and beard that Dali might have envied, painting at an easel. The word ZULLI is painted, carefully, on his back.

Next to him is a wax statue of a man wearing a leather jacket and dark glasses. He has dark hair, and black jeans. He is holding a placard with the word WRITER on it.

"Do you want to hear what he has to say?" asks the Showman.

You shrug. There's a rustling at the edge of the tent; you dart a glance, but see nothing other than wax statues frozen in awkward poses.

The Showman takes a tarnished silver coin from his pocket, and forces it between the lips of the statue. "That's the motto of the lot," he tells you, his voice little more than a whisper. "Put a penny in the slot."

The statue of the writer moves, mechanically. A hand raises, in slow, jerking movements. A head tilts. The lips part, revealing no sign of the coin the showman placed between them.

It begins to talk to us.

I was sitting in my study in England, almost a decade of years ago, when the phone rang. I answered it. I like answering the phone.

"This is Bob Pfeifer. That's P-f-e-i-one-f-e-r. I'm from Epic Records in Los Angeles," he said.

"Hello," I said. I couldn't think why someone from a record company would be calling me. It was, I supposed, vaguely conceivable, that someone had taped me singing in the shower; that a bootleg — The Gaiman Shower Tapes — had been released without my knowledge; it was even conceivable such tapes had made it across the Atlantic all the way to LA. It was slightly more likely that I'd been elected Prime Minister of Lichtenstein and no one had told me.

"Yeah. Anyway. One of my artists is a big fan of yours. Well, we're all big fans of yours. Sandman, all that. My assistant, Jason, he's a huge fan of yours."

"That's nice."

"Yeah. So, like I say. This artist I was talking about. He's going to make a concept album."

"And?"

"Well, we were wondering if you could work with the artist on the concept. Are you interested?"

"Who are we talking about here?"

"Well, that's kind of confidential. But it's Alice Cooper."

Alice Cooper?

I liked Alice Cooper. I liked School's Out and Billion Dollar Babies and Teenage Lament '74. I thought Welcome to My Nightmare was one of the great rock-and-roll records. I thought Trash was a remarkable come-back album.

My head swam with snakes and

swords, top hats and black-rimmed eyes.

"Maybe," I said. "I'd like to meet him first."

Wayne's World had been out a week when I met Alice Cooper, although I hadn't seen it, and knew nothing about it.

I sat in the hotel restaurant with Bob Pfeifer, who is younger and funnier and lankier than he sounds on the phone, and is always magnificently stressed-out. We were in Phoenix, Arizona.

"There he is," said Bob, pointing out of the restaurant window, at a tall man climbing out of a sports car. White t-shirt, blue jeans, long black hair.

Heads turned as he came into the restaurant.

Alice Cooper in person is tall, shaggy, suntanned. His eyes are sharp and good-humoured and alive. He knows more about bad Italian horror movies than anyone who doesn't write books about them for a living.

We ate sandwiches then went up to my hotel room to talk. On the way out of the restaurant a couple ran over to Alice and threw themselves onto their knees.

"We're not worthy," they wailed.

He took it pleasantly. When I asked him about it, he explained that this was but a small token of the respect he was shown in Phoenix; later he admitted that it was from a new movie called *Wayne's World*.

Every time I've seen Alice in public since then, someone has come over to him, bowed low, said "We're not worthy." Every time he has treated them with good humour, nodded, smiled, and bowed back.

In the hotel room we talked about horror fiction, about stories, about what we'd like to do with the story of the album. We talked about the *Grand Guignol*, the French theatre of blood and horror, popular in the early years of this century. We talked about bad Italian Horror movies. We talked about the story of Faust.

Alice Cooper sometimes talked about Alice Cooper in the third person. "Alice wouldn't do that," he explained.

I learned there were two Alice Coopers, the person and the icon.

I found this very comfortable: Alice Cooper the person was his own affair; Alice Cooper the character was something else again. He's larger than life. He's theatre.

Alice Cooper is a horror icon. He's up there with Larry Talbot, and Count Dracula, with Jason and Freddie. Alice Cooper is hung

and guillotined; Alice writhes with snakes and flees the madhouse. He was even the star of his own Marvel comic.

I liked Alice the person enormously. And I liked the idea of creating a story with Alice the character — something that could be used to build an album or a stage show.

Somewhere in there things changed. We were no longer feeling each other out, deciding whether or not we wanted to work together. We *were* working together.

I suggested a few ideas to him. He liked some of them, wasn't as keen on others. We talked about the feel we wanted, the shape, the characters.

I went home to England, talked with Alice some more on the phone, and began to write the story we seemed to be evolving. It was the tale of a boy named Steven, and a strange theatre, and a Showman with a strange resemblance to Alice Cooper — part Machiavellian ghost, part commentator, part demon. It was the story of a deal Steven is offered; of a theatrical performance he attends; of his parents, his school friends, his teachers, and, ultimately, his temptation.

The story wasn't a story I would have come up with alone: it was too clear-cut. God was looking out for the innocent, and the serpent was always looking for a way into your heart. But it was a good story, and it worked.

The next time I saw Alice six months had passed, and we were back in the same hotel in Phoenix. We sat in Bob Pfeifer's hotel room and I listened to tapes of the first few songs they'd written, and I watched Alice and his collaborators write another three songs — while I sat on a bed, occasionally making suggestions for lyrics and song titles.

A lightning storm came in from the desert, and we sat outside on the hotel balcony and watched the storm buffet the eucalyptus trees, while Alice told us about The Time He Met Elvis. Linda Lovelace was in the story, and karate, and guns.

Another few months went by, and now I was in a recording studio in Los Angeles, listening to them record *Lost In America*.

It's odd: one minute it was just a plot in my head, the next it's an honest-to-goodness rock-and-roll concept album. Real musicians. Real Alice Cooper. Dave McKean even agreed to do the album cover.

I'm not sure when it was suggested, or by whom, that we should do a comic.

It wasn't a hard decision to make,

though. I found the idea challenging. Rock stars have been cropping up in comics for decades — Kiss emptied their veins into the first printing of their comic, or so we were told, and Jimmy Olsen, if I remember correctly, was the Stone-Age Beatle of 30,000 B.C. But the comics on the whole (we might as well be honest here, just between ourselves) weren't terribly good. And I didn't see why there *couldn't* be a good rock comic.

There were chunks of plot that hadn't made it onto the album, after all. It would be good to get it all down.

Michael Zulli, Salvador Dali look-alike, artist and co-creator of ecological SF series *Puma Blues*, author of by far the strangest and darkest interpretation of the *Teenage Mutant Ninja Turtles*; occasional interpreter, with me, of *The Sandman*, and my partner in crime in the mysteriously lost *Sweeney Todd, The Demon Barber of Fleet Street*, is one of the most fascinating, grimmest and delightful artists in the business, and would be the perfect artist for the project — if he was interested.

I called him, and he was.

The award-winning Todd Klein was willing to letter the comic.

And the album came out, and the comic came out, and Alice and I stumbled around Europe promoting it. I fulfilled a childhood dream and found myself backstage on BBC TV's *Top of the Pops*, as Alice and the band performed *Lost in America* in front of a 20 foot high reproduction of Michael's double-page splash from part one. We were treated a little like kings in Germany, and a little like gods in Scandinavia.

The reviews were good — people as diverse as the rock critics of the *Times* of London and of *Rolling Stone* proclaimed it Alice's finest album in fifteen years. And it sold pretty well too — it charted all over the world, and continues to sell in respectable numbers to this day.

As for the comic, I wanted to create something that was, essentially, the comics equivalent of several pop singles: nothing too deep, nothing too ambiguous. A campfire tale, that was what I wanted it to be. A comic to read with the album playing in the background. A comic for when the leaves begin to crisp and fall. Light reading for what Ray Bradbury called the October Country.

The wax statue of the writer smiles, nods, closes its mouth and, mechanically, returns to the position it was in to begin with. Its skin has the sheen of old wax, or of a fresh corpse.

The Showman turns to you.

There's something feral in his smile, something wolf-like in his eyes.

"Is there anything else you need to know?" he asks.

You shake your head, nervously, and begin to back away through the tent and the wax people. You would feel far more comfortable back in the graveyard, of that you have no doubt at all.

The Showman gestures.

One by one the candles that illuminate the tent flicker and go out, casting strange shadows across the inside of the tent as they die, shadows that make the wax figures seem to move, to clamber down from their pedestals, to walk towards you.

You aren't moving. You are frozen in place. You can't look away.

"Don't go," says the Showman. "We've got other things to show you." He is fumbling with one gloved hand at the side of his face. "Look."

His face comes away, as if it's hinged, revealing a skull the yellow of old ivory. A tiny snake, the green of a fresh-cut emerald, writhes in an empty eye-socket.

It hisses at you, and bares its fangs.

The spell is broken. You can move once more: you take a step back, then begin to run, looking around frantically for the way out. Somewhere there must be a way out...

You're all alone.

The rustling gets louder now. It seems to come from all around you.

And then the last candle goes out.

Neil Gaiman
1995

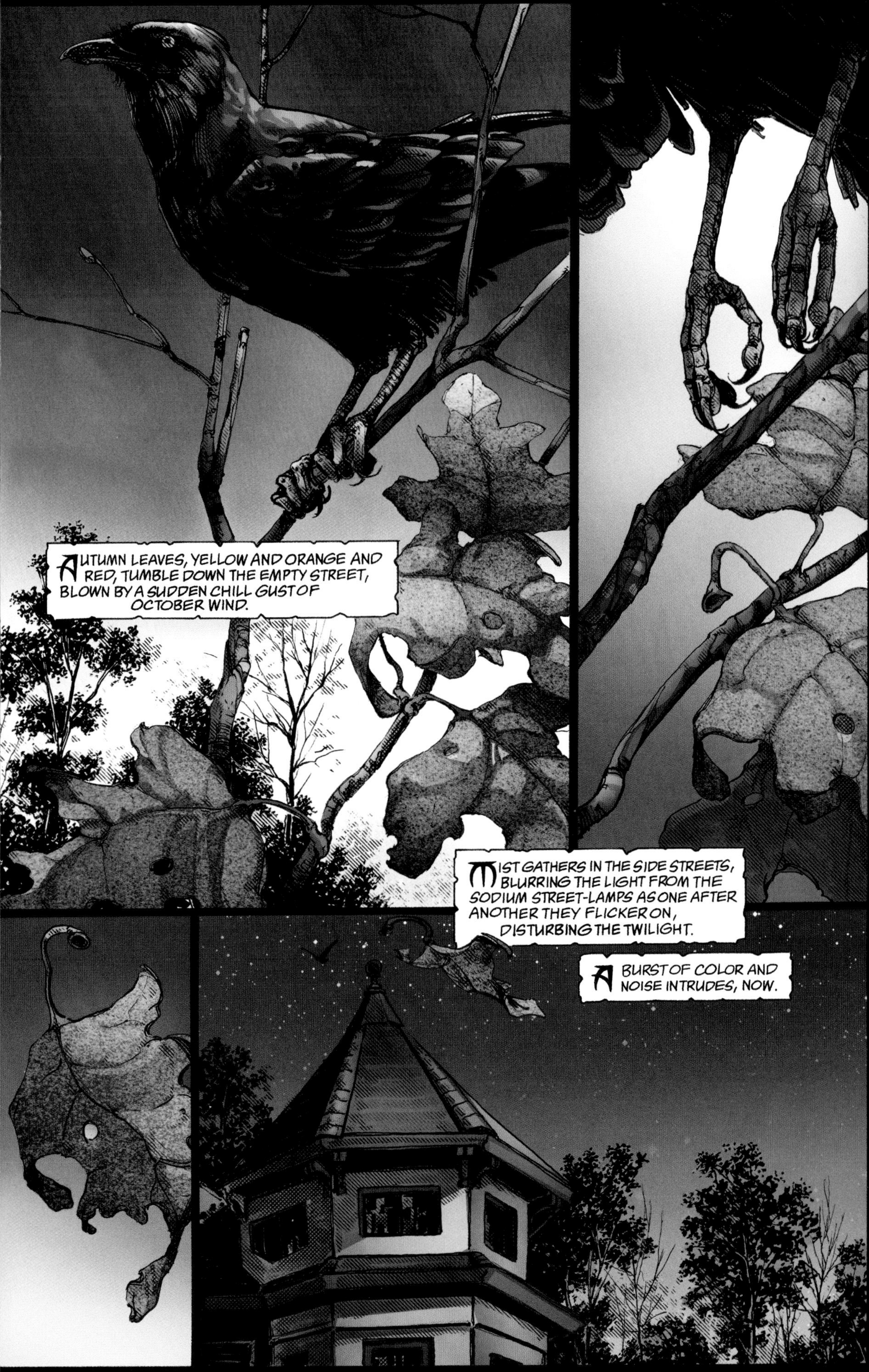
AUTUMN LEAVES, YELLOW AND ORANGE AND RED, TUMBLE DOWN THE EMPTY STREET, BLOWN BY A SUDDEN CHILL GUST OF OCTOBER WIND.
MIST GATHERS IN THE SIDE STREETS, BLURRING THE LIGHT FROM THE SODIUM STREET-LAMPS AS ONE AFTER ANOTHER THEY FLICKER ON, DISTURBING THE TWILIGHT.
A BURST OF COLOR AND NOISE INTRUDES, NOW.

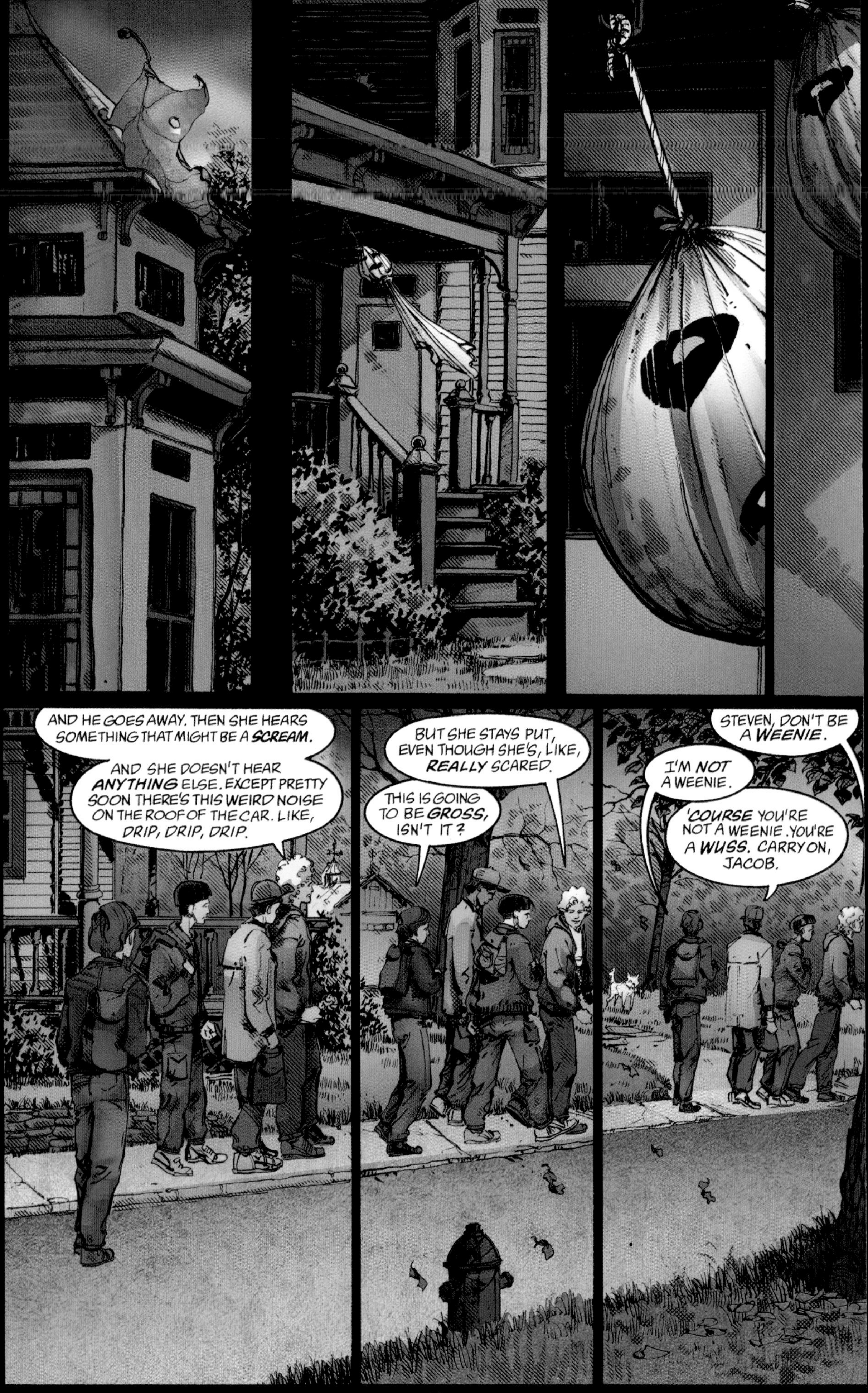
AND HE GOES AWAY. THEN SHE HEARS SOMETHING THAT MIGHT BE A SCREAM.
AND SHE DOESN'T HEAR ANYTHING ELSE. EXCEPT PRETTY SOON THERE'S THIS WEIRD NOISE ON THE ROOF OF THE CAR. LIKE, DRIP, DRIP, DRIP.
BUT SHE STAYS PUT, EVEN THOUGH SHE'S, LIKE, REALLY SCARED.
THIS IS GOING TO BE GROSS, ISN'T IT?
STEVEN, DON'T BE A WEENIE.
I'M NOT A WEENIE.
'COURSE YOU'RE NOT A WEENIE. YOU'RE A WUSS. CARRY ON, JACOB.

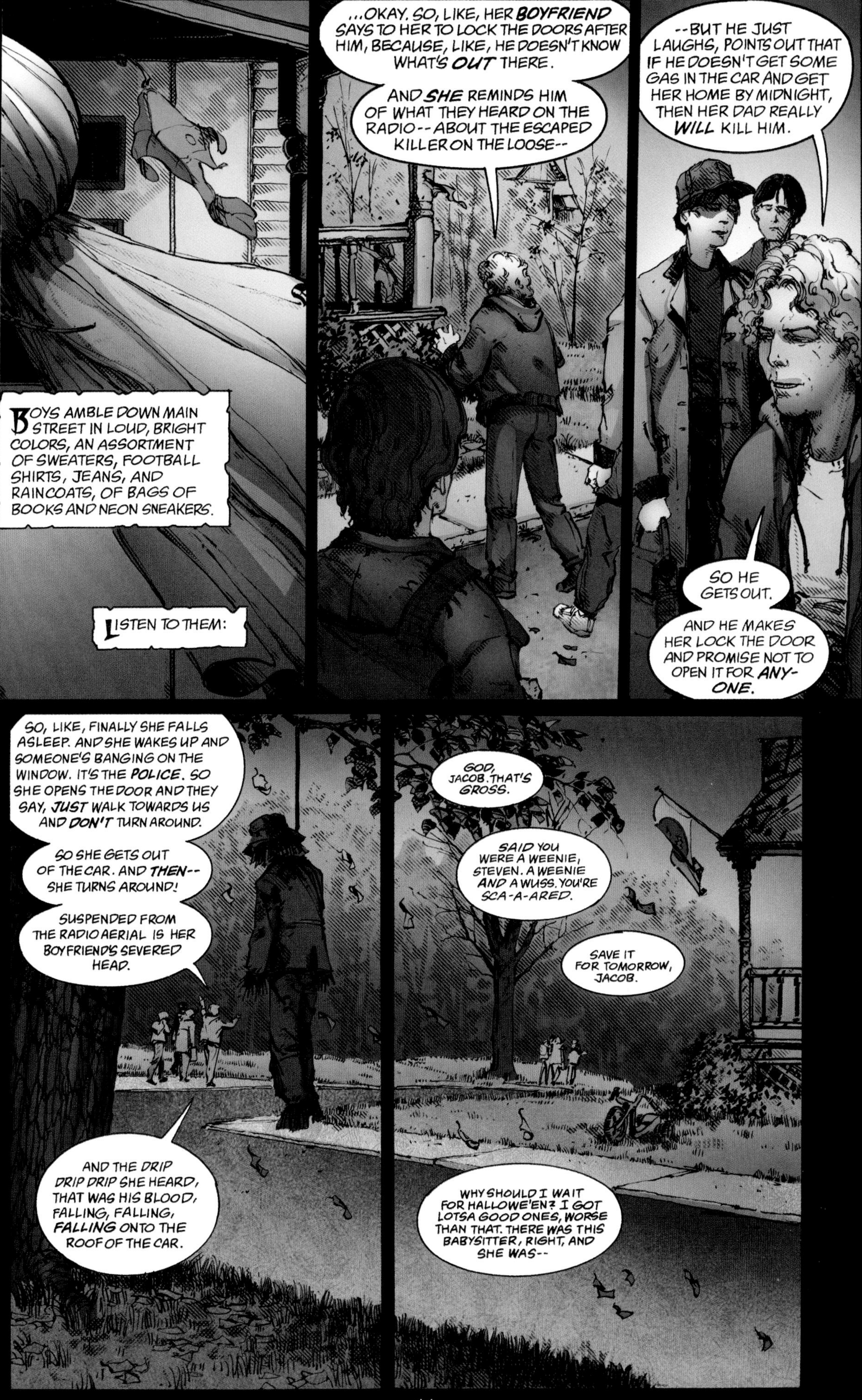
BOYS AMBLE DOWN MAIN STREET IN LOUD, BRIGHT COLORS, AN ASSORTMENT OF SWEATERS, FOOTBALL SHIRTS, JEANS, AND RAINCOATS, OF BAGS OF BOOKS AND NEON SNEAKERS.
LISTEN TO THEM:
...OKAY. SO, LIKE, HER BOYFRIEND SAYS TO HER TO LOCK THE DOORS AFTER HIM, BECAUSE, LIKE, HE DOESN'T KNOW WHAT'S OUT THERE.
AND SHE REMINDS HIM OF WHAT THEY HEARD ON THE RADIO--ABOUT THE ESCAPED KILLER ON THE LOOSE--
--BUT HE JUST LAUGHS, POINTS OUT THAT IF HE DOESN'T GET SOME GAS IN THE CAR AND GET HER HOME BY MIDNIGHT, THEN HER DAD REALLY WILL KILL HIM.
SO HE GETS OUT.
AND HE MAKES HER LOCK THE DOOR AND PROMISE NOT TO OPEN IT FOR ANY-ONE.
SO, LIKE, FINALLY SHE FALLS ASLEEP. AND SHE WAKES UP AND SOMEONE'S BANGING ON THE WINDOW. IT'S THE POLICE. SO SHE OPENS THE DOOR AND THEY SAY, JUST WALK TOWARDS US AND DON'T TURN AROUND.
SO SHE GETS OUT OF THE CAR. AND THEN--SHE TURNS AROUND!
SUSPENDED FROM THE RADIO AERIAL IS HER BOYFRIEND'S SEVERED HEAD.
AND THE DRIP DRIP DRIP SHE HEARD, THAT WAS HIS BLOOD, FALLING, FALLING, FALLING ONTO THE ROOF OF THE CAR.
GOD, JACOB. THAT'S GROSS.
SAID YOU WERE A WEENIE, STEVEN. A WEENIE AND A WUSS. YOU'RE SCA-A-ARED.
SAVE IT FOR TOMORROW, JACOB.
WHY SHOULD I WAIT FOR HALLOWE'EN? I GOT LOTSA GOOD ONES, WORSE THAN THAT. THERE WAS THIS BABYSITTER, RIGHT, AND SHE WAS--

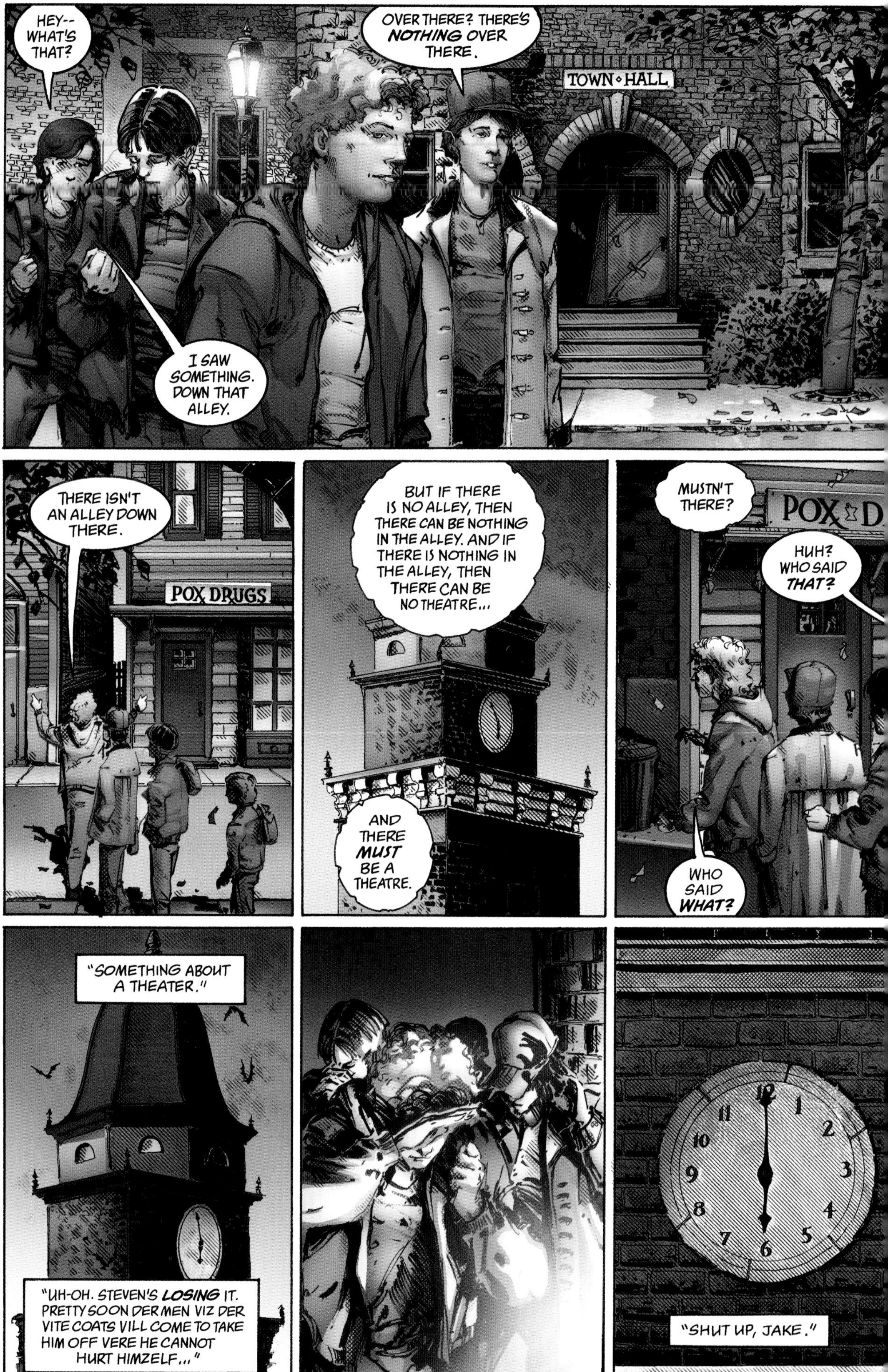
HEY-- WHAT'S THAT?
OVER THERE? THERE'S NOTHING OVER THERE.
TOWN HALL
I SAW SOMETHING. DOWN THAT ALLEY.
THERE ISN'T AN ALLEY DOWN THERE.
POX DRUGS
BUT IF THERE IS NO ALLEY, THEN THERE CAN BE NOTHING IN THE ALLEY. AND IF THERE IS NOTHING IN THE ALLEY, THEN THERE CAN BE NO THEATRE...
AND THERE MUST BE A THEATRE.
MUSTN'T THERE?
HUH? WHO SAID THAT?
WHO SAID WHAT?
"SOMETHING ABOUT A THEATER."
"UH-OH. STEVEN'S LOSING IT. PRETTY SOON DER MEN VIZ DER VITE COATS VILL COME TO TAKE HIM OFF VERE HE CANNOT HURT HIMZELF..."
"SHUT UP, JAKE."

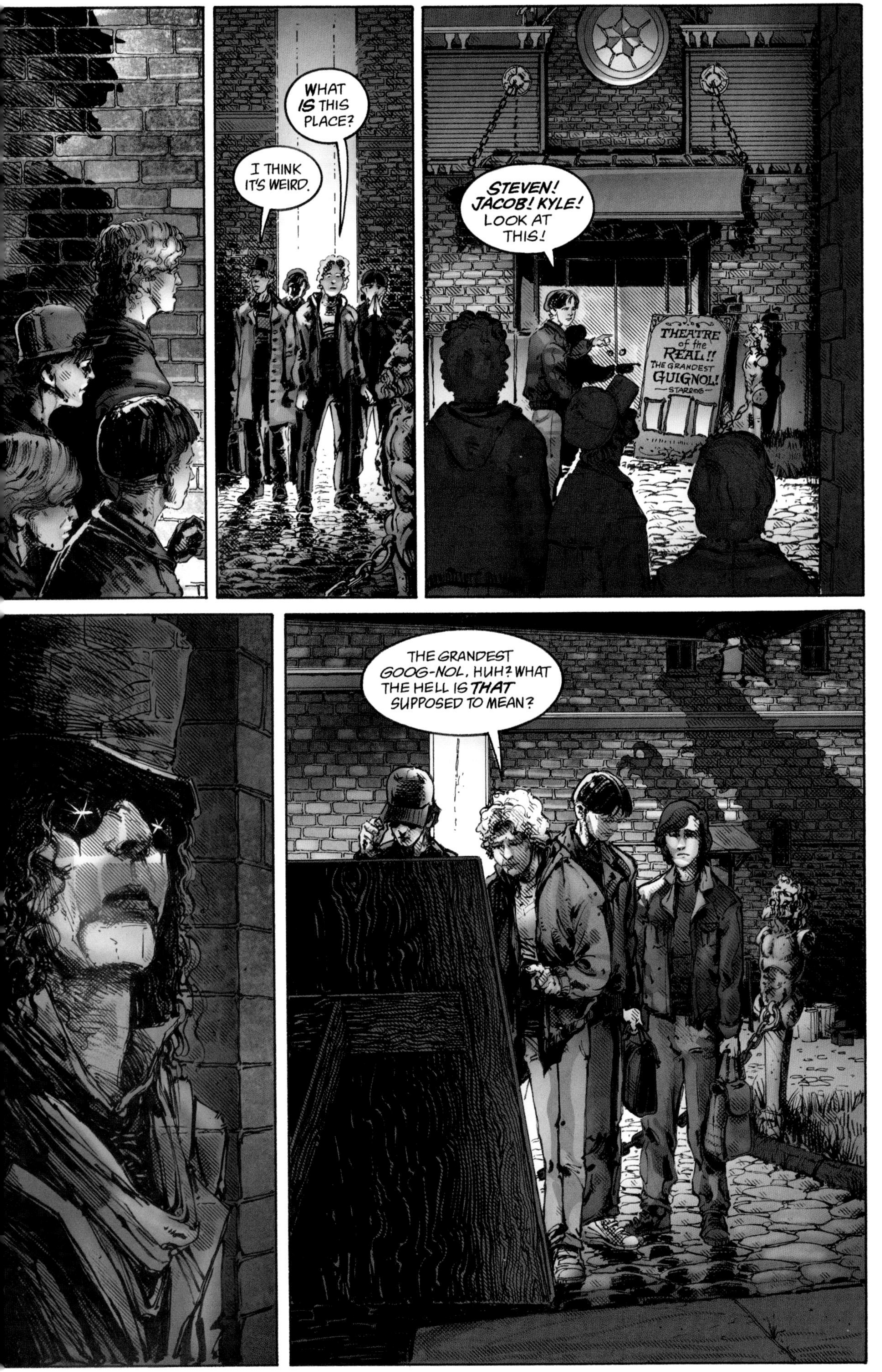
WHAT IS THIS PLACE?
I THINK IT'S WEIRD.
STEVEN! JACOB! KYLE! LOOK AT THIS!
THEATRE of the REAL!! THE GRANDEST GUIGNOL! —STARRING—
THE GRANDEST GOOG-NOL, HUH? WHAT THE HELL IS THAT SUPPOSED TO MEAN?

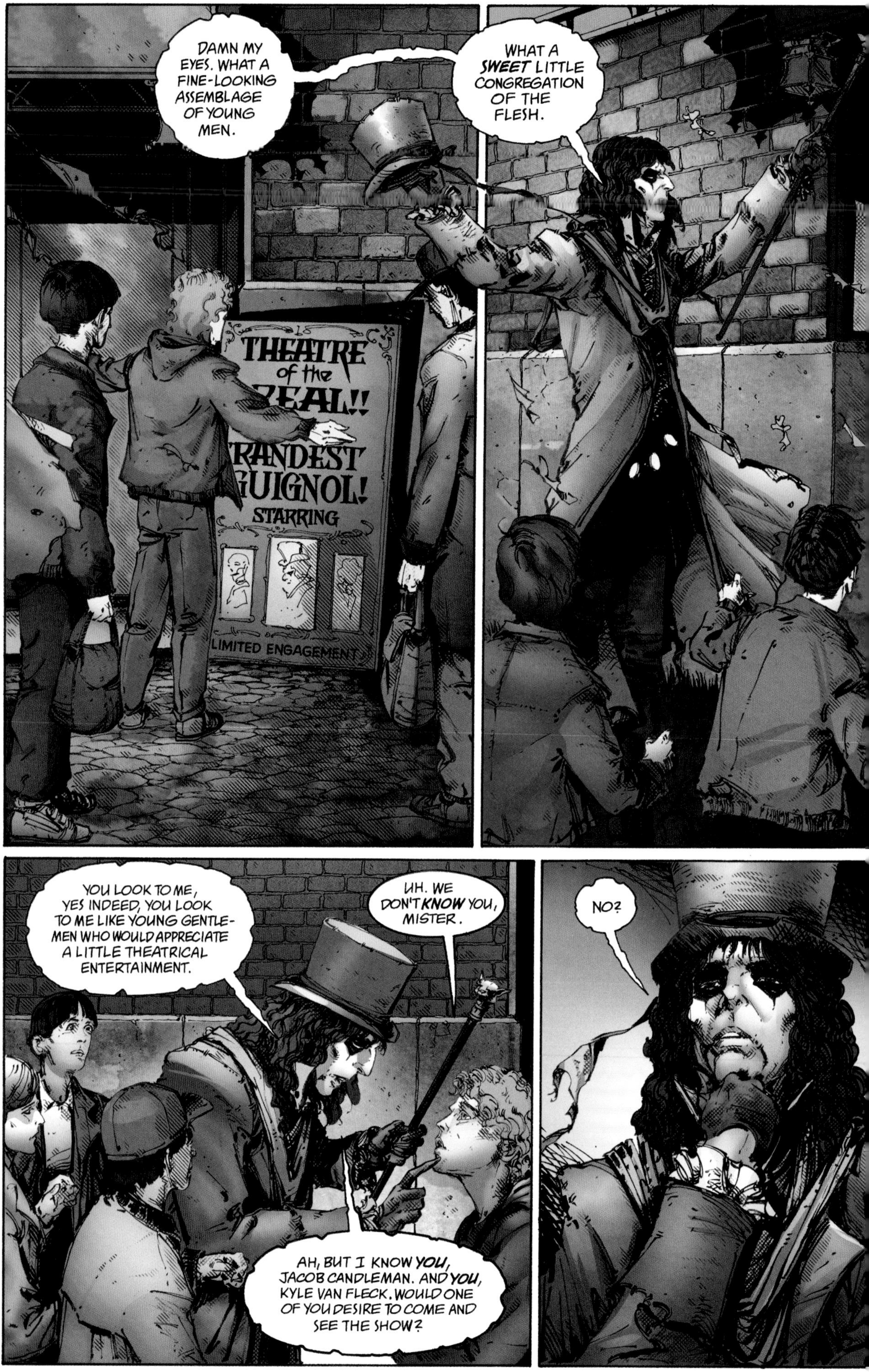
DAMN MY EYES. WHAT A FINE-LOOKING ASSEMBLAGE OF YOUNG MEN.
WHAT A SWEET LITTLE CONGREGATION OF THE FLESH.
THEATRE of the REAL!! GRANDEST GUIGNOL! STARRING
LIMITED ENGAGEMENT
YOU LOOK TO ME, YES INDEED, YOU LOOK TO ME LIKE YOUNG GENTLE-MEN WHO WOULD APPRECIATE A LITTLE THEATRICAL ENTERTAINMENT.
UH. WE DON'T KNOW YOU, MISTER.
AH, BUT I KNOW YOU, JACOB CANDLEMAN. AND YOU, KYLE VAN FLECK. WOULD ONE OF YOU DESIRE TO COME AND SEE THE SHOW?
NO?

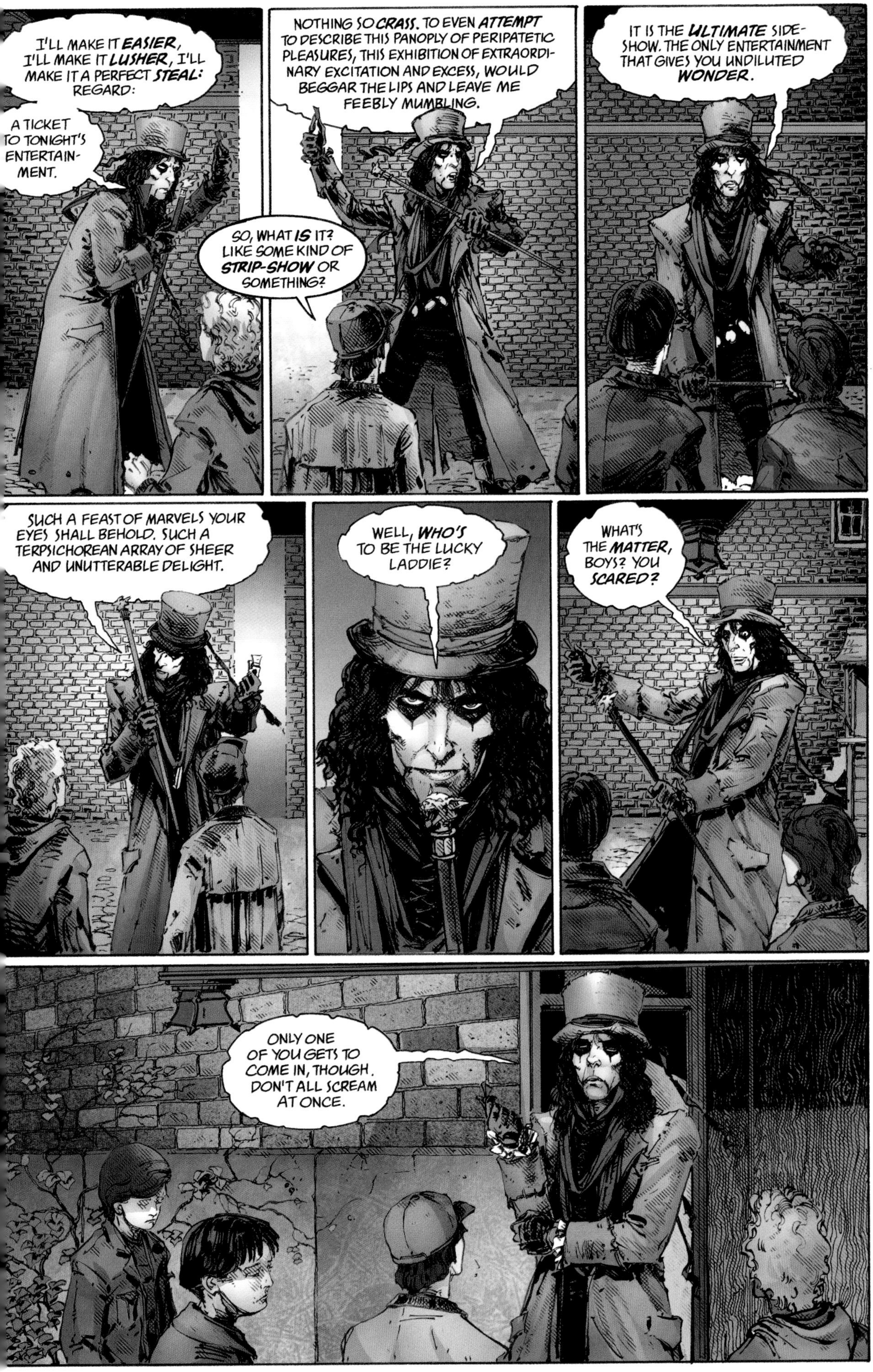
I'LL MAKE IT EASIER, I'LL MAKE IT LUSHER, I'LL MAKE IT A PERFECT STEAL: REGARD:
A TICKET TO TONIGHT'S ENTERTAINMENT.
NOTHING SO CRASS. TO EVEN ATTEMPT TO DESCRIBE THIS PANOPLY OF PERIPATETIC PLEASURES, THIS EXHIBITION OF EXTRAORDINARY EXCITATION AND EXCESS, WOULD BEGGAR THE LIPS AND LEAVE ME FEEBLY MUMBLING.
SO, WHAT IS IT? LIKE SOME KIND OF STRIP-SHOW OR SOMETHING?
IT IS THE ULTIMATE SIDE-SHOW. THE ONLY ENTERTAINMENT THAT GIVES YOU UNDILUTED WONDER.
SUCH A FEAST OF MARVELS YOUR EYES SHALL BEHOLD. SUCH A TERPSICHOREAN ARRAY OF SHEER AND UNUTTERABLE DELIGHT.
WELL, WHO'S TO BE THE LUCKY LADDIE?
WHAT'S THE MATTER, BOYS? YOU SCARED?
ONLY ONE OF YOU GETS TO COME IN, THOUGH. DON'T ALL SCREAM AT ONCE.

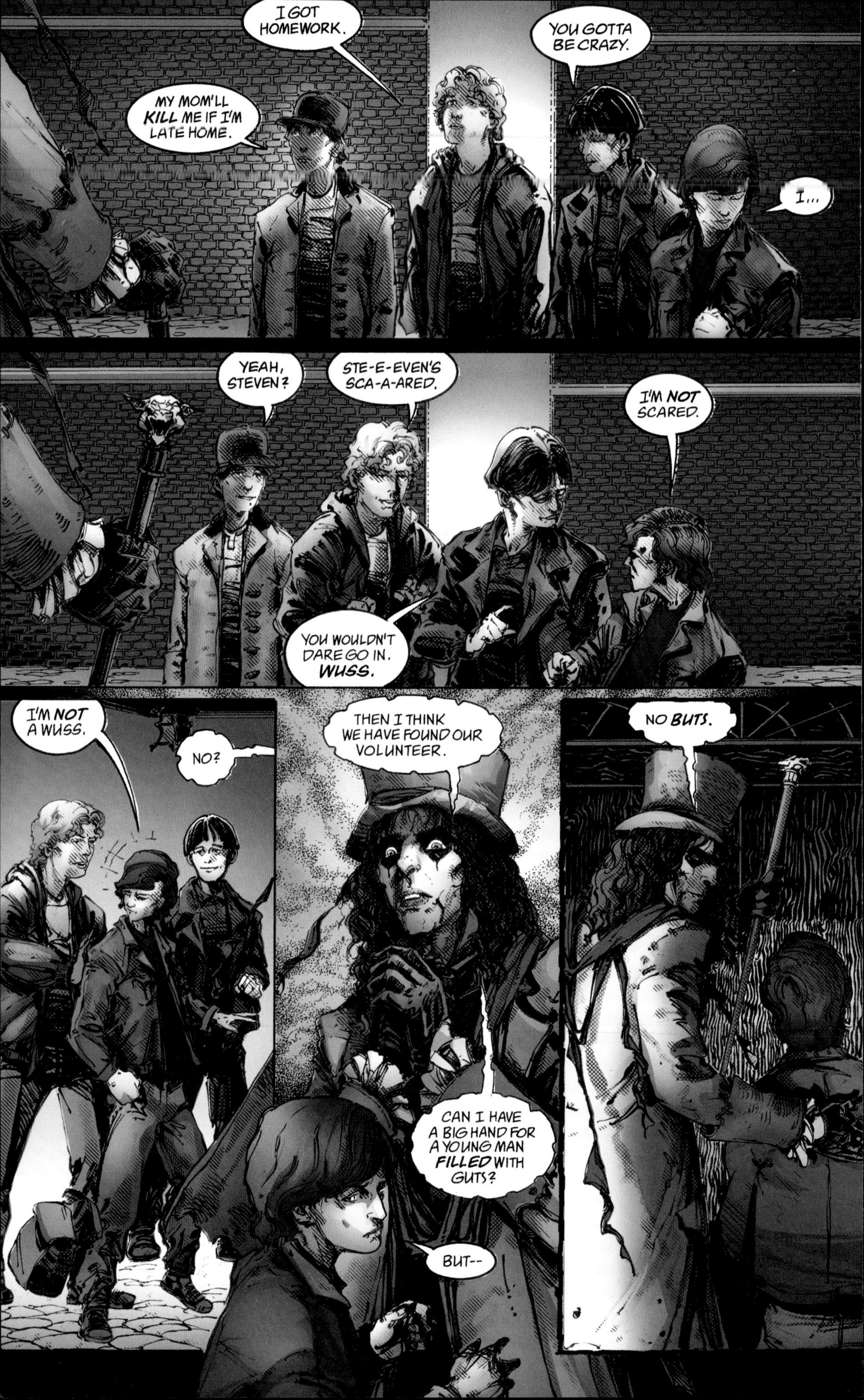
MY MOM'LL **KILL** ME IF I'M LATE HOME.
I GOT HOMEWORK.
YOU GOTTA BE CRAZY.
I...
YEAH, STEVEN?
STE-E-EVEN'S SCA-A-ARED.
I'M **NOT** SCARED.
YOU WOULDN'T DARE GO IN. **WUSS.**
I'M **NOT** A WUSS.
NO?
THEN I THINK WE HAVE FOUND OUR VOLUNTEER.
CAN I HAVE A BIG HAND FOR A YOUNG MAN **FILLED** WITH GUTS?
BUT--
NO **BUTS**.

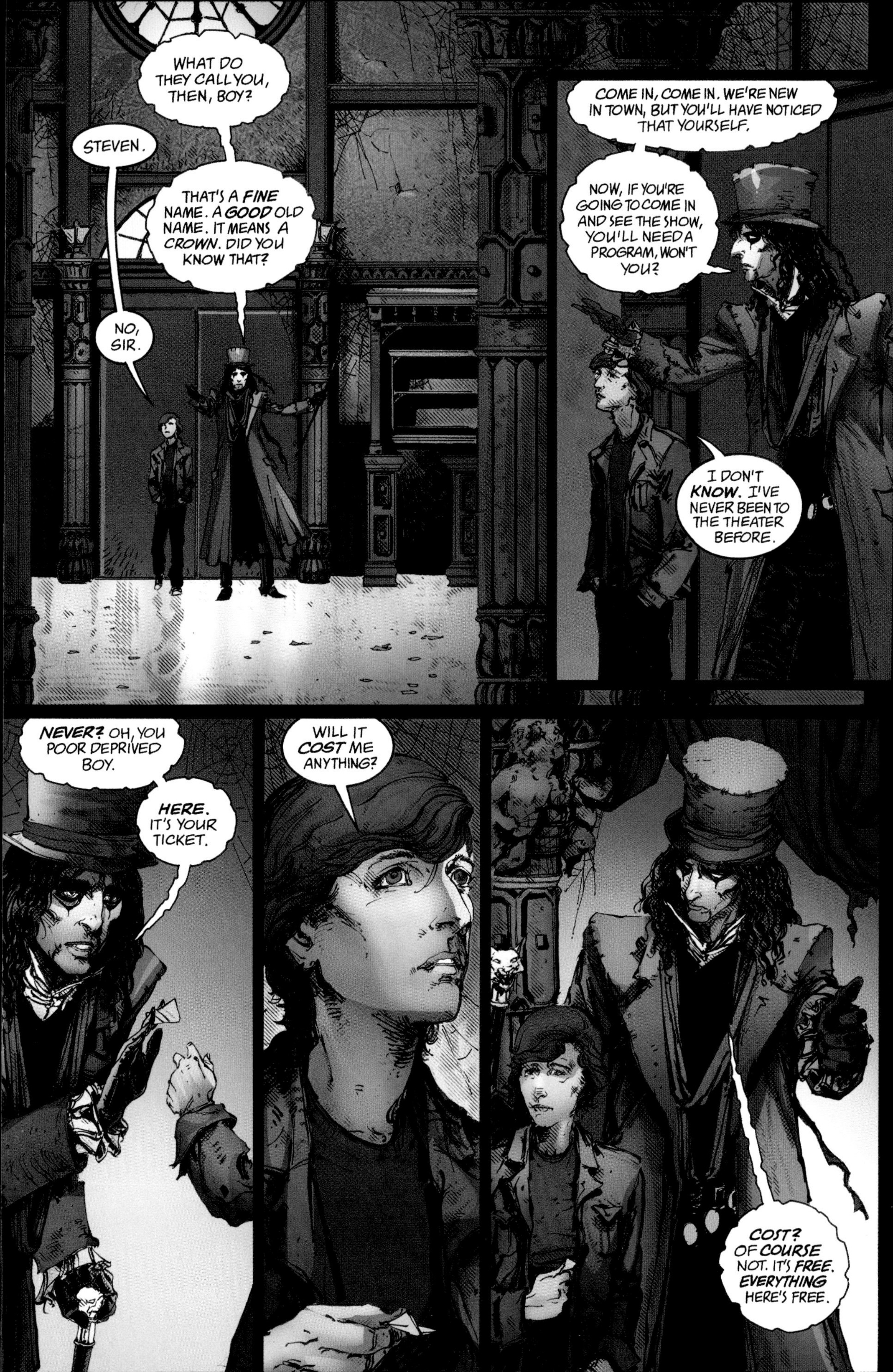
WHAT DO THEY CALL YOU, THEN, BOY?
STEVEN.
THAT'S A *FINE* NAME. A *GOOD* OLD NAME. IT MEANS A *CROWN*. DID YOU KNOW THAT?
NO, SIR.
COME IN, COME IN. WE'RE NEW IN TOWN, BUT YOU'LL HAVE NOTICED THAT YOURSELF.
NOW, IF YOU'RE GOING TO COME IN AND SEE THE SHOW, YOU'LL NEED A PROGRAM, WON'T YOU?
I DON'T **KNOW**. I'VE NEVER BEEN TO THE THEATER BEFORE.
NEVER? OH, YOU POOR DEPRIVED BOY.
HERE. IT'S YOUR TICKET.
WILL IT *COST* ME ANYTHING?
COST? OF *COURSE* NOT. IT'S *FREE*. *EVERYTHING* HERE'S FREE.

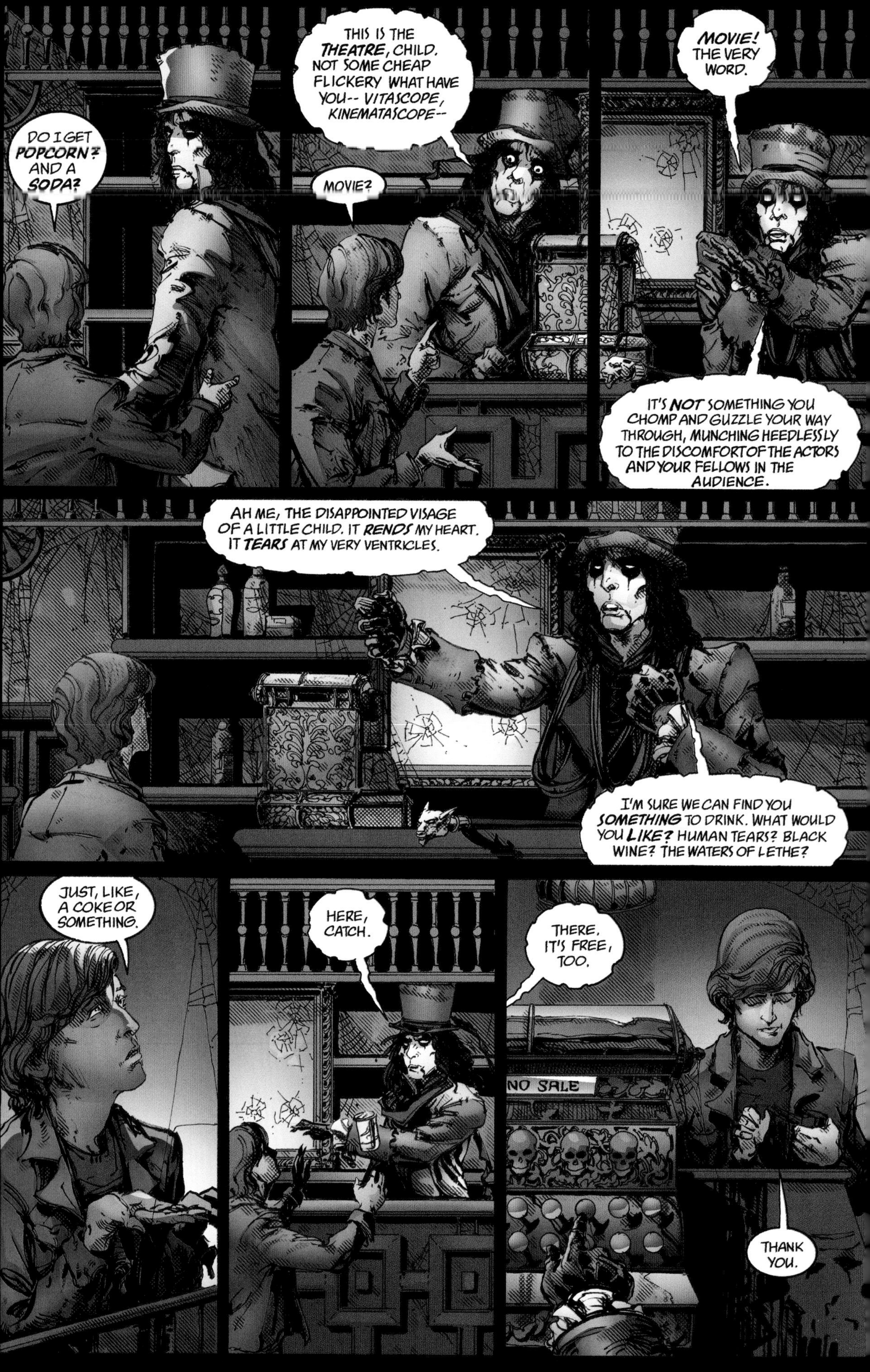
DO I GET POPCORN? AND A SODA?
THIS IS THE THEATRE, CHILD. NOT SOME CHEAP FLICKERY WHAT HAVE YOU-- VITASCOPE, KINEMATASCOPE--
MOVIE?
MOVIE! THE VERY WORD.
IT'S NOT SOMETHING YOU CHOMP AND GUZZLE YOUR WAY THROUGH, MUNCHING HEEDLESSLY TO THE DISCOMFORT OF THE ACTORS AND YOUR FELLOWS IN THE AUDIENCE.
AH ME, THE DISAPPOINTED VISAGE OF A LITTLE CHILD. IT RENDS MY HEART. IT TEARS AT MY VERY VENTRICLES.
I'M SURE WE CAN FIND YOU SOMETHING TO DRINK. WHAT WOULD YOU LIKE? HUMAN TEARS? BLACK WINE? THE WATERS OF LETHE?
JUST, LIKE, A COKE OR SOMETHING.
HERE, CATCH.
THERE, IT'S FREE, TOO.
NO SALE
THANK YOU.

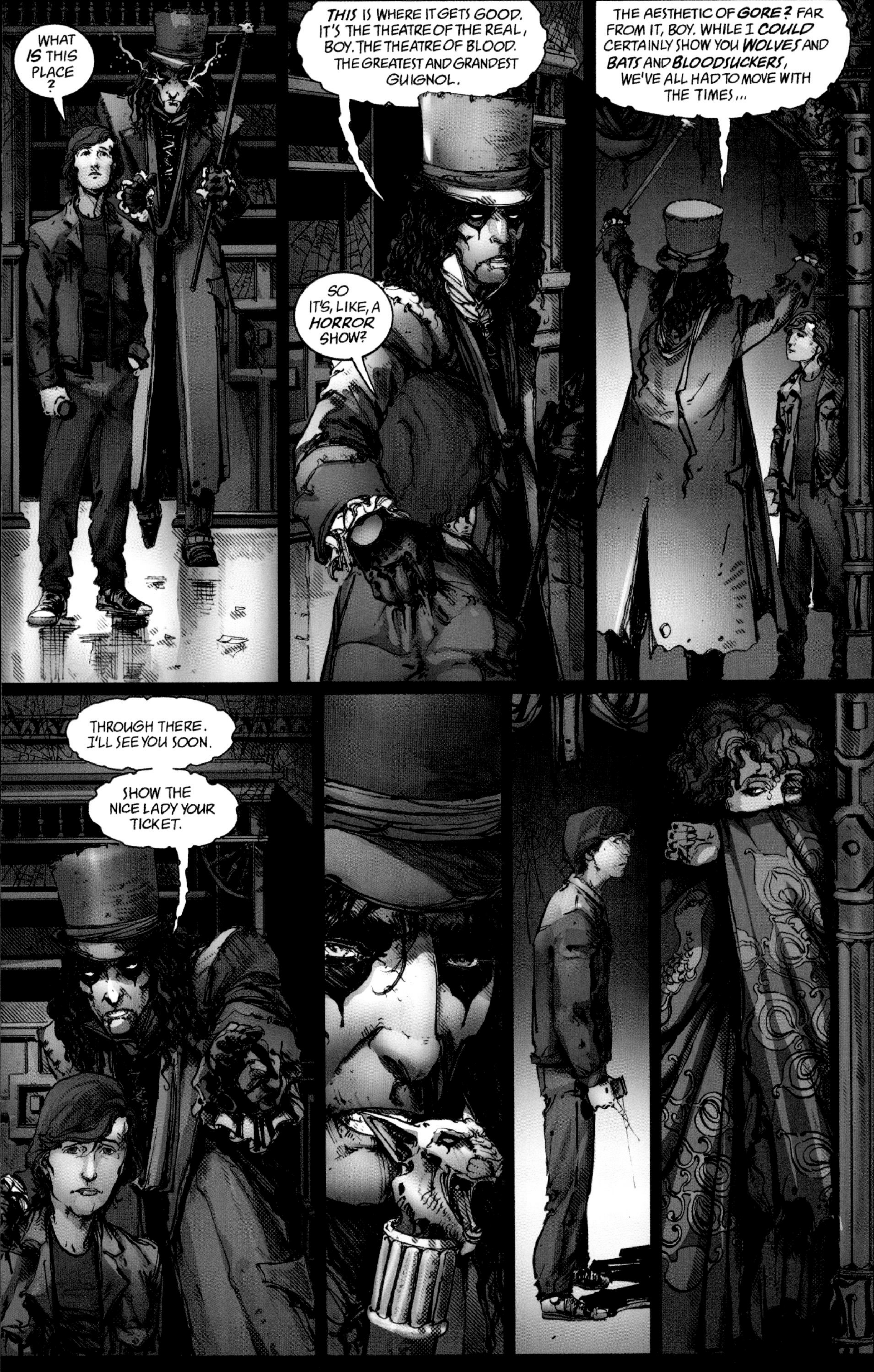
WHAT IS THIS PLACE?
THIS IS WHERE IT GETS GOOD. IT'S THE THEATRE OF THE REAL, BOY. THE THEATRE OF BLOOD. THE GREATEST AND GRANDEST GUIGNOL.
SO IT'S, LIKE, A HORROR SHOW?
THE AESTHETIC OF GORE? FAR FROM IT, BOY. WHILE I COULD CERTAINLY SHOW YOU WOLVES AND BATS AND BLOODSUCKERS, WE'VE ALL HAD TO MOVE WITH THE TIMES...
THROUGH THERE. I'LL SEE YOU SOON.
SHOW THE NICE LADY YOUR TICKET.

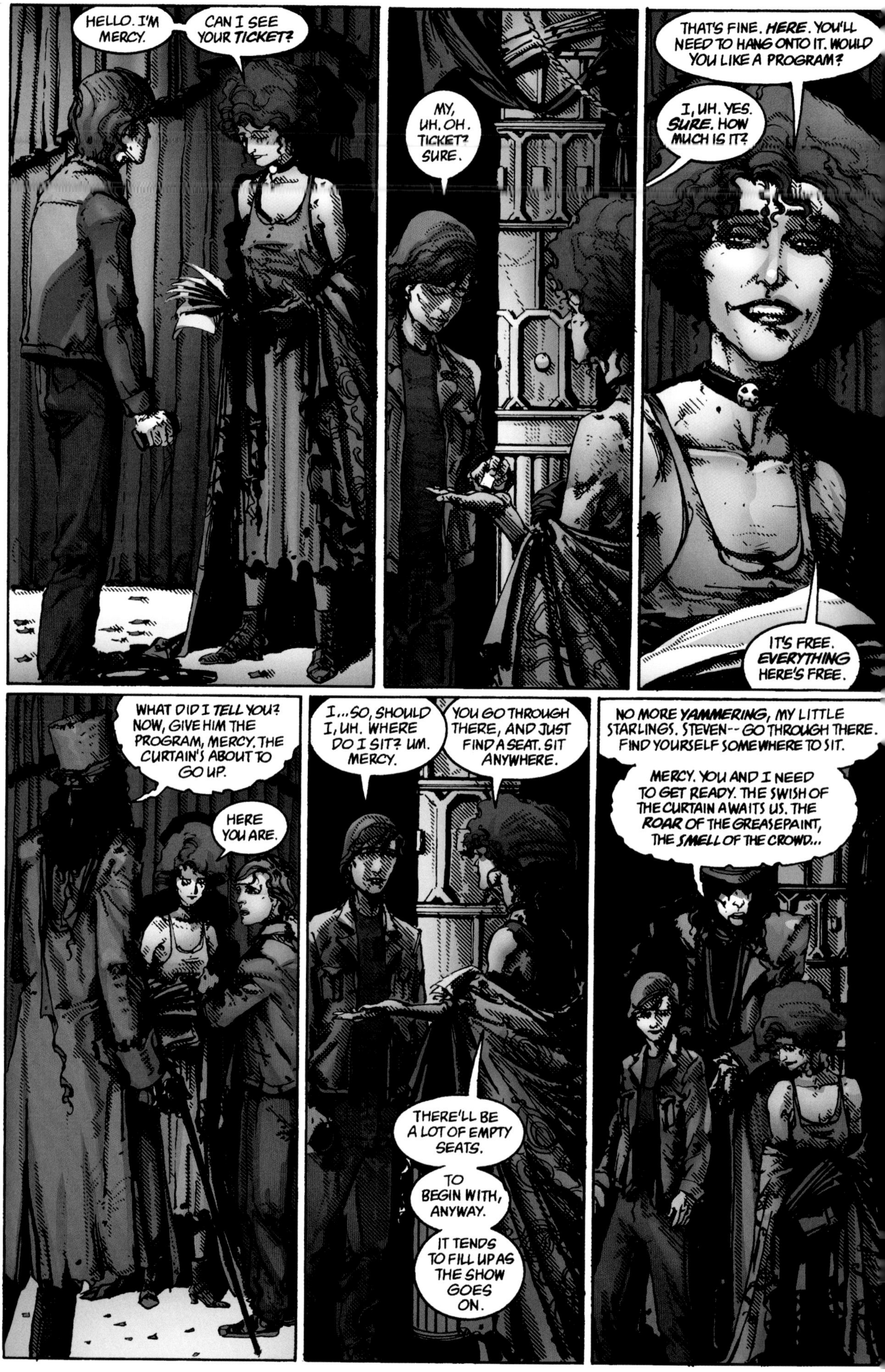
HELLO. I'M MERCY.
CAN I SEE YOUR TICKET?
MY, UH. OH. TICKET? SURE.
THAT'S FINE. HERE. YOU'LL NEED TO HANG ONTO IT. WOULD YOU LIKE A PROGRAM?
I, UH. YES. SURE. HOW MUCH IS IT?
IT'S FREE. EVERYTHING HERE'S FREE.
WHAT DID I TELL YOU? NOW, GIVE HIM THE PROGRAM, MERCY. THE CURTAIN'S ABOUT TO GO UP.
HERE YOU ARE.
I...SO, SHOULD I, UH. WHERE DO I SIT? UM. MERCY.
YOU GO THROUGH THERE, AND JUST FIND A SEAT. SIT ANYWHERE.
THERE'LL BE A LOT OF EMPTY SEATS.
TO BEGIN WITH, ANYWAY.
IT TENDS TO FILL UP AS THE SHOW GOES ON.
NO MORE YAMMERING, MY LITTLE STARLINGS. STEVEN-- GO THROUGH THERE. FIND YOURSELF SOMEWHERE TO SIT.
MERCY. YOU AND I NEED TO GET READY. THE SWISH OF THE CURTAIN AWAITS US. THE ROAR OF THE GREASEPAINT, THE SMELL OF THE CROWD...

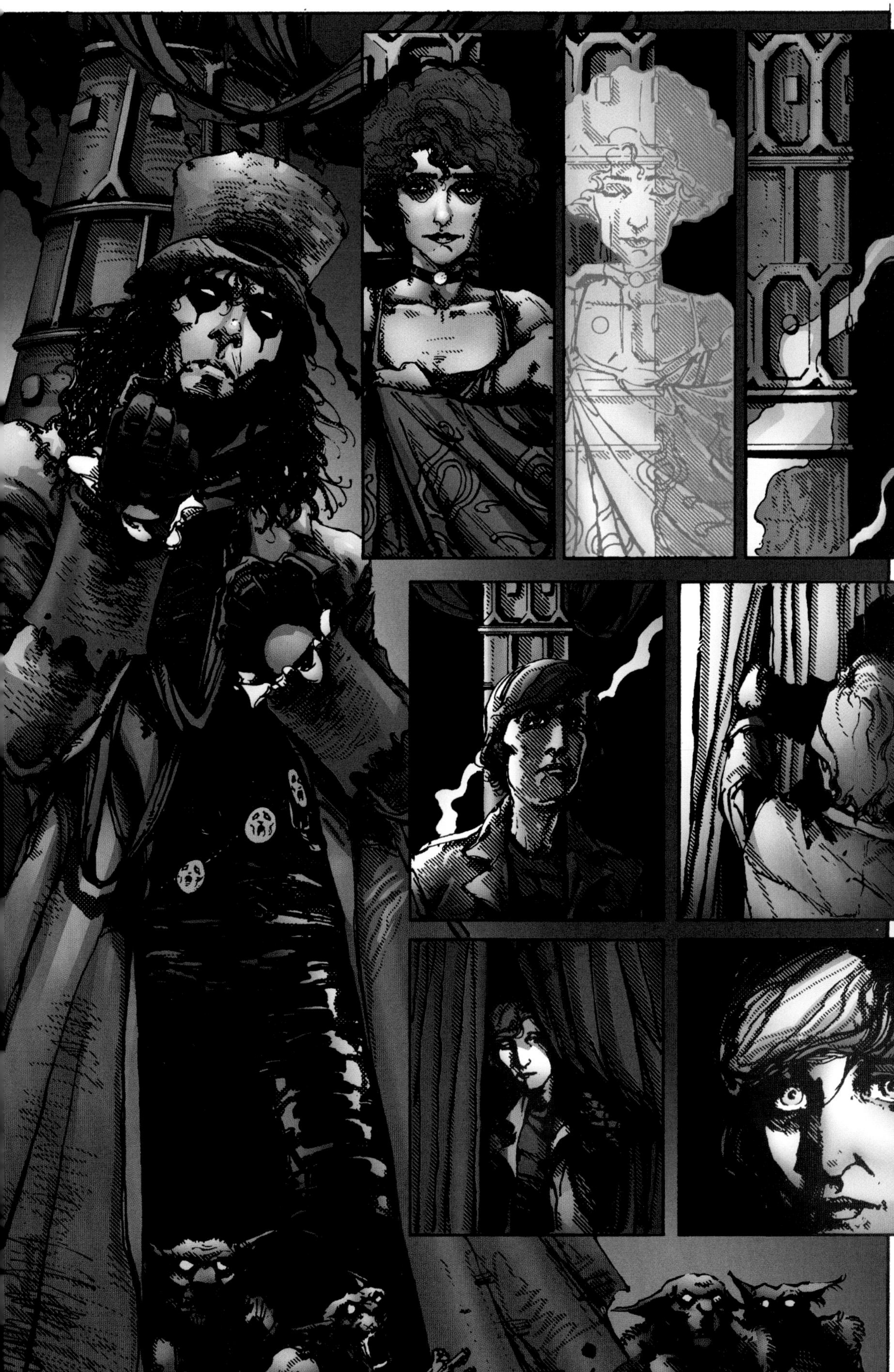

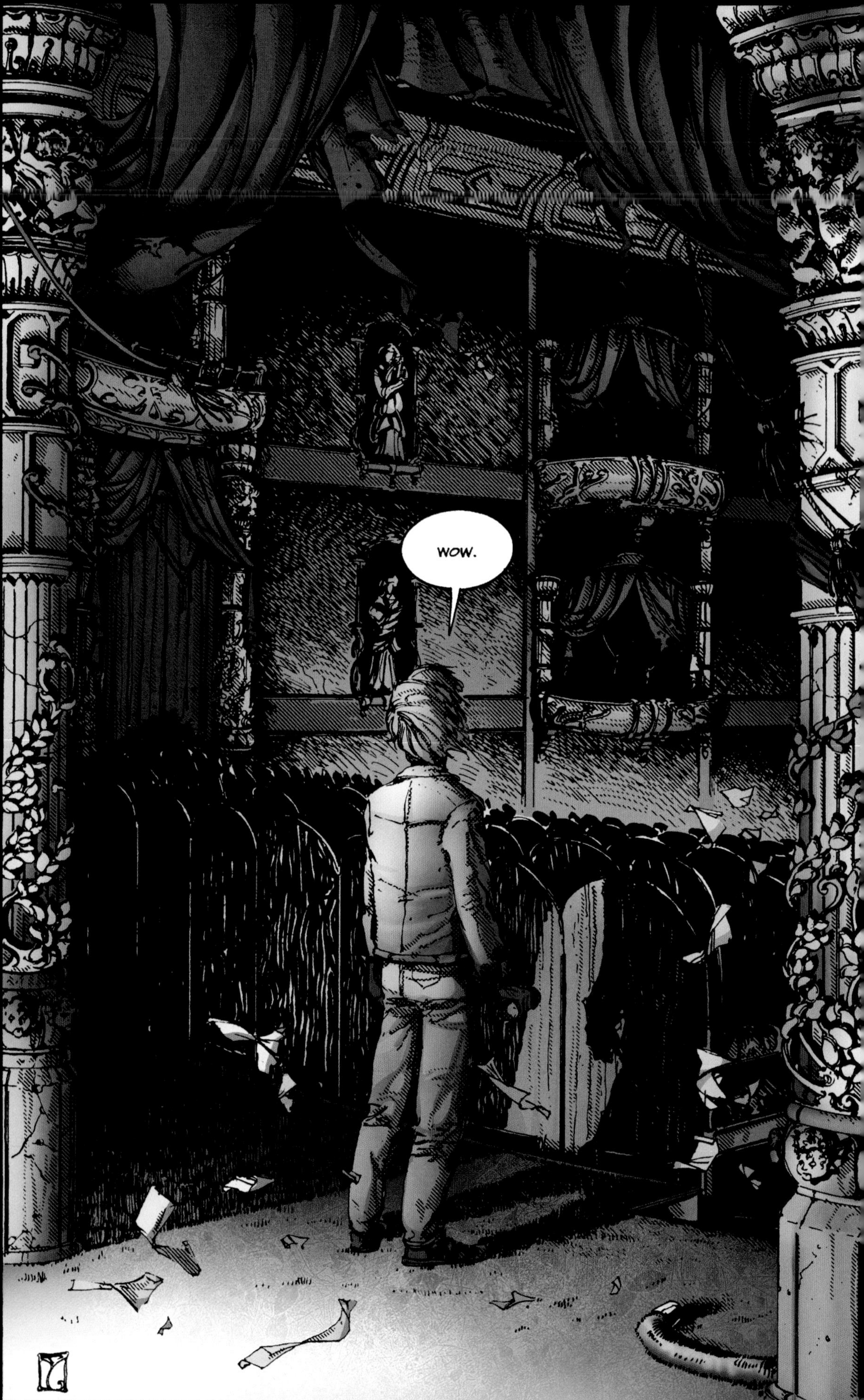
WOW.

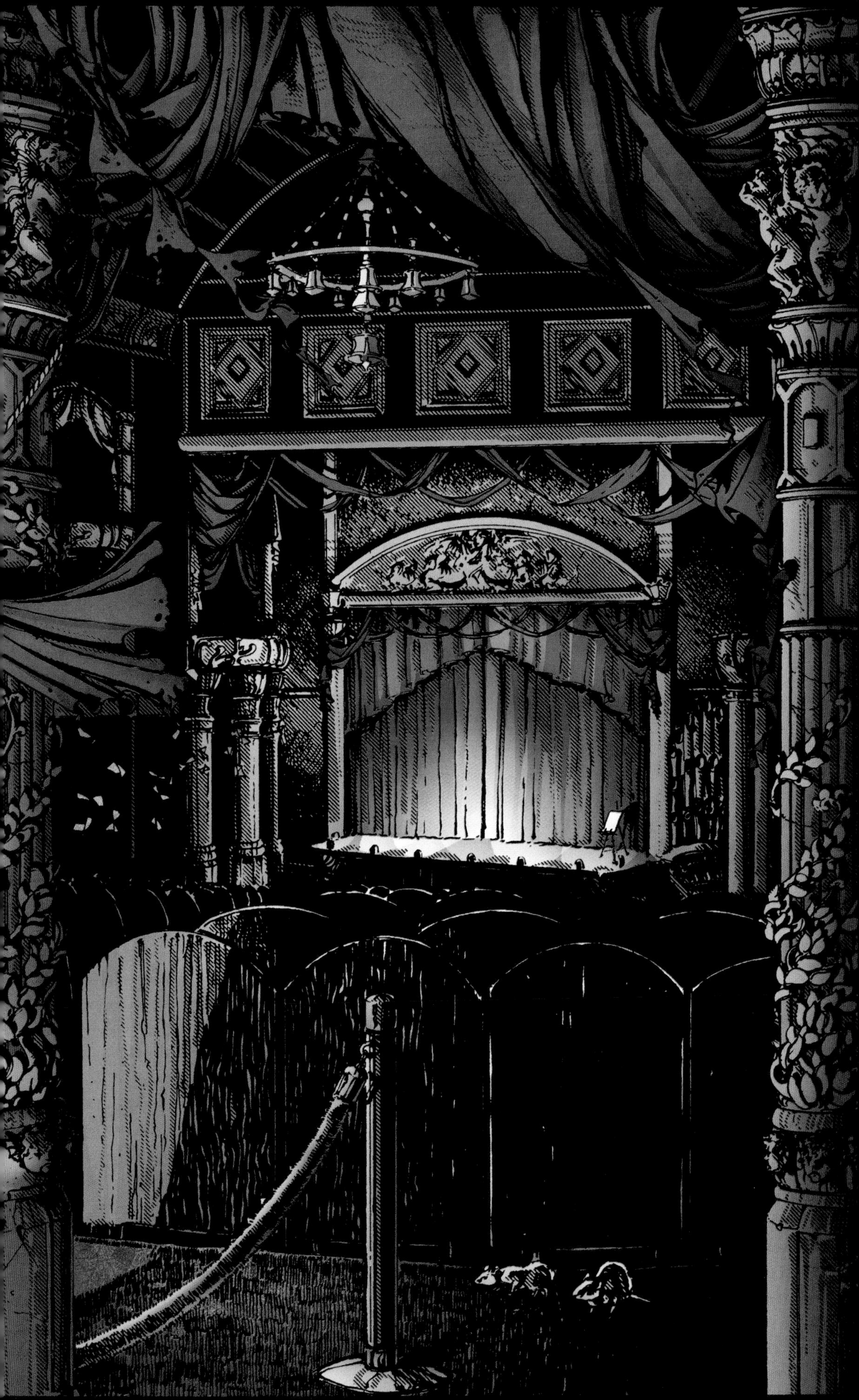

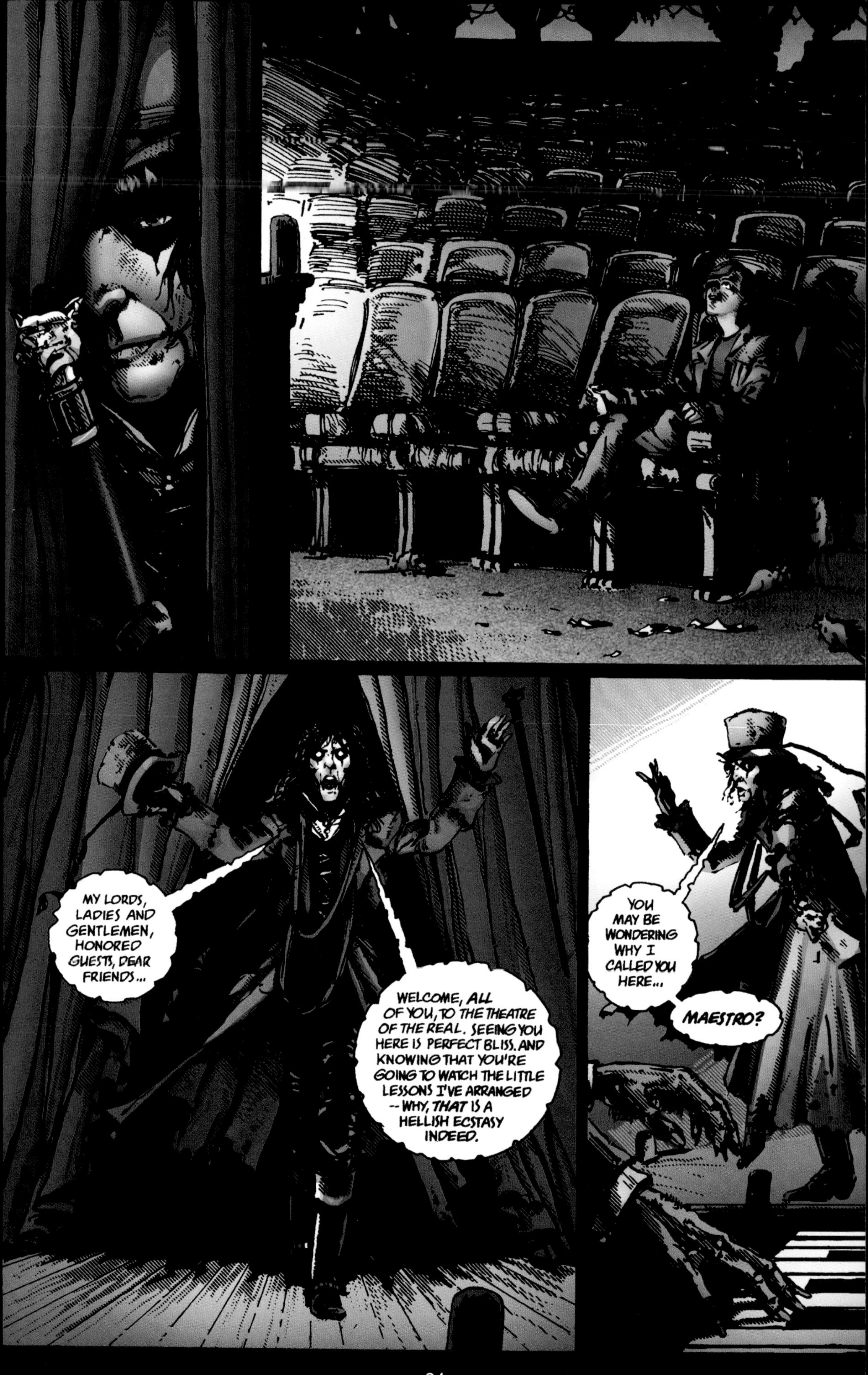
MY LORDS, LADIES AND GENTLEMEN, HONORED GUESTS, DEAR FRIENDS...
WELCOME, ALL OF YOU, TO THE THEATRE OF THE REAL. SEEING YOU HERE IS PERFECT BLISS. AND KNOWING THAT YOU'RE GOING TO WATCH THE LITTLE LESSONS I'VE ARRANGED -- WHY, THAT IS A HELLISH ECSTASY INDEED.
YOU MAY BE WONDERING WHY I CALLED YOU HERE...
MAESTRO?

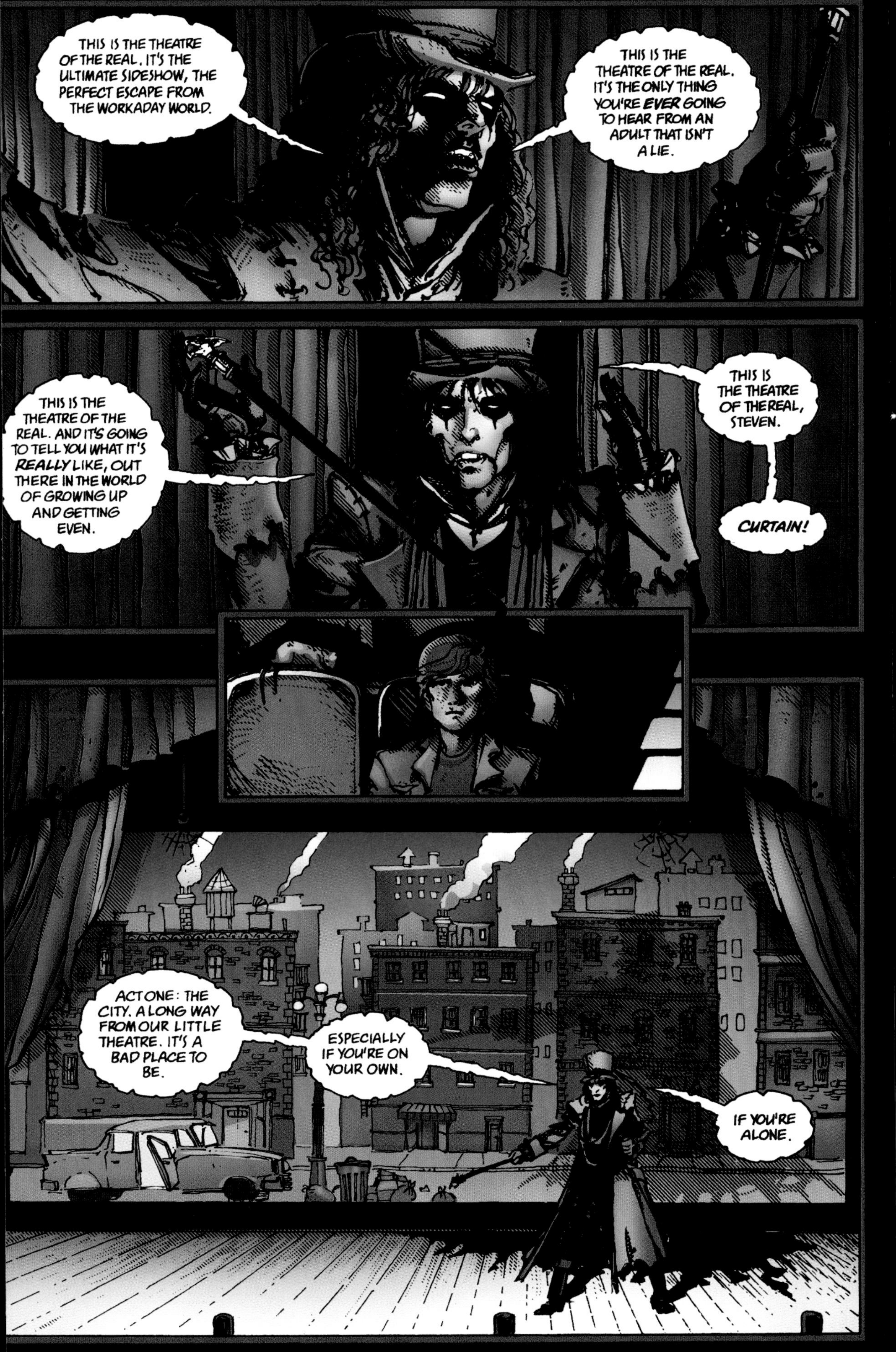
THIS IS THE THEATRE OF THE REAL. IT'S THE ULTIMATE SIDESHOW, THE PERFECT ESCAPE FROM THE WORKADAY WORLD.
THIS IS THE THEATRE OF THE REAL. IT'S THE ONLY THING YOU'RE EVER GOING TO HEAR FROM AN ADULT THAT ISN'T A LIE.
THIS IS THE THEATRE OF THE REAL. AND IT'S GOING TO TELL YOU WHAT IT'S REALLY LIKE, OUT THERE IN THE WORLD OF GROWING UP AND GETTING EVEN.
THIS IS THE THEATRE OF THE REAL, STEVEN.
CURTAIN!
ACT ONE: THE CITY. A LONG WAY FROM OUR LITTLE THEATRE. IT'S A BAD PLACE TO BE.
ESPECIALLY IF YOU'RE ON YOUR OWN.
IF YOU'RE ALONE.

27

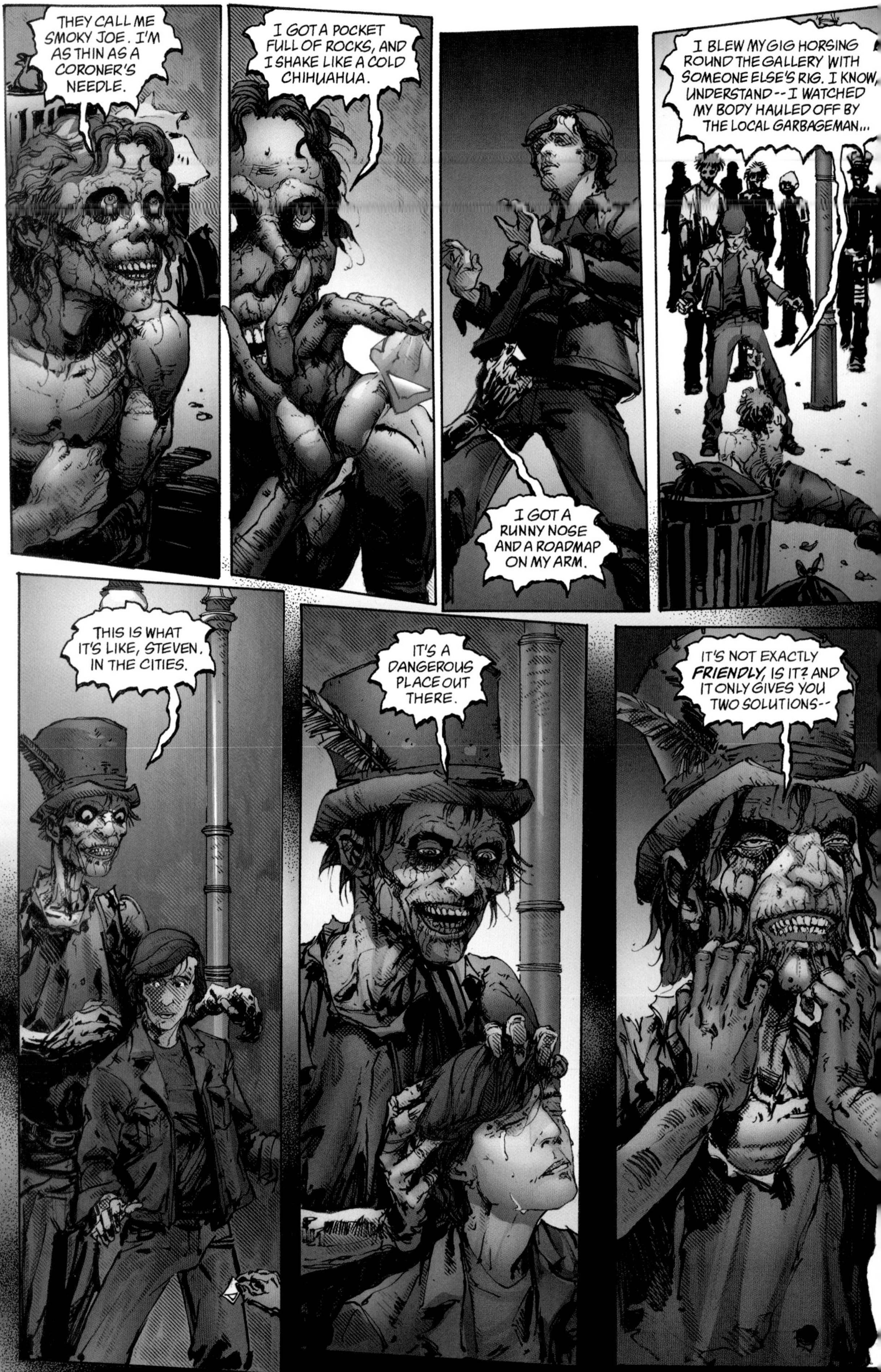
THEY CALL ME SMOKY JOE. I'M AS THIN AS A CORONER'S NEEDLE.
I GOT A POCKET FULL OF ROCKS, AND I SHAKE LIKE A COLD CHIHUAHUA.
I GOT A RUNNY NOSE AND A ROADMAP ON MY ARM.
I BLEW MY GIG HORSING ROUND THE GALLERY WITH SOMEONE ELSE'S RIG. I KNOW, UNDERSTAND--I WATCHED MY BODY HAULED OFF BY THE LOCAL GARBAGEMAN...
THIS IS WHAT IT'S LIKE, STEVEN, IN THE CITIES.
IT'S A DANGEROUS PLACE OUT THERE.
IT'S NOT EXACTLY **FRIENDLY**, IS IT? AND IT ONLY GIVES YOU TWO SOLUTIONS--

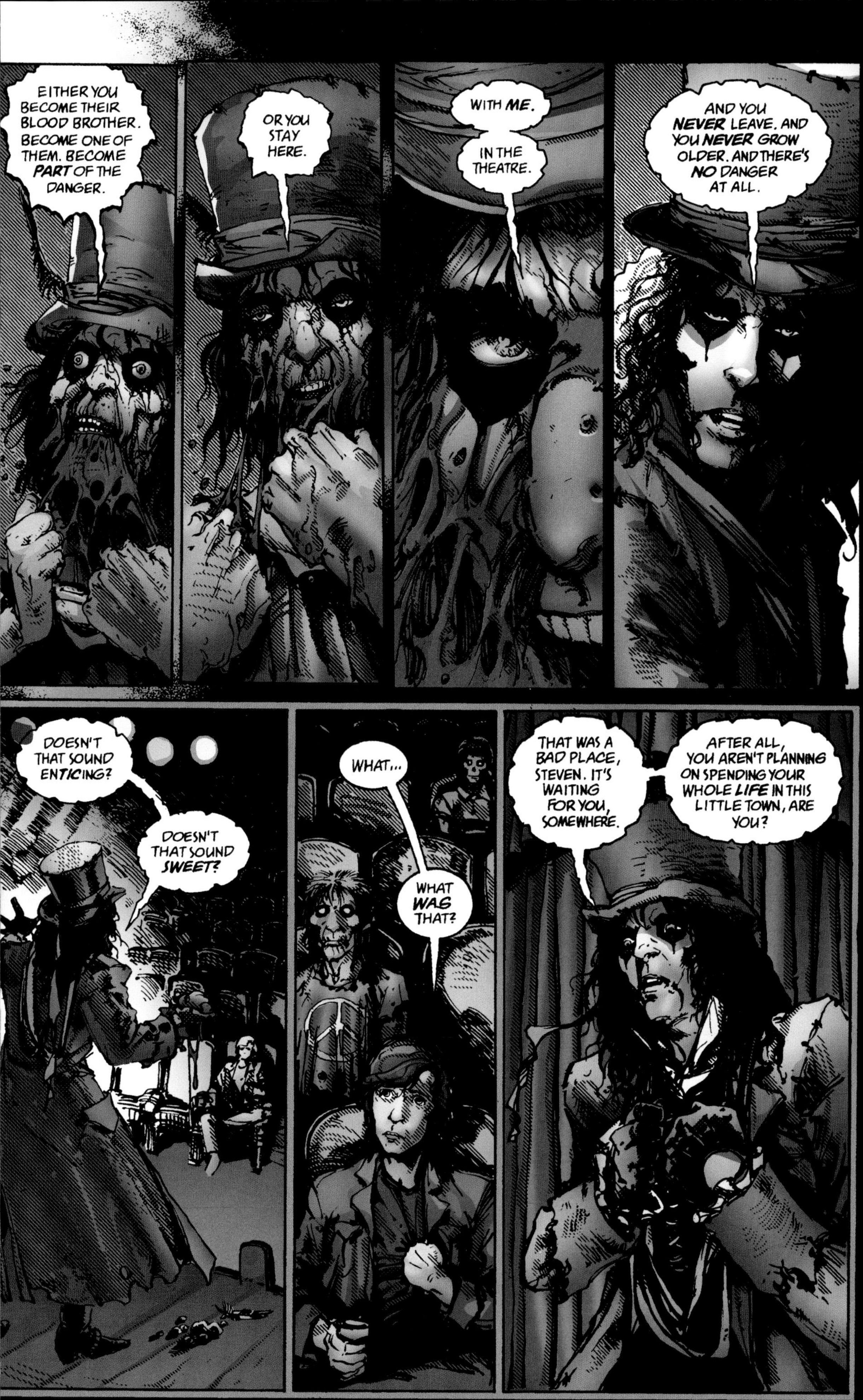
EITHER YOU BECOME THEIR BLOOD BROTHER. BECOME ONE OF THEM. BECOME PART OF THE DANGER.
OR YOU STAY HERE.
WITH ME.
IN THE THEATRE.
AND YOU NEVER LEAVE. AND YOU NEVER GROW OLDER. AND THERE'S NO DANGER AT ALL.
DOESN'T THAT SOUND ENTICING?
DOESN'T THAT SOUND SWEET?
WHAT...
WHAT WAS THAT?
THAT WAS A BAD PLACE, STEVEN. IT'S WAITING FOR YOU, SOMEWHERE.
AFTER ALL, YOU AREN'T PLANNING ON SPENDING YOUR WHOLE LIFE IN THIS LITTLE TOWN, ARE YOU?

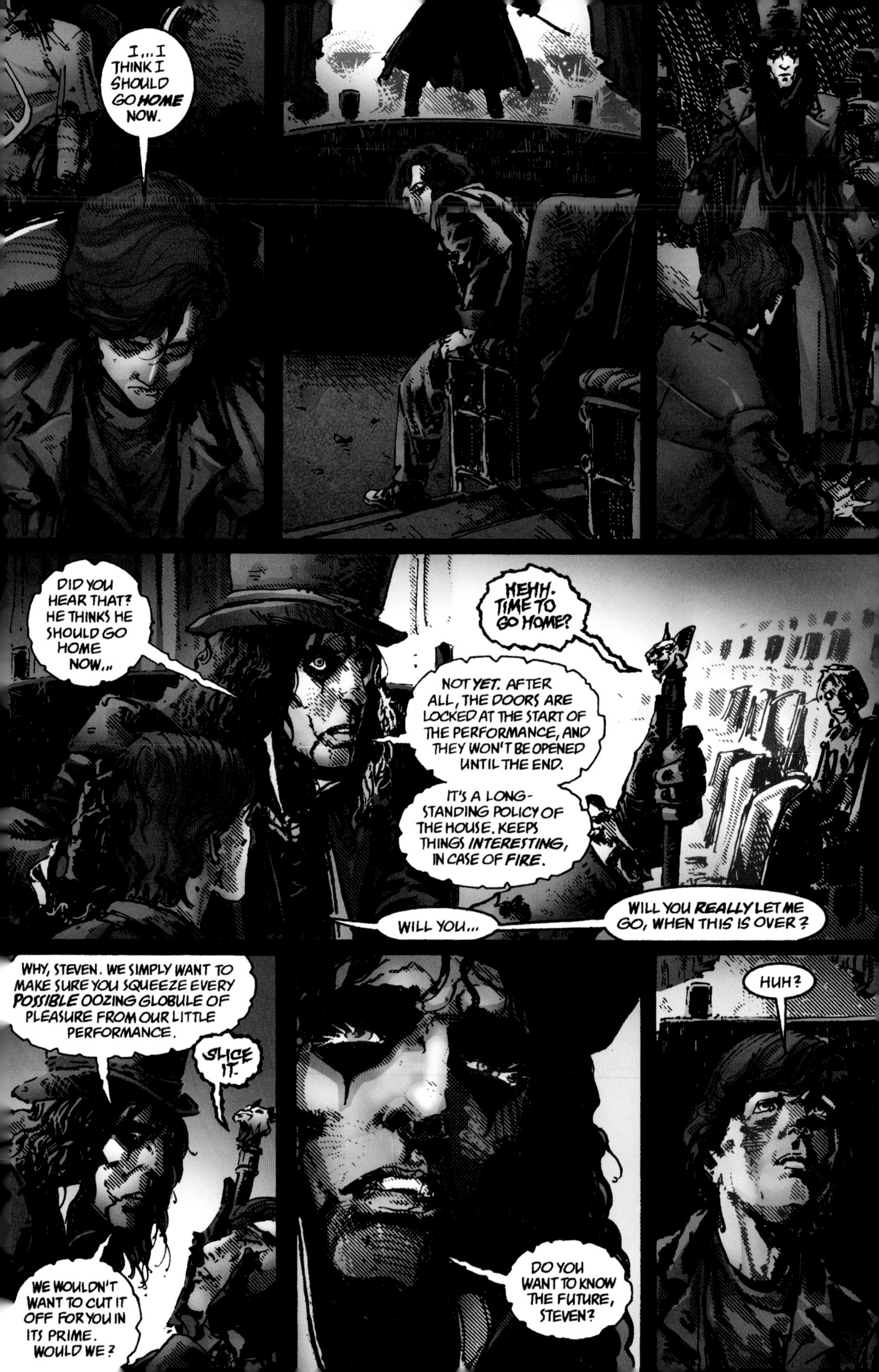

I... I THINK I SHOULD GO HOME NOW.
DID YOU HEAR THAT? HE THINKS HE SHOULD GO HOME NOW...
HEHH. TIME TO GO HOME?
NOT YET. AFTER ALL, THE DOORS ARE LOCKED AT THE START OF THE PERFORMANCE, AND THEY WON'T BE OPENED UNTIL THE END.
IT'S A LONG-STANDING POLICY OF THE HOUSE. KEEPS THINGS INTERESTING, IN CASE OF FIRE.
WILL YOU...
WILL YOU REALLY LET ME GO, WHEN THIS IS OVER?
WHY, STEVEN. WE SIMPLY WANT TO MAKE SURE YOU SQUEEZE EVERY POSSIBLE OOZING GLOBULE OF PLEASURE FROM OUR LITTLE PERFORMANCE.
SLICE IT.
WE WOULDN'T WANT TO CUT IT OFF FOR YOU IN ITS PRIME. WOULD WE?
DO YOU WANT TO KNOW THE FUTURE, STEVEN?
HUH?

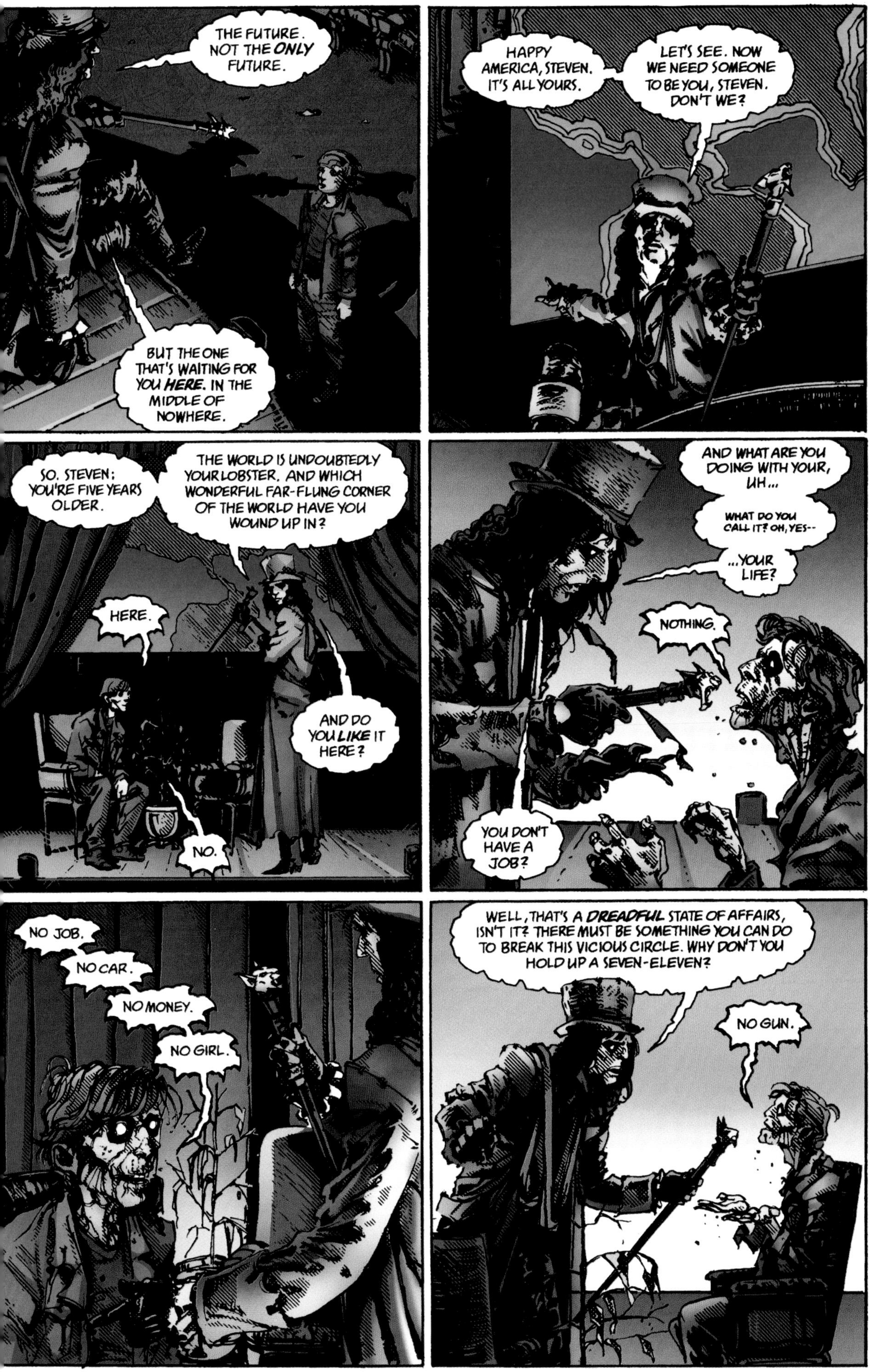
THE FUTURE. NOT THE ONLY FUTURE.
BUT THE ONE THAT'S WAITING FOR YOU HERE. IN THE MIDDLE OF NOWHERE.
HAPPY AMERICA, STEVEN. IT'S ALL YOURS.
LET'S SEE. NOW WE NEED SOMEONE TO BE YOU, STEVEN. DON'T WE?
SO. STEVEN: YOU'RE FIVE YEARS OLDER.
THE WORLD IS UNDOUBTEDLY YOUR LOBSTER. AND WHICH WONDERFUL FAR-FLUNG CORNER OF THE WORLD HAVE YOU WOUND UP IN?
HERE.
AND DO YOU LIKE IT HERE?
NO.
AND WHAT ARE YOU DOING WITH YOUR, UH...
WHAT DO YOU CALL IT? OH, YES--
...YOUR LIFE?
NOTHING.
YOU DON'T HAVE A JOB?
NO JOB.
NO CAR.
NO MONEY.
NO GIRL.
WELL, THAT'S A DREADFUL STATE OF AFFAIRS, ISN'T IT? THERE MUST BE SOMETHING YOU CAN DO TO BREAK THIS VICIOUS CIRCLE. WHY DON'T YOU HOLD UP A SEVEN-ELEVEN?
NO GUN.

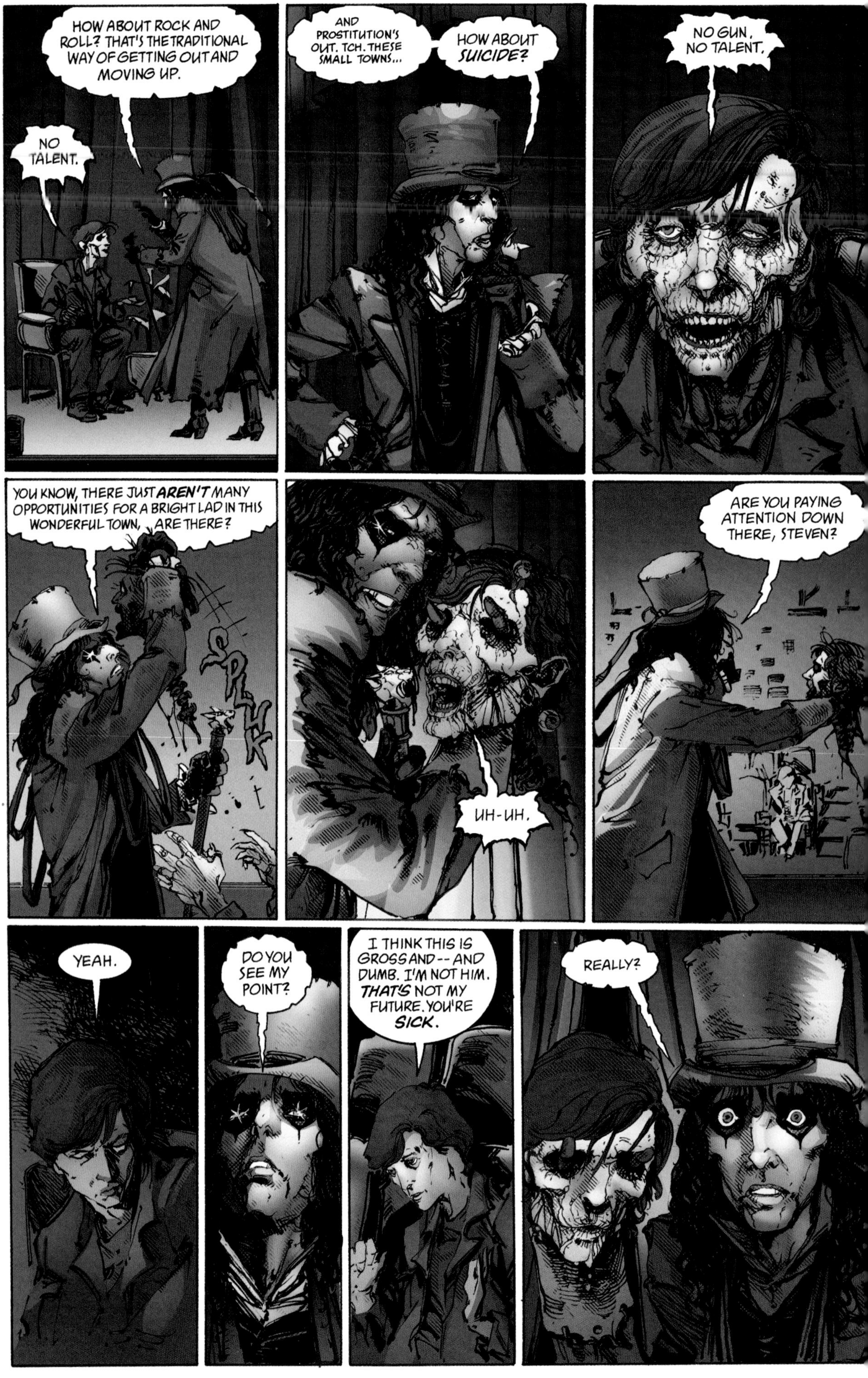
HOW ABOUT ROCK AND ROLL? THAT'S THE TRADITIONAL WAY OF GETTING OUT AND MOVING UP.
NO TALENT.
AND PROSTITUTION'S OUT. TCH. THESE SMALL TOWNS...
HOW ABOUT SUICIDE?
NO GUN, NO TALENT.
YOU KNOW, THERE JUST AREN'T MANY OPPORTUNITIES FOR A BRIGHT LAD IN THIS WONDERFUL TOWN, ARE THERE?
SPLHK
UH-UH.
ARE YOU PAYING ATTENTION DOWN THERE, STEVEN?
YEAH.
DO YOU SEE MY POINT?
I THINK THIS IS GROSS AND -- AND DUMB. I'M NOT HIM. THAT'S NOT MY FUTURE. YOU'RE SICK.
REALLY?

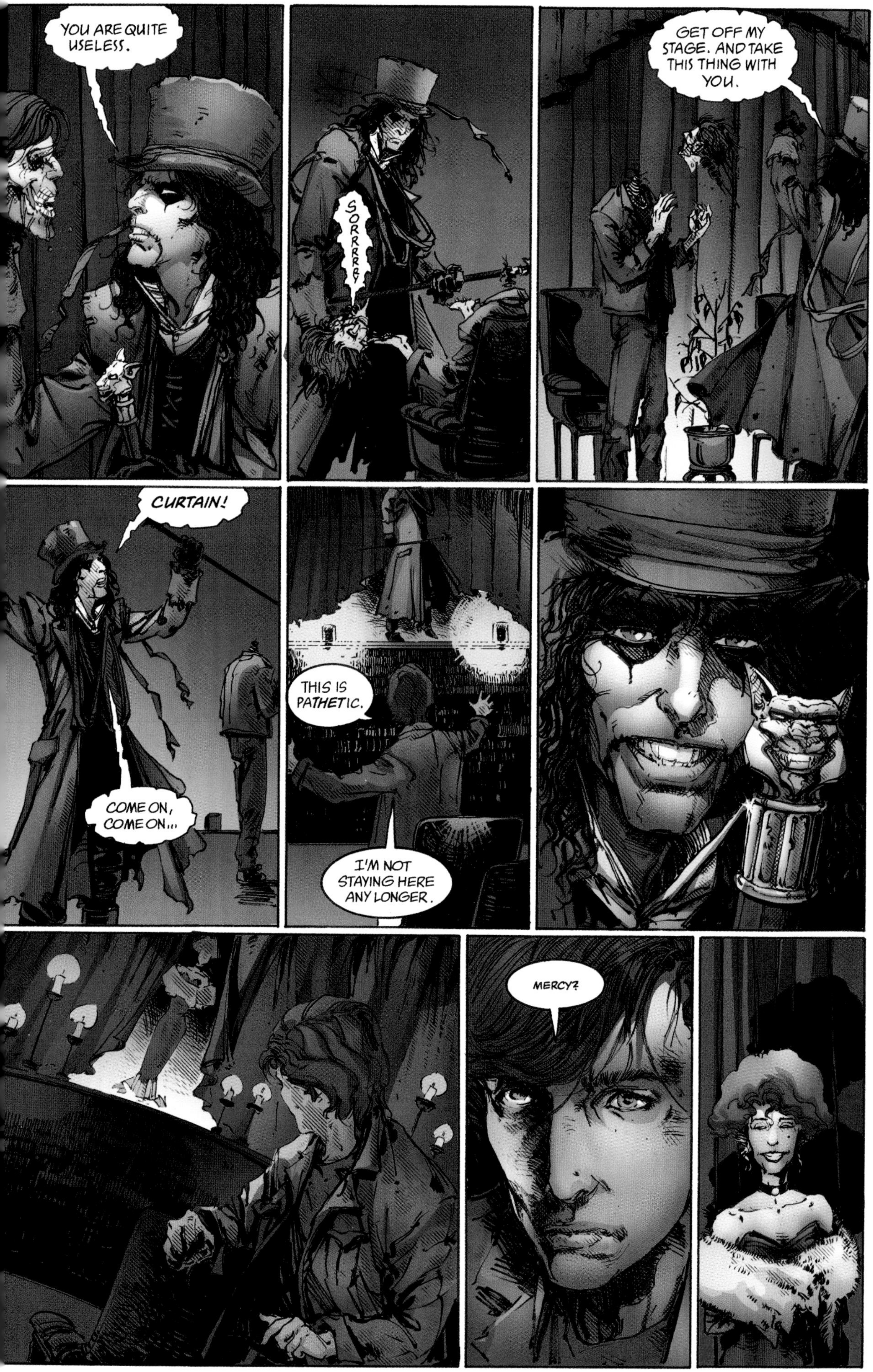
YOU ARE QUITE USELESS.
SORRRRRY
GET OFF MY STAGE. AND TAKE THIS THING WITH YOU.
CURTAIN!
COME ON, COME ON...
THIS IS PATHETIC.
I'M NOT STAYING HERE ANY LONGER.
MERCY?

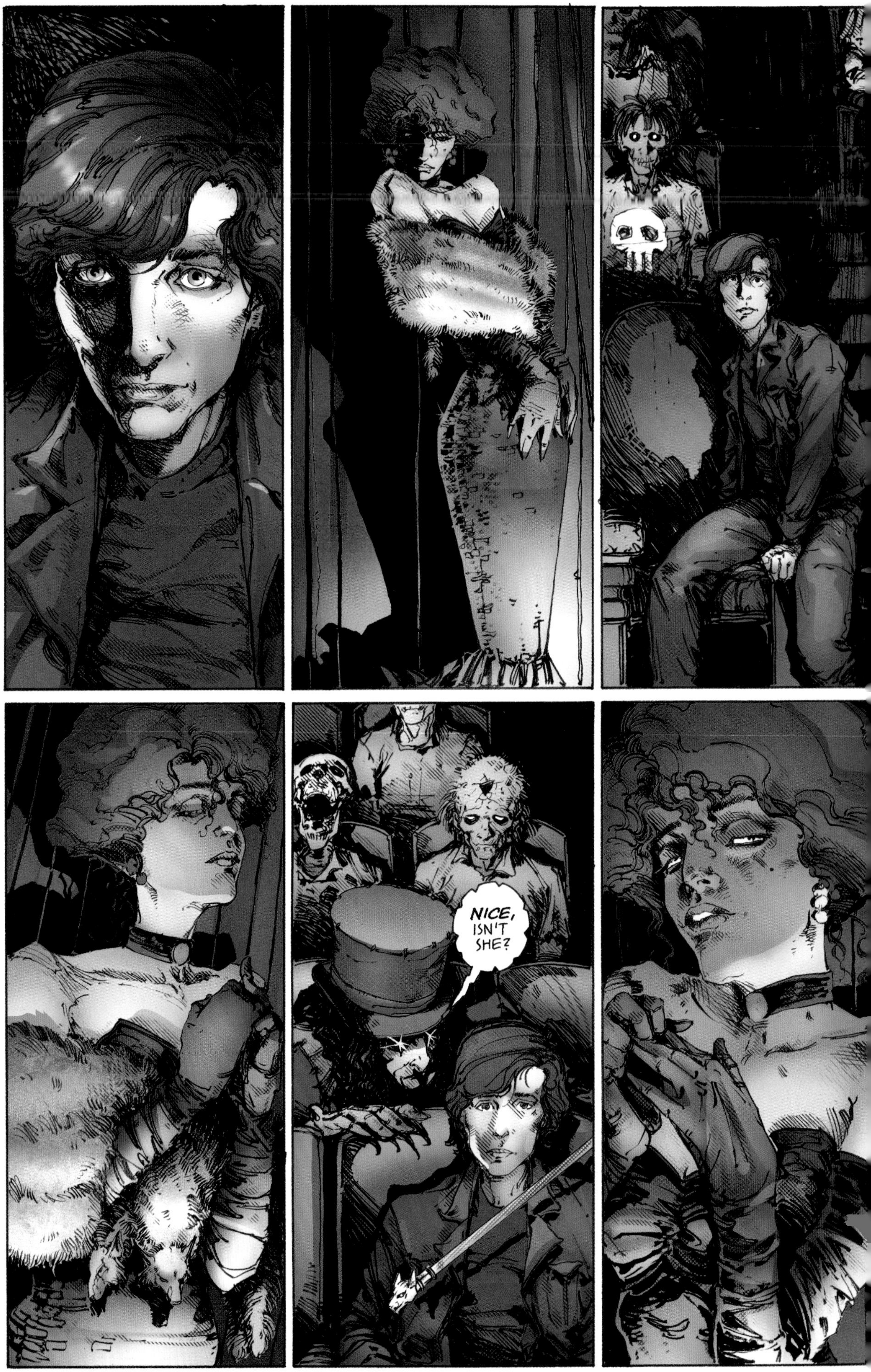
NICE, ISN'T SHE?

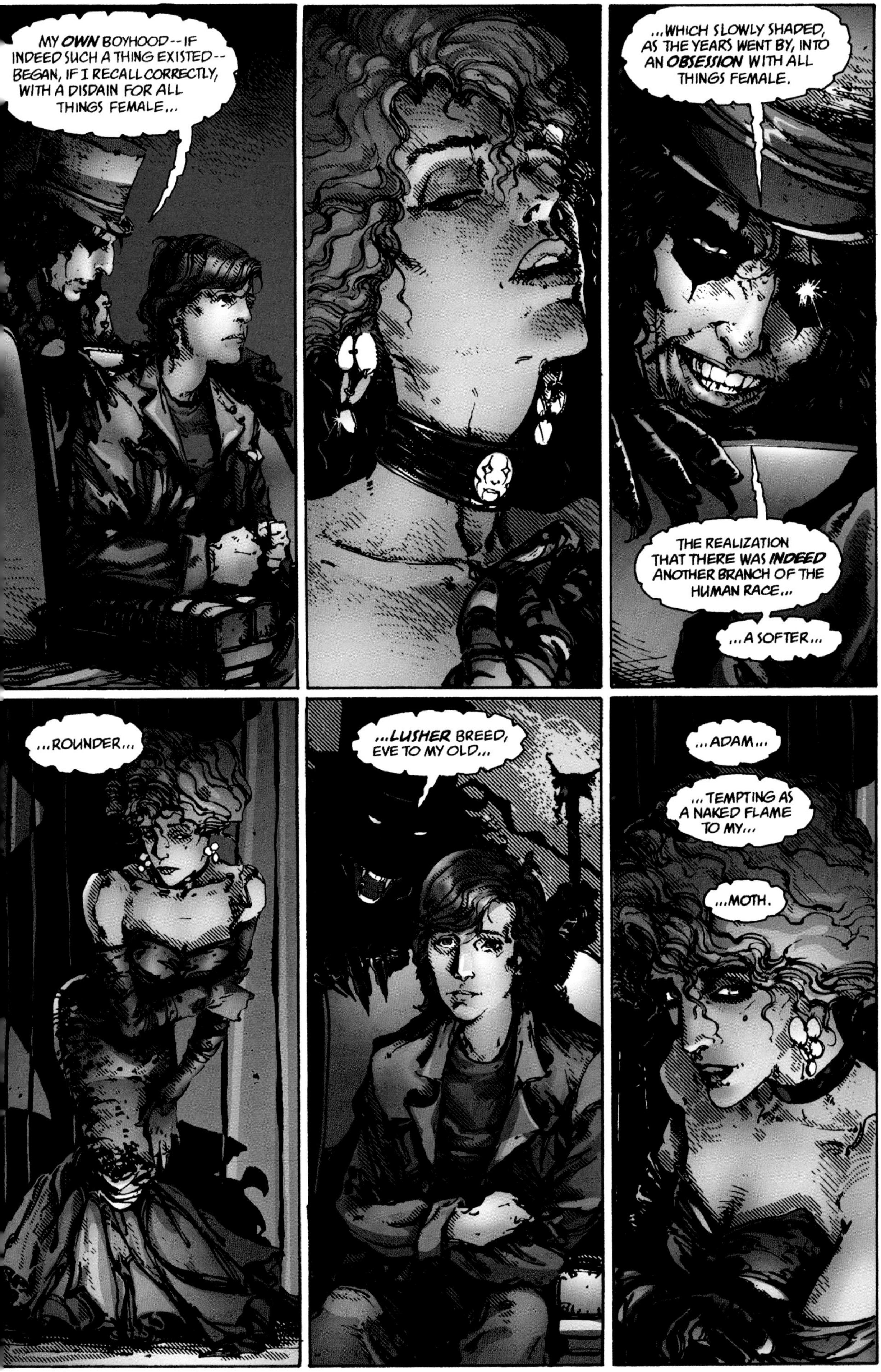
MY OWN BOYHOOD--IF INDEED SUCH A THING EXISTED--BEGAN, IF I RECALL CORRECTLY, WITH A DISDAIN FOR ALL THINGS FEMALE...
...WHICH SLOWLY SHADED, AS THE YEARS WENT BY, INTO AN OBSESSION WITH ALL THINGS FEMALE.
THE REALIZATION THAT THERE WAS INDEED ANOTHER BRANCH OF THE HUMAN RACE...
...A SOFTER...
...ROUNDER...
...LUSHER BREED, EVE TO MY OLD...
...ADAM...
...TEMPTING AS A NAKED FLAME TO MY...
...MOTH.

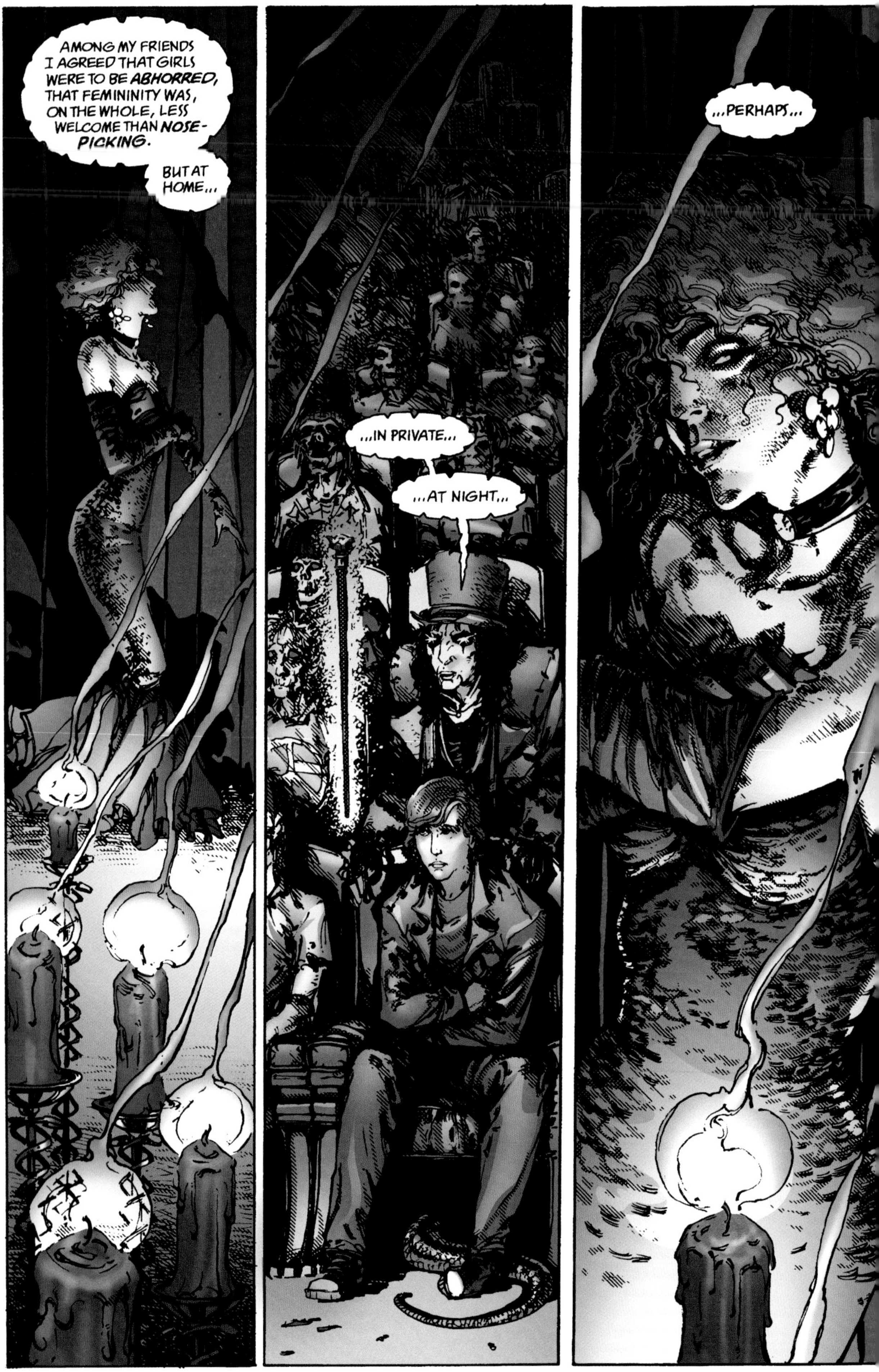
AMONG MY FRIENDS I AGREED THAT GIRLS WERE TO BE ABHORRED, THAT FEMININITY WAS, ON THE WHOLE, LESS WELCOME THAN NOSE-PICKING.
BUT AT HOME...
...IN PRIVATE...
...AT NIGHT...
...PERHAPS...

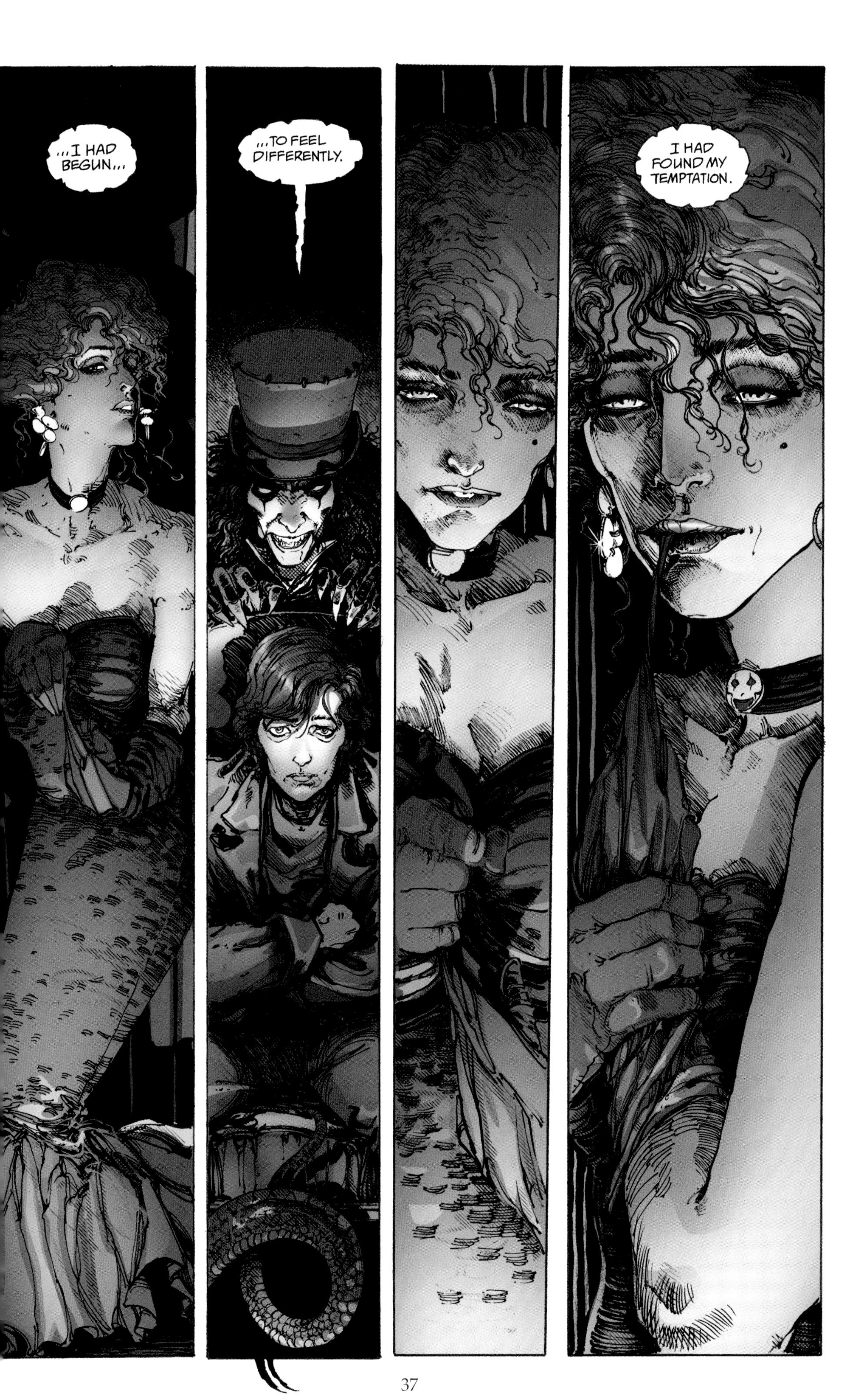
...I HAD BEGUN...
...TO FEEL DIFFERENTLY.
I HAD FOUND MY TEMPTATION.

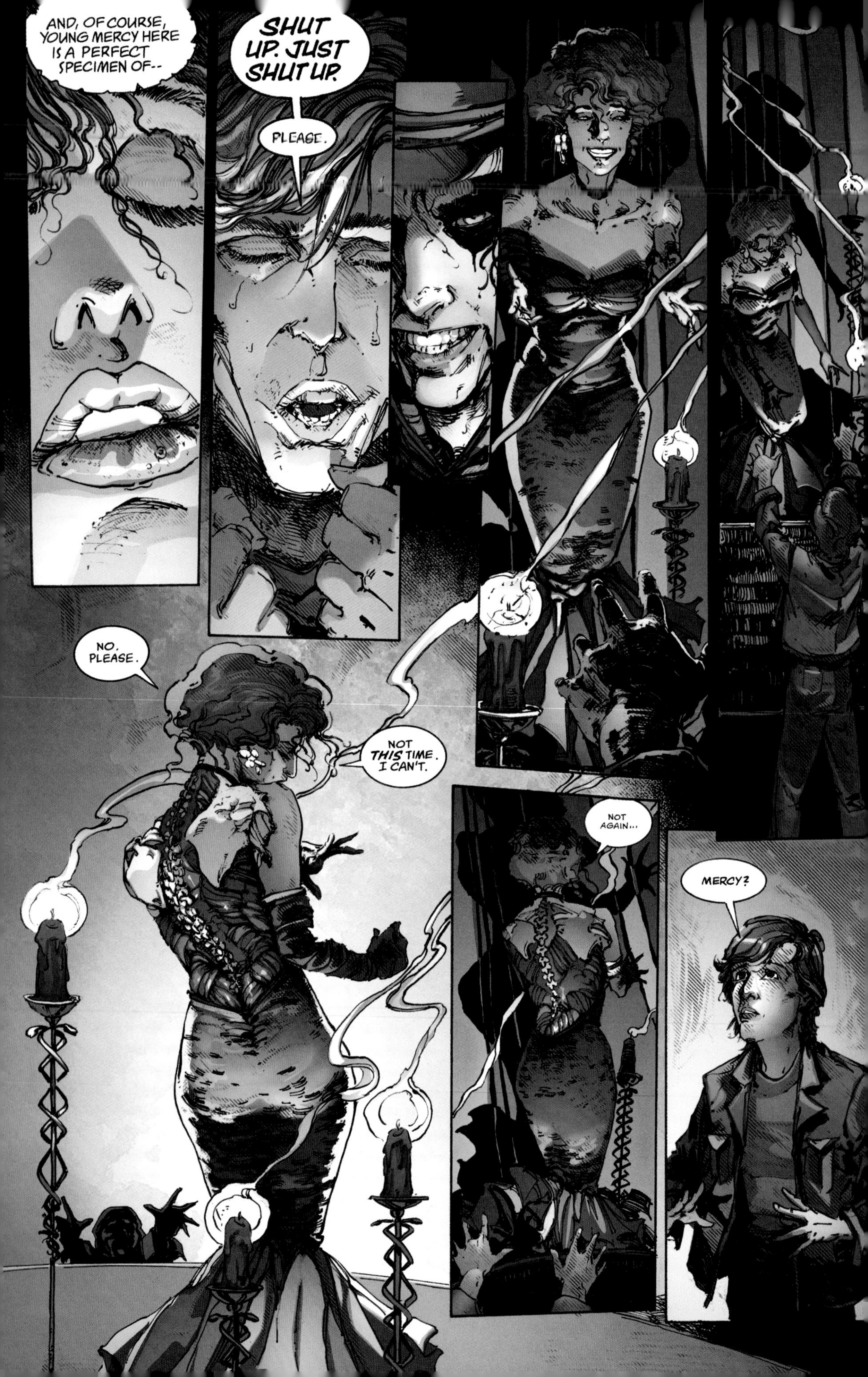
AND, OF COURSE, YOUNG MERCY HERE IS A PERFECT SPECIMEN OF--
SHUT UP. JUST SHUT UP.
PLEASE.
NO. PLEASE.
NOT THIS TIME. I CAN'T.
NOT AGAIN...
MERCY?

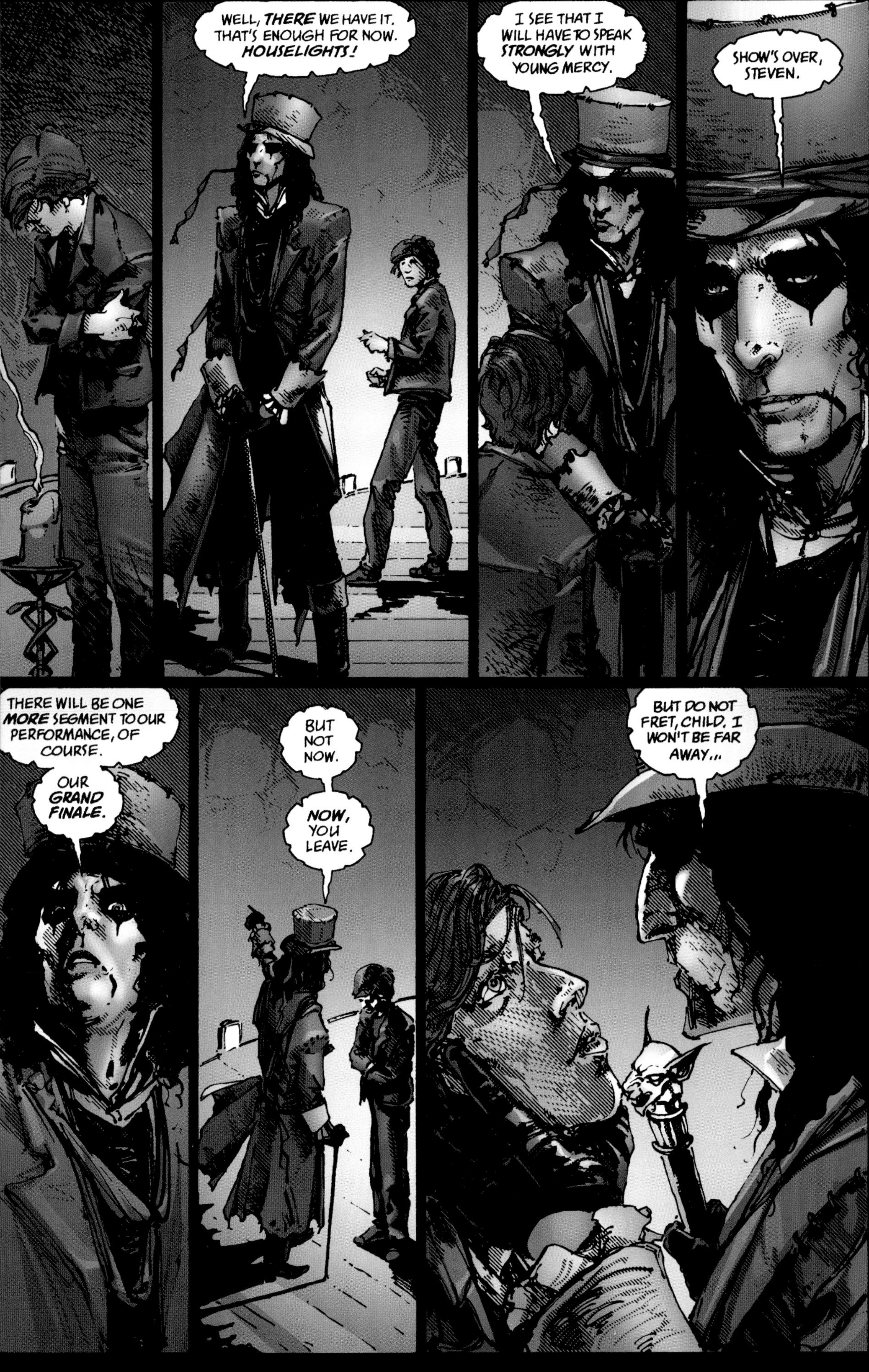
WELL, THERE WE HAVE IT. THAT'S ENOUGH FOR NOW. HOUSELIGHTS!
I SEE THAT I WILL HAVE TO SPEAK STRONGLY WITH YOUNG MERCY.
SHOW'S OVER, STEVEN.
THERE WILL BE ONE MORE SEGMENT TO OUR PERFORMANCE, OF COURSE.
OUR GRAND FINALE.
BUT NOT NOW.
NOW, YOU LEAVE.
BUT DO NOT FRET, CHILD. I WON'T BE FAR AWAY...

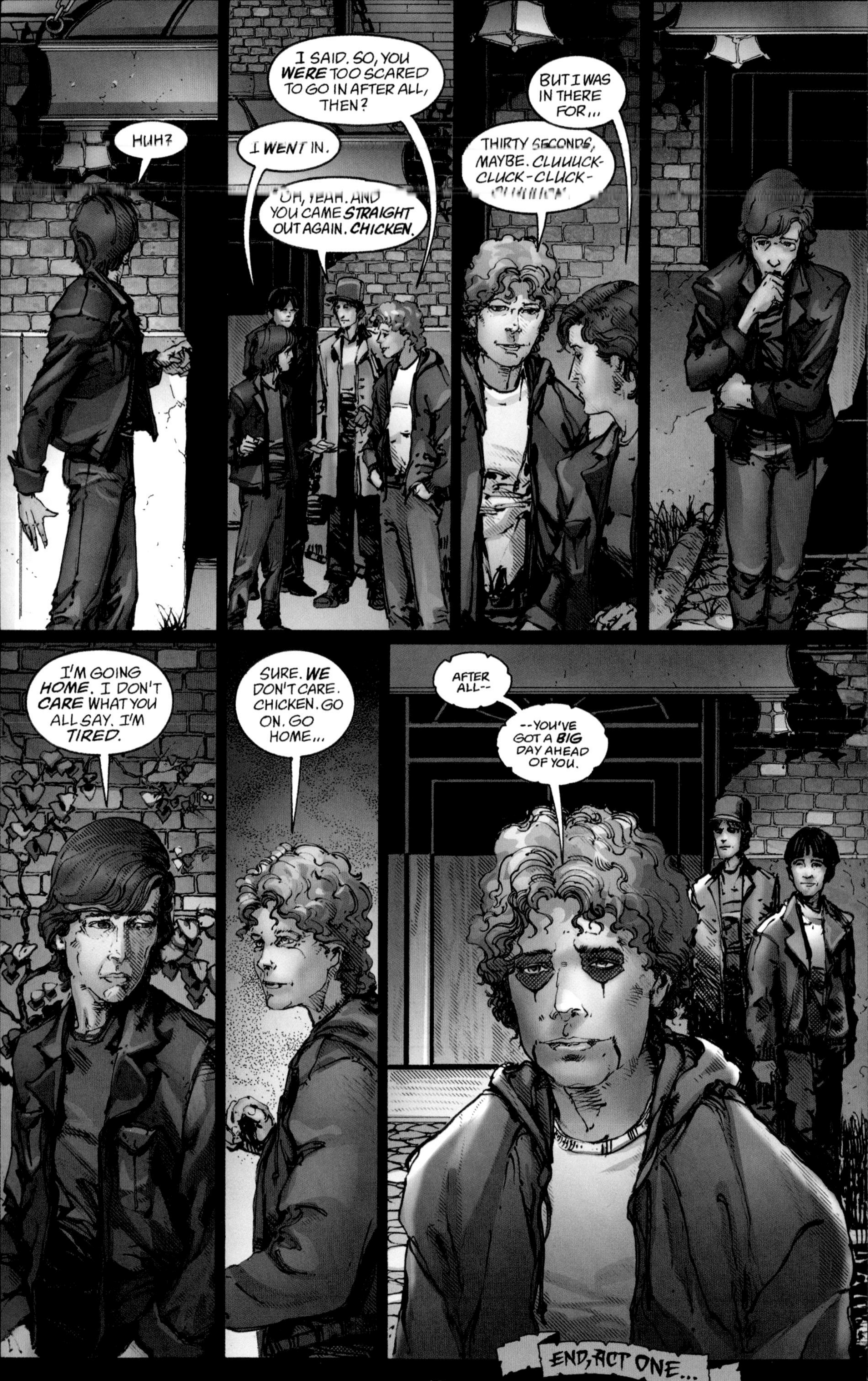
HUH?
I SAID. SO, YOU WERE TOO SCARED TO GO IN AFTER ALL, THEN?
I WENT IN.
OH, YEAH. AND YOU CAME STRAIGHT OUT AGAIN. CHICKEN.
BUT I WAS IN THERE FOR...
THIRTY SECONDS, MAYBE. CLUUUCK-CLUCK-CLUCK-
I'M GOING HOME. I DON'T CARE WHAT YOU ALL SAY. I'M TIRED.
SURE. WE DON'T CARE. CHICKEN. GO ON. GO HOME...
AFTER ALL--
--YOU'VE GOT A BIG DAY AHEAD OF YOU.
END, ACT ONE...

ACT TWO: UNHOLY WAR

HIS NAME IS STEVEN. AFTER SCHOOL TODAY HE SAW A SHOW IN A THEATER THAT DOESN'T EXIST.

LEAVING IT, AT FIRST, HE WALKED AWAY. SLOWLY. ALMOST CARELESSLY.

SOON HE BEGAN TO HURRY.

FINALLY HE BEGAN TO RUN.

TO RUN HEEDLESSLY, BLINDLY, AS IF ALL THE POWERS OF HELL WERE CLOSE BEHIND HIM.

STRANGER THINGS HAVE HAPPENED, AFTER ALL...

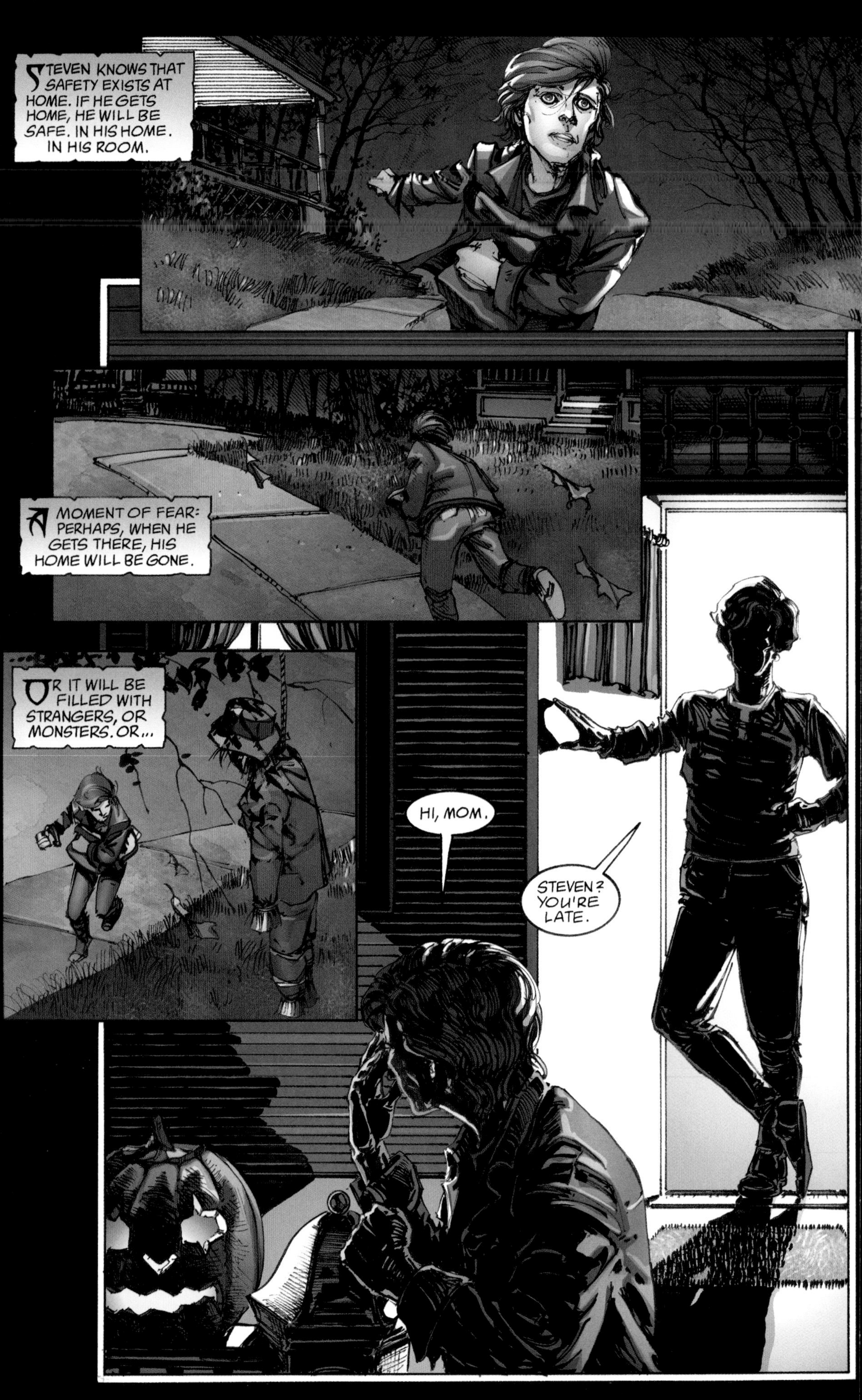
STEVEN KNOWS THAT SAFETY EXISTS AT HOME. IF HE GETS HOME, HE WILL BE SAFE. IN HIS HOME. IN HIS ROOM.
A MOMENT OF FEAR: PERHAPS, WHEN HE GETS THERE, HIS HOME WILL BE GONE.
OR IT WILL BE FILLED WITH STRANGERS, OR MONSTERS. OR...
HI, MOM.
STEVEN? YOU'RE LATE.

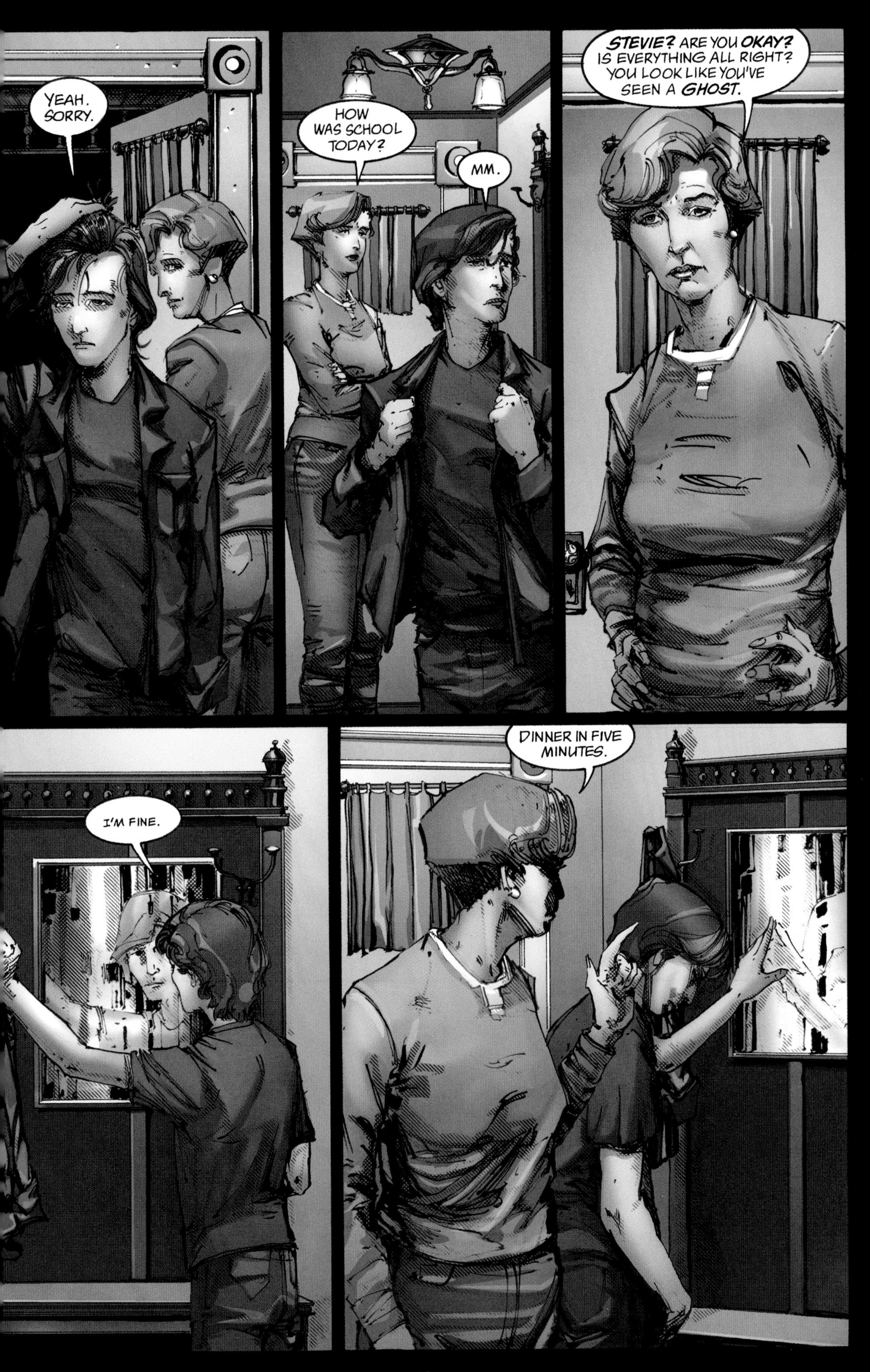

YEAH. SORRY.
HOW WAS SCHOOL TODAY?
MM.
STEVIE? ARE YOU OKAY? IS EVERYTHING ALL RIGHT? YOU LOOK LIKE YOU'VE SEEN A GHOST.
I'M FINE.
DINNER IN FIVE MINUTES.

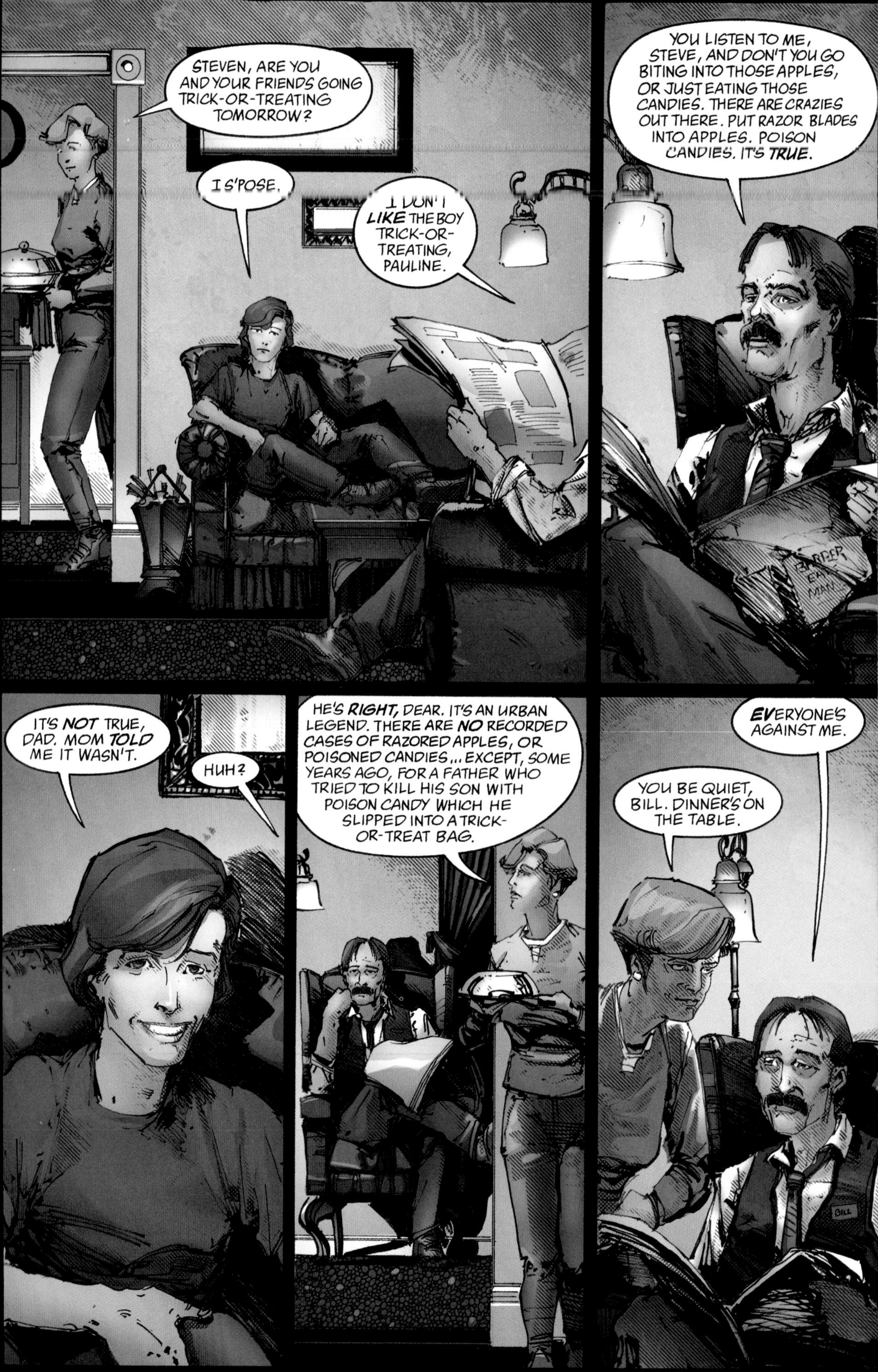
STEVEN, ARE YOU AND YOUR FRIENDS GOING TRICK-OR-TREATING TOMORROW?
I S'POSE.
I DON'T LIKE THE BOY TRICK-OR-TREATING, PAULINE.
YOU LISTEN TO ME, STEVE, AND DON'T YOU GO BITING INTO THOSE APPLES, OR JUST EATING THOSE CANDIES. THERE ARE CRAZIES OUT THERE. PUT RAZOR BLADES INTO APPLES. POISON CANDIES. IT'S TRUE.
IT'S NOT TRUE, DAD. MOM TOLD ME IT WASN'T.
HUH?
HE'S RIGHT, DEAR. IT'S AN URBAN LEGEND. THERE ARE NO RECORDED CASES OF RAZORED APPLES, OR POISONED CANDIES... EXCEPT, SOME YEARS AGO, FOR A FATHER WHO TRIED TO KILL HIS SON WITH POISON CANDY WHICH HE SLIPPED INTO A TRICK-OR-TREAT BAG.
EVERYONE'S AGAINST ME.
YOU BE QUIET, BILL. DINNER'S ON THE TABLE.

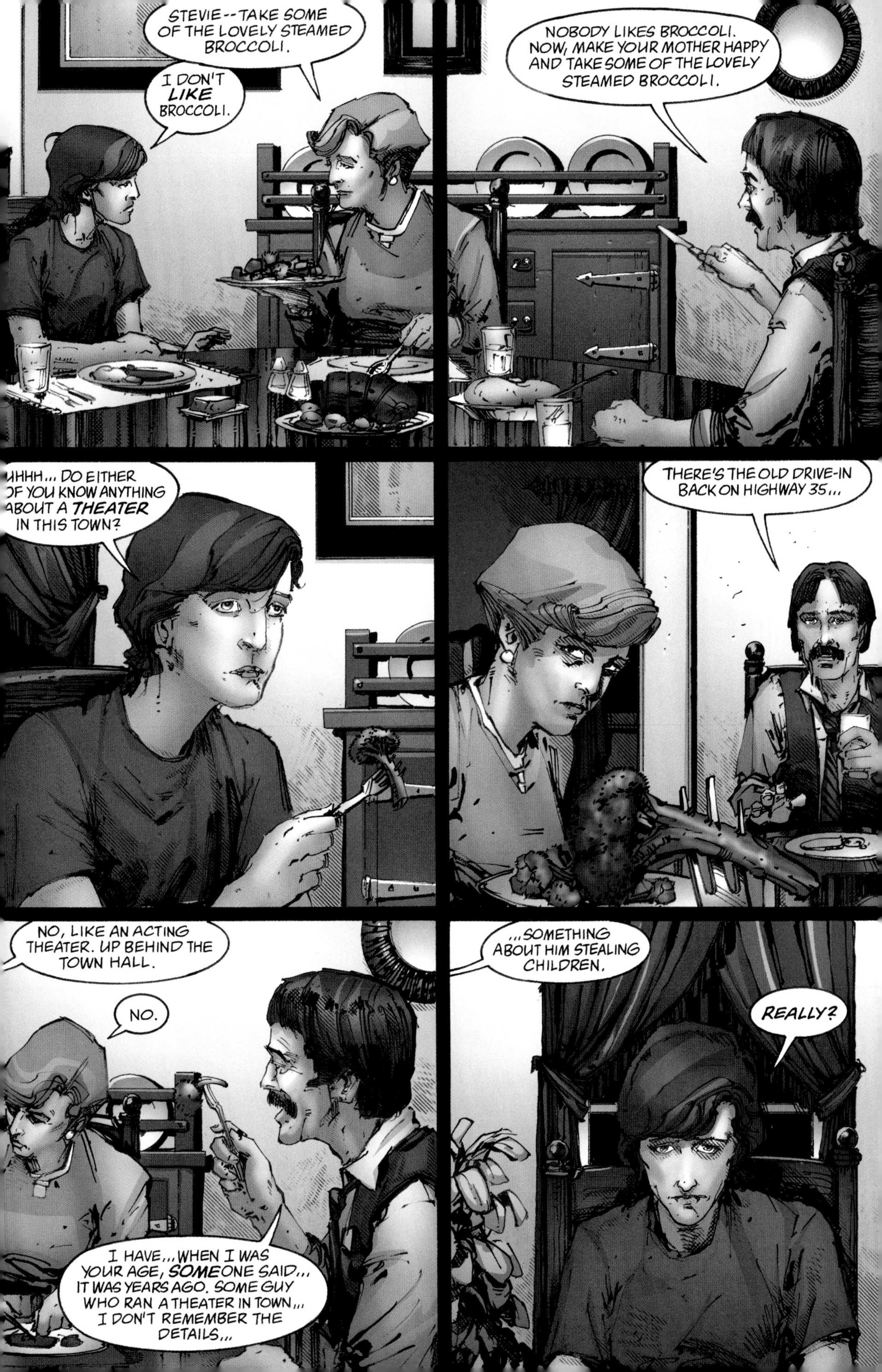
STEVIE--TAKE SOME OF THE LOVELY STEAMED BROCCOLI.
I DON'T LIKE BROCCOLI.
NOBODY LIKES BROCCOLI. NOW, MAKE YOUR MOTHER HAPPY AND TAKE SOME OF THE LOVELY STEAMED BROCCOLI.
UHHH... DO EITHER OF YOU KNOW ANYTHING ABOUT A THEATER IN THIS TOWN?
THERE'S THE OLD DRIVE-IN BACK ON HIGHWAY 35...
NO, LIKE AN ACTING THEATER. UP BEHIND THE TOWN HALL.
NO.
I HAVE... WHEN I WAS YOUR AGE, SOMEONE SAID... IT WAS YEARS AGO. SOME GUY WHO RAN A THEATER IN TOWN... I DON'T REMEMBER THE DETAILS...
...SOMETHING ABOUT HIM STEALING CHILDREN.
REALLY?

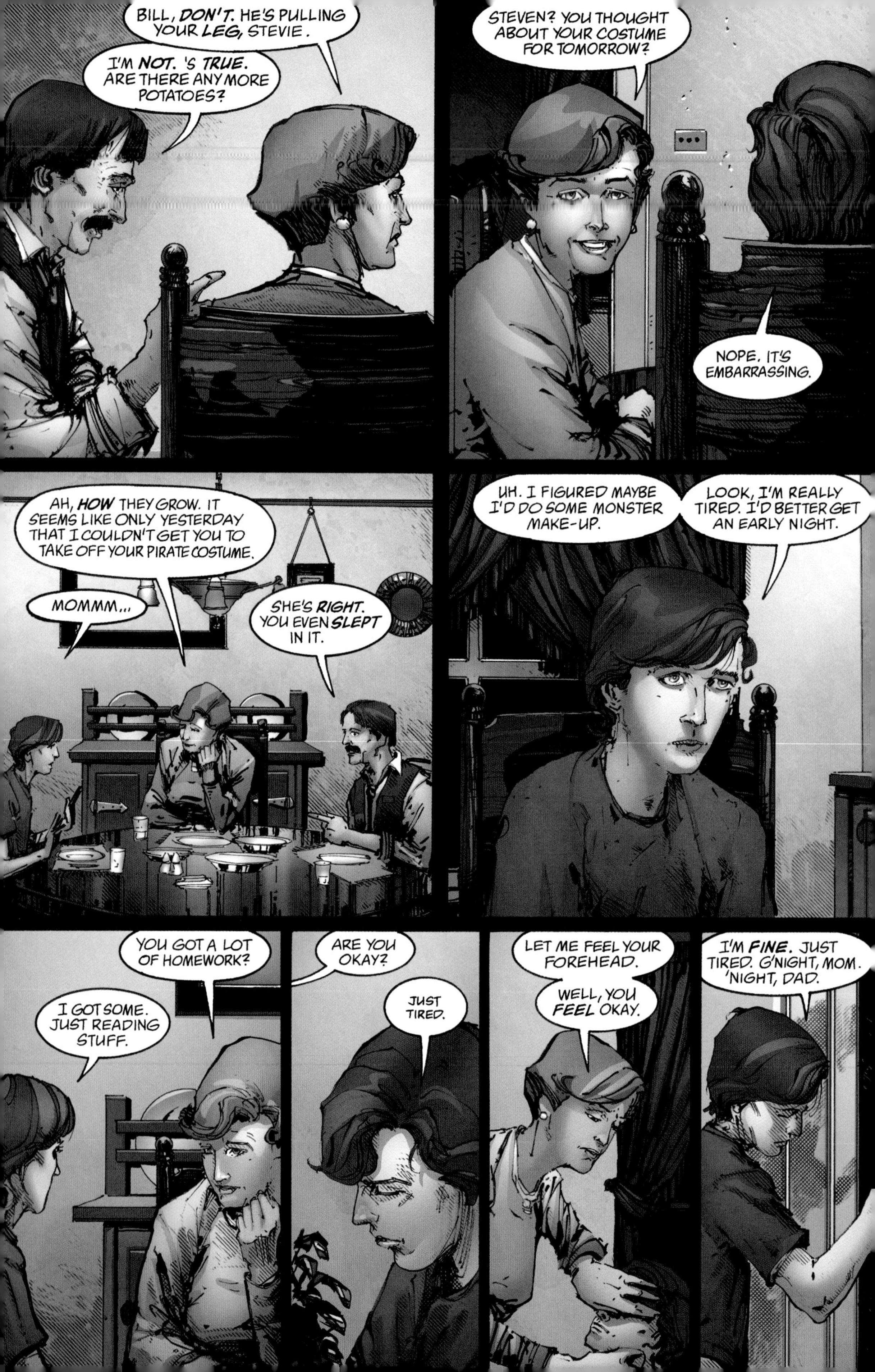
BILL, DON'T. HE'S PULLING YOUR LEG, STEVIE.
I'M NOT. 'S TRUE. ARE THERE ANY MORE POTATOES?
STEVEN? YOU THOUGHT ABOUT YOUR COSTUME FOR TOMORROW?
NOPE. IT'S EMBARRASSING.
AH, HOW THEY GROW. IT SEEMS LIKE ONLY YESTERDAY THAT I COULDN'T GET YOU TO TAKE OFF YOUR PIRATE COSTUME.
MOMMM...
SHE'S RIGHT. YOU EVEN SLEPT IN IT.
UH. I FIGURED MAYBE I'D DO SOME MONSTER MAKE-UP.
LOOK, I'M REALLY TIRED. I'D BETTER GET AN EARLY NIGHT.
YOU GOT A LOT OF HOMEWORK?
I GOT SOME. JUST READING STUFF.
ARE YOU OKAY?
JUST TIRED.
LET ME FEEL YOUR FOREHEAD.
WELL, YOU FEEL OKAY.
I'M FINE. JUST TIRED. G'NIGHT, MOM. 'NIGHT, DAD.

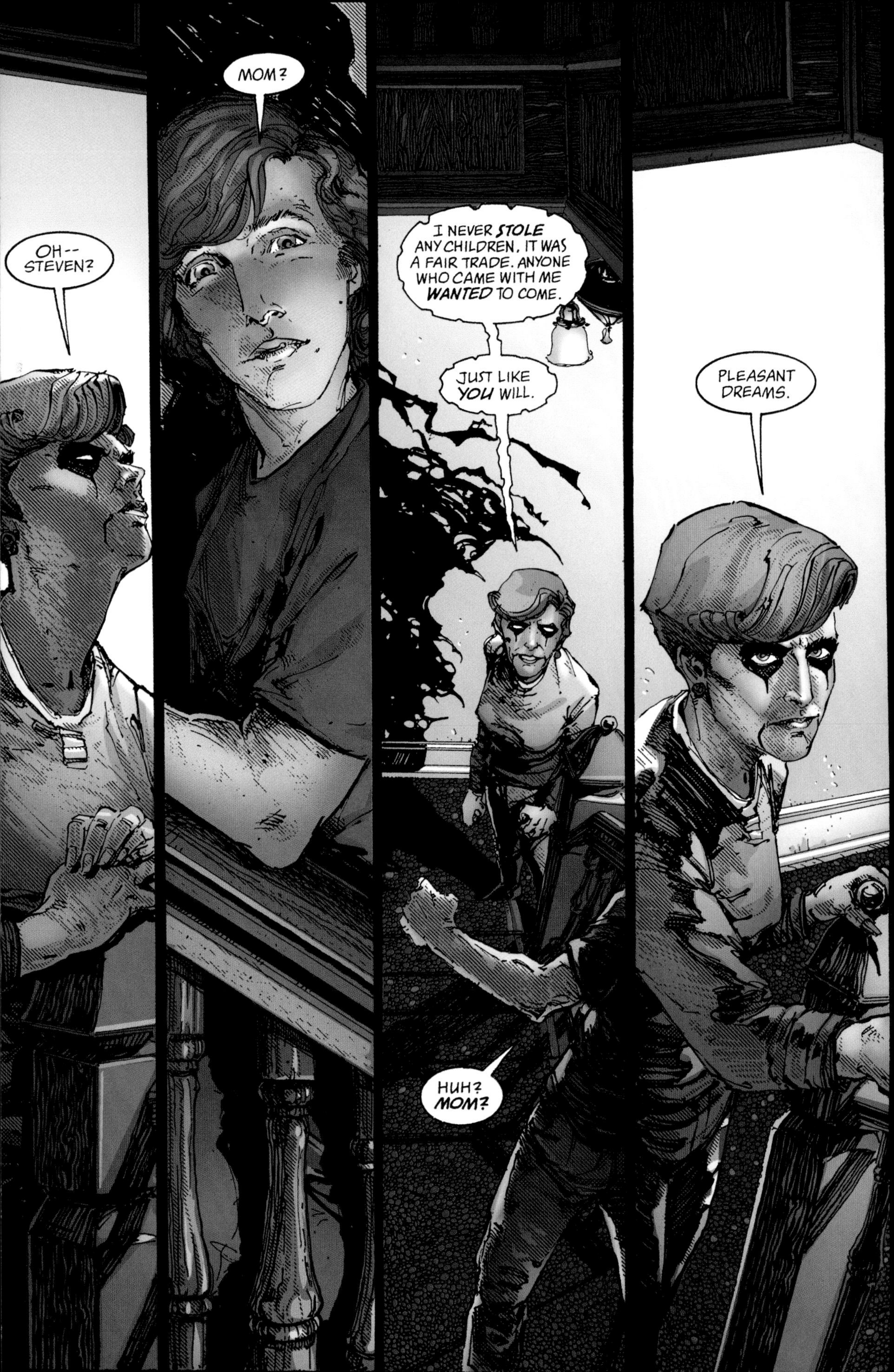
MOM?
OH-- STEVEN?
I NEVER STOLE ANY CHILDREN. IT WAS A FAIR TRADE. ANYONE WHO CAME WITH ME WANTED TO COME.
JUST LIKE YOU WILL.
HUH? MOM?
PLEASANT DREAMS.

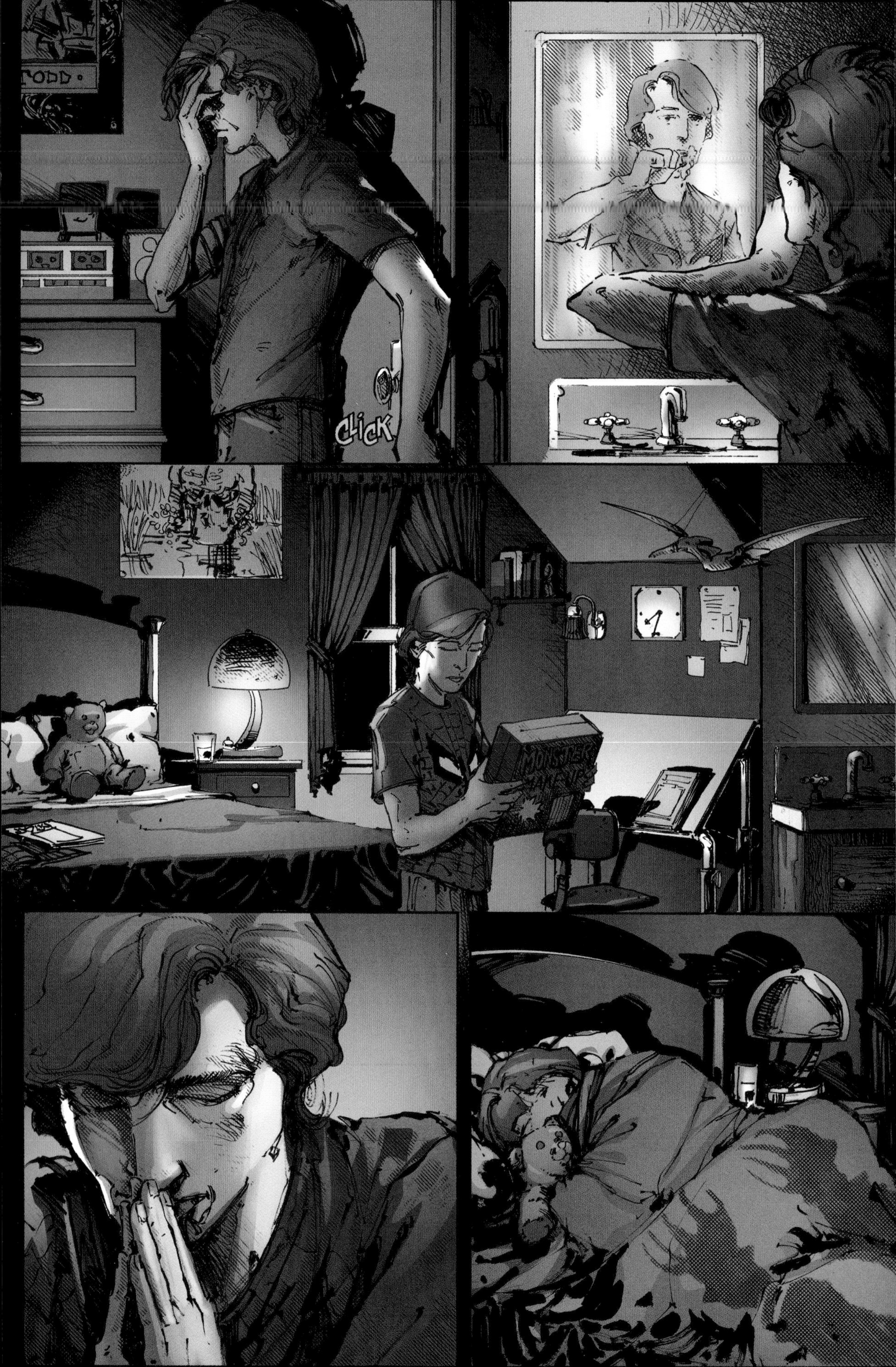
TODD
CLICK
MONSTER MAKE-UP

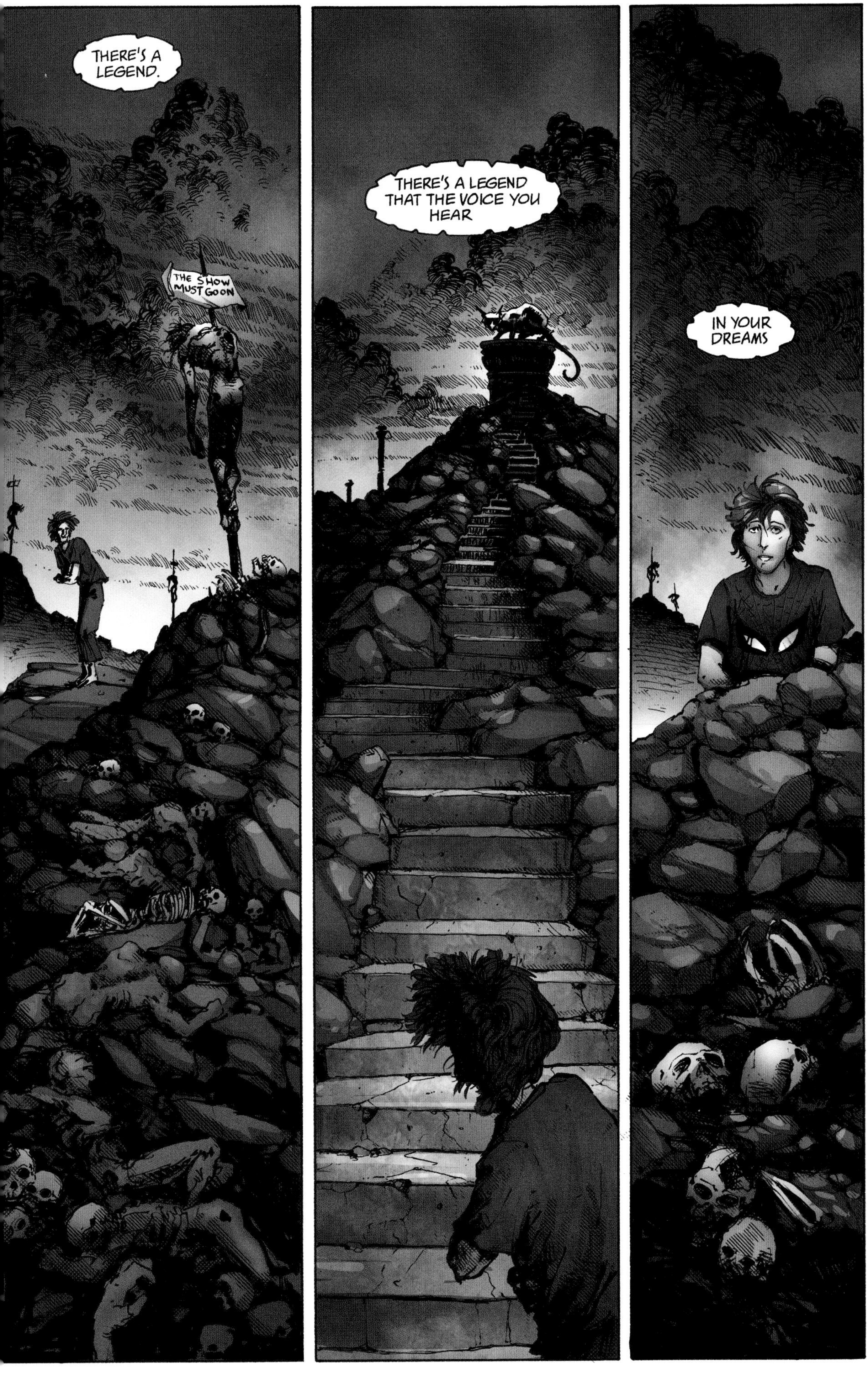
THERE'S A LEGEND.
THE SHOW MUST GO ON
THERE'S A LEGEND THAT THE VOICE YOU HEAR
IN YOUR DREAMS

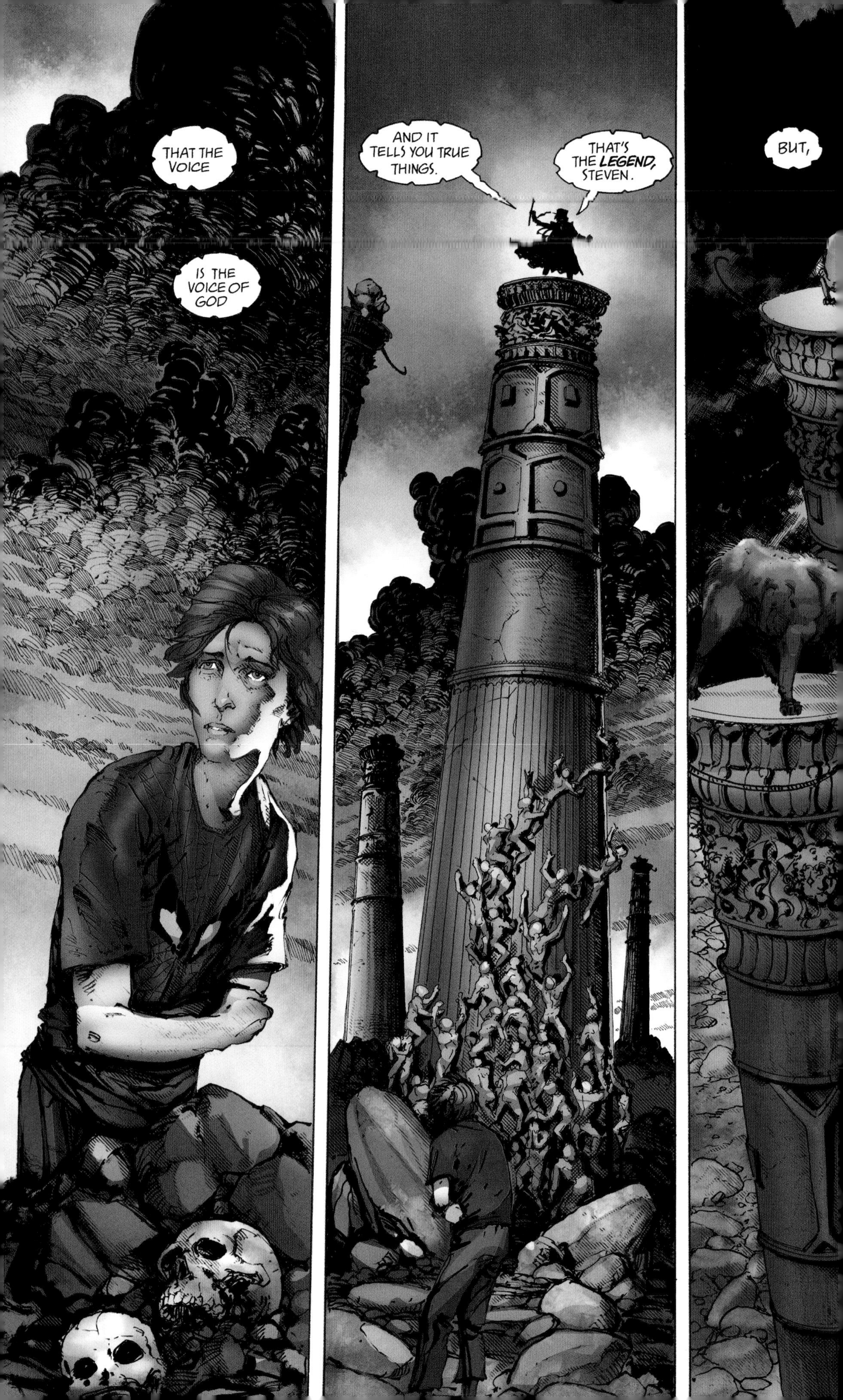
THAT THE VOICE
IS THE VOICE OF GOD
AND IT TELLS YOU TRUE THINGS.
THAT'S THE LEGEND, STEVEN.
BUT,

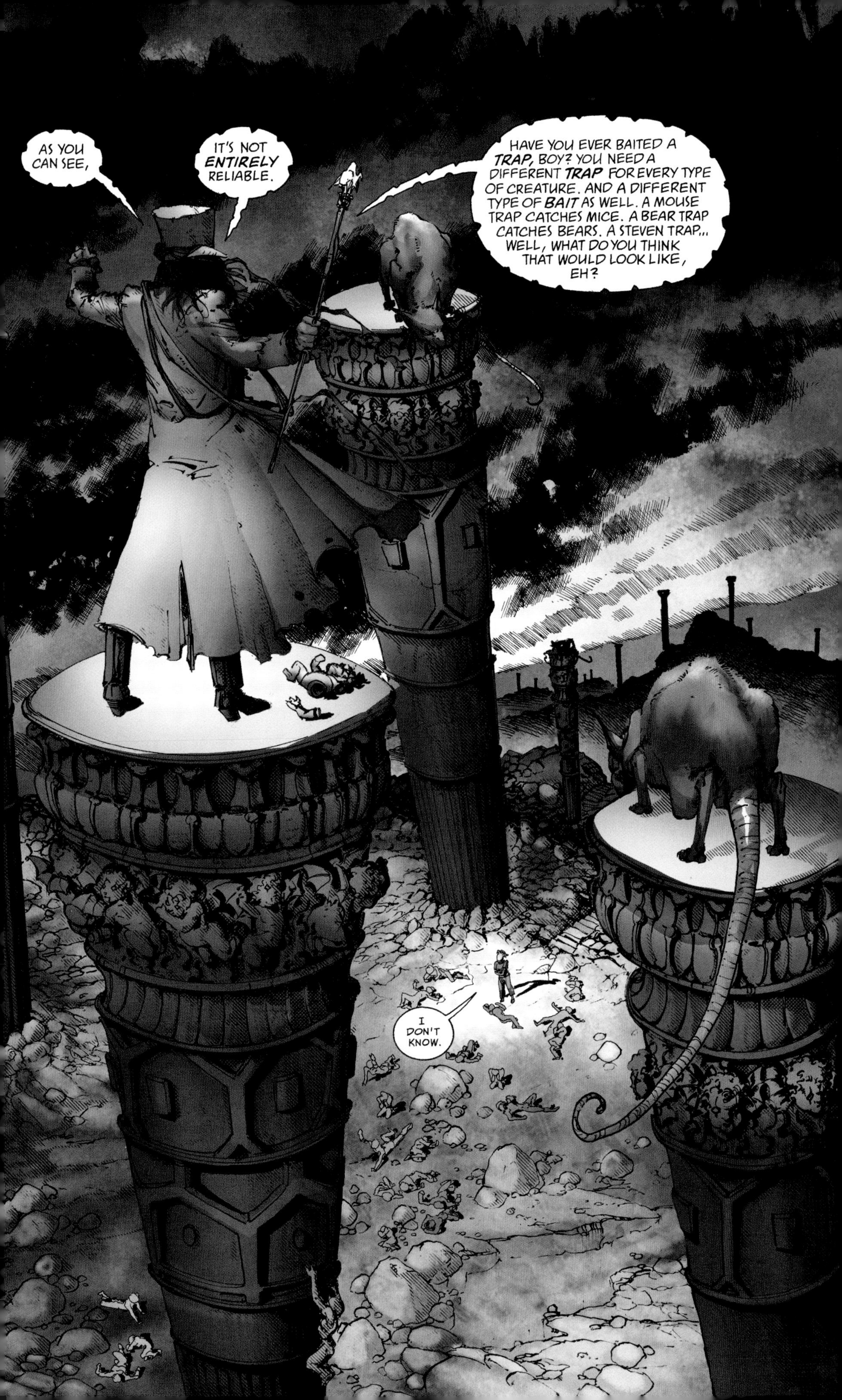
AS YOU CAN SEE,
IT'S NOT ENTIRELY RELIABLE.
HAVE YOU EVER BAITED A TRAP, BOY? YOU NEED A DIFFERENT TRAP FOR EVERY TYPE OF CREATURE. AND A DIFFERENT TYPE OF BAIT AS WELL. A MOUSE TRAP CATCHES MICE. A BEAR TRAP CATCHES BEARS. A STEVEN TRAP... WELL, WHAT DO YOU THINK THAT WOULD LOOK LIKE, EH?
I DON'T KNOW.

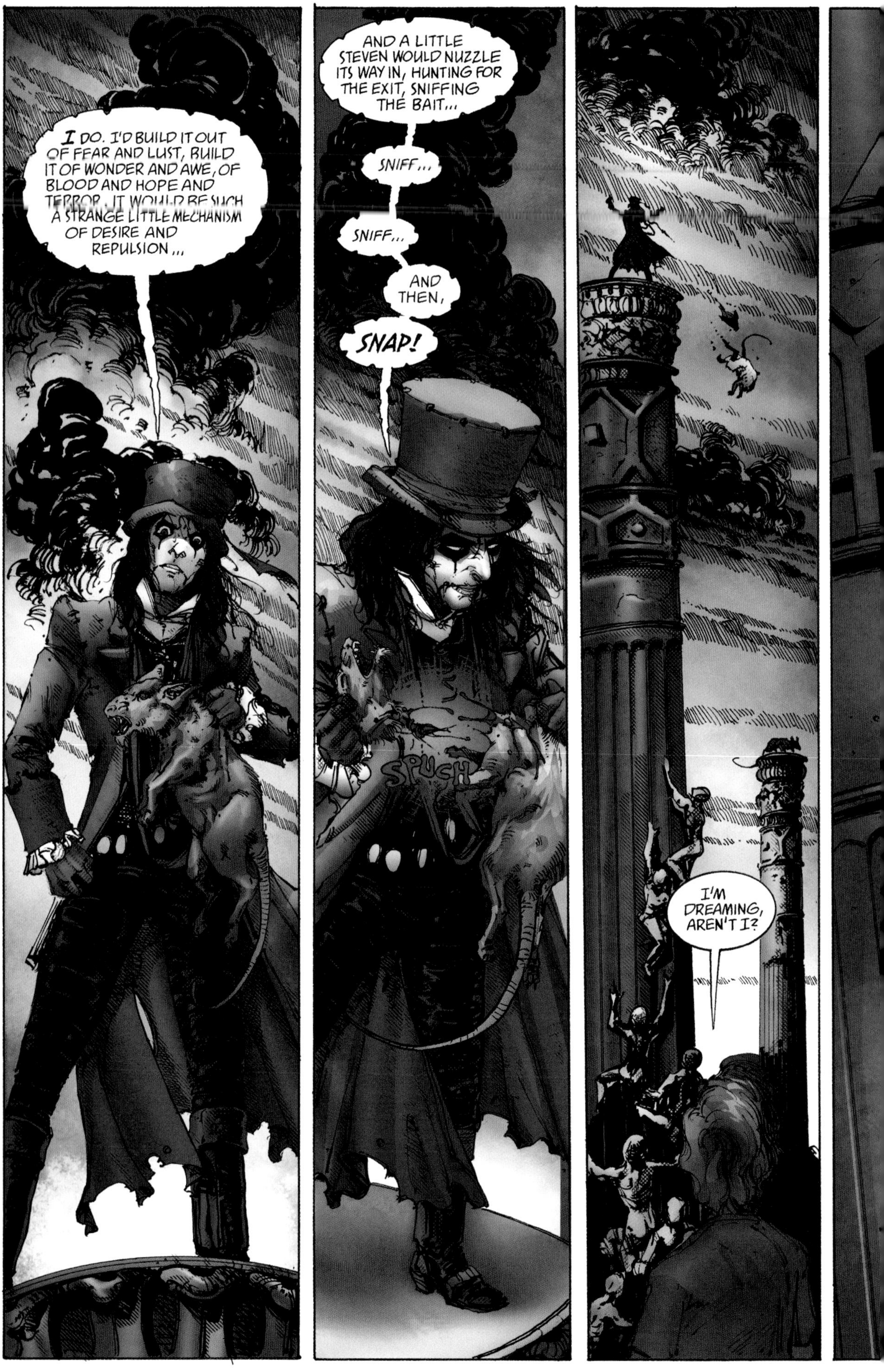
I DO. I'D BUILD IT OUT OF FEAR AND LUST, BUILD IT OF WONDER AND AWE, OF BLOOD AND HOPE AND TERROR. IT WOULD BE SUCH A STRANGE LITTLE MECHANISM OF DESIRE AND REPULSION...
AND A LITTLE STEVEN WOULD NUZZLE ITS WAY IN, HUNTING FOR THE EXIT, SNIFFING THE BAIT...
SNIFF...
SNIFF...
AND THEN,
SNAP!
SPUCH
I'M DREAMING, AREN'T I?

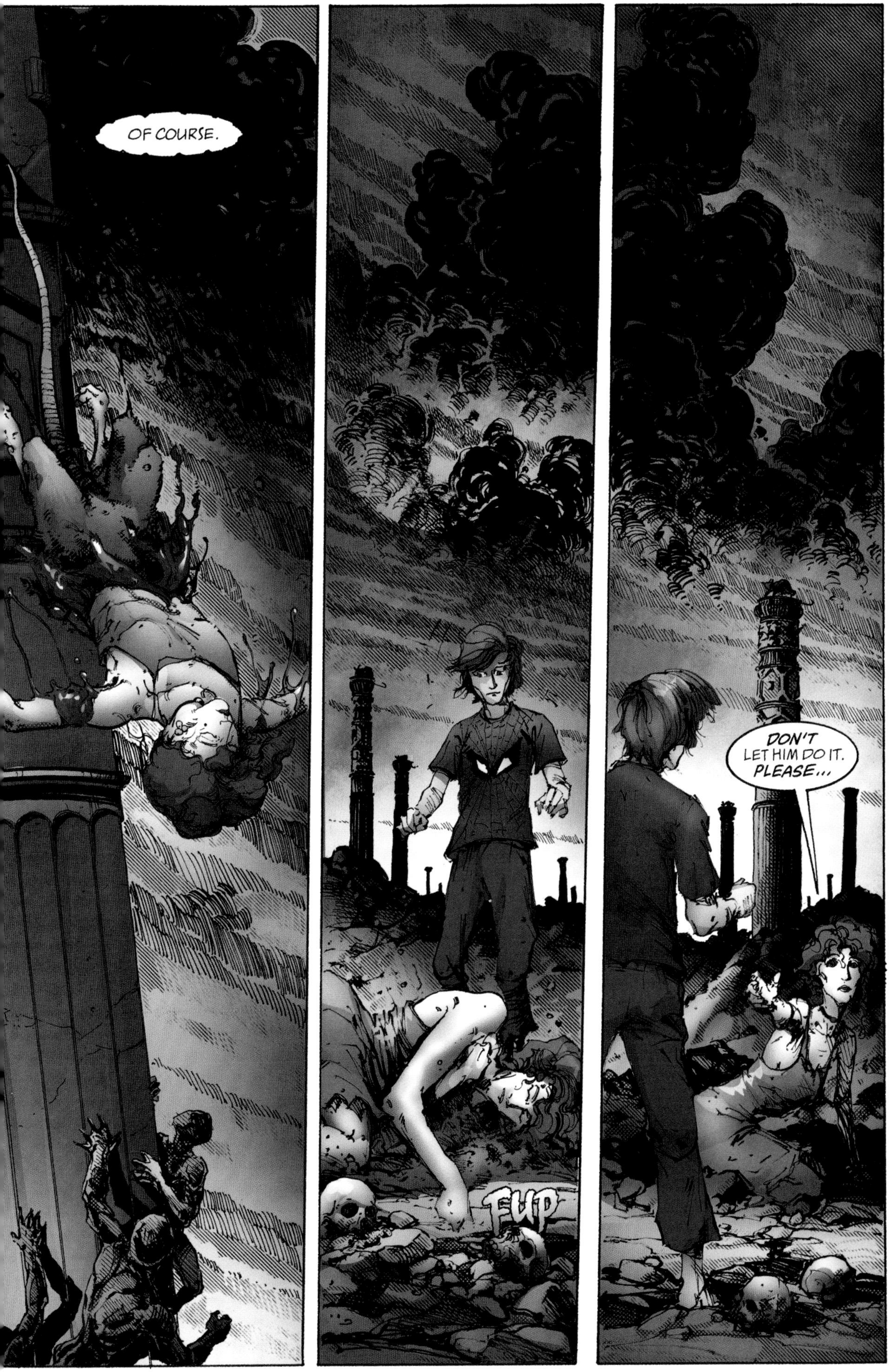

OF COURSE.
FUP
DON'T LET HIM DO IT. PLEASE...

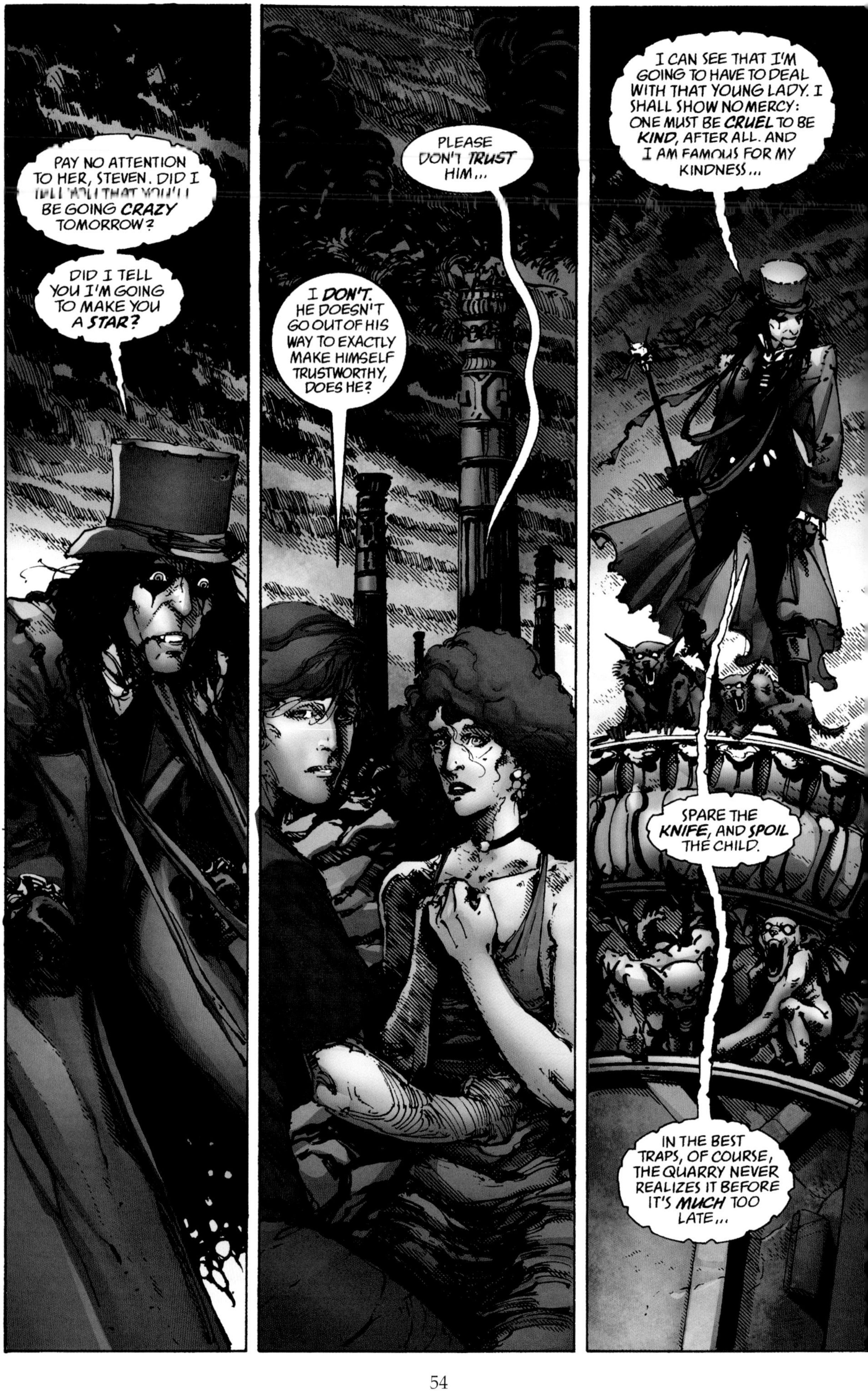
PAY NO ATTENTION TO HER, STEVEN. DID I TELL YOU THAT YOU'LL BE GOING *CRAZY* TOMORROW?
DID I TELL YOU I'M GOING TO MAKE YOU A *STAR?*
PLEASE DON'T *TRUST* HIM...
I *DON'T.* HE DOESN'T GO OUT OF HIS WAY TO EXACTLY MAKE HIMSELF TRUSTWORTHY, DOES HE?
I CAN SEE THAT I'M GOING TO HAVE TO DEAL WITH THAT YOUNG LADY. I SHALL SHOW NO MERCY: ONE MUST BE *CRUEL* TO BE *KIND*, AFTER ALL. AND I AM FAMOUS FOR MY KINDNESS...
SPARE THE *KNIFE*, AND *SPOIL* THE CHILD.
IN THE BEST TRAPS, OF COURSE, THE QUARRY NEVER REALIZES IT BEFORE IT'S *MUCH* TOO LATE...

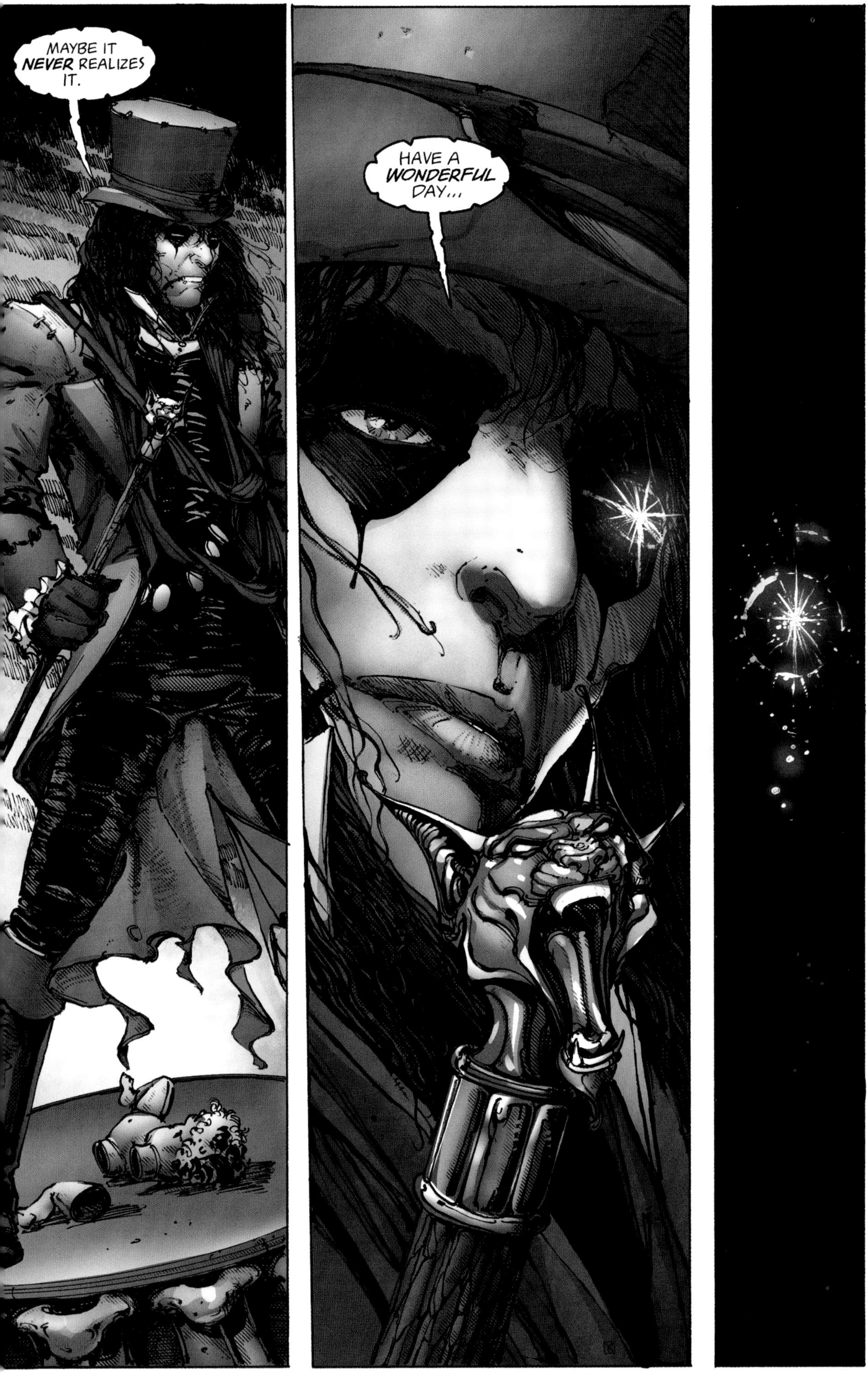
MAYBE IT NEVER REALIZES IT.
HAVE A WONDERFUL DAY...

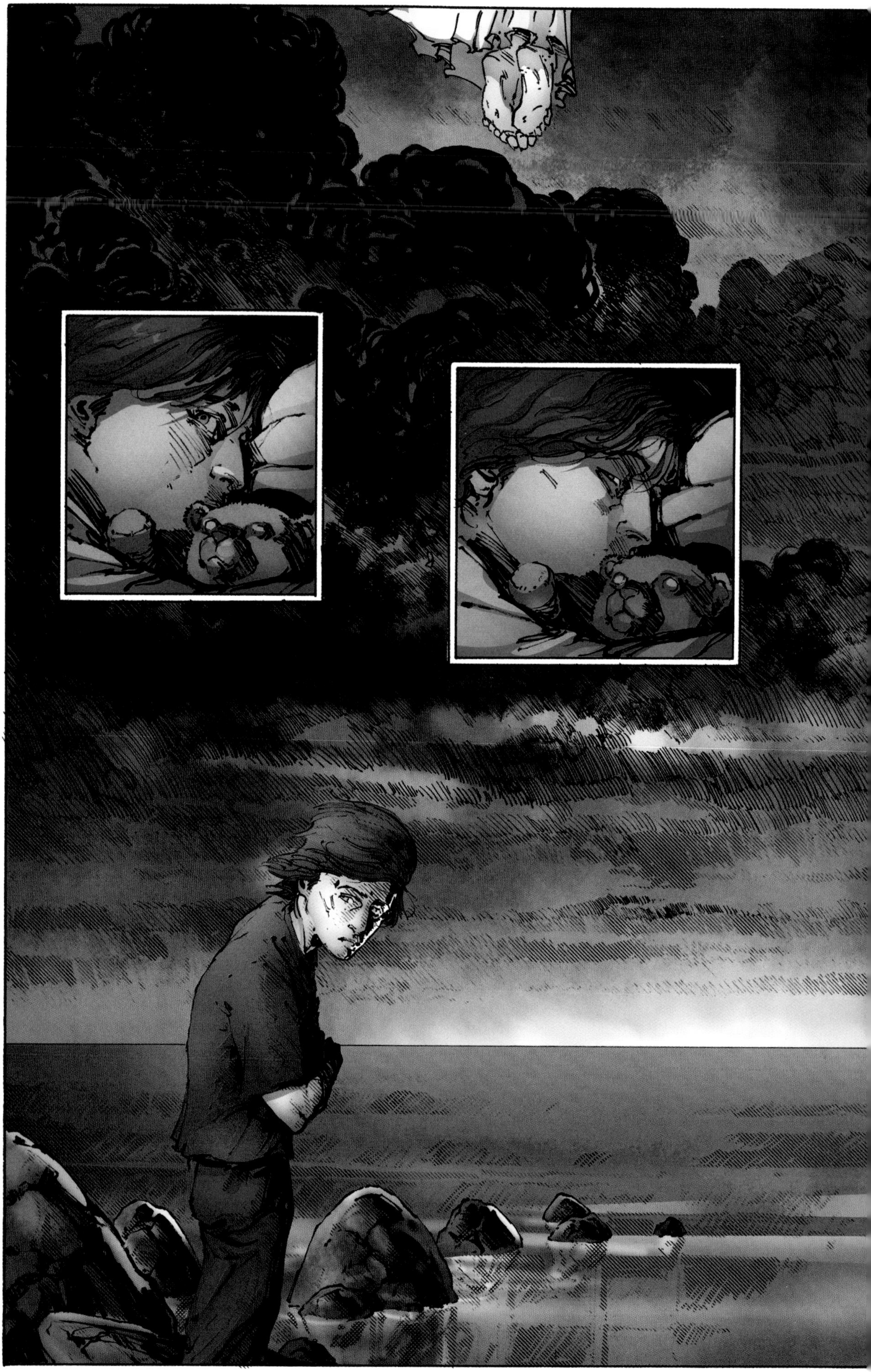

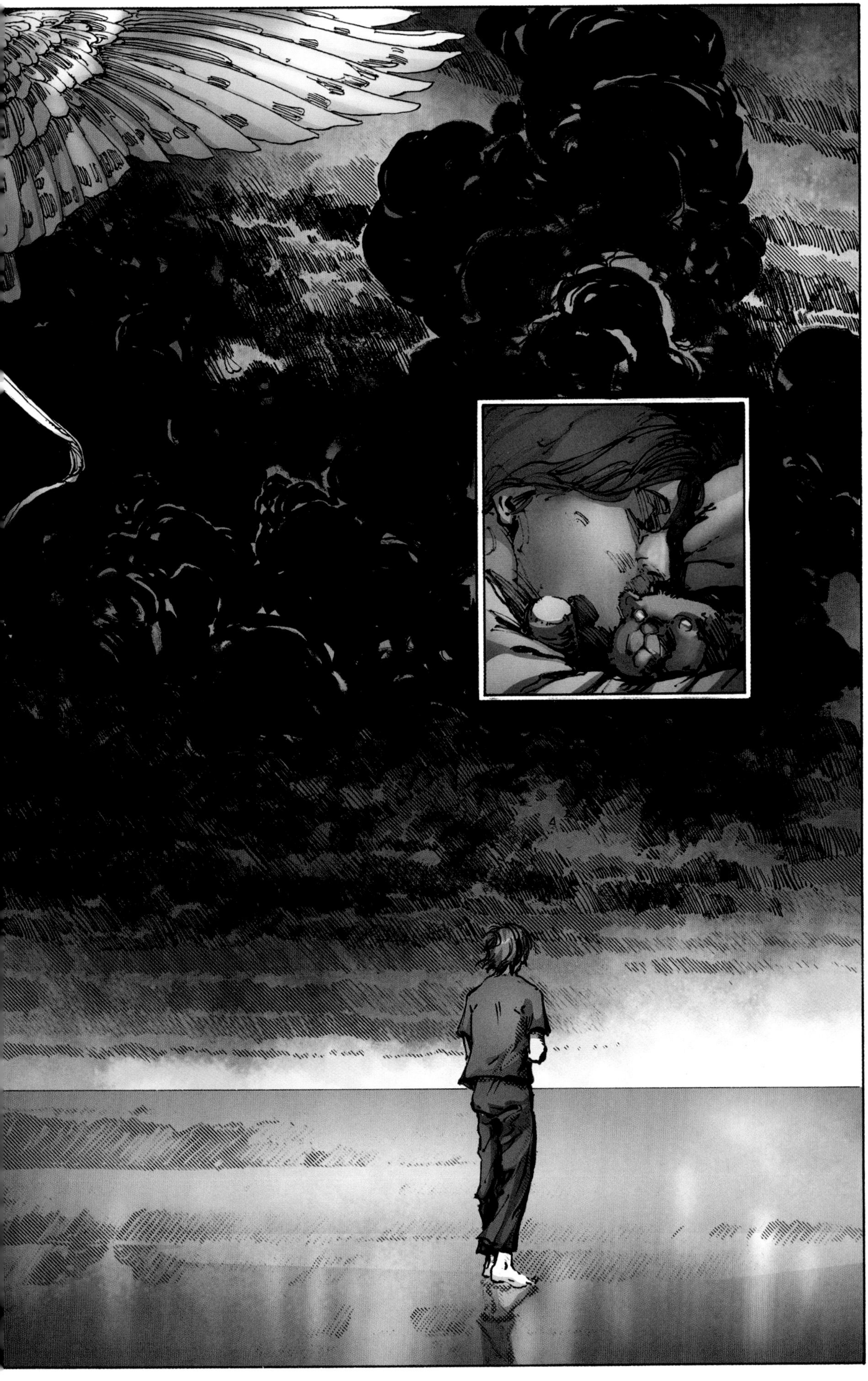

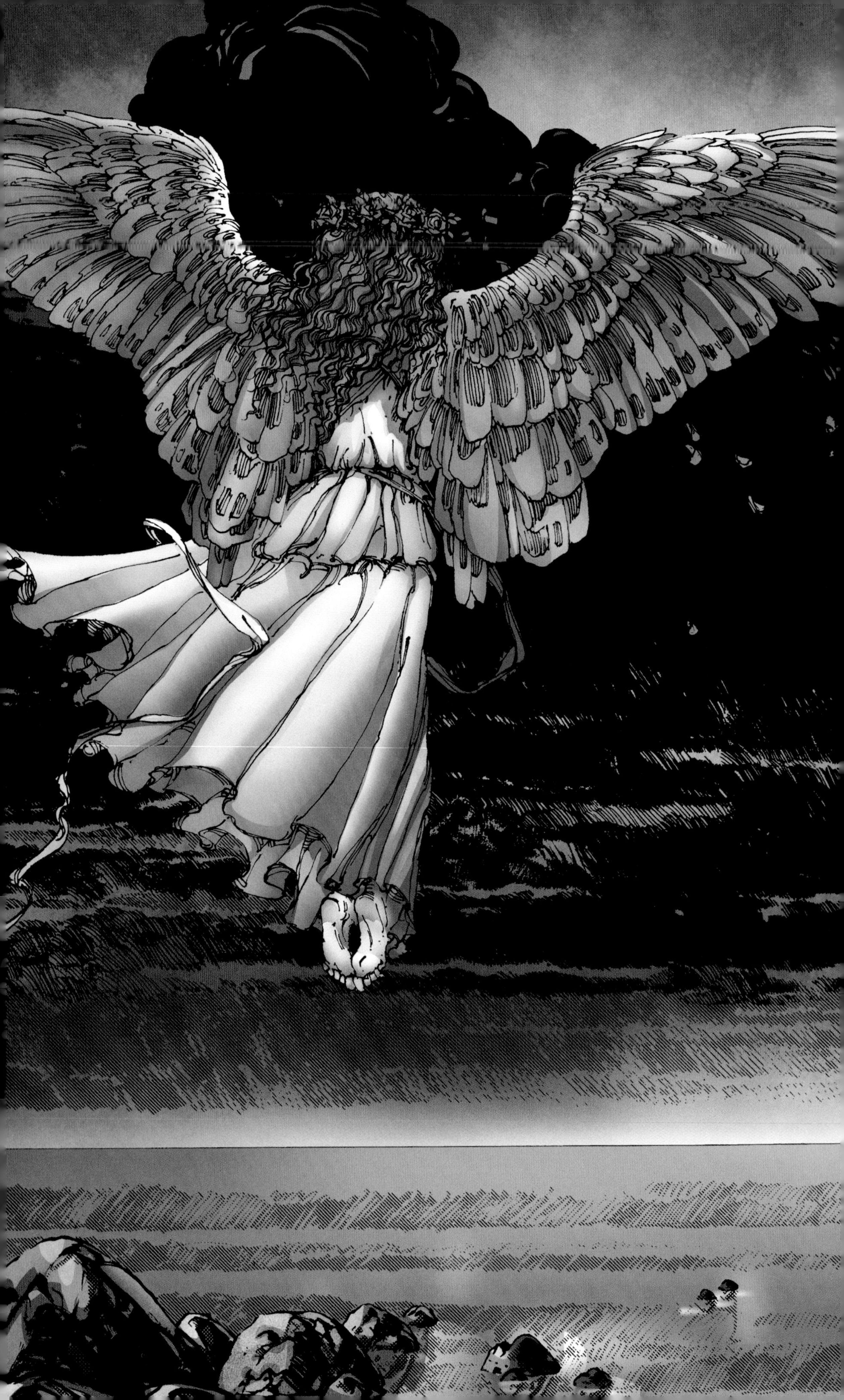

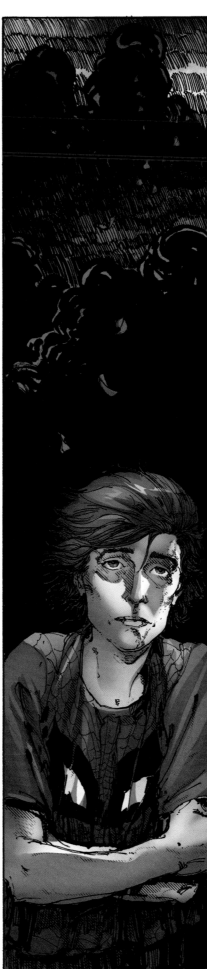

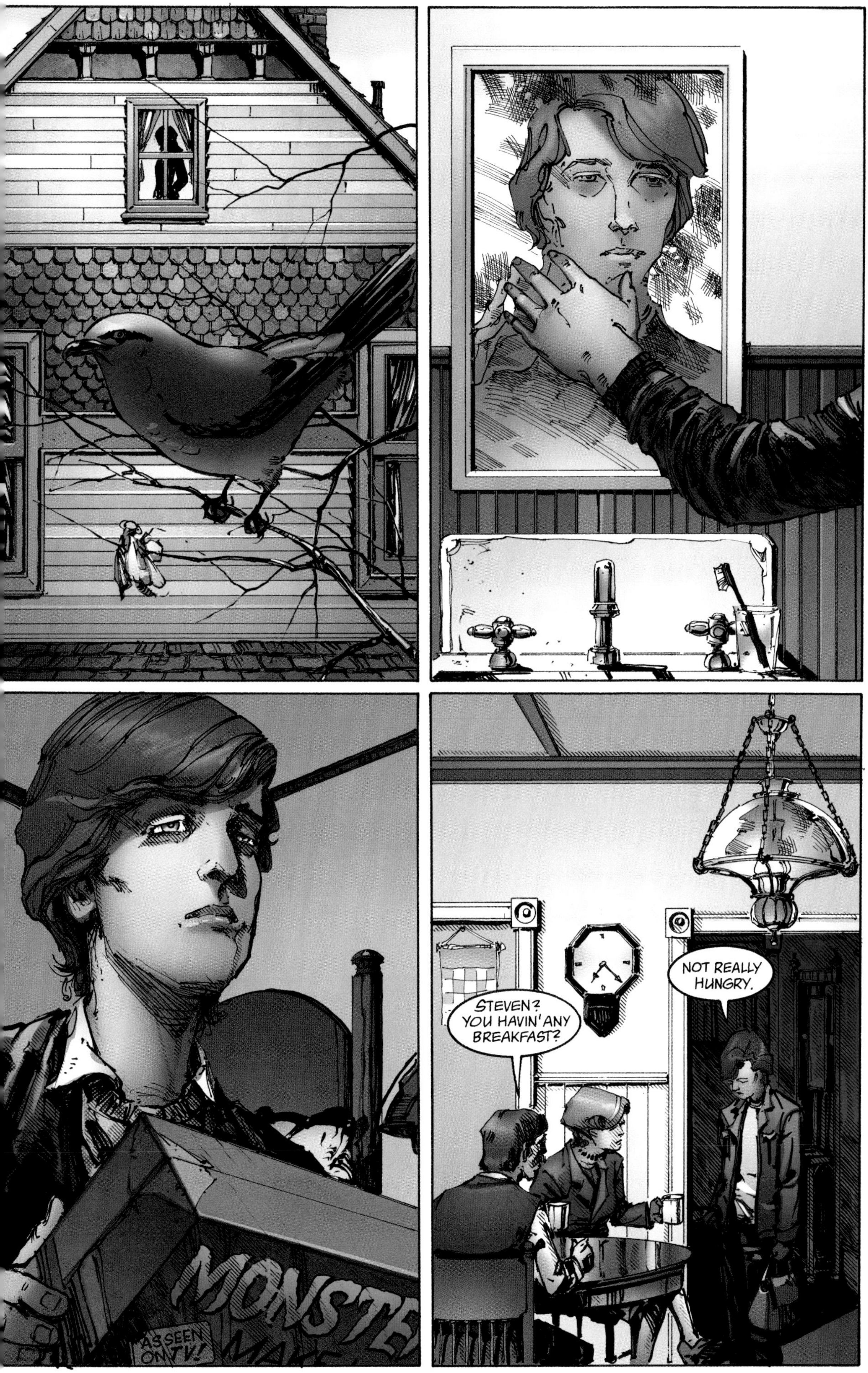
AS SEEN ON TV!
STEVEN? YOU HAVIN' ANY BREAKFAST?
NOT REALLY HUNGRY.

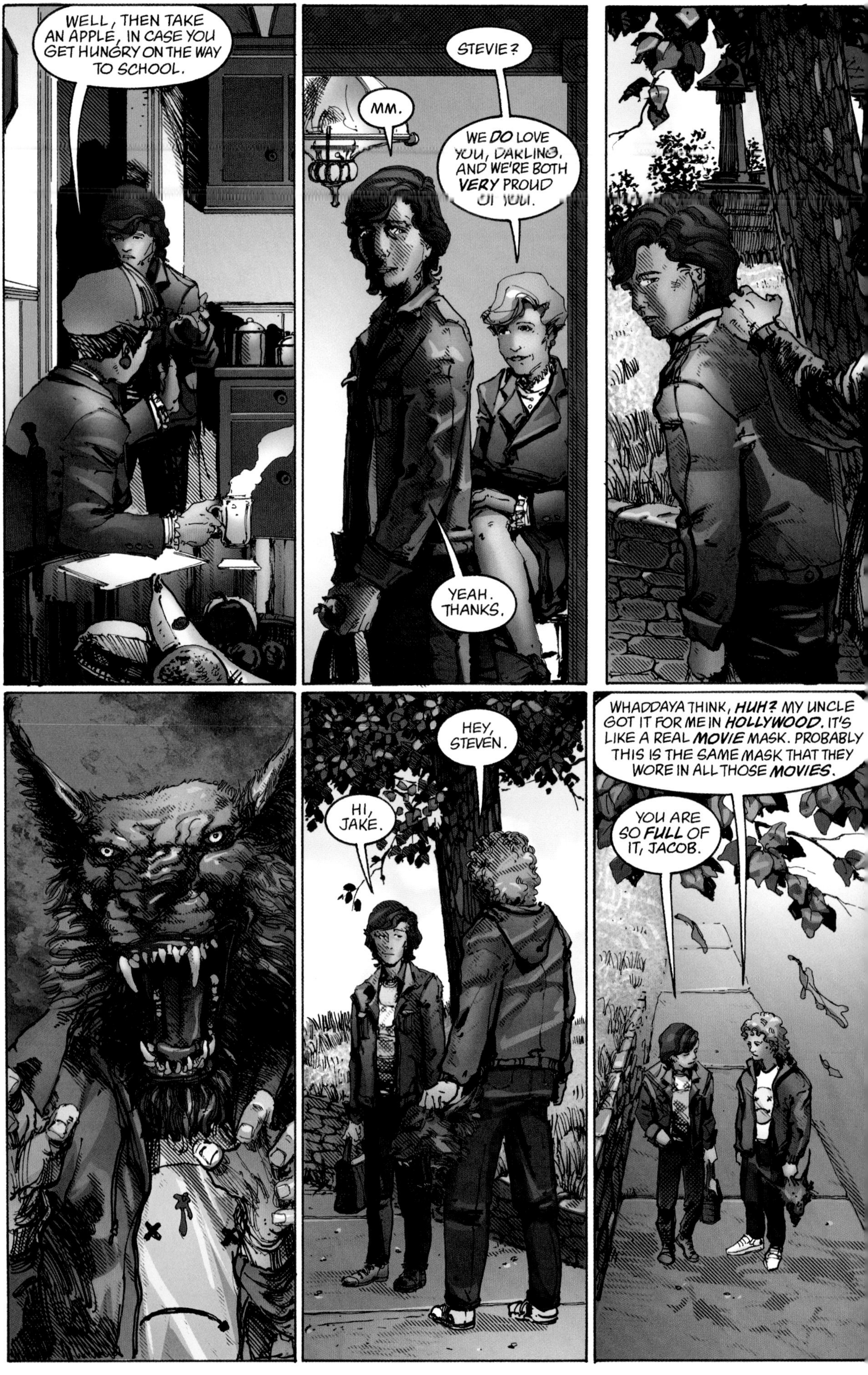
WELL, THEN TAKE AN APPLE, IN CASE YOU GET HUNGRY ON THE WAY TO SCHOOL.
STEVIE?
MM.
WE DO LOVE YOU, DARLING. AND WE'RE BOTH VERY PROUD OF YOU.
YEAH. THANKS.
HEY, STEVEN.
HI, JAKE.
WHADDAYA THINK, HUH? MY UNCLE GOT IT FOR ME IN HOLLYWOOD. IT'S LIKE A REAL MOVIE MASK. PROBABLY THIS IS THE SAME MASK THAT THEY WORE IN ALL THOSE MOVIES.
YOU ARE SO FULL OF IT, JACOB.

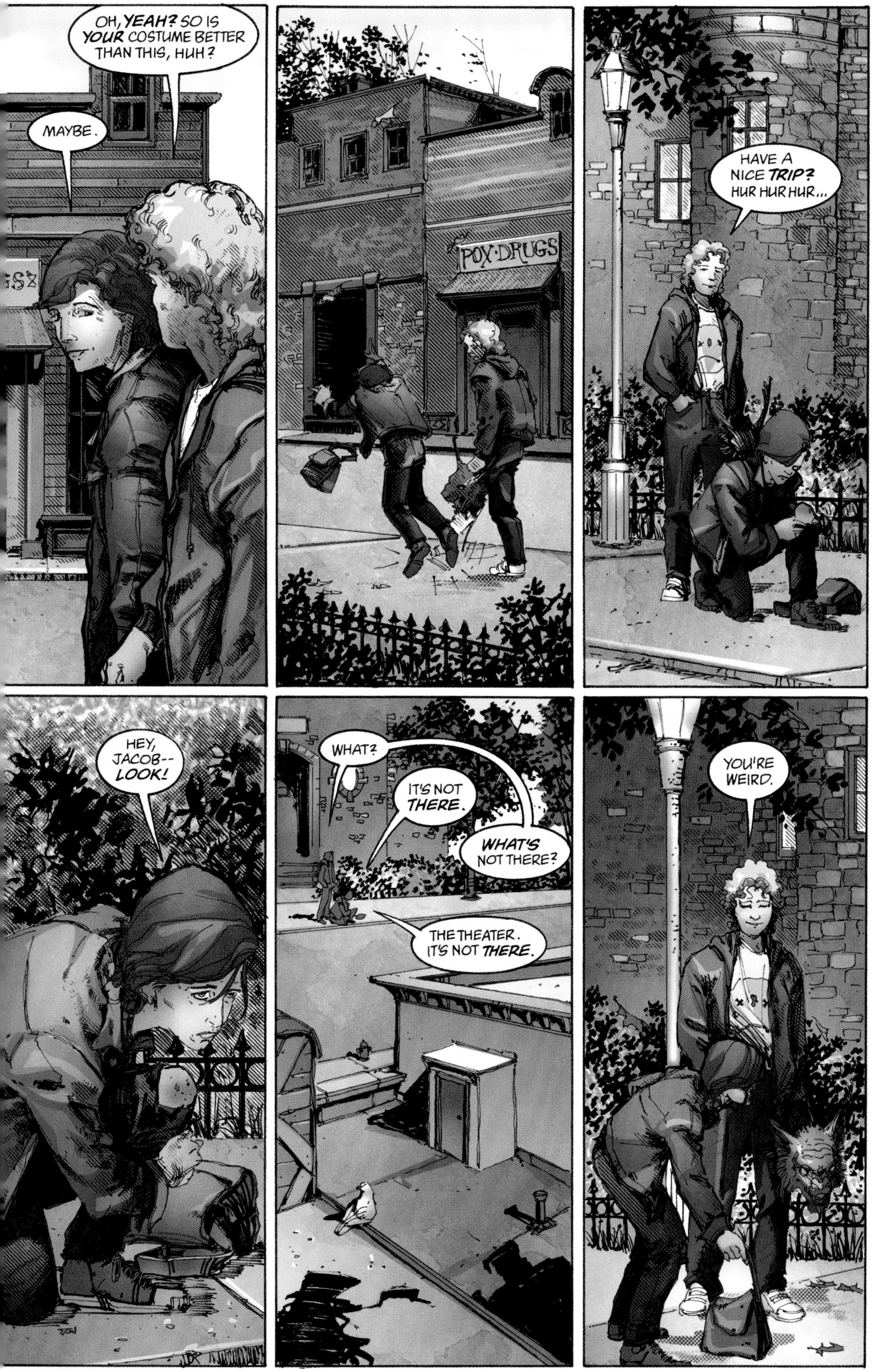
OH, YEAH? SO IS YOUR COSTUME BETTER THAN THIS, HUH?
MAYBE.
POX·DRUGS
HAVE A NICE TRIP? HUR HUR HUR...
HEY, JACOB-- LOOK!
WHAT?
IT'S NOT THERE.
WHAT'S NOT THERE?
THE THEATER. IT'S NOT THERE.
YOU'RE WEIRD.

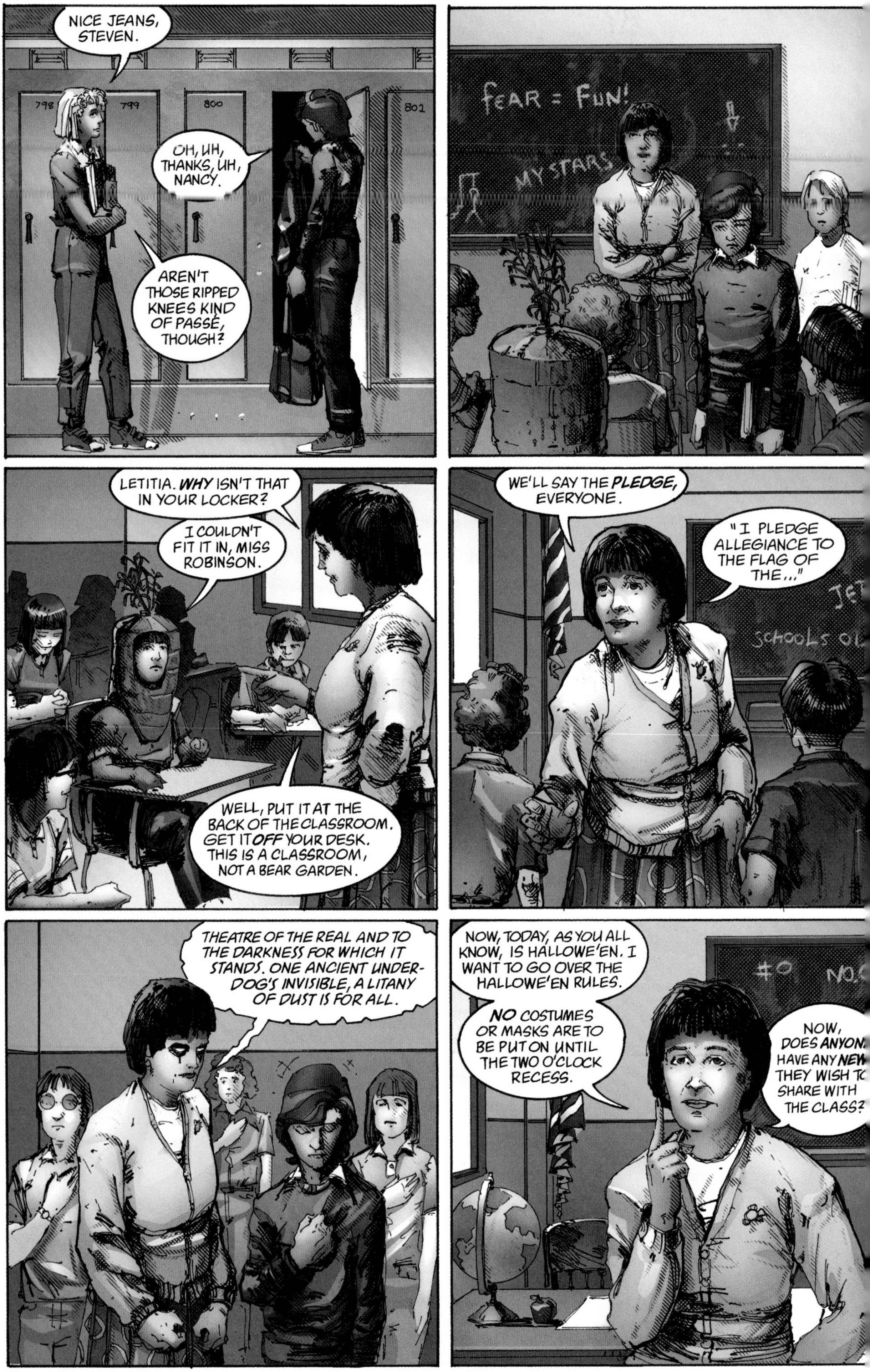
NICE JEANS, STEVEN.
OH, UH, THANKS, UH, NANCY.
AREN'T THOSE RIPPED KNEES KIND OF PASSÉ, THOUGH?
FEAR = FUN!
MY STARS
LETITIA. WHY ISN'T THAT IN YOUR LOCKER?
I COULDN'T FIT IT IN, MISS ROBINSON.
WELL, PUT IT AT THE BACK OF THE CLASSROOM. GET IT OFF YOUR DESK. THIS IS A CLASSROOM, NOT A BEAR GARDEN.
WE'LL SAY THE PLEDGE, EVERYONE.
"I PLEDGE ALLEGIANCE TO THE FLAG OF THE..."
THEATRE OF THE REAL AND TO THE DARKNESS FOR WHICH IT STANDS. ONE ANCIENT UNDER-DOG'S INVISIBLE, A LITANY OF DUST IS FOR ALL.
NOW, TODAY, AS YOU ALL KNOW, IS HALLOWE'EN. I WANT TO GO OVER THE HALLOWE'EN RULES.
NO COSTUMES OR MASKS ARE TO BE PUT ON UNTIL THE TWO O'CLOCK RECESS.
NOW, DOES ANYON HAVE ANY NEW THEY WISH TO SHARE WITH THE CLASS?

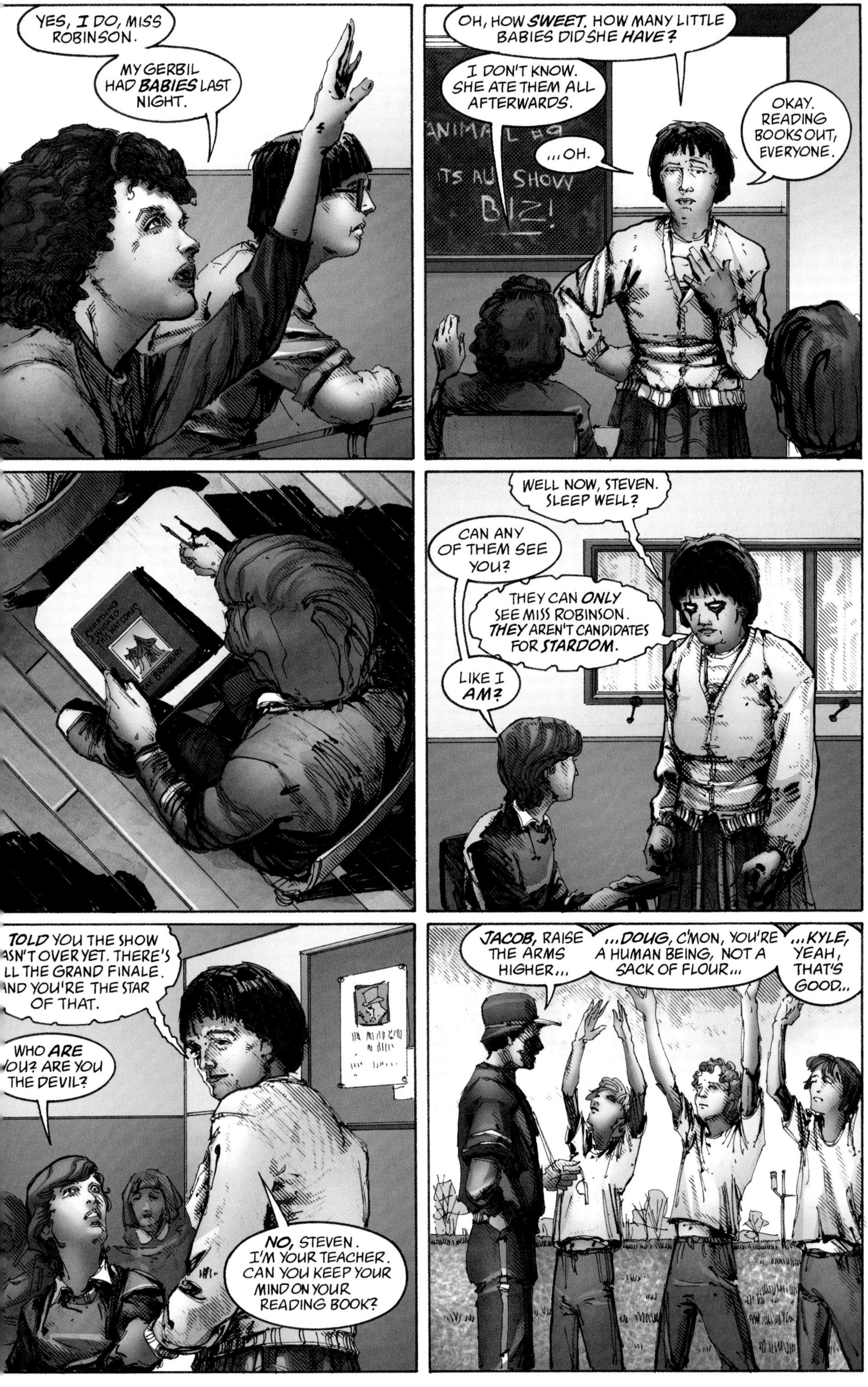
YES, I DO, MISS ROBINSON.
MY GERBIL HAD BABIES LAST NIGHT.
OH, HOW SWEET. HOW MANY LITTLE BABIES DID SHE HAVE?
I DON'T KNOW. SHE ATE THEM ALL AFTERWARDS.
...OH.
OKAY. READING BOOKS OUT, EVERYONE.
WELL NOW, STEVEN. SLEEP WELL?
CAN ANY OF THEM SEE YOU?
THEY CAN ONLY SEE MISS ROBINSON. THEY AREN'T CANDIDATES FOR STARDOM.
LIKE I AM?
TOLD YOU THE SHOW ASN'T OVER YET. THERE'S LL THE GRAND FINALE. ND YOU'RE THE STAR OF THAT.
WHO ARE OU? ARE YOU THE DEVIL?
NO, STEVEN. I'M YOUR TEACHER. CAN YOU KEEP YOUR MIND ON YOUR READING BOOK?
JACOB, RAISE THE ARMS HIGHER...
...DOUG, C'MON, YOU'RE A HUMAN BEING, NOT A SACK OF FLOUR...
...KYLE, YEAH, THAT'S GOOD...

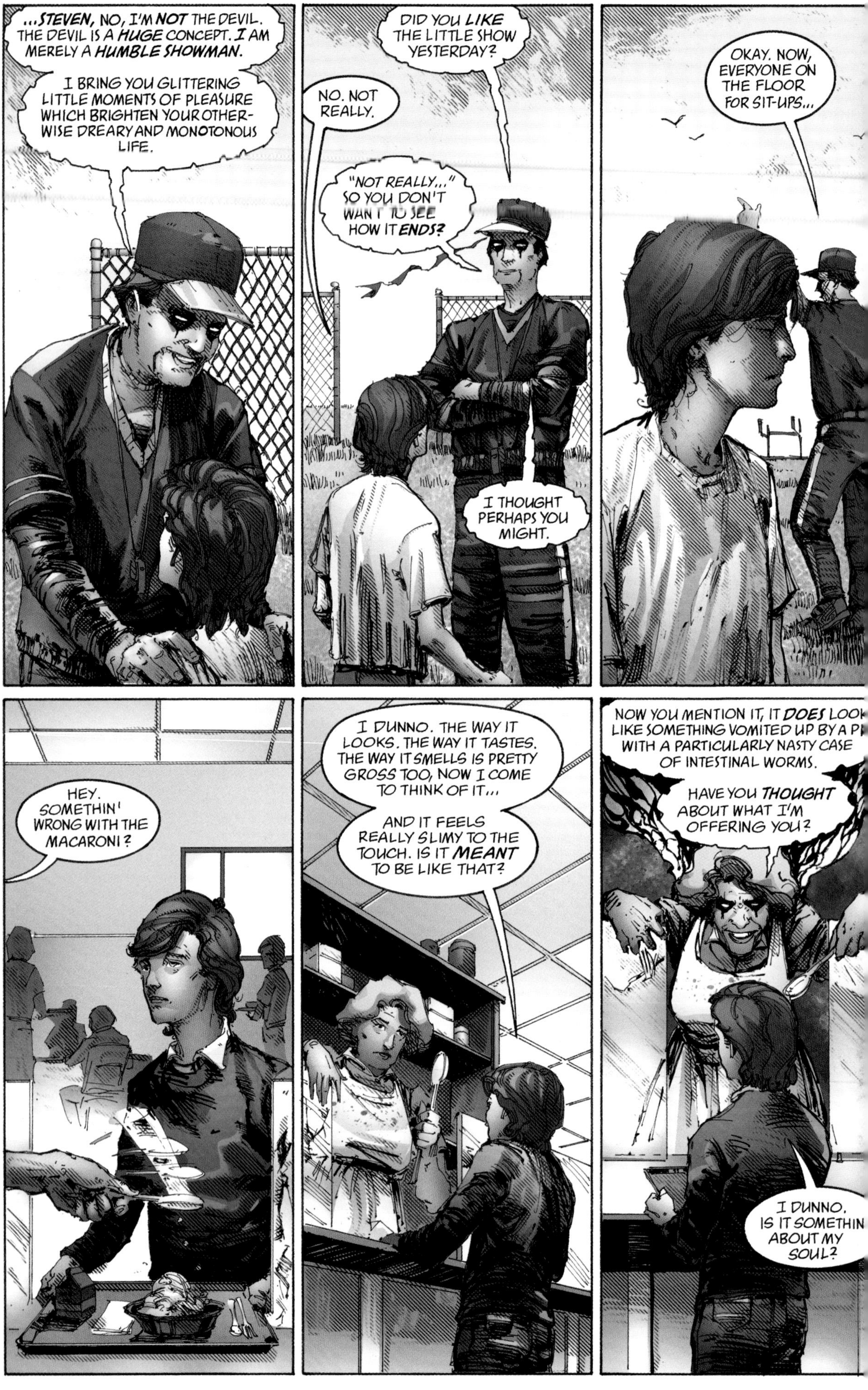
...STEVEN, NO, I'M NOT THE DEVIL. THE DEVIL IS A HUGE CONCEPT. I AM MERELY A HUMBLE SHOWMAN.
I BRING YOU GLITTERING LITTLE MOMENTS OF PLEASURE WHICH BRIGHTEN YOUR OTHER-WISE DREARY AND MONOTONOUS LIFE.
DID YOU LIKE THE LITTLE SHOW YESTERDAY?
NO. NOT REALLY.
"NOT REALLY..." SO YOU DON'T WANT TO SEE HOW IT ENDS?
I THOUGHT PERHAPS YOU MIGHT.
OKAY. NOW, EVERYONE ON THE FLOOR FOR SIT-UPS...
HEY. SOMETHIN' WRONG WITH THE MACARONI?
I DUNNO. THE WAY IT LOOKS. THE WAY IT TASTES. THE WAY IT SMELLS IS PRETTY GROSS TOO, NOW I COME TO THINK OF IT...
AND IT FEELS REALLY SLIMY TO THE TOUCH. IS IT MEANT TO BE LIKE THAT?
NOW YOU MENTION IT, IT DOES LOO LIKE SOMETHING VOMITED UP BY A P WITH A PARTICULARLY NASTY CASE OF INTESTINAL WORMS.
HAVE YOU THOUGHT ABOUT WHAT I'M OFFERING YOU?
I DUNNO. IS IT SOMETHIN ABOUT MY SOUL?

I DON'T BUY **SOULS**. I'M AN IMPRE**SARIO**, NOT A **COSTERMONGER**. YOUR SOUL'S HEALTH IS YOUR **OWN** AFFAIR. WOULD I LIE TO YOU?

JELL-O?

YEAH, THE JELL-O'S OKAY.

BUT THERE **IS** A DEAL. AND IT'S A **GOOD** DEAL. I WANT YOU TO JOIN THE **CAST**.

YOU'VE **SEEN** YOUR FUTURE, STEVEN. IT'S A NOTHING PLACE, AN EMPTY JOKE.

SO?

SO... I'M GIVING YOU THE OPPORTUNITY TO **CHANGE** ALL THAT. **WHAT**-- YOU ASK ME-- AM I **OFFERING** YOU?

NO, I DIDN'T. I **DIDN'T** ASK YOU.

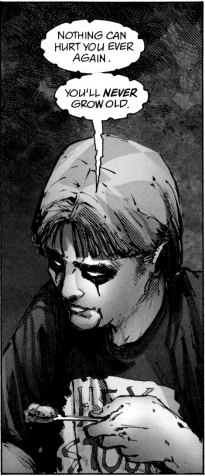

NOTHING CAN HURT YOU EVER AGAIN.

YOU'LL **NEVER** GROW OLD.

TASTES WORSE THAN IT LOOKS, EH? THAT'S **QUITE** AN ACHIEVEMENT.

ALL YOU NEED DO IS JOIN THE CAST OF MY LITTLE THEATRE. THE BLOOD'S JUST GREASEPAINT. YOU **DO** BELIEVE THAT, DON'T YOU?

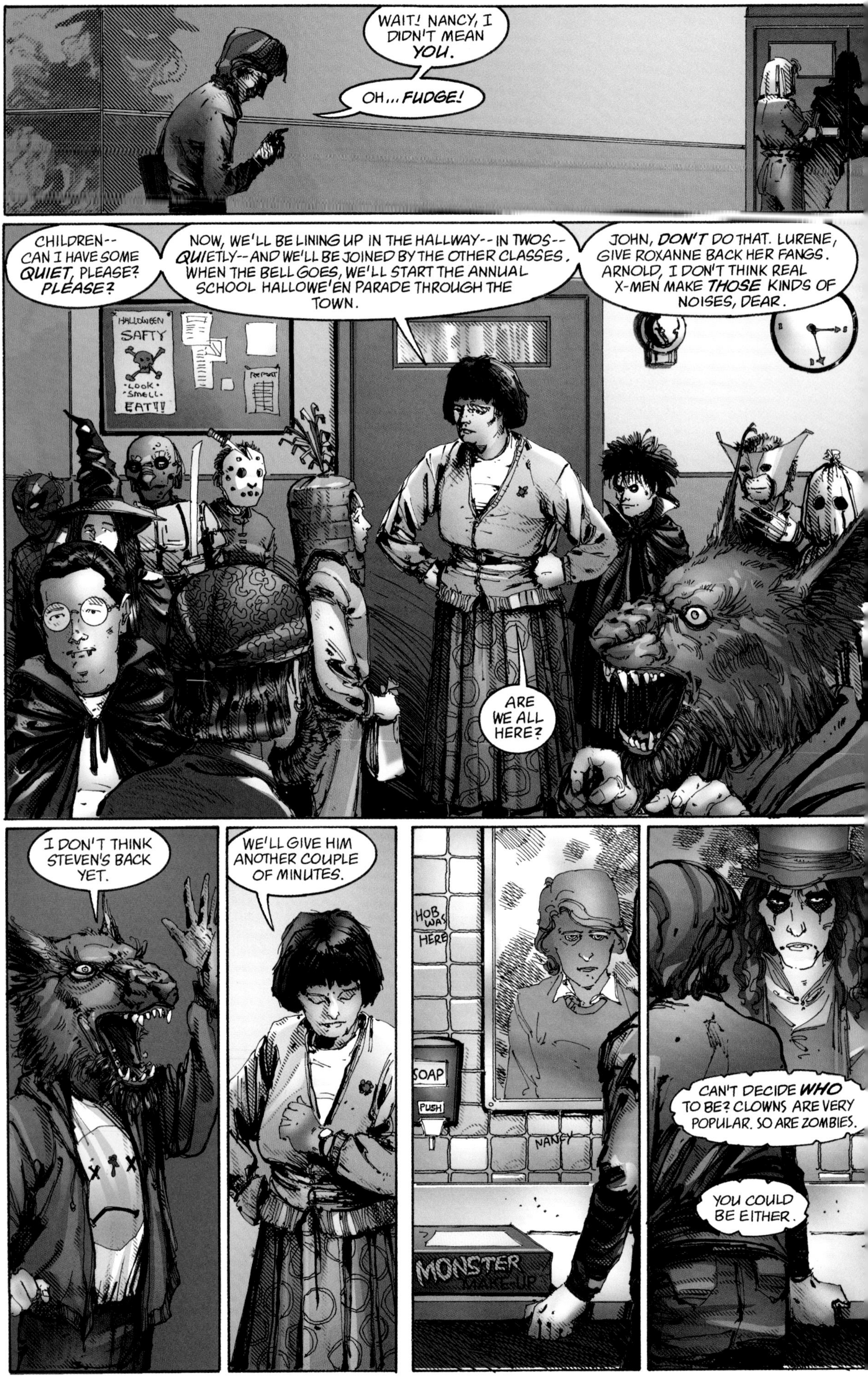
WAIT! NANCY, I DIDN'T MEAN ***YOU***.
OH... ***FUDGE!***
CHILDREN-- CAN I HAVE SOME ***QUIET***, PLEASE? ***PLEASE?***
NOW, WE'LL BE LINING UP IN THE HALLWAY-- IN TWOS-- ***QUI***ETLY-- AND WE'LL BE JOINED BY THE OTHER CLASSES. WHEN THE BELL GOES, WE'LL START THE ANNUAL SCHOOL HALLOWE'EN PARADE THROUGH THE TOWN.
JOHN, ***DON'T*** DO THAT. LURENE, GIVE ROXANNE BACK HER FANGS. ARNOLD, I DON'T THINK REAL X-MEN MAKE ***THOSE*** KINDS OF NOISES, DEAR.
HALLOWEEN SAFTY
•LOOK• •SMELL• EAT!!!
REPORT
ARE WE ALL HERE?
I DON'T THINK STEVEN'S BACK YET.
WE'LL GIVE HIM ANOTHER COUPLE OF MINUTES.
HOB WAS HERE
SOAP
PUSH
NANCY
MONSTER MAKE-UP
CAN'T DECIDE ***WHO*** TO BE? CLOWNS ARE VERY POPULAR. SO ARE ZOMBIES.
YOU COULD BE EITHER.

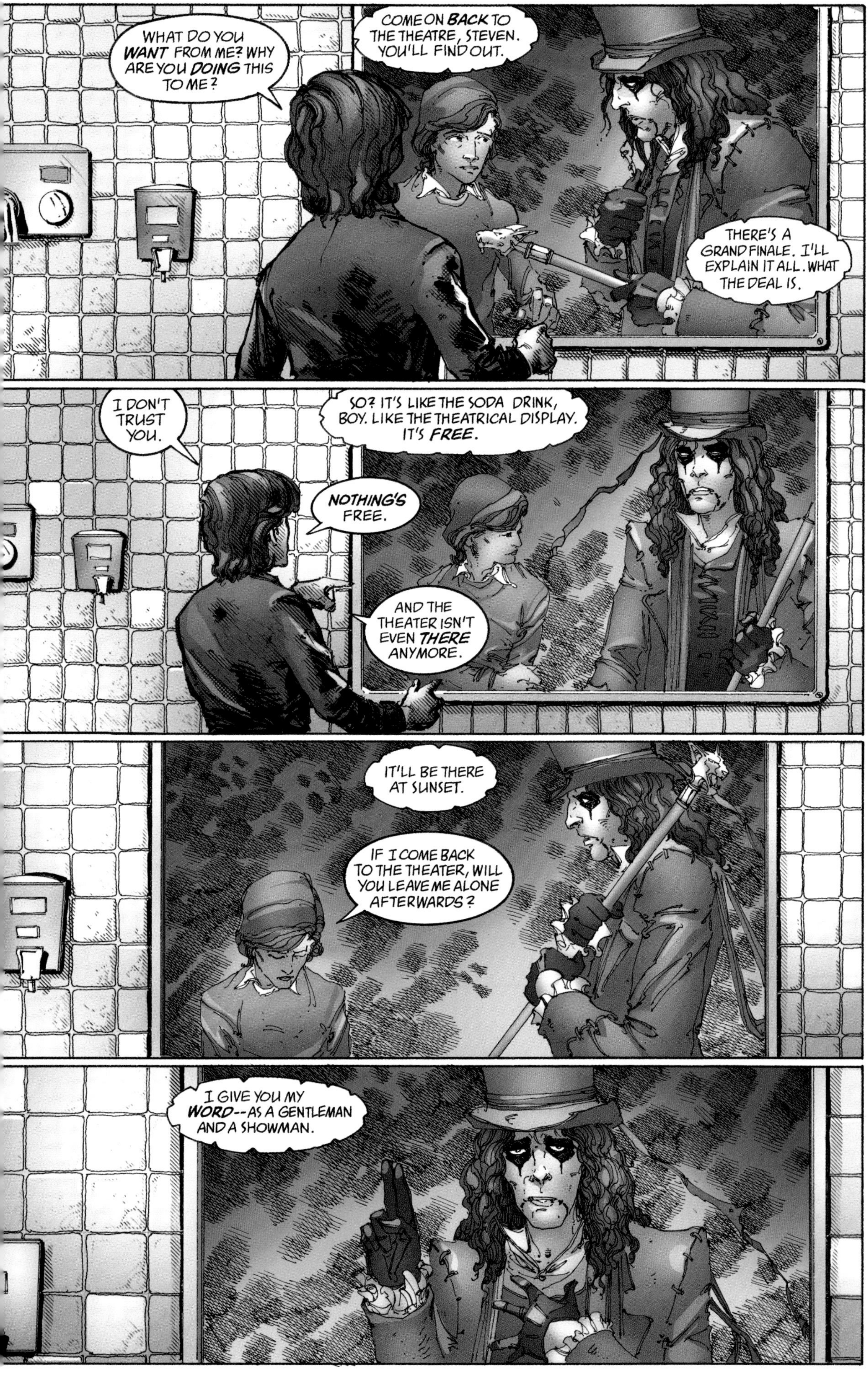
WHAT DO YOU WANT FROM ME? WHY ARE YOU DOING THIS TO ME?
COME ON BACK TO THE THEATRE, STEVEN. YOU'LL FIND OUT.
THERE'S A GRAND FINALE. I'LL EXPLAIN IT ALL. WHAT THE DEAL IS.
I DON'T TRUST YOU.
SO? IT'S LIKE THE SODA DRINK, BOY. LIKE THE THEATRICAL DISPLAY. IT'S FREE.
NOTHING'S FREE.
AND THE THEATER ISN'T EVEN THERE ANYMORE.
IT'LL BE THERE AT SUNSET.
IF I COME BACK TO THE THEATER, WILL YOU LEAVE ME ALONE AFTERWARDS?
I GIVE YOU MY WORD--AS A GENTLEMAN AND A SHOWMAN.

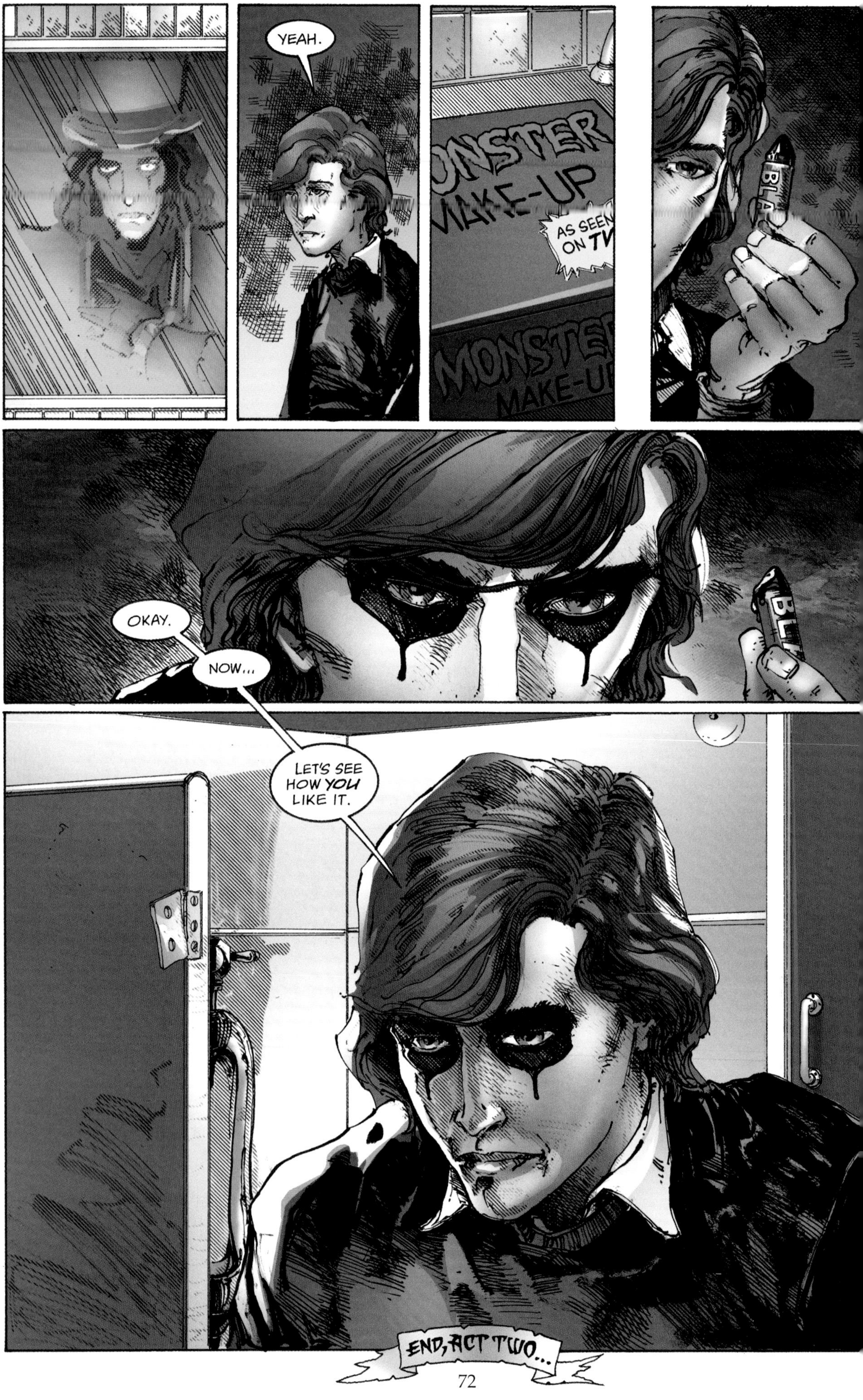
YEAH.
MONSTER MAKE-UP
AS SEEN ON TV
MONSTER MAKE-UP
OKAY.
NOW...
LET'S SEE HOW YOU LIKE IT.
END, ACT TWO...

Act Three: Cleansed by Fire

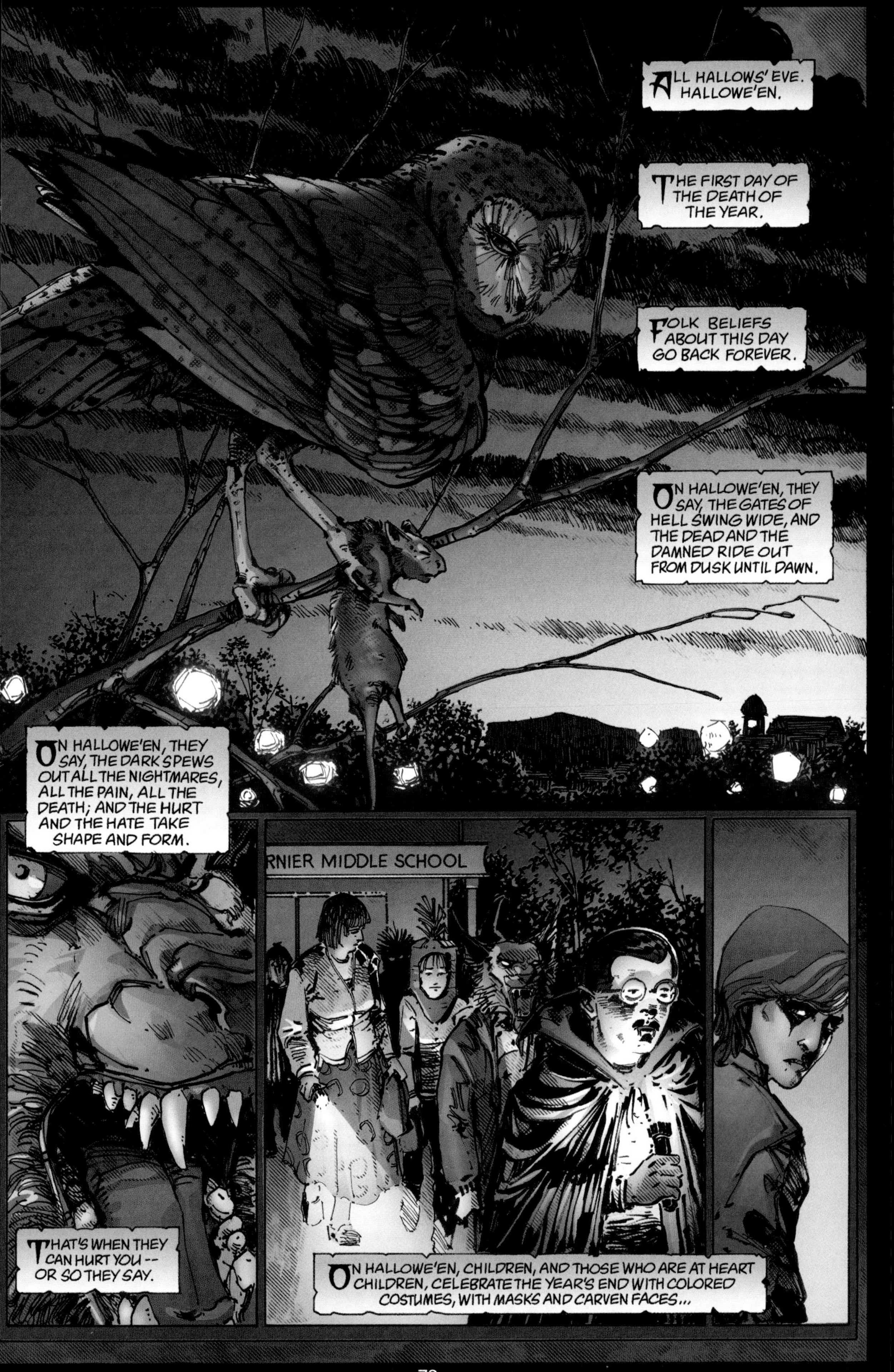
ALL HALLOWS' EVE. HALLOWE'EN.
THE FIRST DAY OF THE DEATH OF THE YEAR.
FOLK BELIEFS ABOUT THIS DAY GO BACK FOREVER.
ON HALLOWE'EN, THEY SAY, THE GATES OF HELL SWING WIDE, AND THE DEAD AND THE DAMNED RIDE OUT FROM DUSK UNTIL DAWN.
ON HALLOWE'EN, THEY SAY, THE DARK SPEWS OUT ALL THE NIGHTMARES, ALL THE PAIN, ALL THE DEATH; AND THE HURT AND THE HATE TAKE SHAPE AND FORM.
THAT'S WHEN THEY CAN HURT YOU -- OR SO THEY SAY.
RNIER MIDDLE SCHOOL
ON HALLOWE'EN, CHILDREN, AND THOSE WHO ARE AT HEART CHILDREN, CELEBRATE THE YEAR'S END WITH COLORED COSTUMES, WITH MASKS AND CARVEN FACES...

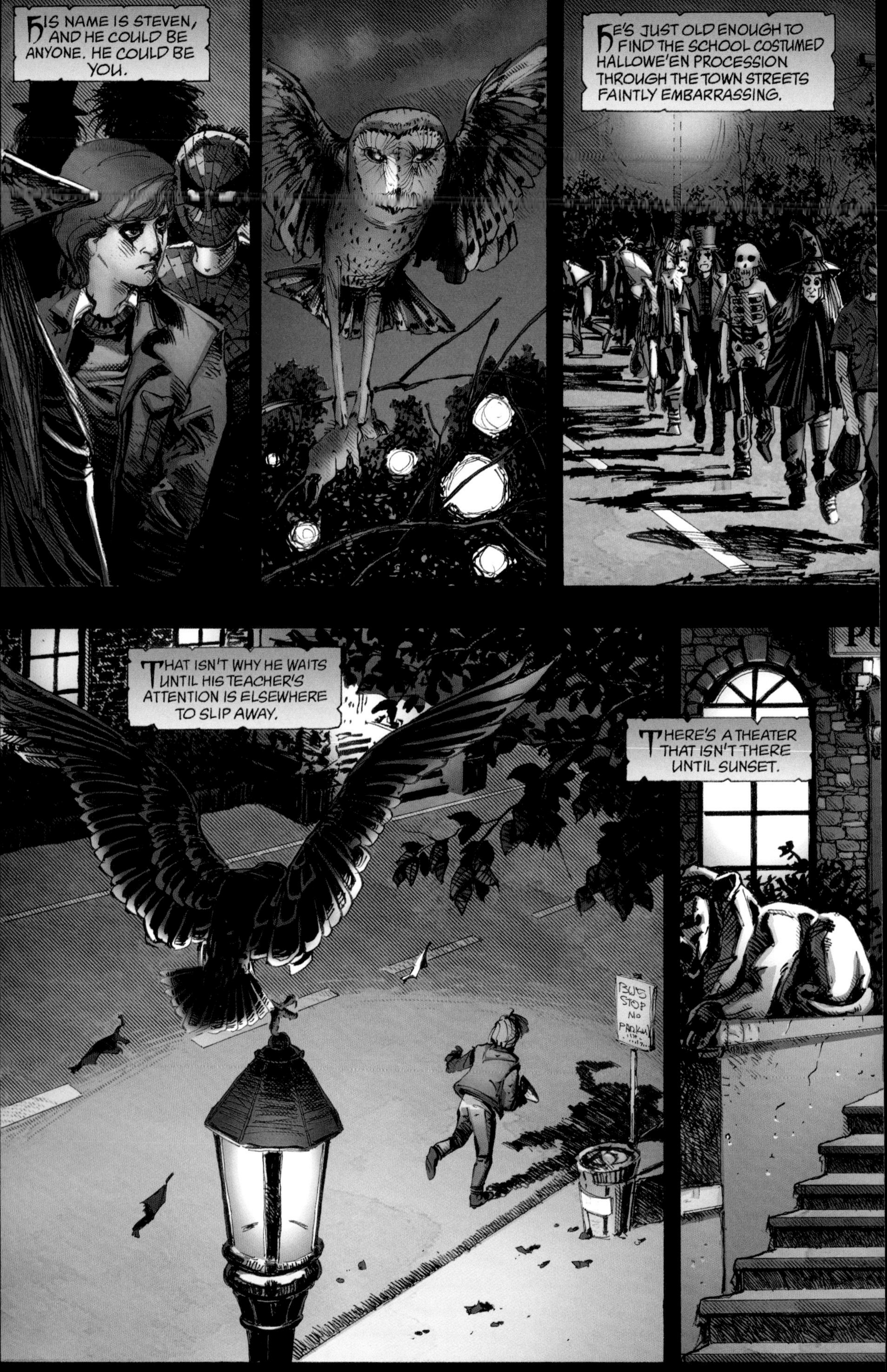
HIS NAME IS STEVEN, AND HE COULD BE ANYONE. HE COULD BE YOU.
HE'S JUST OLD ENOUGH TO FIND THE SCHOOL COSTUMED HALLOWE'EN PROCESSION THROUGH THE TOWN STREETS FAINTLY EMBARRASSING.
THAT ISN'T WHY HE WAITS UNTIL HIS TEACHER'S ATTENTION IS ELSEWHERE TO SLIP AWAY.
BUS STOP NO PARKING
THERE'S A THEATER THAT ISN'T THERE UNTIL SUNSET.

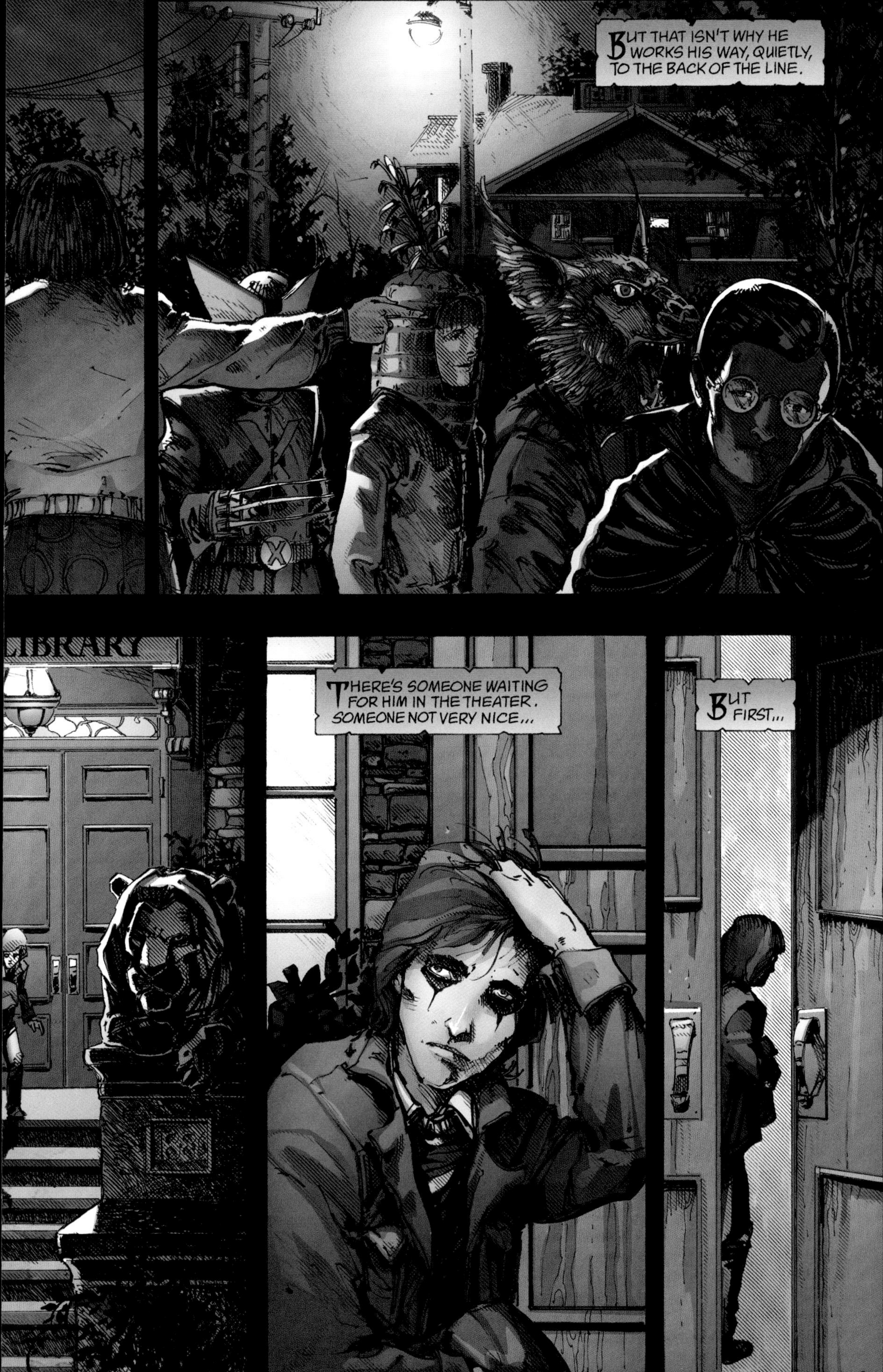
BUT THAT ISN'T WHY HE WORKS HIS WAY, QUIETLY, TO THE BACK OF THE LINE.
LIBRARY
THERE'S SOMEONE WAITING FOR HIM IN THE THEATER. SOMEONE NOT VERY NICE...
BUT FIRST...

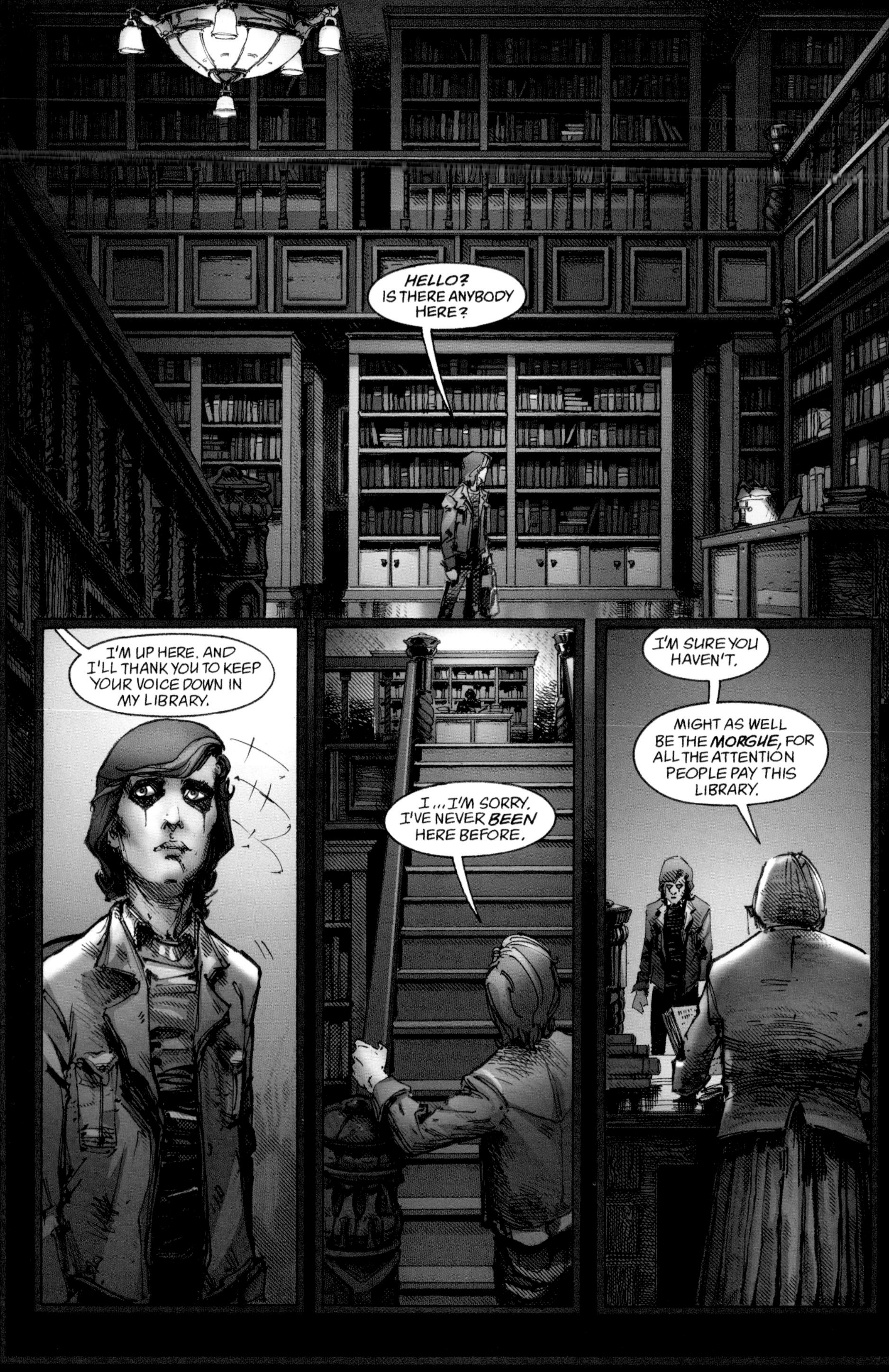
HELLO? IS THERE ANYBODY HERE?
I'M UP HERE. AND I'LL THANK YOU TO KEEP YOUR VOICE DOWN IN MY LIBRARY.
I... I'M SORRY. I'VE NEVER BEEN HERE BEFORE.
I'M SURE YOU HAVEN'T.
MIGHT AS WELL BE THE MORGUE, FOR ALL THE ATTENTION PEOPLE PAY THIS LIBRARY.

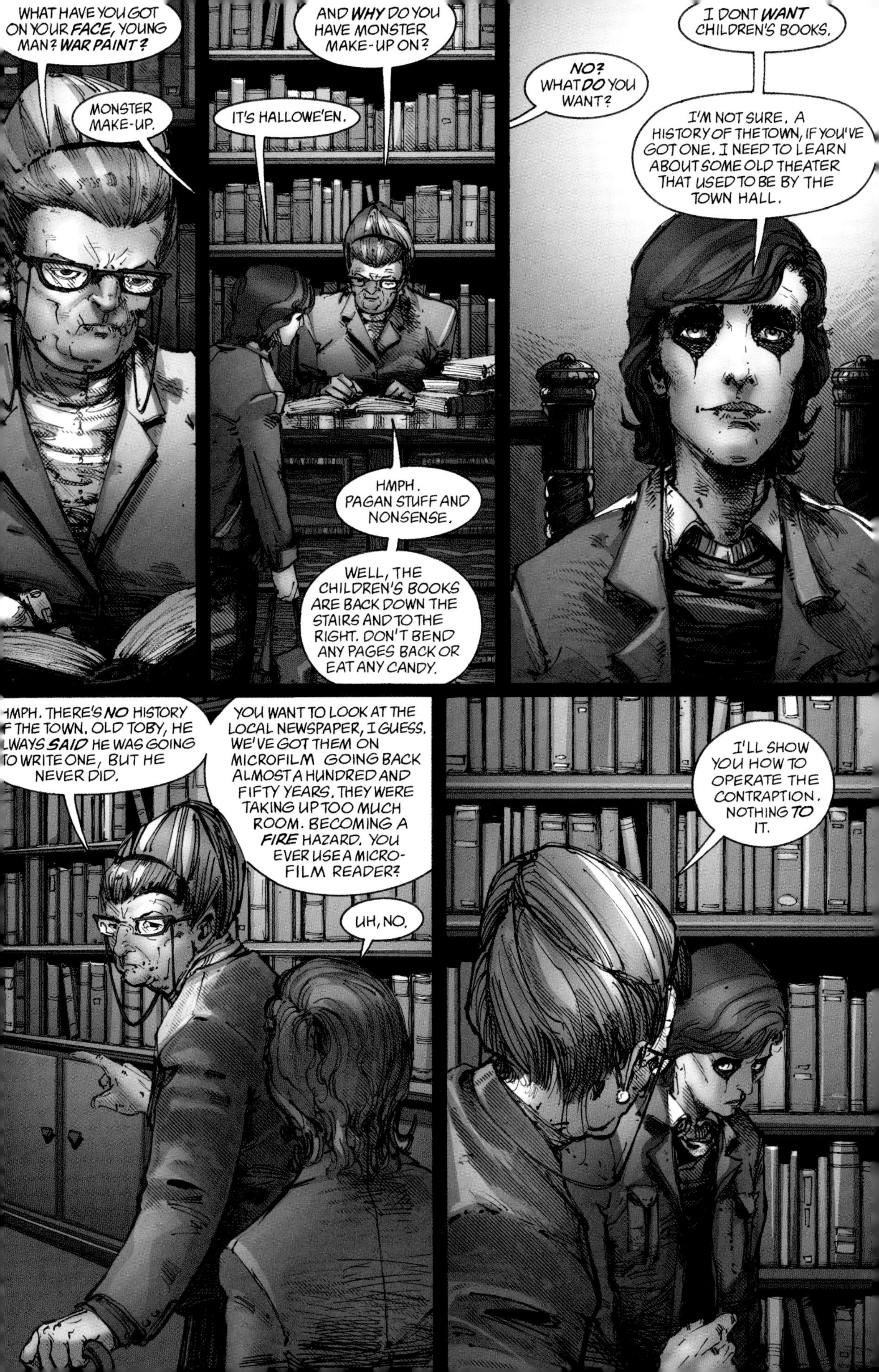

WHAT HAVE YOU GOT ON YOUR FACE, YOUNG MAN? WAR PAINT?
MONSTER MAKE-UP.
AND WHY DO YOU HAVE MONSTER MAKE-UP ON?
IT'S HALLOWE'EN.
HMPH. PAGAN STUFF AND NONSENSE.
WELL, THE CHILDREN'S BOOKS ARE BACK DOWN THE STAIRS AND TO THE RIGHT. DON'T BEND ANY PAGES BACK OR EAT ANY CANDY.
I DONT WANT CHILDREN'S BOOKS.
NO? WHAT DO YOU WANT?
I'M NOT SURE. A HISTORY OF THE TOWN, IF YOU'VE GOT ONE. I NEED TO LEARN ABOUT SOME OLD THEATER THAT USED TO BE BY THE TOWN HALL.
HMPH. THERE'S NO HISTORY OF THE TOWN. OLD TOBY, HE ALWAYS SAID HE WAS GOING TO WRITE ONE, BUT HE NEVER DID.
YOU WANT TO LOOK AT THE LOCAL NEWSPAPER, I GUESS. WE'VE GOT THEM ON MICROFILM GOING BACK ALMOST A HUNDRED AND FIFTY YEARS. THEY WERE TAKING UP TOO MUCH ROOM. BECOMING A FIRE HAZARD. YOU EVER USE A MICRO-FILM READER?
UH, NO.
I'LL SHOW YOU HOW TO OPERATE THE CONTRAPTION. NOTHING TO IT.

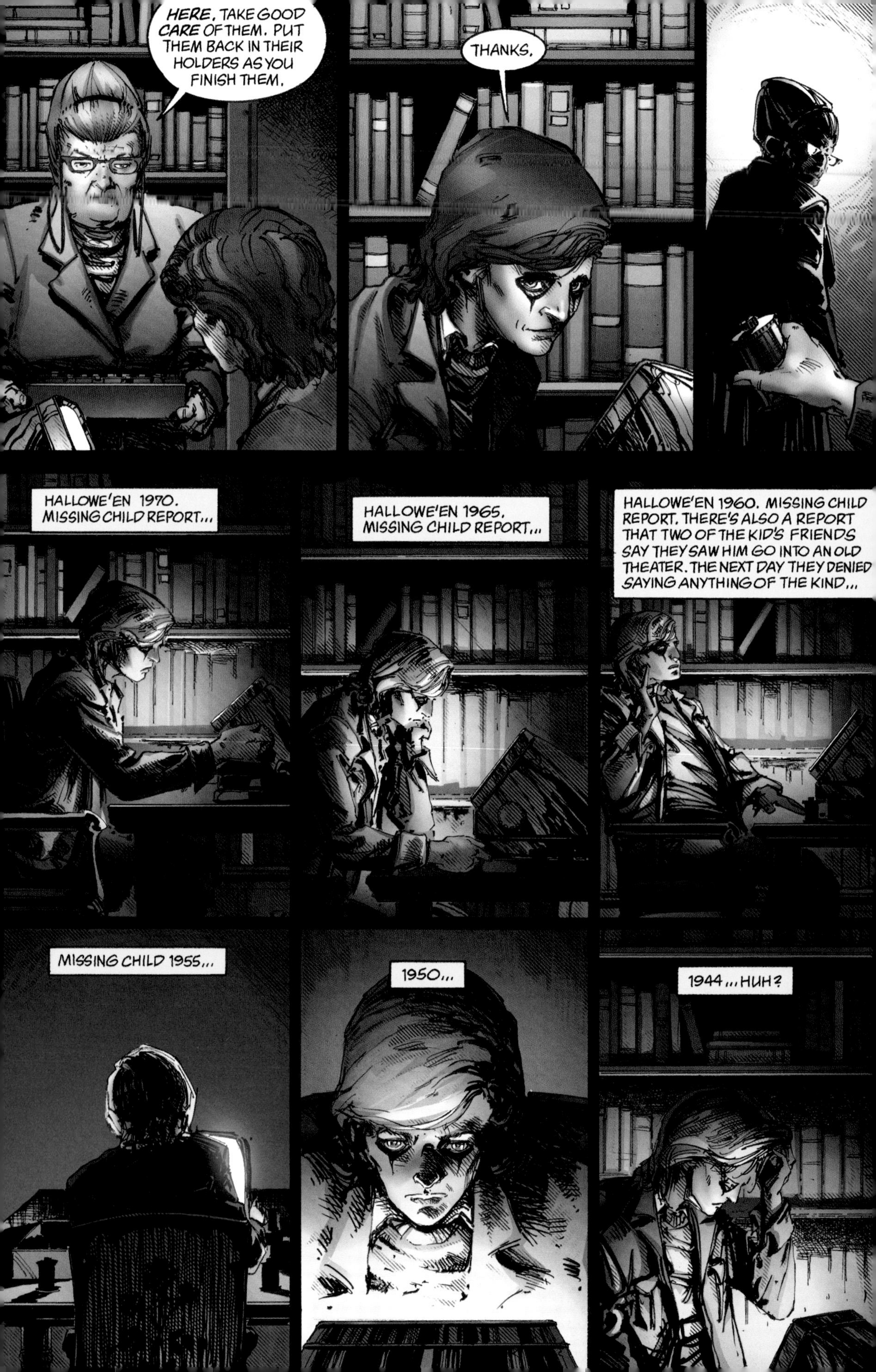
HERE. TAKE GOOD CARE OF THEM. PUT THEM BACK IN THEIR HOLDERS AS YOU FINISH THEM.
THANKS.
HALLOWE'EN 1970. MISSING CHILD REPORT...
HALLOWE'EN 1965. MISSING CHILD REPORT...
HALLOWE'EN 1960. MISSING CHILD REPORT. THERE'S ALSO A REPORT THAT TWO OF THE KID'S FRIENDS SAY THEY SAW HIM GO INTO AN OLD THEATER. THE NEXT DAY THEY DENIED SAYING ANYTHING OF THE KIND...
MISSING CHILD 1955...
1950...
1944... HUH?

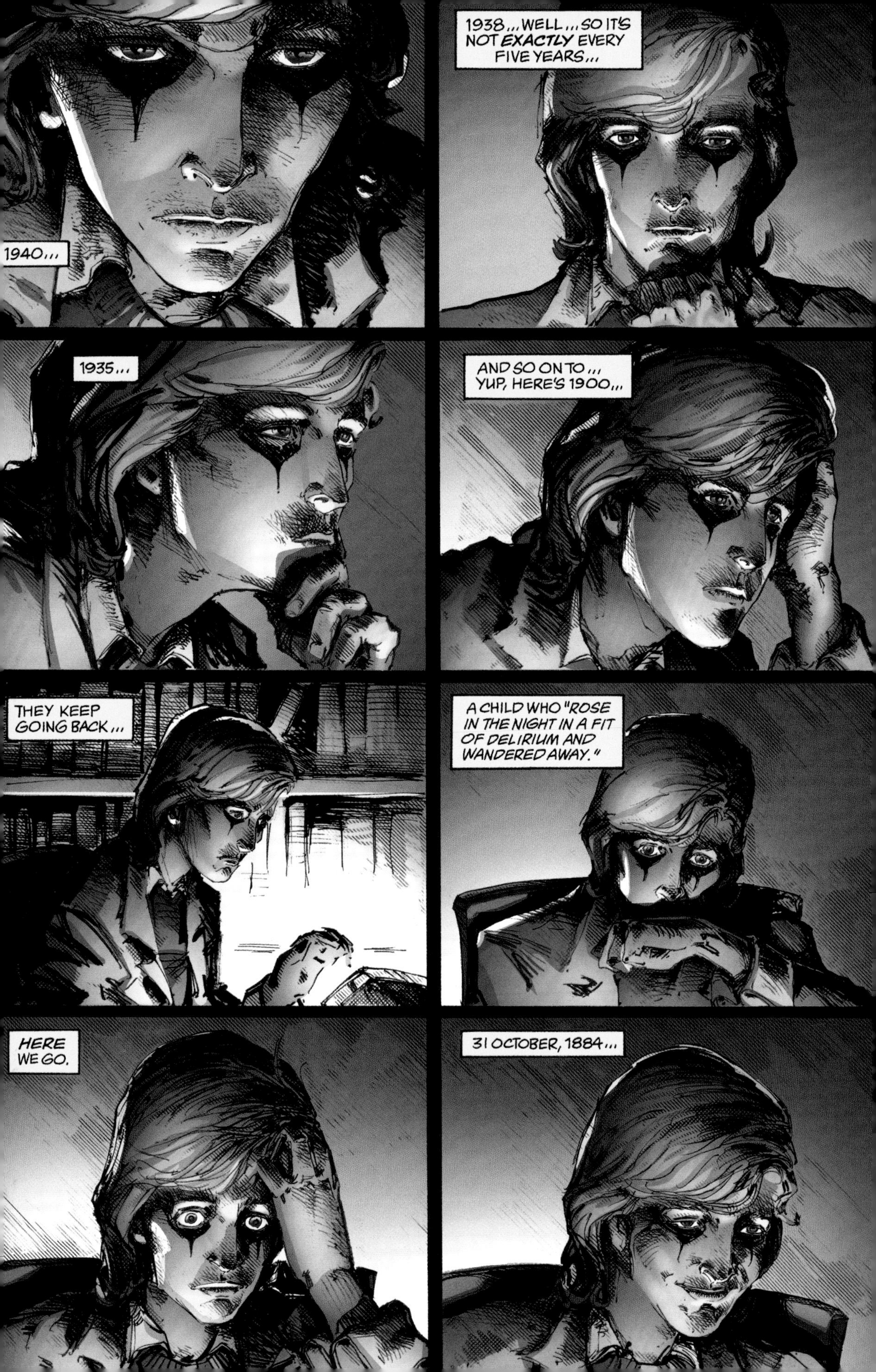
1940...
1938... WELL... SO IT'S NOT EXACTLY EVERY FIVE YEARS...
1935...
AND SO ON TO... YUP, HERE'S 1900...
THEY KEEP GOING BACK...
A CHILD WHO "ROSE IN THE NIGHT IN A FIT OF DELIRIUM AND WANDERED AWAY."
HERE WE GO.
31 OCTOBER, 1884...

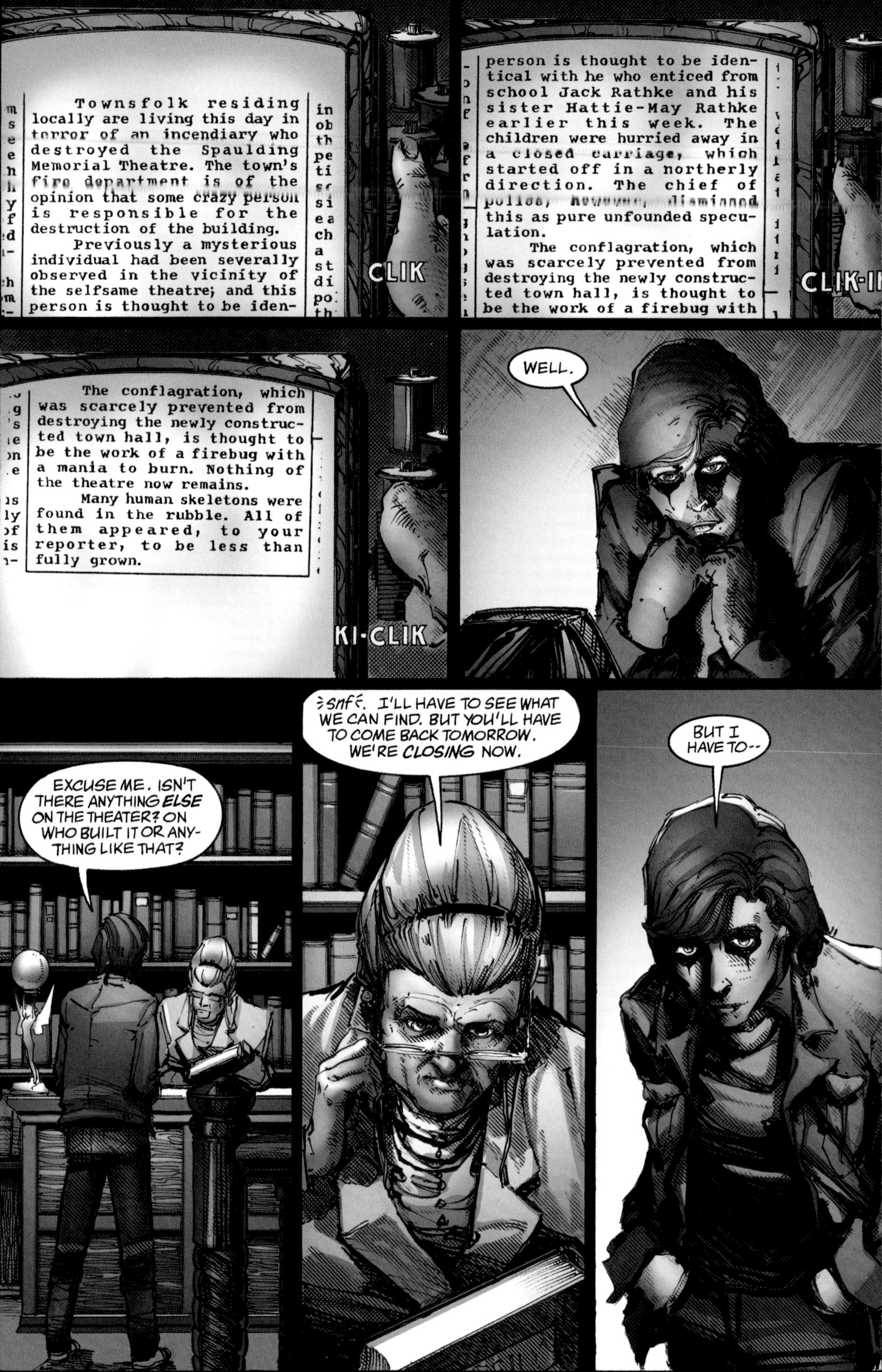
Townsfolk residing locally are living this day in terror of an incendiary who destroyed the Spaulding Memorial Theatre. The town's fire department is of the opinion that some crazy person is responsible for the destruction of the building.
Previously a mysterious individual had been severally observed in the vicinity of the selfsame theatre; and this person is thought to be iden-
CLIK
person is thought to be identical with he who enticed from school Jack Rathke and his sister Hattie-May Rathke earlier this week. The children were hurried away in a closed carriage, which started off in a northerly direction. The chief of police, however, dismissed this as pure unfounded speculation.
The conflagration, which was scarcely prevented from destroying the newly constructed town hall, is thought to be the work of a firebug with
CLIK-IK
The conflagration, which was scarcely prevented from destroying the newly constructed town hall, is thought to be the work of a firebug with a mania to burn. Nothing of the theatre now remains.
Many human skeletons were found in the rubble. All of them appeared, to your reporter, to be less than fully grown.
KI-CLIK
WELL.
EXCUSE ME. ISN'T THERE ANYTHING ELSE ON THE THEATER? ON WHO BUILT IT OR ANYTHING LIKE THAT?
snf. I'LL HAVE TO SEE WHAT WE CAN FIND. BUT YOU'LL HAVE TO COME BACK TOMORROW. WE'RE CLOSING NOW.
BUT I HAVE TO--

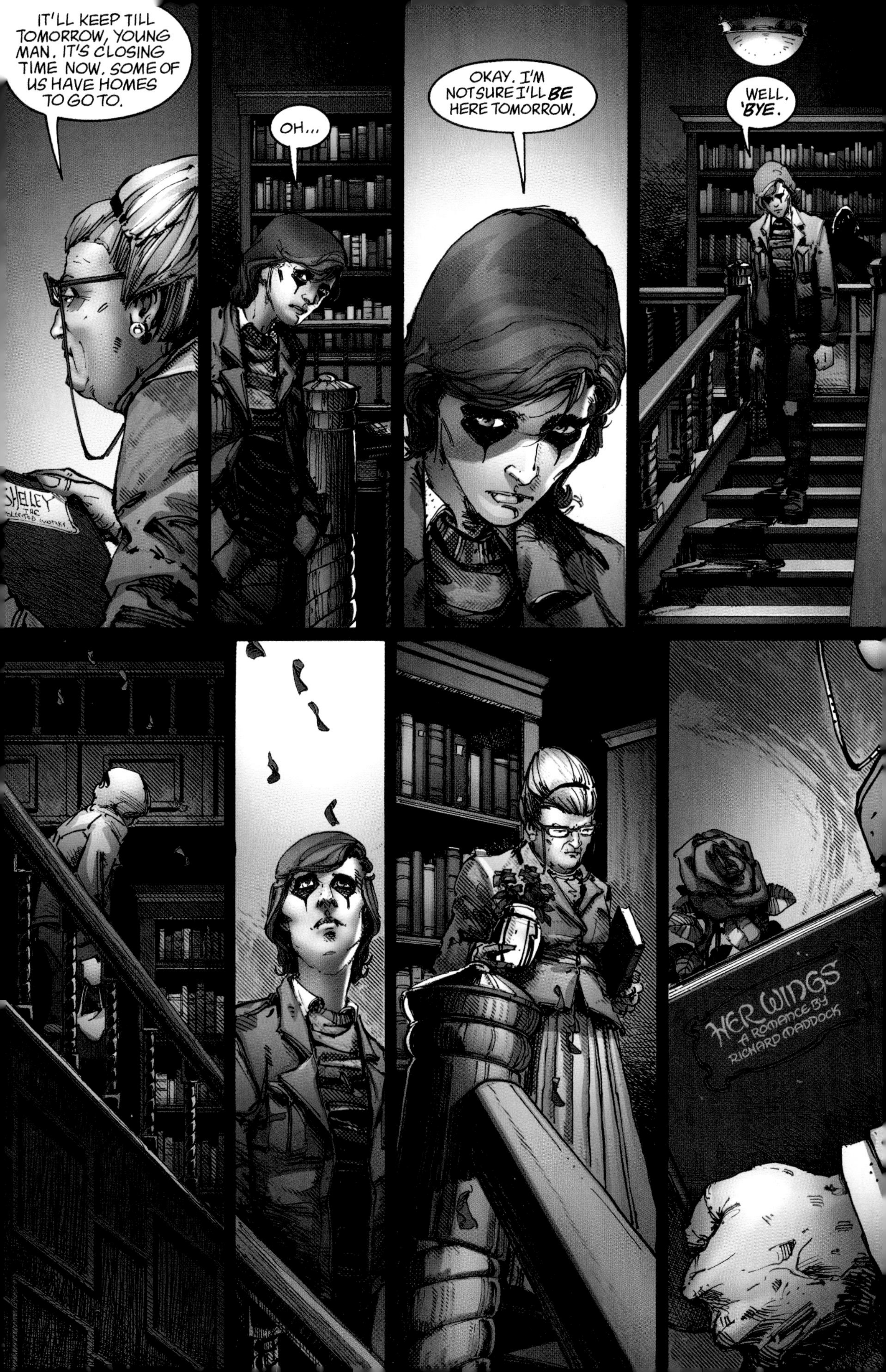
IT'LL KEEP TILL TOMORROW, YOUNG MAN. IT'S CLOSING TIME NOW. SOME OF US HAVE HOMES TO GO TO.
SHELLEY THE SELECTED WORKS
OH...
OKAY. I'M NOT SURE I'LL BE HERE TOMORROW.
WELL. 'BYE.
HER WINGS
A ROMANCE BY RICHARD MADDOCK

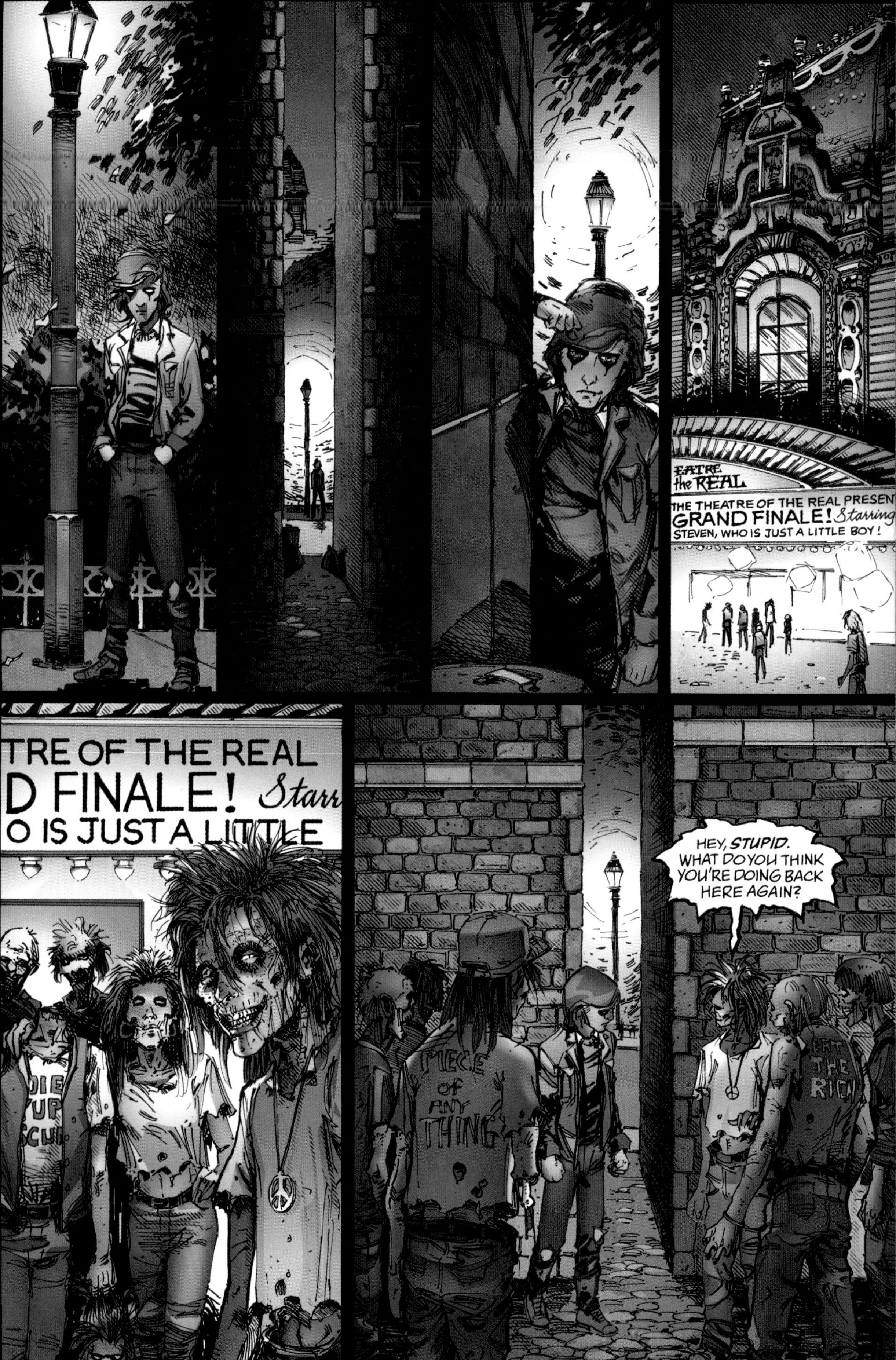
EATRE the REAL
THE THEATRE OF THE REAL PRESEN
GRAND FINALE! Starring
STEVEN, WHO IS JUST A LITTLE BOY!
TRE OF THE REAL
D FINALE! Starr
O IS JUST A LITTLE
DIE UP SCHL
PIECE of ANY THING
HEY, STUPID. WHAT DO YOU THINK YOU'RE DOING BACK HERE AGAIN?
EAT THE RICH

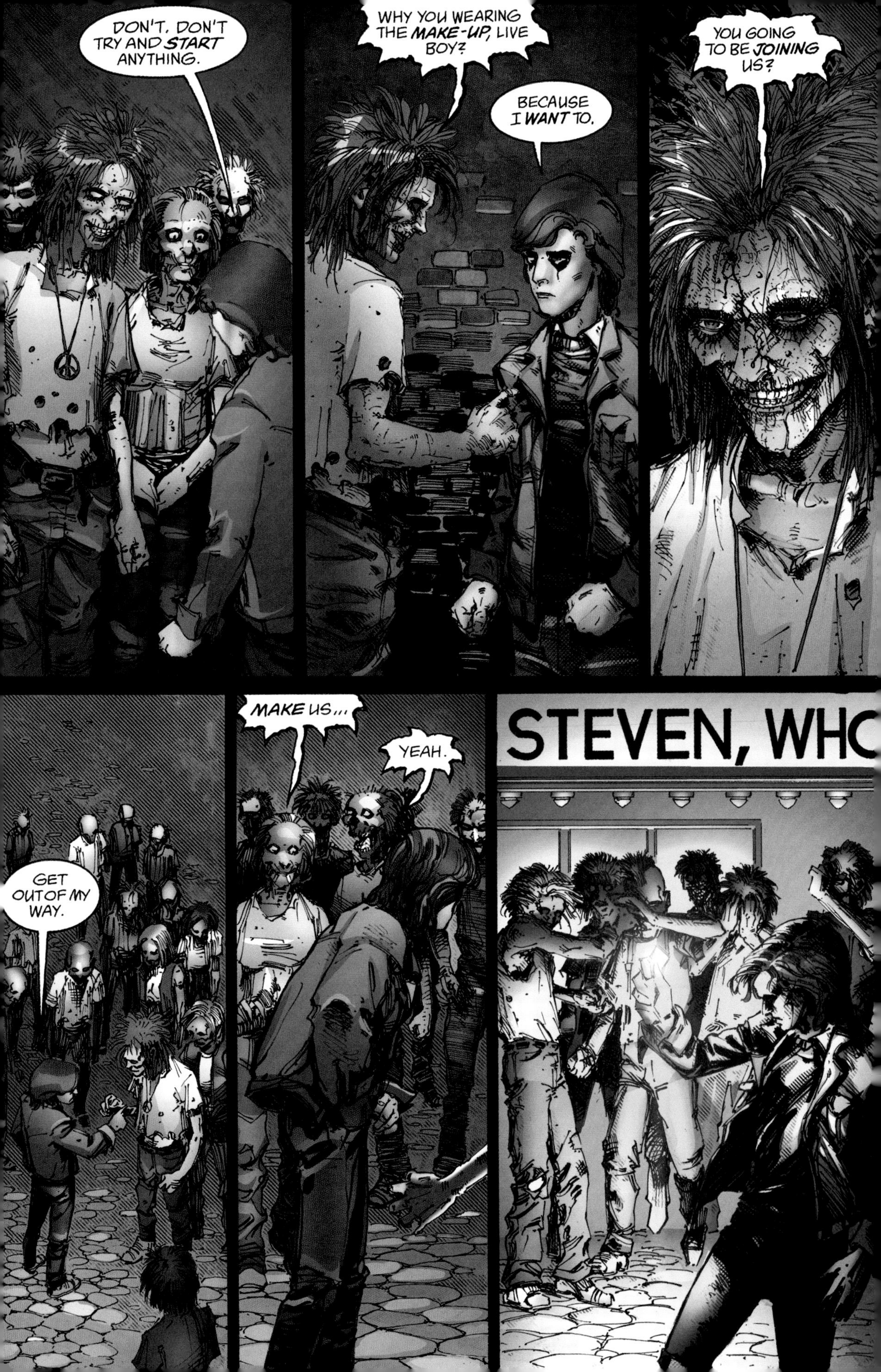
DON'T. DON'T TRY AND START ANYTHING.
WHY YOU WEARING THE MAKE-UP, LIVE BOY?
BECAUSE I WANT TO.
YOU GOING TO BE JOINING US?
GET OUT OF MY WAY.
MAKE US...
YEAH.
STEVEN, WHO

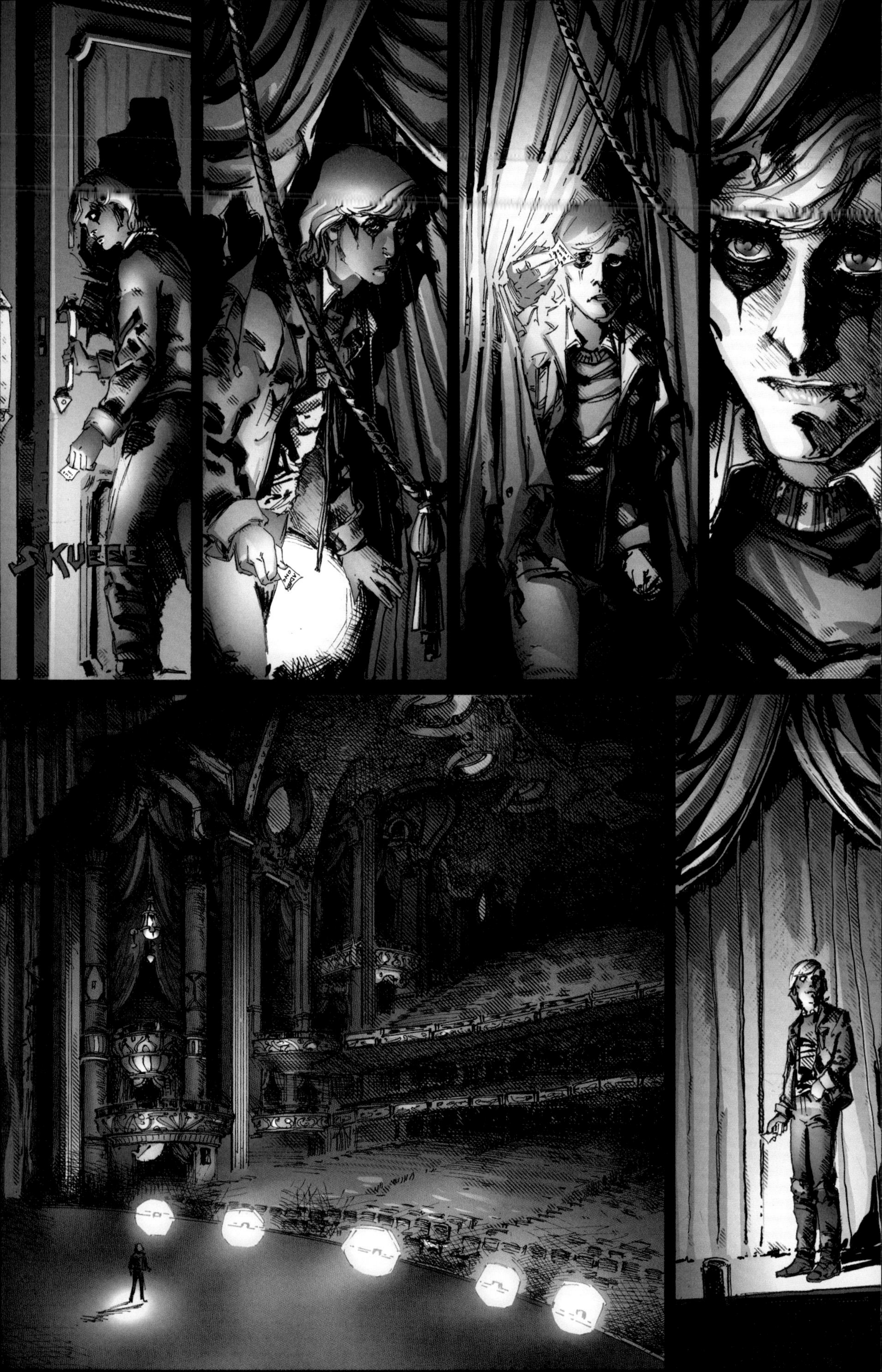
SKUEEE

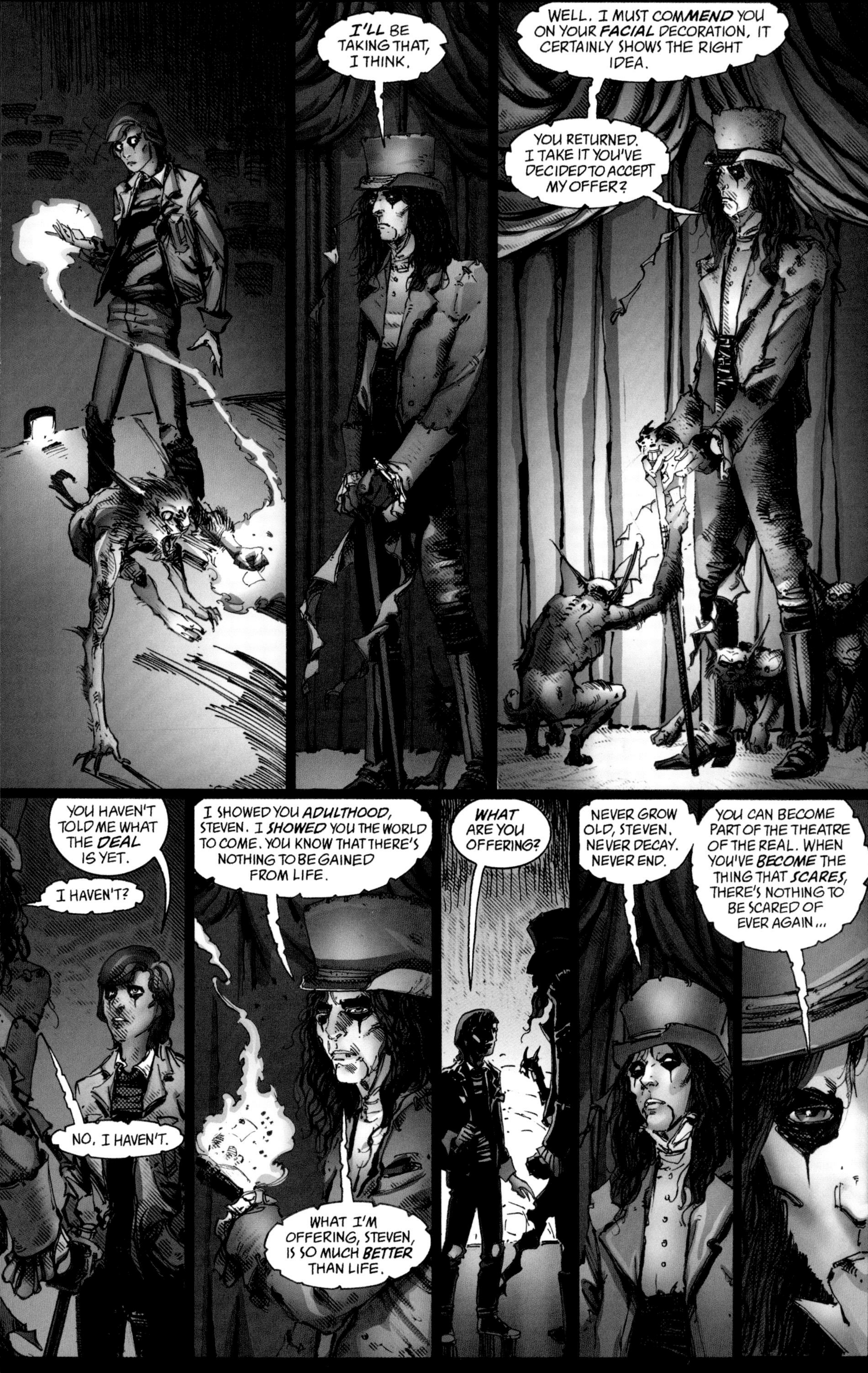
I'LL BE TAKING THAT, I THINK.
WELL. I MUST COMMEND YOU ON YOUR FACIAL DECORATION, IT CERTAINLY SHOWS THE RIGHT IDEA.
YOU RETURNED. I TAKE IT YOU'VE DECIDED TO ACCEPT MY OFFER?
YOU HAVEN'T TOLD ME WHAT THE DEAL IS YET.
I HAVEN'T?
NO. I HAVEN'T.
I SHOWED YOU ADULTHOOD, STEVEN. I SHOWED YOU THE WORLD TO COME. YOU KNOW THAT THERE'S NOTHING TO BE GAINED FROM LIFE.
WHAT I'M OFFERING, STEVEN, IS SO MUCH BETTER THAN LIFE.
WHAT ARE YOU OFFERING?
NEVER GROW OLD, STEVEN. NEVER DECAY. NEVER END.
YOU CAN BECOME PART OF THE THEATRE OF THE REAL. WHEN YOU'VE BECOME THE THING THAT SCARES, THERE'S NOTHING TO BE SCARED OF EVER AGAIN...

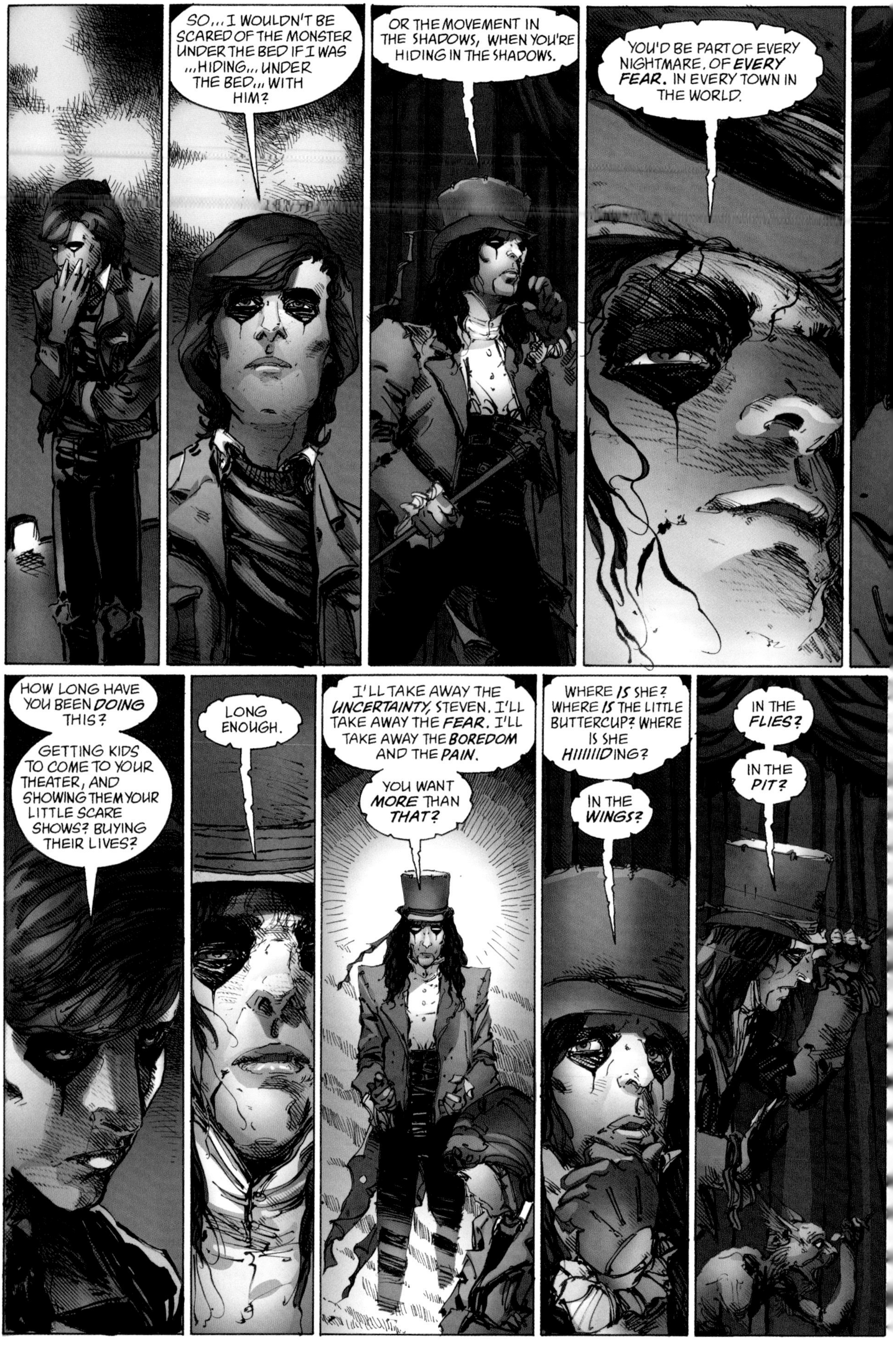
SO... I WOULDN'T BE SCARED OF THE MONSTER UNDER THE BED IF I WAS ...HIDING... UNDER THE BED... WITH HIM?
OR THE MOVEMENT IN THE SHADOWS, WHEN YOU'RE HIDING IN THE SHADOWS.
YOU'D BE PART OF EVERY NIGHTMARE, OF EVERY FEAR. IN EVERY TOWN IN THE WORLD.
HOW LONG HAVE YOU BEEN DOING THIS?
GETTING KIDS TO COME TO YOUR THEATER, AND SHOWING THEM YOUR LITTLE SCARE SHOWS? BUYING THEIR LIVES?
LONG ENOUGH.
I'LL TAKE AWAY THE UNCERTAINTY, STEVEN. I'LL TAKE AWAY THE FEAR. I'LL TAKE AWAY THE BOREDOM AND THE PAIN.
YOU WANT MORE THAN THAT?
WHERE IS SHE? WHERE IS THE LITTLE BUTTERCUP? WHERE IS SHE HIIIIIDING?
IN THE WINGS?
IN THE FLIES?
IN THE PIT?

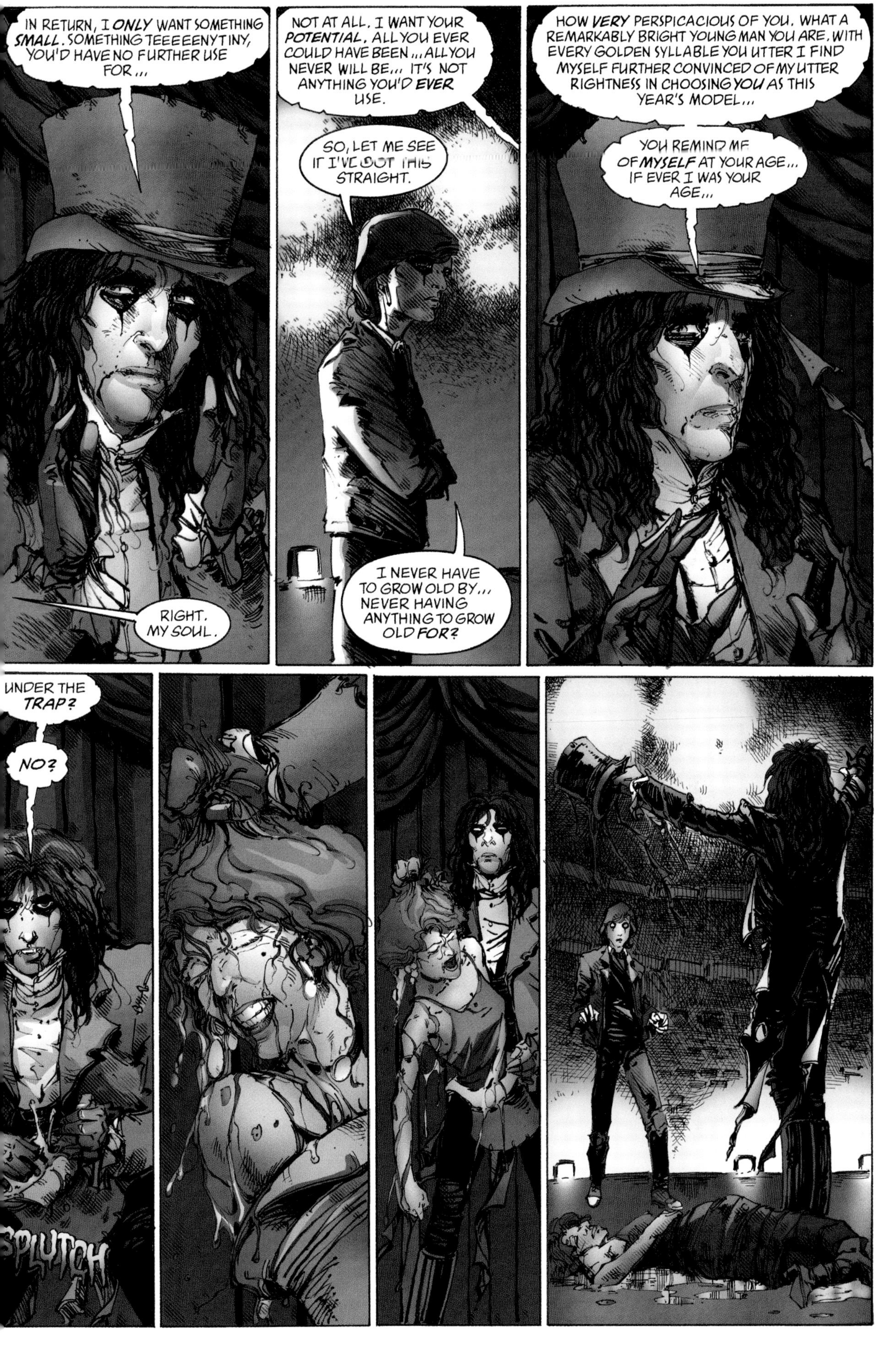
IN RETURN, I ONLY WANT SOMETHING SMALL. SOMETHING TEEEEENYTINY, YOU'D HAVE NO FURTHER USE FOR...
RIGHT. MY SOUL.
NOT AT ALL. I WANT YOUR POTENTIAL. ALL YOU EVER COULD HAVE BEEN... ALL YOU NEVER WILL BE... IT'S NOT ANYTHING YOU'D EVER USE.
SO, LET ME SEE IF I'VE GOT THIS STRAIGHT.
I NEVER HAVE TO GROW OLD BY... NEVER HAVING ANYTHING TO GROW OLD FOR?
HOW VERY PERSPICACIOUS OF YOU. WHAT A REMARKABLY BRIGHT YOUNG MAN YOU ARE. WITH EVERY GOLDEN SYLLABLE YOU UTTER I FIND MYSELF FURTHER CONVINCED OF MY UTTER RIGHTNESS IN CHOOSING YOU AS THIS YEAR'S MODEL...
YOU REMIND ME OF MYSELF AT YOUR AGE... IF EVER I WAS YOUR AGE...
UNDER THE TRAP?
NO?
SPLUTCH

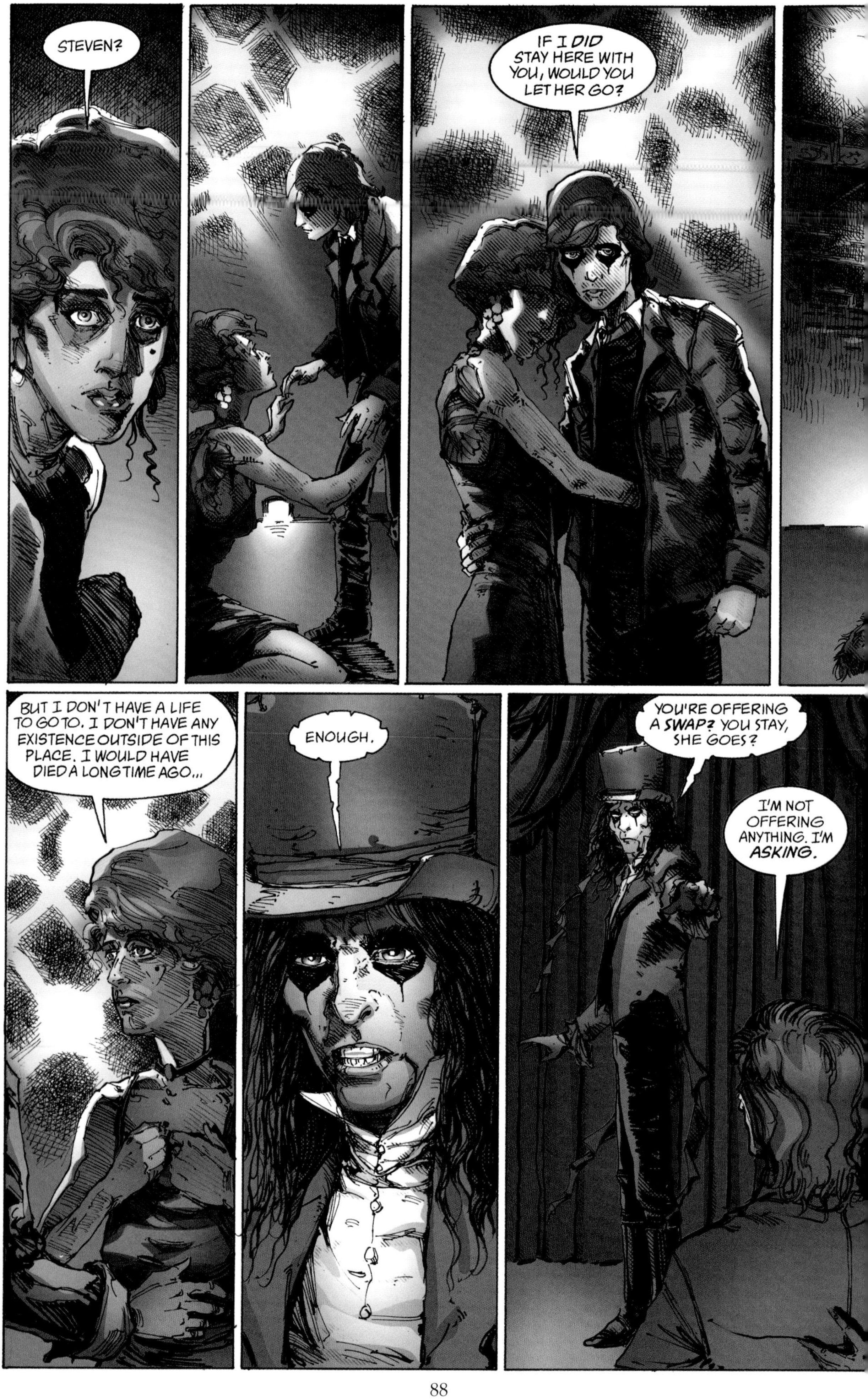
STEVEN?
IF I DID STAY HERE WITH YOU, WOULD YOU LET HER GO?
BUT I DON'T HAVE A LIFE TO GO TO. I DON'T HAVE ANY EXISTENCE OUTSIDE OF THIS PLACE. I WOULD HAVE DIED A LONG TIME AGO...
ENOUGH.
YOU'RE OFFERING A SWAP? YOU STAY, SHE GOES?
I'M NOT OFFERING ANYTHING. I'M ASKING.

NOW, *THERE'S* AN INTERESTING PROPOSITION, WORTHY INDEED OF A CERTAIN AMOUNT OF NEGOTIATION.

STEVEN. YOU *CAN'T*. YOU *MUSTN'T*. REALLY.

I CAN.

THE FURTHER THIS GOES, THE MORE I SUSPECT THAT I MIGHT HAVE MADE IT EASIER ON MYSELF, HAD I PICKED ANOTHER HALLOWE'EN CHILD...

NO. I WOULD *NEVER* PERMIT HER TO LEAVE. MERCY IS PART OF THE SHOW.

THE SHOW'S THE THING.

THE SHOW.

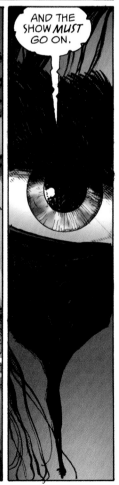

AND THE SHOW *MUST* GO ON.

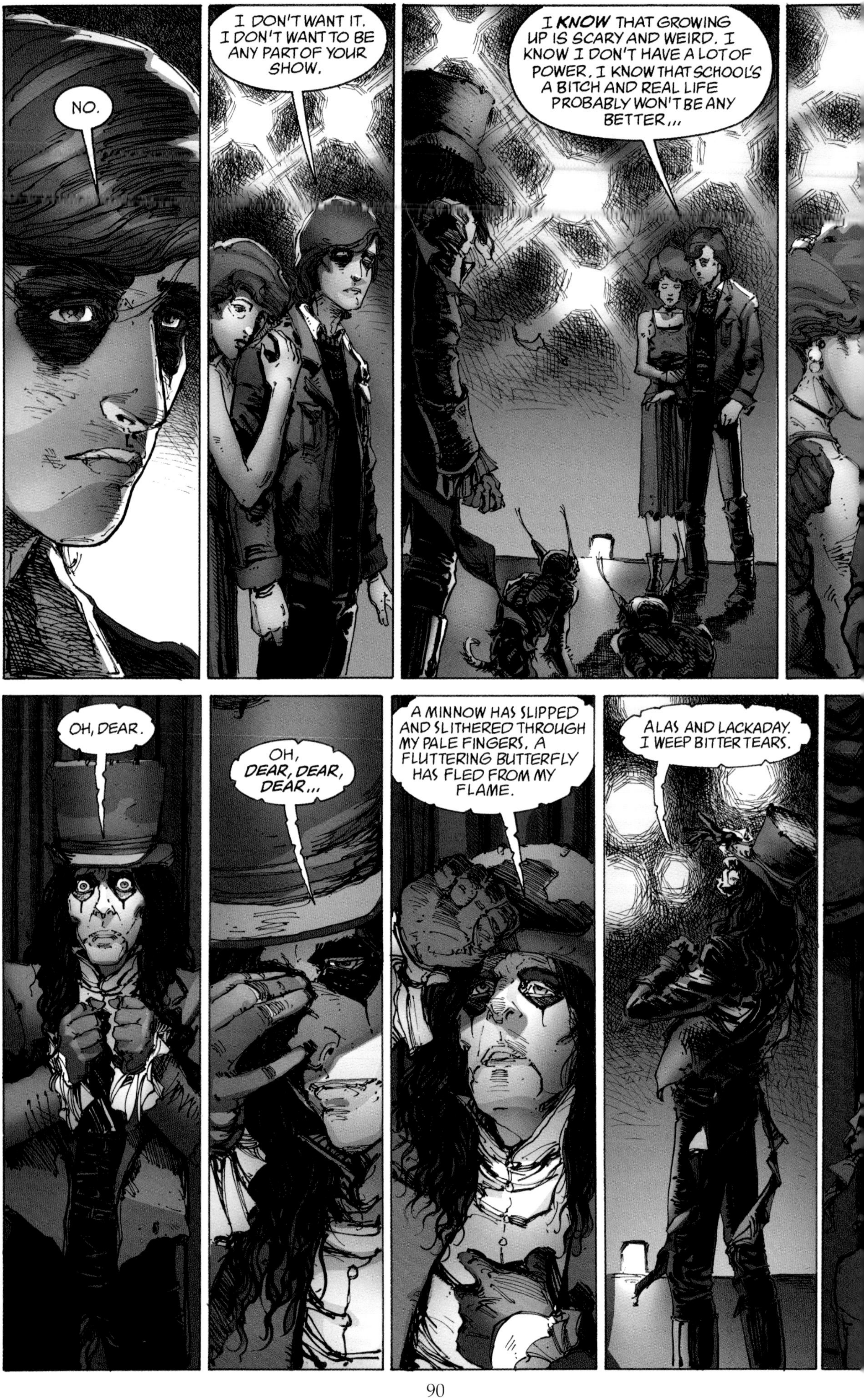
NO.
I DON'T WANT IT. I DON'T WANT TO BE ANY PART OF YOUR SHOW.
I **KNOW** THAT GROWING UP IS SCARY AND WEIRD. I KNOW I DON'T HAVE A LOT OF POWER. I KNOW THAT SCHOOL'S A BITCH AND REAL LIFE PROBABLY WON'T BE ANY BETTER...
OH, DEAR.
OH, *DEAR, DEAR, DEAR...*
A MINNOW HAS SLIPPED AND SLITHERED THROUGH MY PALE FINGERS. A FLUTTERING BUTTERFLY HAS FLED FROM MY FLAME.
ALAS AND LACKADAY. I WEEP BITTER TEARS.

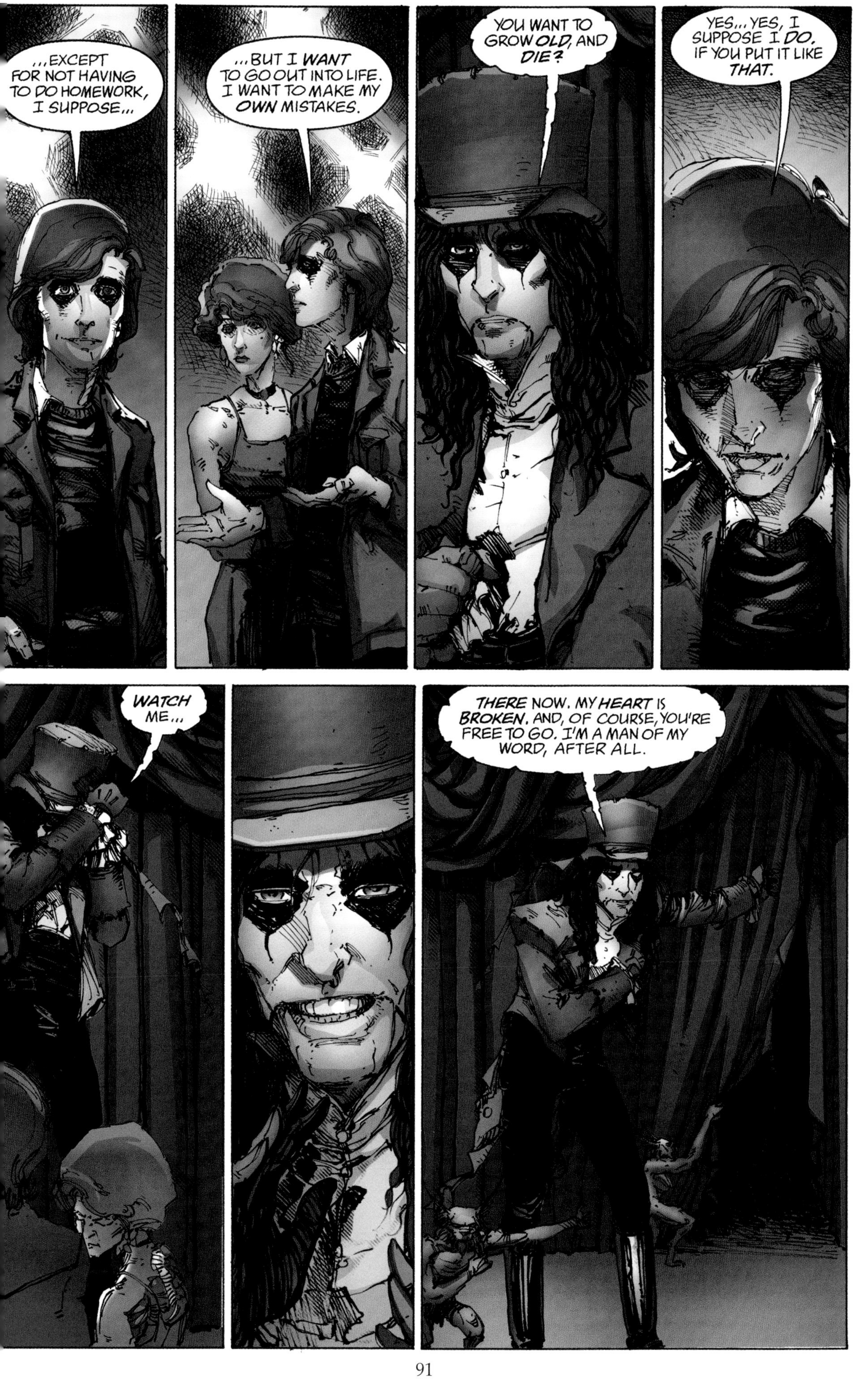
...EXCEPT FOR NOT HAVING TO DO HOMEWORK, I SUPPOSE...
...BUT I WANT TO GO OUT INTO LIFE. I WANT TO MAKE MY OWN MISTAKES.
YOU WANT TO GROW OLD, AND DIE?
YES... YES, I SUPPOSE I DO. IF YOU PUT IT LIKE THAT.
WATCH ME...
THERE NOW. MY HEART IS BROKEN. AND, OF COURSE, YOU'RE FREE TO GO. I'M A MAN OF MY WORD, AFTER ALL.

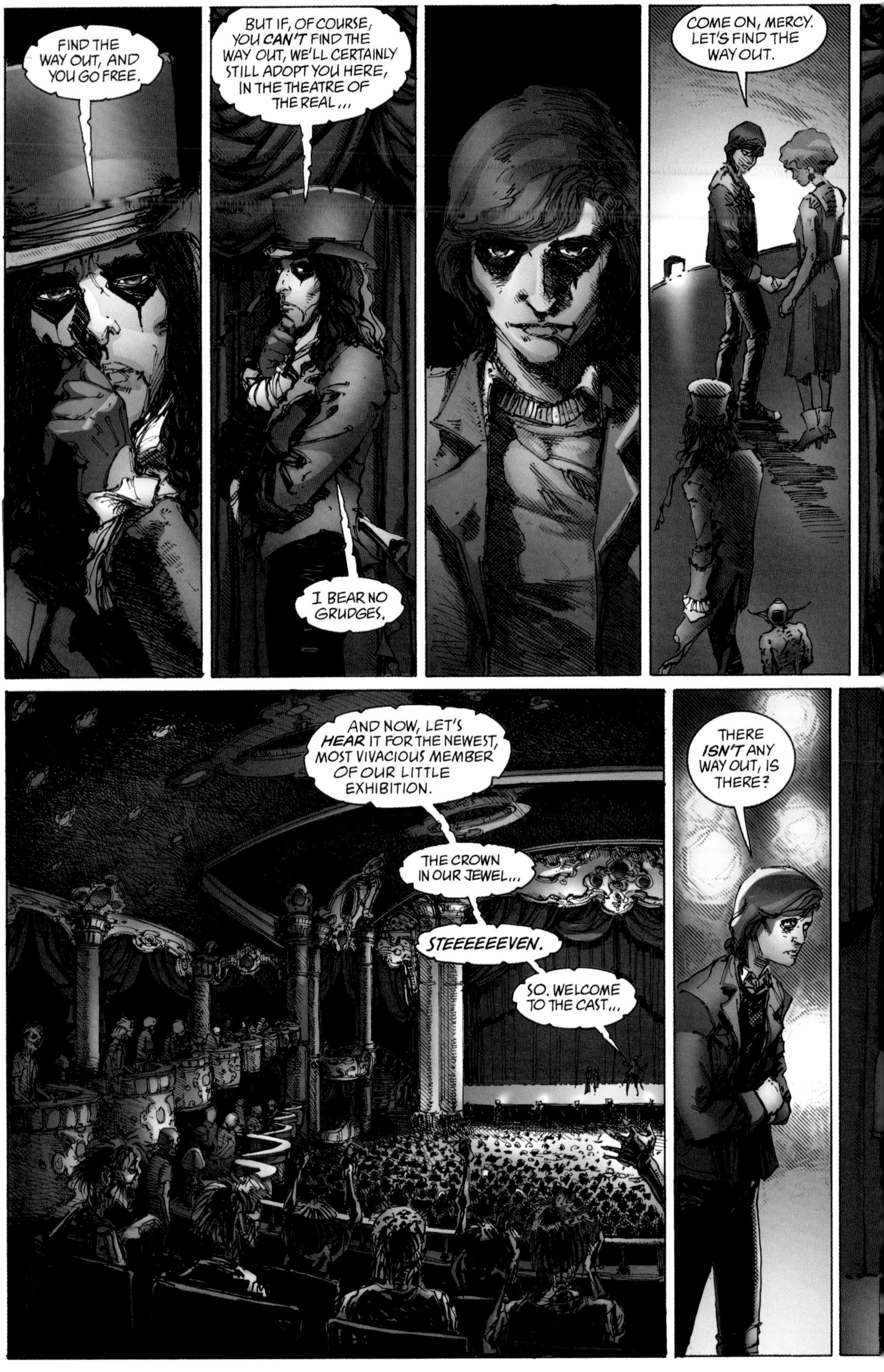
FIND THE WAY OUT, AND YOU GO FREE.
BUT IF, OF COURSE, YOU *CAN'T* FIND THE WAY OUT, WE'LL CERTAINLY STILL ADOPT YOU HERE, IN THE THEATRE OF THE REAL...
I BEAR NO GRUDGES.
COME ON, MERCY. LET'S FIND THE WAY OUT.
AND NOW, LET'S *HEAR* IT FOR THE NEWEST, MOST VIVACIOUS MEMBER OF OUR LITTLE EXHIBITION.
THE CROWN IN OUR JEWEL...
STEEEEEEVEN.
SO. WELCOME TO THE CAST...
THERE *ISN'T* ANY WAY OUT, IS THERE?

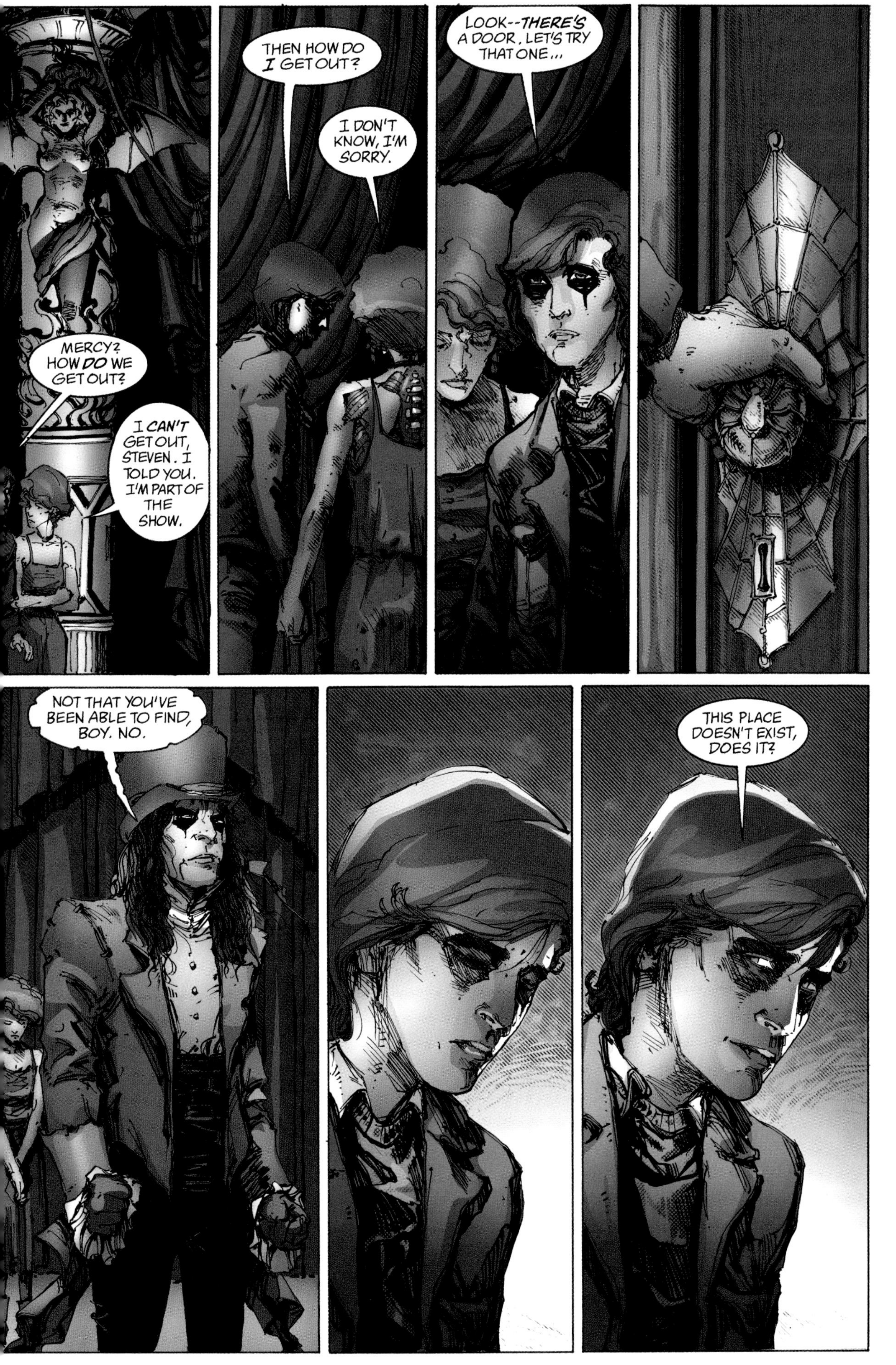
MERCY? HOW DO WE GET OUT?
I CAN'T GET OUT, STEVEN. I TOLD YOU. I'M PART OF THE SHOW.
THEN HOW DO I GET OUT?
I DON'T KNOW, I'M SORRY.
LOOK--THERE'S A DOOR, LET'S TRY THAT ONE...
NOT THAT YOU'VE BEEN ABLE TO FIND, BOY. NO.
THIS PLACE DOESN'T EXIST, DOES IT?

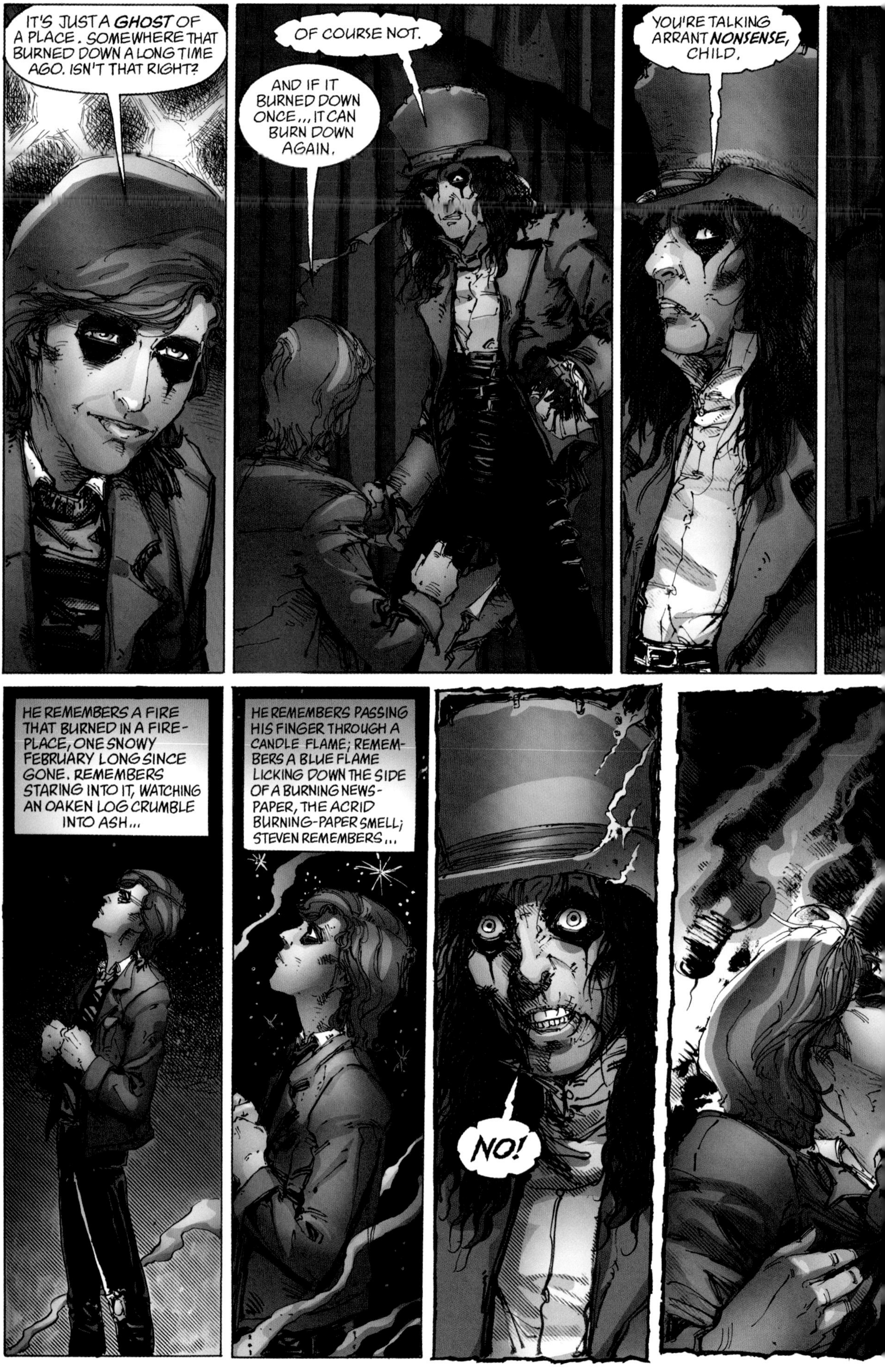
IT'S JUST A GHOST OF A PLACE. SOMEWHERE THAT BURNED DOWN A LONG TIME AGO. ISN'T THAT RIGHT?
OF COURSE NOT.
AND IF IT BURNED DOWN ONCE,,, IT CAN BURN DOWN AGAIN.
YOU'RE TALKING ARRANT NONSENSE, CHILD.
HE REMEMBERS A FIRE THAT BURNED IN A FIRE-PLACE, ONE SNOWY FEBRUARY LONG SINCE GONE. REMEMBERS STARING INTO IT, WATCHING AN OAKEN LOG CRUMBLE INTO ASH...
HE REMEMBERS PASSING HIS FINGER THROUGH A CANDLE FLAME; REMEMBERS A BLUE FLAME LICKING DOWN THE SIDE OF A BURNING NEWS-PAPER, THE ACRID BURNING-PAPER SMELL; STEVEN REMEMBERS...
NO!

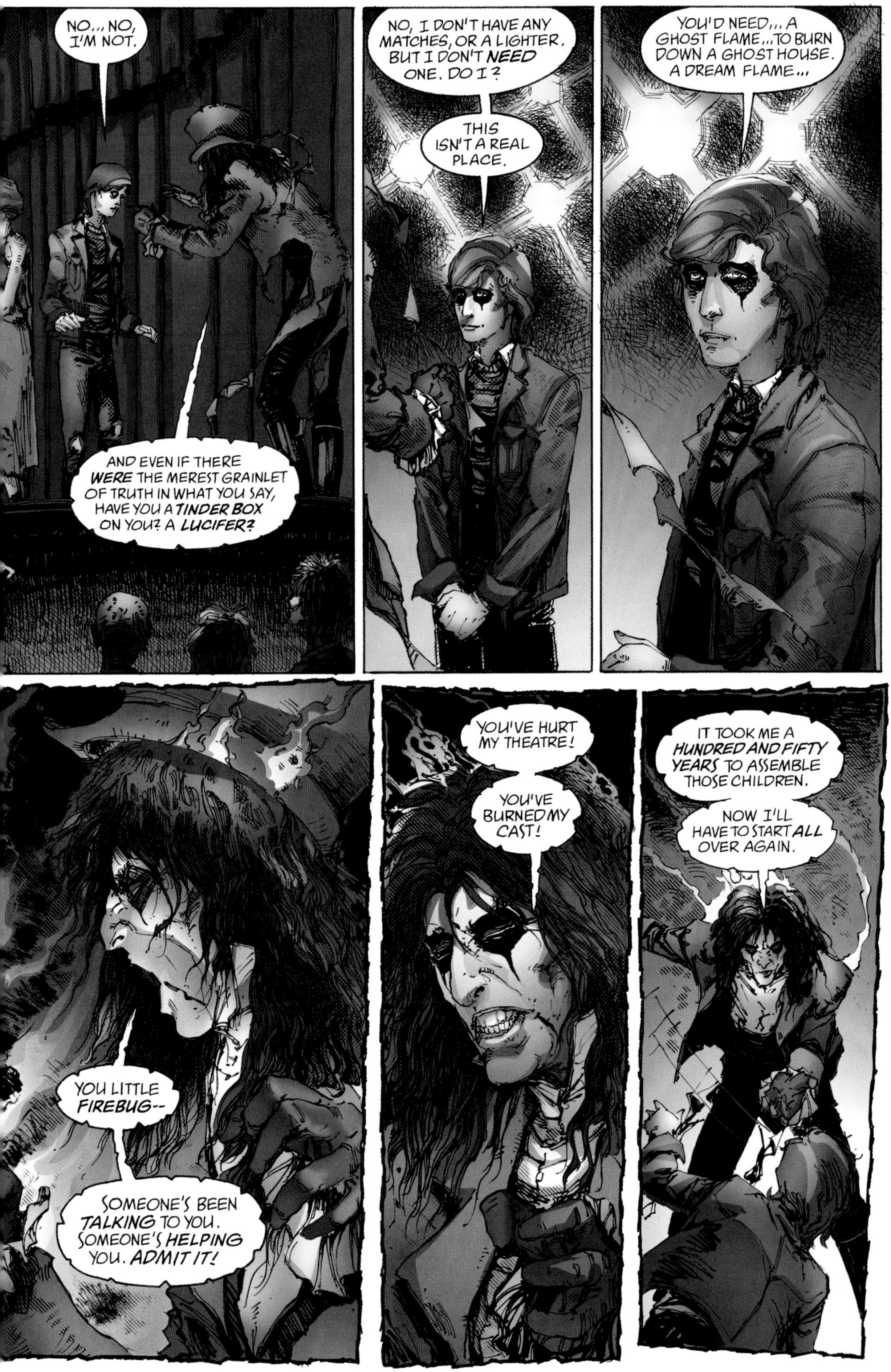
NO,.. NO, I'M NOT.
AND EVEN IF THERE WERE THE MEREST GRAINLET OF TRUTH IN WHAT YOU SAY, HAVE YOU A TINDER BOX ON YOU? A LUCIFER?
NO, I DON'T HAVE ANY MATCHES, OR A LIGHTER. BUT I DON'T NEED ONE. DO I?
THIS ISN'T A REAL PLACE.
YOU'D NEED... A GHOST FLAME... TO BURN DOWN A GHOST HOUSE. A DREAM FLAME...
YOU LITTLE FIREBUG--
SOMEONE'S BEEN TALKING TO YOU. SOMEONE'S HELPING YOU. ADMIT IT!
YOU'VE HURT MY THEATRE!
YOU'VE BURNED MY CAST!
IT TOOK ME A HUNDRED AND FIFTY YEARS TO ASSEMBLE THOSE CHILDREN.
NOW I'LL HAVE TO START ALL OVER AGAIN.

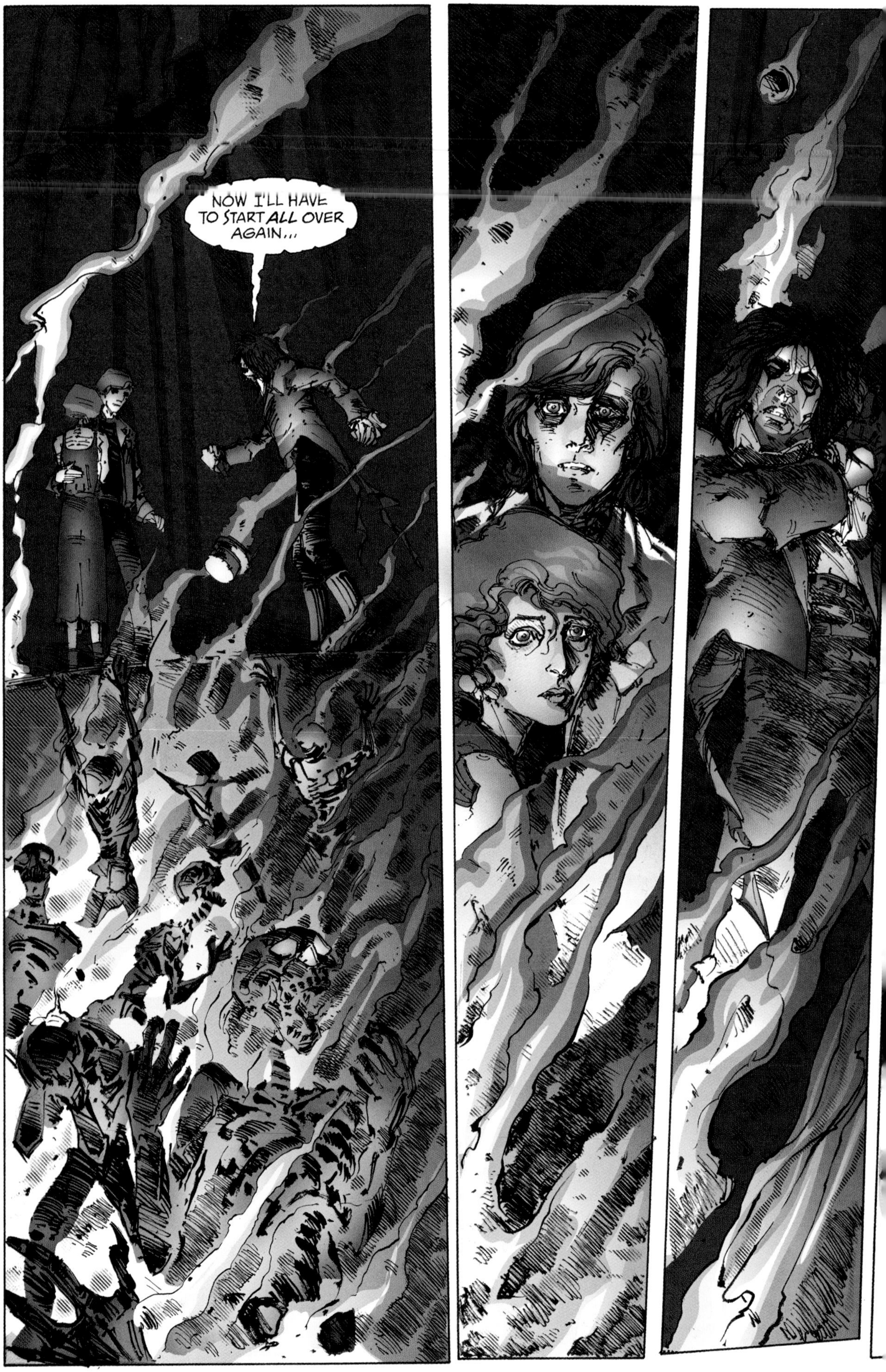
NOW I'LL HAVE TO START ALL OVER AGAIN...

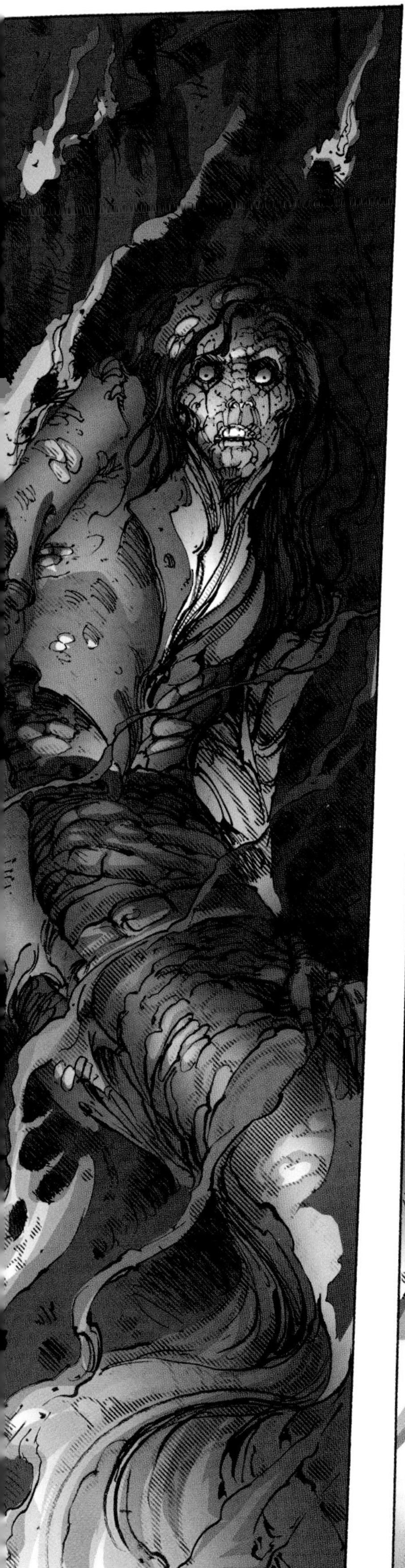

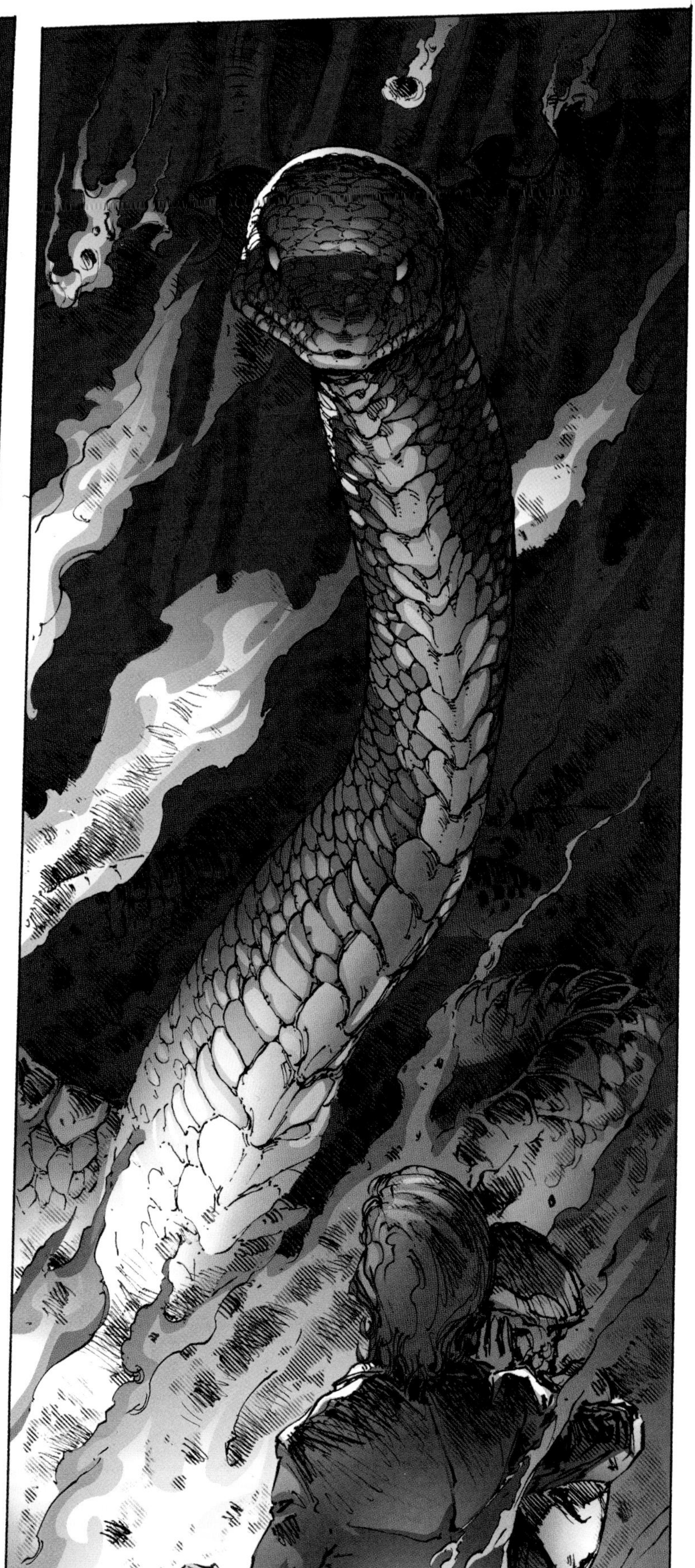

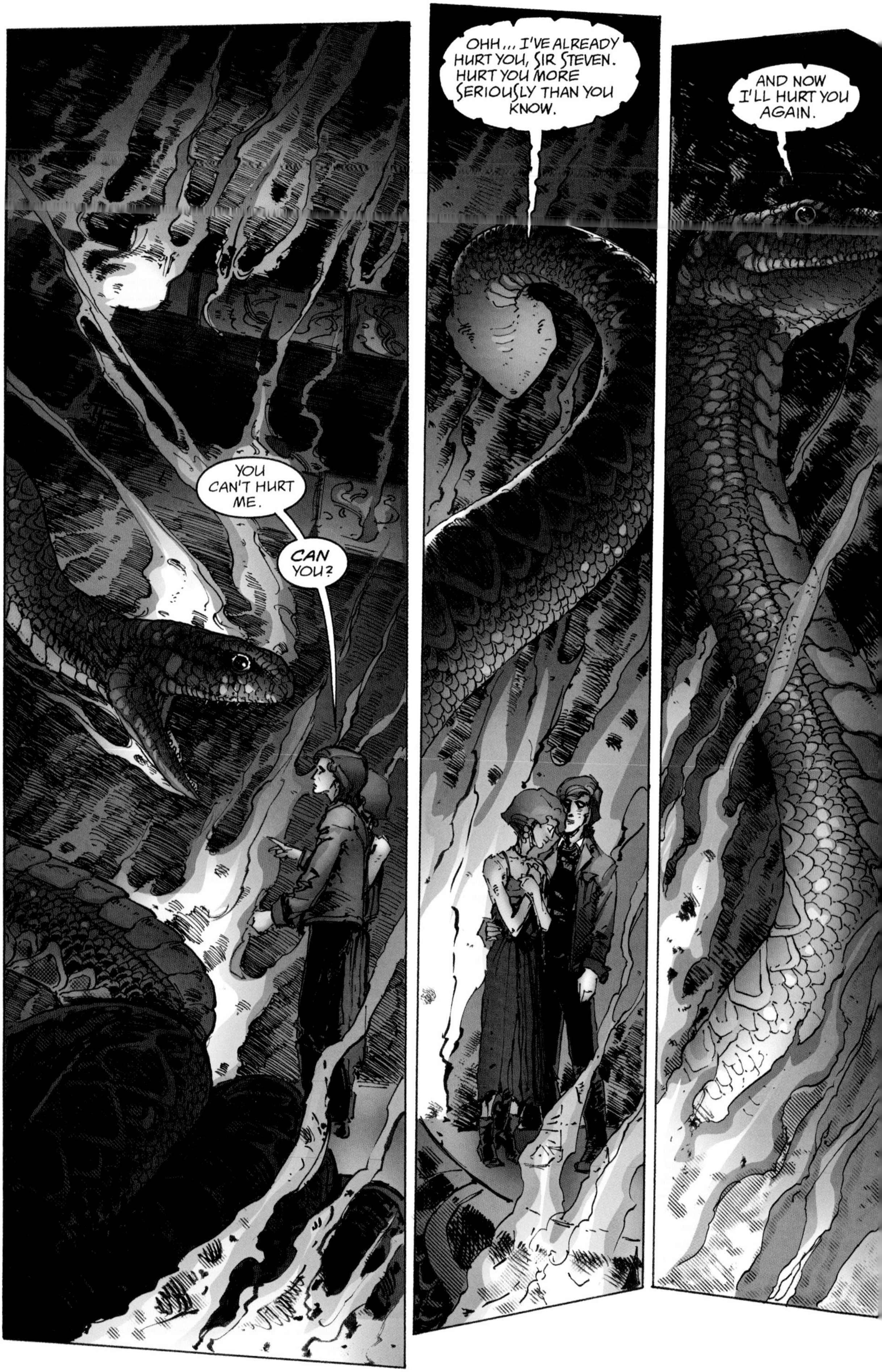
YOU CAN'T HURT ME.
CAN YOU?
OHH... I'VE ALREADY HURT YOU, SIR STEVEN. HURT YOU MORE SERIOUSLY THAN YOU KNOW.
AND NOW I'LL HURT YOU AGAIN.

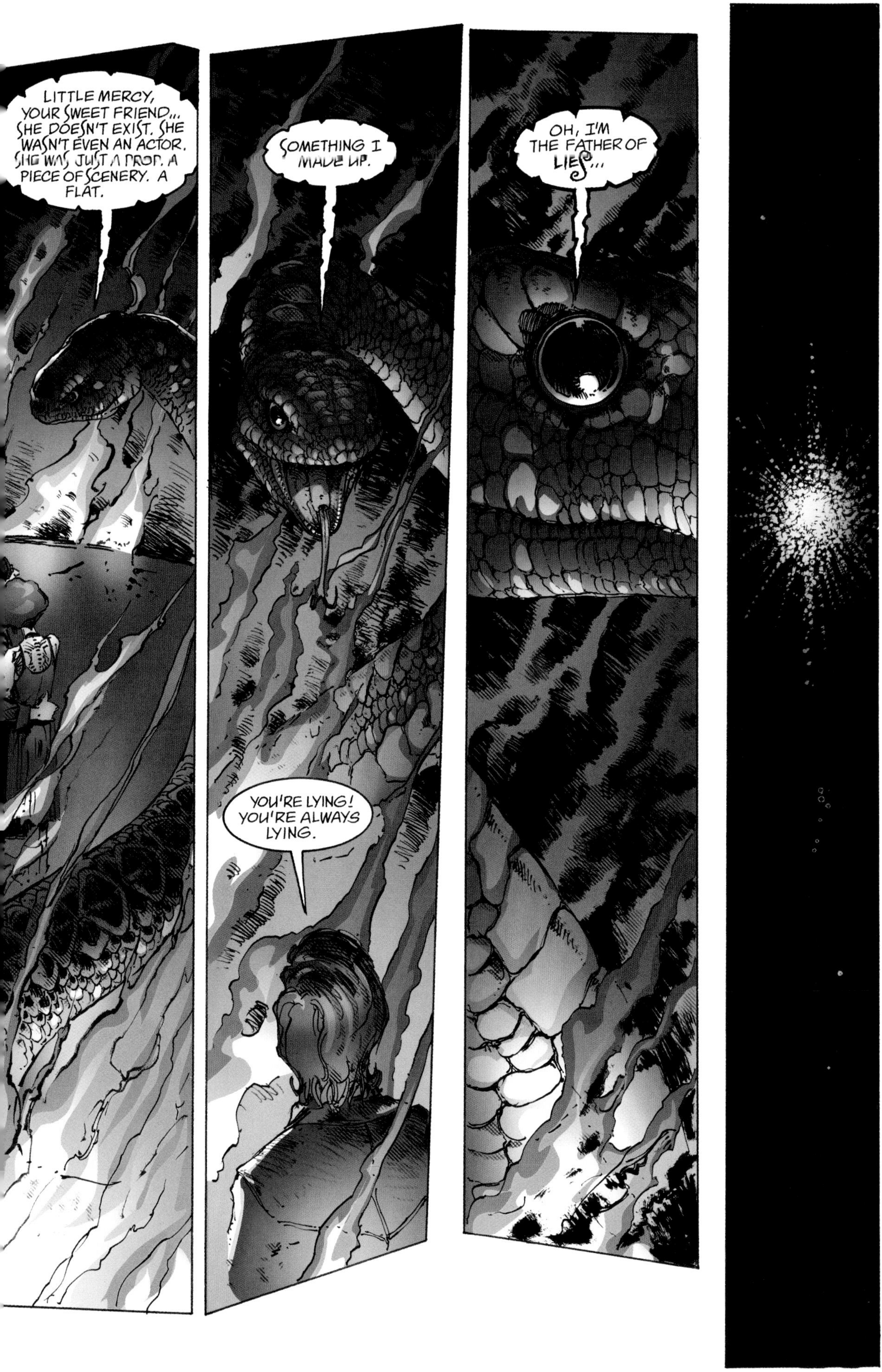
LITTLE MERCY, YOUR SWEET FRIEND... SHE DOESN'T EXIST. SHE WASN'T EVEN AN ACTOR. SHE WAS JUST A PROP. A PIECE OF SCENERY. A FLAT.
SOMETHING I MADE UP.
YOU'RE LYING! YOU'RE ALWAYS LYING.
OH, I'M THE FATHER OF LIES...

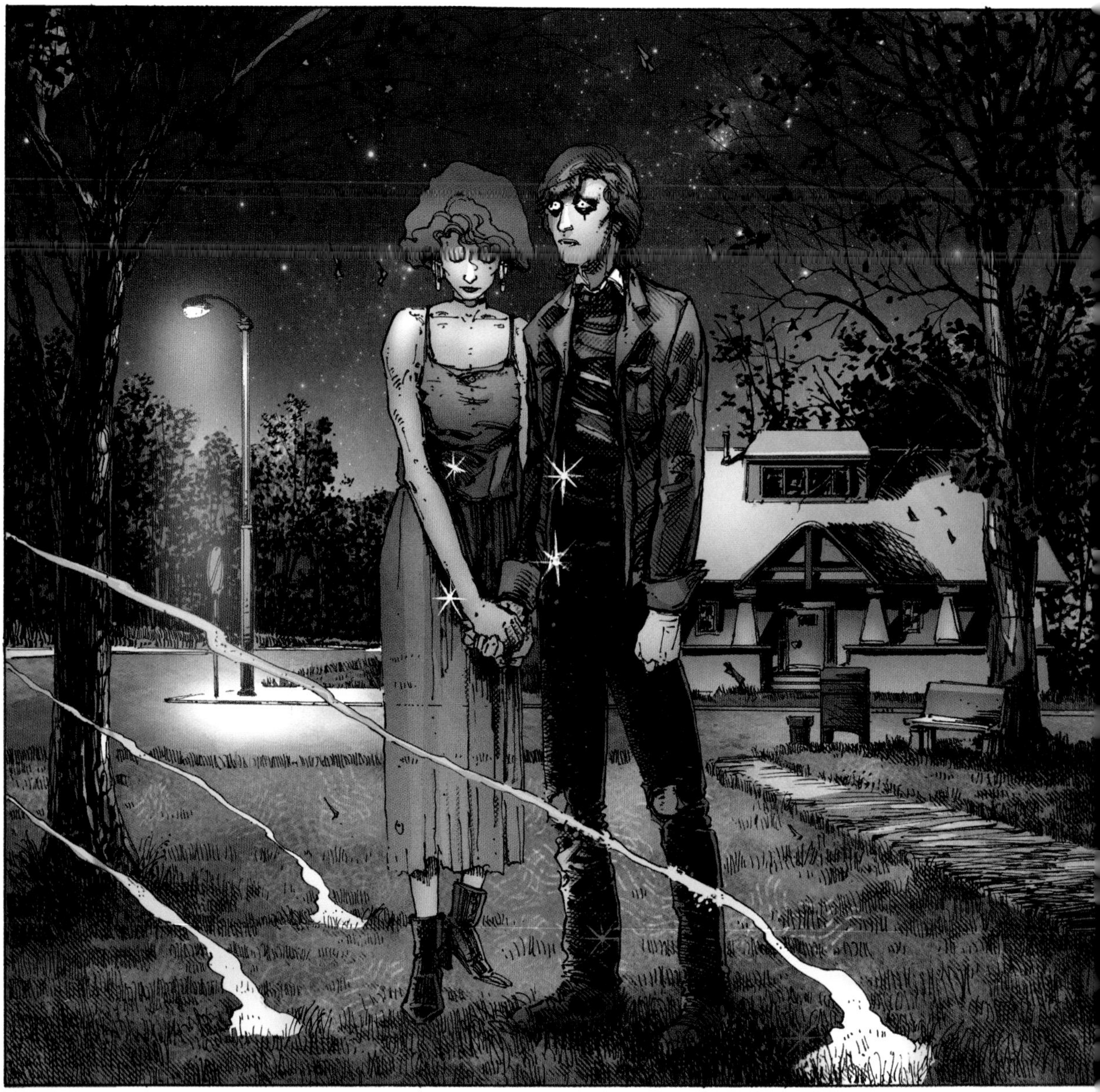

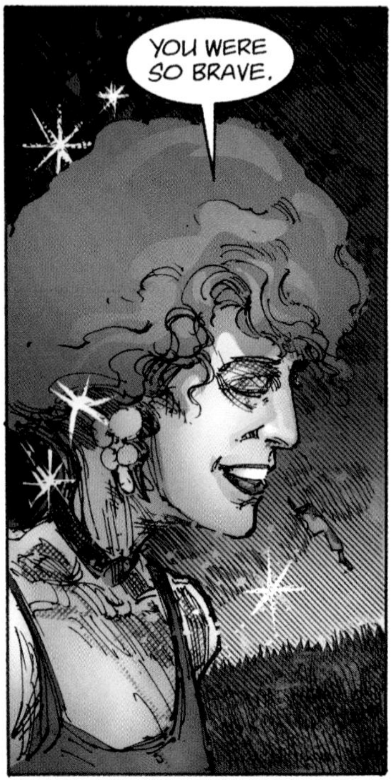
YOU WERE SO BRAVE.

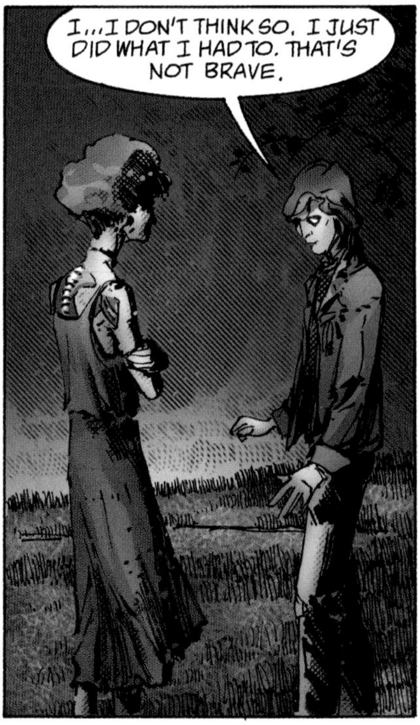
I...I DON'T THINK SO. I JUST DID WHAT I HAD TO. THAT'S NOT BRAVE.

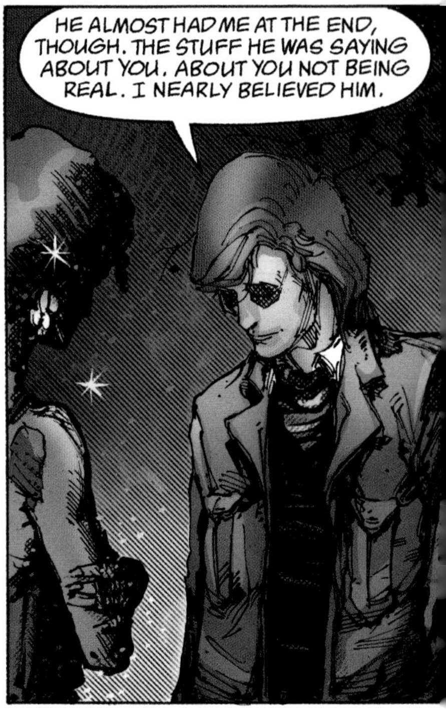
HE ALMOST HAD ME AT THE END, THOUGH. THE STUFF HE WAS SAYING ABOUT YOU. ABOUT YOU NOT BEING REAL. I NEARLY BELIEVED HIM.

THAT *WASN'T* A LIE, STEVEN.

I WASN'T EVEN A GHOST, I'M *SORRY...*

SSSSSS

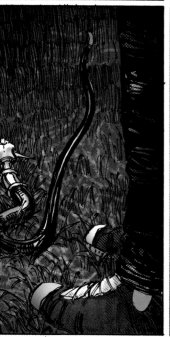

HOW WAS HALLOWE'EN?

DID YOU HAVE FUN, TRICK-OR-TREATING?

FINE.

I SUPPOSE.

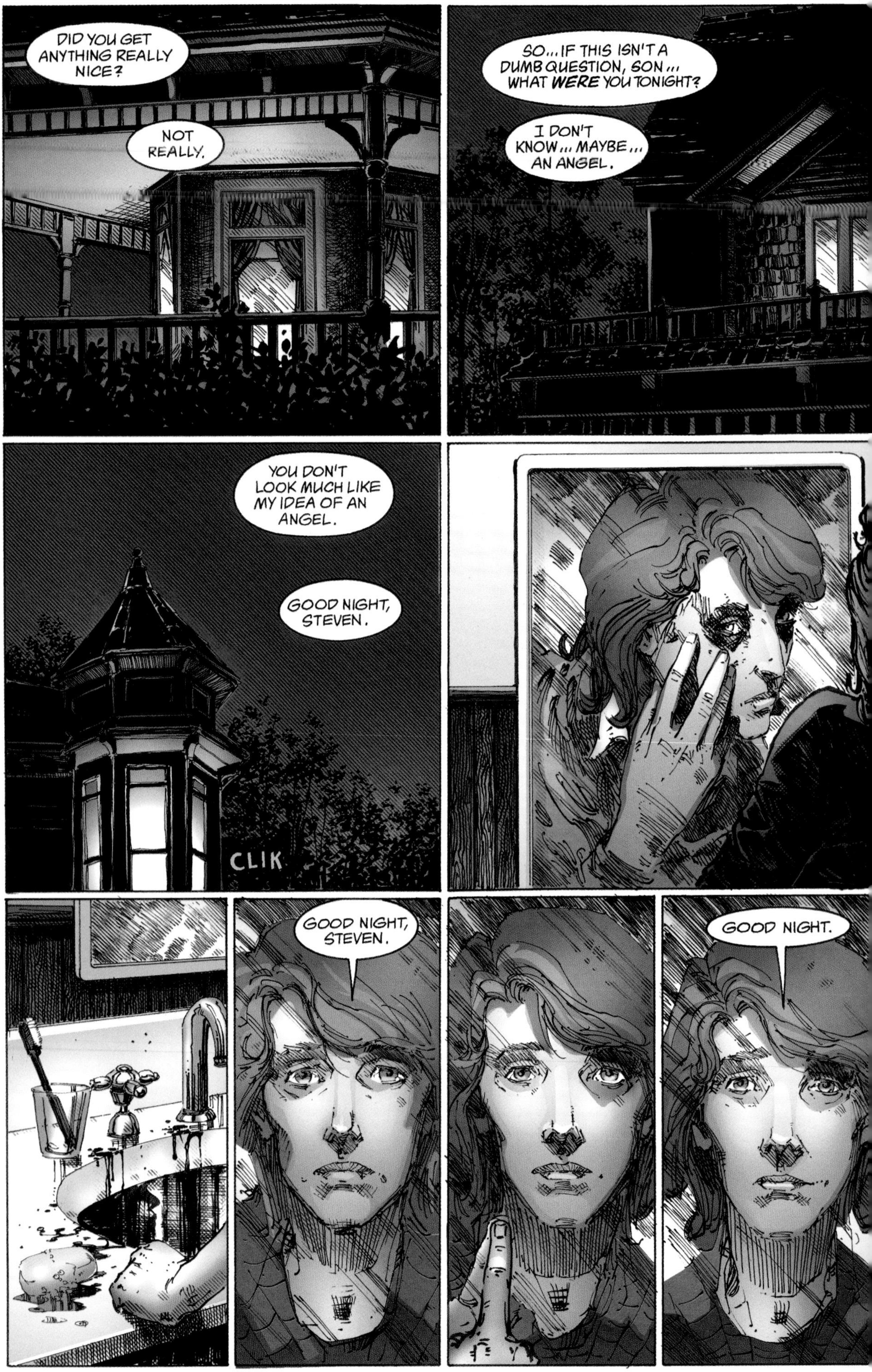
DID YOU GET ANYTHING REALLY NICE?
NOT REALLY.
SO... IF THIS ISN'T A DUMB QUESTION, SON... WHAT *WERE* YOU TONIGHT?
I DON'T KNOW... MAYBE... AN ANGEL.
YOU DON'T LOOK MUCH LIKE MY IDEA OF AN ANGEL.
GOOD NIGHT, STEVEN.
CLIK
GOOD NIGHT, STEVEN.
GOOD NIGHT.

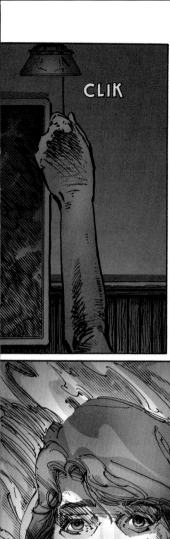

CLIK

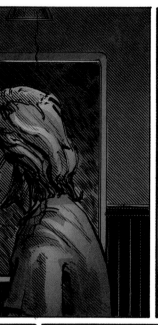

THERE, BOY.

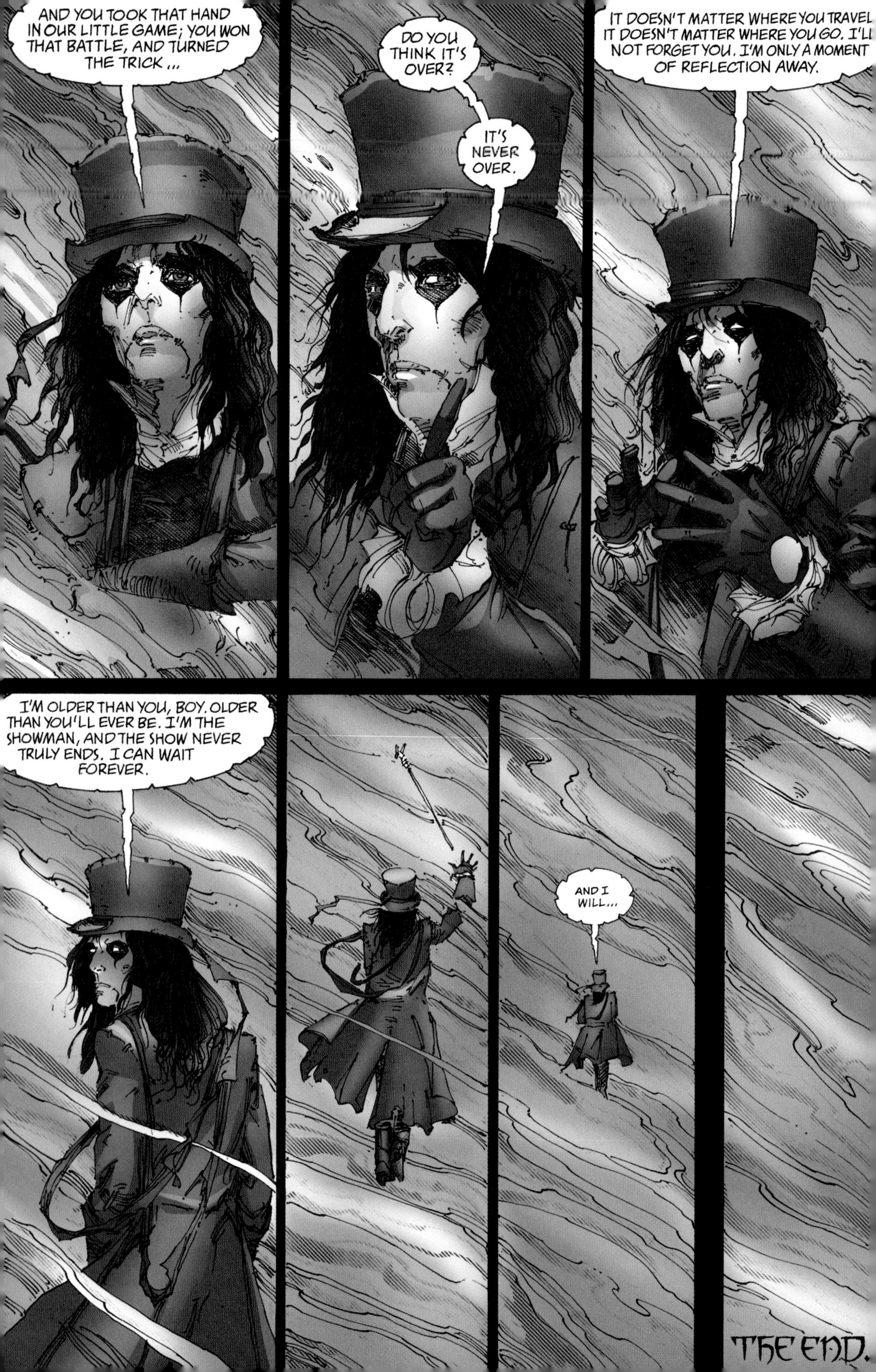

AND YOU TOOK THAT HAND IN OUR LITTLE GAME; YOU WON THAT BATTLE, AND TURNED THE TRICK ...
DO YOU THINK IT'S OVER?
IT'S NEVER OVER.
IT DOESN'T MATTER WHERE YOU TRAVEL IT DOESN'T MATTER WHERE YOU GO. I'LL NOT FORGET YOU. I'M ONLY A MOMENT OF REFLECTION AWAY.
I'M OLDER THAN YOU, BOY. OLDER THAN YOU'LL EVER BE. I'M THE SHOWMAN, AND THE SHOW NEVER TRULY ENDS. I CAN WAIT FOREVER.
AND I WILL...
THE END.

AFTERWORD BY MICHAEL ZULLI
"HAVE YOU A LUCIFER?"

I desperately wanted to title this bit, *"what becomes a legend most?"* If you're familiar with the late and, well, legendary Lou Reed you would have made a connection here. But I am writing about an altogether *different* legend. One Alice Cooper, specifically. Whereas Lou was all New York City, Alice is, in many, many ways pure Detroit.

Okay.

Imagine this: you are walking down a Detroit sidewalk and you just happen to trip over a crack in the pavement. Then, as if you've fallen into a B movie, time slows down as you watch as the sidewalk rise to meet your face. You see the cracks in the pavement, the weeds struggling through in spots, a broken beer bottle in the gutter, a few old cigarette butts and a fast food wrapper scuttle by in slo-mo. The one thing you are totally convinced of, is that this is *really*, really going to hurt.

But there is something else that runs through your mind and— much like driving by the scene of a car wreck— you *cannot* look away. This whole elongated sequence of seconds seem strangely beautiful.

That's when time pops back to normal speed and bone meets concrete. Oh yeah, it **really, really** hurts.

Welcome to Detroit. Welcome to Alice Cooper, and yes, welcome to the nightmare; the knife in the dark, the howling D.T's in a cheap apartment, the needle abscess behind your left knee.

Welcome to the Theater of the Real.

When I willingly entered the Showman's world, my fee for entering was the price of perhaps fifteen CD's just to play catch-up; and from the offices, a huge envelope stuffed full of clippings of Alice on stage. To say I received feedback would be an understatement. I confess now that the years have passed— that I listened politely for a bit, and then simply as *ever*, did it my way. Another confession. When the Alice Copper Band's first record (remember those? Large black flat things that you actually had to *turn over*?) came out, I was into a far different kind of musical world. The band just was not on my personal radar.

Drawing *The Last Temptation* made me listen, and by God, did I listen. I listened so hard my ears leaked and stained my pillowcase with bits of brains. And I loved every minute of it.

Meeting Alice in person simply confirmed what I already knew— I had him pinned: body movement, a subtle turn of the head, a narrowing of the eyes here, a sinister smile there. Now, when I say that the Showman (aka Alice Copper on stage) is very little like the real living, breathing, puts-his-pants-on-in-the-morning Alice Copper you'd best believe it. I think that's why the creature on stage didn't die in a hotel room strangling on his own vomit at twenty-seven. In person, the flesh and bone Alice is a truly wonderful person to hang out with. Intelligent, humorous, and wise to the world, he is a totally grounded and decent human being. To this day, I feel graced to have been involved *at all* in this project. My only regret is that I wish I had done better, because for an Artist with a big "A" you can always do better. And as the work faded as it always does, I lost track of Alice and the amazing world that he's built around himself. Now, I'm not blowing smoke my friend— I very much mean it. If you know me at all, you would know that sort of thing just does not fly with me.

I mean it man.

So, thank you Neil, and thank you Alice, I'd like to hear from you someday. That would be the nazz.

From the middle of nowhere,

On a day pass, closely supervised,

lucky to be out at all.

Michael Zulli.

July, 2014.

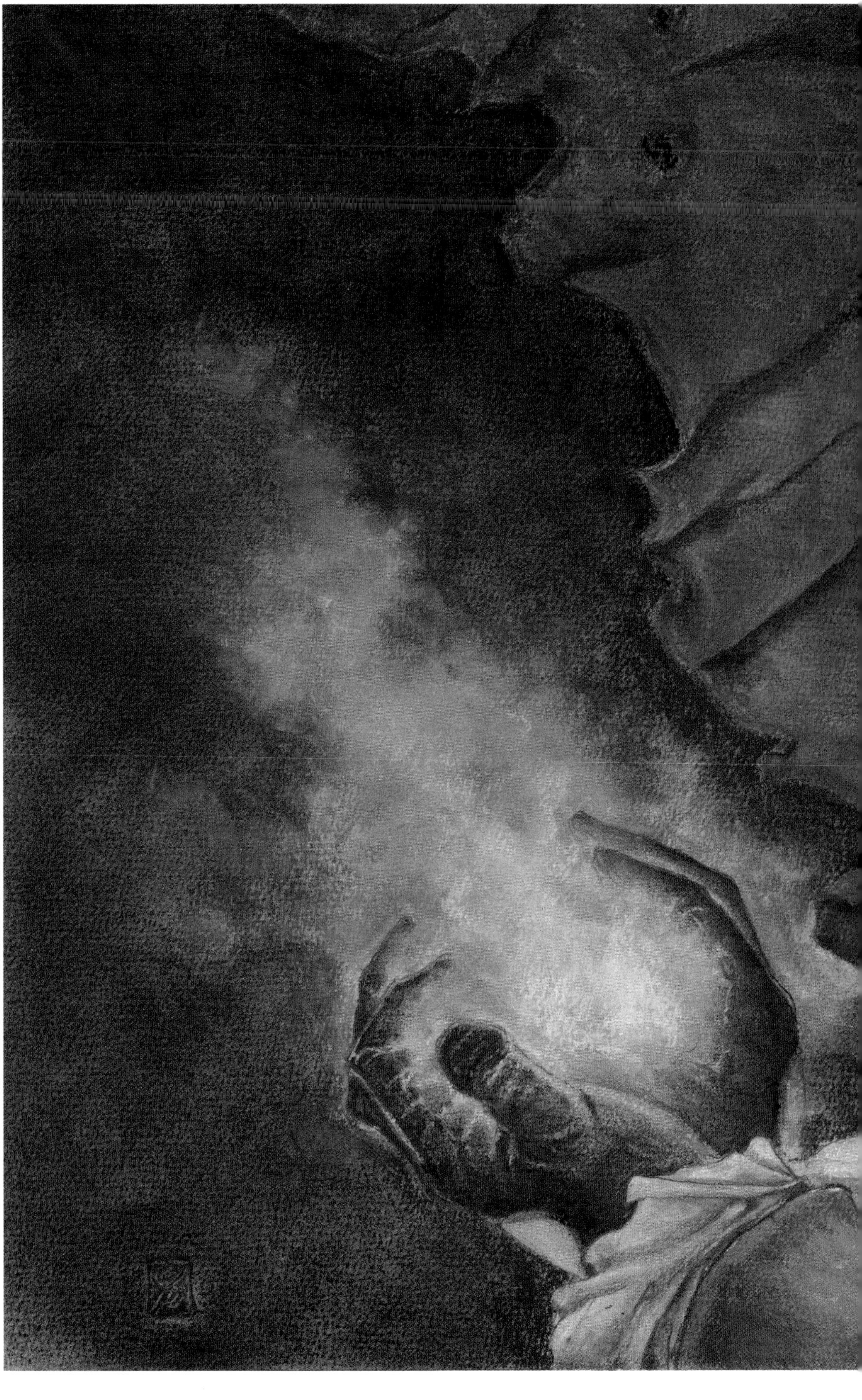

pin-up art by Michael Zulli (2014)

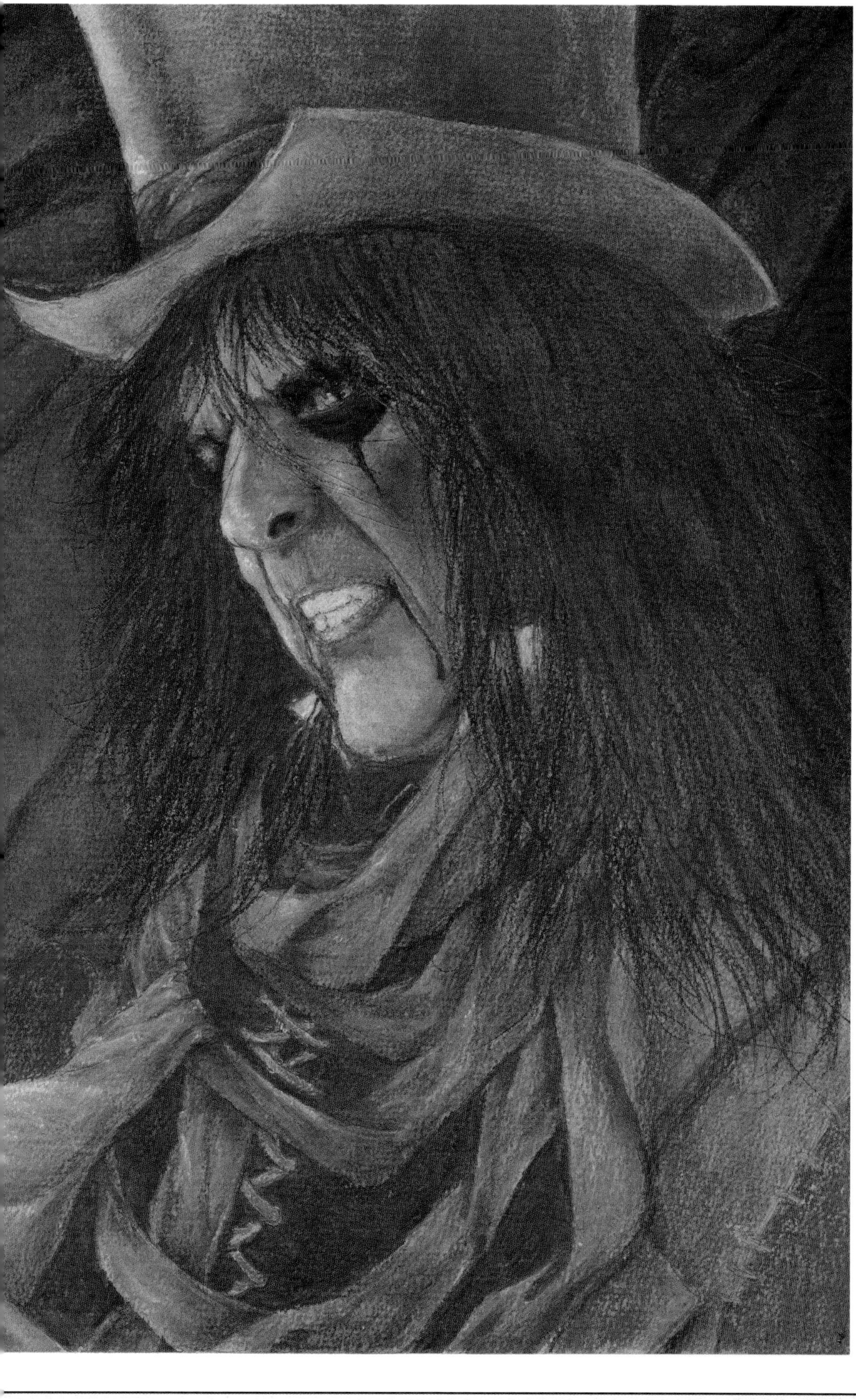

NEIL GAIMAN'S FIRST LETTER TO ALICE COOPER

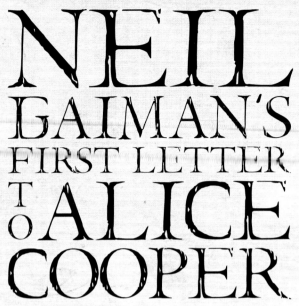

Dear Alice,

Well, I hear from my agent that the deal is getting done, and I've been thinking about the Project a lot, so I figure it's time to start those ol' fax lines flying across the Atlantic.

Let me know what you think.

I've taken it on a little from our conversations in Phoenix, added some more plot and played around with it: and I'm sure you've done some song stuff already which'll feed back into this.

Anyway, here's the loose plot for your eyes only at this point, really as something to take and start talking about, in one direction or another.

I don't think I've missed out anything important...

AS-YET-UNTITLED-PROJECT.

We begin with Steven and his friends; kids in the grey zone between childhood and adolescence, a place where adult life and responsibility is visible as something coming over the horizon toward them like a Scud Missile. Sooner or later you have to face up to it.

It's small-town America. The time is now. We could be in anytown. It's early evening, in Autumn, and dead leaves blow down Main Street. Steven and the other kids are walking home from school.

There's a red light flashing; an alleyway, where there wasn't an alleyway before. They stop and look down the alleyway. Standing in the shadows is The Showman, extolling the virtues of the little theatre.

The Showman is wearing Alice make-up.

"Hey, kids. C'mon in. You want to see a show? I'll show you something you've never seen before. It's the show of a lifetime. It's a whole new world, and it's all real, and it's all free...

"I'll show you life, and blood, and all the secrets that no-one's going to tell you. It's the Theatre of the Real, boys..."

He lists delights waiting for them, inside the Theatre.

The kids are scared – Steven as much as any of the others. They begin a low undercurrent of "Go on – go on in – I dare you, are you scared? Heck, I'm not scared, well, why don't you? well, why don't YOU? I think you're scared. I'm not scared."

Gradually they begin to focus on Steven. He's the one they're all accusing of being scared – of just being a little kid.

"I'm not scared. I dare," says Steven, scared. And he goes down the alleyway. The other kids scatter.

The Showman takes him into the theatre, gives him a ticket.

Steven walks into the empty theatre. The curtain is down. He's the only one in there. He takes a seat.

The music begins and the curtain goes up. And the show begins...

And as the show begins the theatre is no longer empty. There are other people sitting on the red velvet seats. Strange, shadowy people, waiting in silence.

The Showman comes on, dressed differently.

"Okay," he says. "This is what's waiting for you."

And the show begins.

The kid watches, open-mouthed and scared as the strange little Grand Guignol shows begin.

The kid is being shown adult-hood – not as something that carries with it any kind of responsibility or pride, but as something terrifying, something to be feared.

Now, to some extent what he sees is dependent on which songs we go for here, but topics we've talked about include:

MECHANISED DEATH
Machines, Cars and death on the road. Steel crumpling, glass shattering, people impaled on steering wheels, bodies being cut from blazing wrecks. A world in which we're surrounded by machines, in which death becomes more impersonal. Blood glittering on diamonds of broken glass and razors of fractured chrome. The fear you feel as headlights weave towards you on a darkened road. Fear on the highways, mechanised Death.

BAD PLACE ALONE
The fear of Big Cities, of taking the wrong turn into the wrong places, of the gleam of lies and knives; of gang warfare; being knocked to the ground, having cigarettes ground out on your skin; of being robbed, raped or killed.

BLOOD LINE
What happens when families unravel and break. The loss of stability and security which occur. Listening to parents screaming, listening to the sound of blows. Helplessness.

HIDDEN PERSUADERS
The world of media manipulation, a world in which everyone's trying to sell you something. Sell you ideas. Sell you products. Sell you themselves.

These are all possibilities, and there are others that we can use here. Each of them is a tiny playlet put on by the Showman and his little cast: grand guignol for the 1990s, blood-washed excursions into fear, revolving around the nightmares of adulthood, of growing up. Money. Responsibility. Death.

One that we should do something with, obviously, is the world of sex – this might well be the duet we were talking about in Phoenix. Anyway, however we work this...

After some hours, the show's over. The curtain goes down, the lights go up. The theatre is once again empty.

Steven gets up, shaken. He walks out.

We follow him out of the alleyway, back onto the sidewalk: his friends – the ones from Dare You – are waiting there for him.

"We said you were scared. We said you wouldn't dare to go in."

Steven's puzzled, upset. He *did* go in. As far as they're concerned he was inside for 30 seconds or less...

He goes home, fleeing their jeers.

Home: his parents are there, as sweet and solicitous as usual. But things seem strangely off-kilter, disturbing: his parents tell him that they're *so* proud of their little boy. But when he catches glimpses of them from the corner of his eye they're wearing the Alice make-up that the Showman was wearing.

At school the next day – Steven is taken aside by various teachers, other pupils – maybe even the cutest girl in the school. Each of them has Alice make-up that only he can see; each of the is, in some way, the Showman himself, talking through these people.

Steven's being offered a deal.

"Never grow old," says the Showman. "Nothing has to be real. Nothing has to hurt you. Join the show. The blood's just paint. You can have anything you want and never pay for it – and it'll last forever."

He tells Steven to come back to the theatre after school.

It's Hallowe'en. The masks are on, the kids are wandering the streets, tricking and treating; and Steven goes looking for the theatre.

It isn't there. Where it was is just a blank wall, or maybe a dusty old storefront, long empty and shut up.

The sun sets; and as the sun sets the storefront shimmers and becomes the theatre. The alley's there.

Steven goes in. The Showman is up on the stage. The audience is seated in the seats, staring up at the Showman. He pulls Steven up on the stage.

Steven looks down, realises that the audience is an audience of corpses: dried, desiccated people, grinning the grins of the dead, hands clapping awkwardly.

The Showman explains to Steven what he needs: he wants – they all want – to feed on Steven's life, on his blood, on his potential and his fear. In exchange, Steven can be a child forever. Never grow old. Never decay.

Steven can become part of their blood-line. Part of the Theatre of the Real. In every little town of America. In every child's mind. Steven can be like them – the monsters under the bed, the movements in the shadows.

And then?

Well, then we have the grand finale, which is Steven fighting back, and getting out. Possibly Steven burns the theatre down – the audience melts like waxen dummies, and the showman is destroyed. We need to think this through – there are lots of different ways to do this: one possibility is to have Steven simply refuse to be afraid, to refuse to fear growing up, to realise that everything has to be paid for, and to have the theatre and its inhabitants melt and deliquesce and fade, until once again, Steven's on his own on the sidewalk, with the dead leaves blowing past him. We should talk about this – it's got to be the big Wagnerian production number at the end.

Steven goes home.

He goes up to his room. He looks in the mirror. His reflection wavers, and becomes, first Steven in Alice make-up, then The Showman. And the Showman sings Steven a love song. Almost a lullaby. "I'll come back to you," he sings. "It doesn't matter where you travel. It doesn't matter where you go. It doesn't matter what you did to me. I'll never forget you. I'll wait for you forever. I'm here. I'll come back to you."

Steven backs away. But the reflection stays where it is. "One day you'll need me, one day you'll call me," it tells him. "I'll come back to you."

End

Okay. That's a very loose sketch of the kind of thing we're looking at I think.

-Neil Gaiman

ORIGINAL OUTLINE BY NEIL GAIMAN

It's small-town America. The time is now. We could be in anytown: it's early evening, in Autumn, and dead leaves blow down Main Street.

We begin with Steven and his friends; kids in that grey zone between childhood and adolescence, a place where adult life and responsibility is visible as something coming over the horizon toward them like a Scud Missile. Sooner or later you'll have to face up to it.

Steven and the other kids are walking home from school.

There's a red light flashing that draws them over; there's an alleyway where there wasn't an alleyway before. They stop and look down the alleyway. There's a theatre there, an old awning calling them in. Standing in the shadows is the Showman, extolling the virtues of the little theatre.

The Showman is wearing Alice make-up.

"Hey, kids. C'mon in. You want to see a show? I'll show you something you've never seen before. It's the show of a lifetime. It's a whole new world, and it's all real, and it's all free...

"I'll show you life, and blood, and all the secrets that no-one's going to tell you. It's the Theatre of the Real, boys..."

He lists delights that are waiting for them inside the Theatre.

The kids are scared – Steven as much as any of the others. They begin a low undercurrent of "Go on – go on in – I dare you, are you scared? Heck, I'm not scared, well, why don't you? well, why don't YOU? I think you're scared. I'm not scared."

Gradually they begin to focus on Steven. He's the one they're all accusing of being scared – of just being a little kid.

"I'm not scared. I dare," says Steven, scared. And he goes down the alleyway. The other kids scatter.

The Showman takes him into the theatre, gives him a ticket. "Tonight – for you? It's free!"

Steven walks into the empty theatre. The curtain is down. He's the only one in there.

He takes a seat.

The music begins and the curtain goes up. And the show begins...

And as the show begins the theatre is, somehow, no longer empty. There are other people sitting on the red velvet seats. Strange, shadowy people, waiting in silence in the dark.

The footlights light. The Showman comes on, dressed as the host of the show.

"Okay," he says. "This is what's waiting for you."

The curtain goes up.

And the show begins.

Steven watches, open-mouthed and scared, as the strange little Grand Guignol shows begin.

He is being shown adult-hood – not as something that carries with it any kind of responsibility or pride, but as something terrifying, something to be feared and rejected – as a series of blind alleys.

He watches a sequence of little plays, performed by a cast of people who look more or less dead.

BAD PLACE ALONE – the fear of Big Cities, of taking the wrong turn into the wrong places, of the gleam of lies and knives; of gang warfare; being knocked to the ground, having cigarettes ground out on your skin; of being robbed, raped or killed.

LOST IN AMERICA – what it's like to be a dead-end teenager, no car, no money, no girl, no possibilities.

Each of them is a tiny playlet put on by the Showman and his little cast: grand guignol for the 1990s, blood-washed excursions into fear, revolving around the nightmares of adulthood, of growing up. Money. Responsibility. Death.

And, of course, the other magnet that draws kids into adulthood: Sex.

The girl-woman of Steven's dreams comes onto the stage. 'I'M YOUR TEMPTATION' she tells him.

The show's over. The curtain goes down, the lights go up. The theatre is once again empty.

Steven gets up, shaken. He walks out.

We follow him out of the alleyway, back onto the sidewalk: his friends are waiting there for him.

"We said you were scared. We said you wouldn't dare to go in."

Steven's puzzled, upset. He did go in. But as far as they're concerned he was inside for 30 seconds, or less. He just walked in and came out again.

He goes home, fleeing their jeers.

Home: his parents are there, as sweet and solicitous as usual. But things seem strangely off-kilter, disturbing: his parents tell him that they're so proud of their little boy. But when he catches glimpses of them from the corner of his eye they're wearing the Alice make-up that the Showman was wearing.

At school the next day – Steven is taken aside by various teachers, other pupils – maybe even the cutest girl in the school. Each of them has Alice make-up that only he can see; each of them is, in some way, the Showman himself, talking through these people.

"Are you ready to deal, yet? It's free. Everything's free."

Steven's being offered a deal.

"Never grow old," says the Showman. "Nothing has to be real. Nothing has to hurt you. Join the

show. The blood's just paint. You can have anything you want and never pay for it – and it'll last forever."

He tells Steven to come back to the theatre after school.

It's Hallowe'en. The masks are on, the kids are wandering the streets, tricking and treating; and Steven goes looking for the theatre.

It isn't there. Where it was is just a blank wall, or maybe a dusty old storefront, long empty and shut up.

The sun sets; and as the sun sets the storefront shimmers and becomes the theatre. The alley's there.

Steven goes in. The Showman is up on the stage. The audience is seated in the seats, staring up at the Showman. He pulls Steven up on the stage.

Steven looks down, realises that the audience is an audience of corpses: dried, desiccated people, grinning the grins of the dead, hands clapping awkwardly.

The Showman explains to Steven what he needs: he wants – they all want – to feed on Steven's life, on his blood, on his potential and his fear. In exchange, Steven can be a child forever. Never grow old. Never decay.

Steven can become part of their blood-line. Part of the Theatre of the Real. In every little town of America. In every child's mind. Steven can be like them – the monsters under the bed, the movements in the shadows.

The Showman brings out his final card: the wonderful girl from "I'm your temptation". But as she turns around, he sees that she's dead: the bones of her spine stick out from her back, her flesh is rotting and falling away.

Come with us – it's free.

And that's when Steven realises that Nothing's Free.

Steven fights back, rejects the Theatre and the Showman, and getting out.

Possibly Steven burns the theatre down – the audience melts like waxen dummies, and the Showman is destroyed. Steven simply refuses to be afraid, to refuse to fear growing up, to realise that everything has to be paid for, and to have the theatre and its inhabitants melt and deliquesce and fade, until once again, Steven's on his own on the sidewalk, with the dead leaves blowing past him.

Steven goes home.

He goes up to his room. He looks in the mirror. His reflection wavers, and becomes, first Steven in Alice make-up, then the Showman. And the Showman sings Steven a love song. Almost a lullaby.

"It doesn't matter where you travel. It doesn't matter where you go. It doesn't matter what you did to me. I'll never forget you. I'll wait for you forever. I'm here. I'll come back to you. It's me," he sings. "It's me you're looking for."

Steven backs away. But the reflection stays where it is. "One day you'll need me, one day you'll call me," it tells him. "It's me."

End

This is a rough outline.

The project began with an outline much like this; the outline then went to Alice Cooper who began work on songs inspired by it; these songs and themes have now been incorporated into the outline – and will continue to be as the album continues to get written.

The comic would be in three monthly parts of 24-32 pages each, then a collected book edition that would come out the month after the last comic, and would contain a number of pages at the back with original material – photos, scrapbook type material, handwritten lyrics, background on the project and so forth.

The release date of the comic would need to be tied to the release date of the CD.

-Neil Gaiman

ALICE COOPER: THE LAST TEMPTATION
Book One Script by Neil Gaiman

Part One:
For Michael Zulli.

Hi Michael,

Right. Now, I loved your sketches for the project.

I have a theory, that everyone is allowed to do a story like this once in their lives. A story that will scare the bejasus out of fourteen year old boys all over the world.

It's a rotting Hallowe'en story; a gothic baroque; and a coming-of-age story.

The Alice character, the Showman, is the centre of it all: he is, after all, the star of the show, in all senses. He's not Alice - or if he is, he's the apotheosis of Alice Cooper, the persona, not the person.

It's the idea of Alice as something dangerous and nasty and actually threatening - a power that lures the young away from, whatever, normalcy, mundanity, boredom, "The establishment" - with the power that idea has.

I'm not sure we'd ever want to be as explicit as to say that The Showman is the Devil - or even some kind of demon. He might be, I suppose, and he definitely is in Alice's lyrics, but I tend to think of him as something old and strange and dangerous and evil: he's not dealing in souls - he's dealing in dreams and hopes and potential. I'm sure he's not the Big Devil - a devil, I suppose, or another Damned Soul with big ideas.

Steven is a little bundle of potential and fear.

The town is any american small town, Michael. Architecturally, you'd probably be best advised to go local to you - that New England baroque. Northhampton, for example, or any of those towns with generic main streets filled with old houses. Enough trees on the street to be able to drop leaves.

It's just before hallowe'en. You should be able to get an idea of appropriate decorations from the next few weeks...

I need to talk to Mort Todd, but I'm going to proceed from the supposition that we've got 32 pages to fill; I don't know whether any of those pages are adverts. If they aren't, I think we ought to put a few scrapbook pages in the back - sketches, notes, photos, maybe a note from Alice. All that.

I'll break this down for you by page, Michael, but do it more like we did Sweeney than Sandman - stage directions where needed, but otherwise you get to pick the pictures...

Book 1.   BAD
                 PLACE
                 ALONE.

Page 1:

The captions should be in slightly raggedy-edged boxes, Todd.

caption: Autumn leaves, yellow and orange and red, tumble down the empty street, blown by a
                 sudden chill gust of October wind.

cap: Mist gathers in the side streets, blurring the light from the sodium street-lamps
as
                 one afer another they flicker on, disturbing the twilight.

cap: A burst of colour and noise intrudes, now.

Page 2

cap: Boys amble down Main Street in loud, bright colours, an assortment of sweaters,
                 football shirts, jeans and raincoats, of bags of books and neon sneakers.

cap: Listen to them:

Jacob, a self-assured young kid, is in the lead. There are four or five of them. Steven's in the rear. He looks awkward, like he's not enjoying hearing what he's listening to.

Jacob: ...okay. So, like her <u>boyfriend</u> says to her to lock the doors after him, because, like, he doesn't know what's <u>out</u> there.

Jacob: And <u>she</u> reminds him of what they heard on the radio - about the escaped killer on the loose - but he just laughs, points out that if he doesn't get some gas in the car and get her home by midnight then her dad really <u>will</u> kill him.

Jacob: So he gets out.

                    And he makes her lock the door and promise not to open it for <u>anyone.</u> And he goes away. Then she hears something that might be a <u>scream.</u>

                    And she doesn't hear <u>anything</u> else. Except pretty soon there's this weird noise on the roof of the car. Like, *drip, drip, drip...*

Page 3

Jacob: But she stays put, even though she's, like, <u>really</u> scared.

Steven: This is going to be <u>gross,</u> isn't it?

Jacob: Steven, don't be a <u>weenie.</u>

Steven: I'm <u>not</u> a weenie.
Kyle: <u>Course</u> you're not a weenie. You're a <u>wuss.</u> Carry on, Jacob.

Jacob: So like, finally she falls asleep. And she wakes up and someone's banging on the window. It's the <u>police.</u> So she opens the door and they say, <u>just</u> walk towards us and <u>don't</u> turn around.

Jacob: She gets out the car. And <u>then</u> - she turns around!

Jacob: Suspended from the radio aerial is her boyfriend's severed head. And the *drip drip drip* she heard, that was his blood, falling, falling, <u>falling</u> onto the the roof of the car...

Steven: <u>God,</u> Jacob. That's <u>gross.</u>

Jacob: <u>Said</u> you were a weenie, Steven. A weenie <u>and</u> a wuss. You're sca-a-ared.

Kyle: Save it for tomorrow Jacob.

Jacob: Why should I wait for Hallowe'en? I got lotsa good ones, worse than that. There was this babysitter, right, and she was-

Page 4

The sun has not quite set. Now, down an alleyway, we see something flicker strangely.

Steven: Hey - what's that?

Kyle: Over there? There's <u>nothing</u> over there.

Steven: I saw something. Down that alley.
Jacob: There isn't an alley down there.

A voice comes from off-panel. Nobody hears it but Steven.

off-panel voice: But if there is no alley, then there can be nothing in the alley. And if there is nothing in the alley then there can be no theatre...

Off-panel voice: And there <u>must</u> be a theatre.

Off panel voice: Mustn't there?

Steven: Huh? Who said <u>that?</u>

Jacob: Who said <u>what?</u>

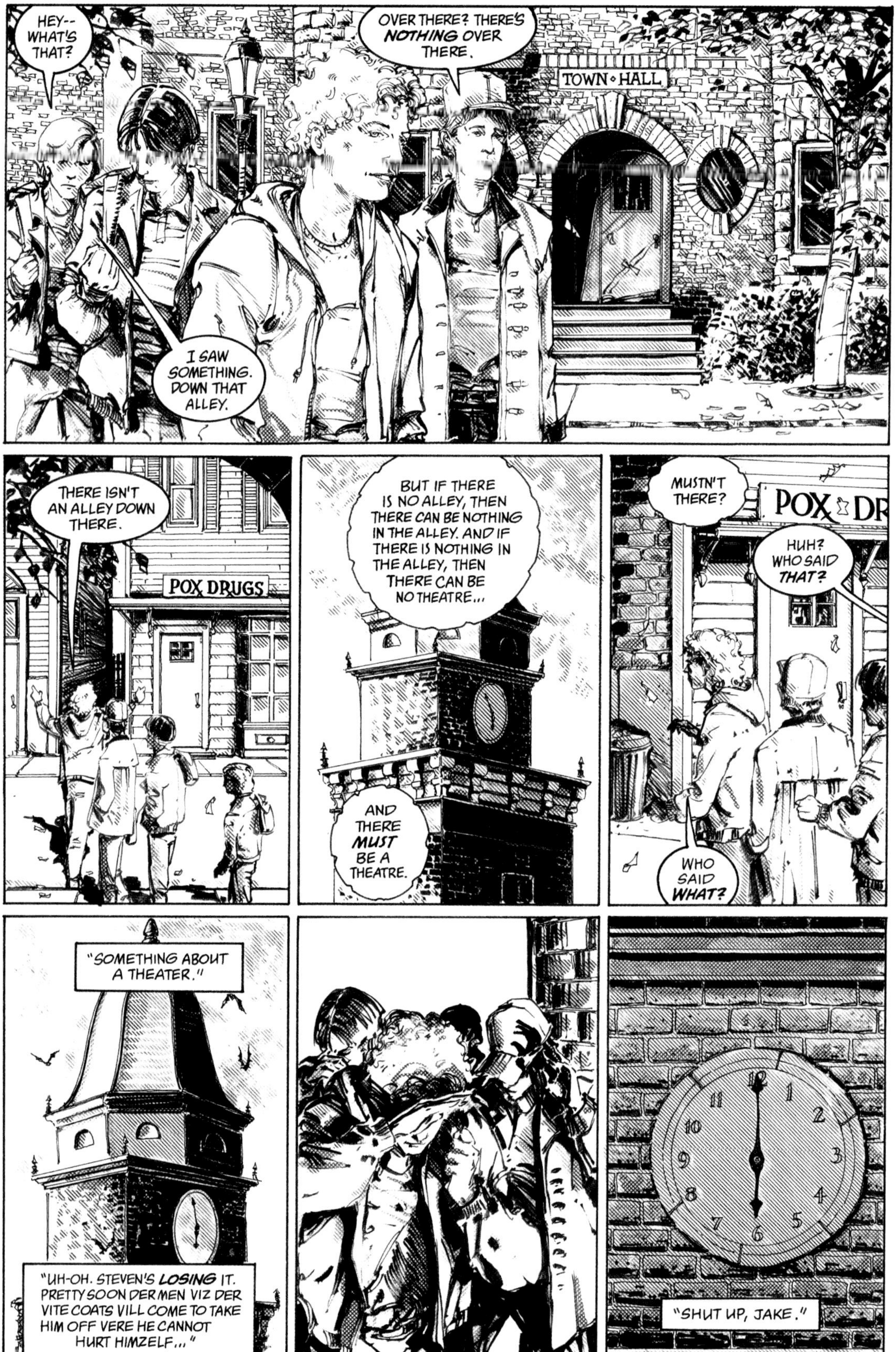
HEY-- WHAT'S THAT?
OVER THERE? THERE'S NOTHING OVER THERE.
TOWN HALL
I SAW SOMETHING. DOWN THAT ALLEY.
THERE ISN'T AN ALLEY DOWN THERE.
POX DRUGS
BUT IF THERE IS NO ALLEY, THEN THERE CAN BE NOTHING IN THE ALLEY. AND IF THERE IS NOTHING IN THE ALLEY, THEN THERE CAN BE NO THEATRE...
AND THERE MUST BE A THEATRE.
MUSTN'T THERE?
POX DR
HUH? WHO SAID THAT?
WHO SAID WHAT?
"SOMETHING ABOUT A THEATER."
"UH-OH. STEVEN'S LOSING IT. PRETTY SOON DER MEN VIZ DER VITE COATS VILL COME TO TAKE HIM OFF VERE HE CANNOT HURT HIMZELF..."
"SHUT UP, JAKE."

final page 4 inked art by Michael Zulli

Steven:	Something about a theatre.
Jacob:	Uh-oh. Steven's <u>losing</u> it. Pretty soon der men viz der vite coats vill come to take himm off vere he cannot hurt himzelf...
Steven:	Shut up, Jake.

Page 5

By now they've reached the alleyway. It's filled with crumbling old wooden shops, empty and dusty, with empty windows. The last orange flare of sunset catches an empty shop window, glares and flares and burns.

And now we're there aren't any old shops. There's a decaying theatre frontage, half-way between a carnival sideshow, a bavarian castle, and an honest-to-goodness victorian theatre.

The kids walk down to the alley.

Jacob:	What <u>is</u> this place?
Kyle:	I think it's weird.
Ben:	<u>Steven! Jacob! Kyle!</u> Look at this!

*There's a sign up outside - **The Theatre of the Real**, and underneath, in smaller letters, the **Grandest Guignol**, Pictures of the stars, including the pretty red-headed girl.*

THE SHOWMAN stands in the shadows. Just eyes...

Jacob:	The grandest *goog-nol*. Huh? What the hell is <u>that</u> meant to mean?

Page 6

The Showman steps out of the shadows, as if on cue. He raises a battered hat to them, and grins like a fox eating shit from a barbed-wire fence.

Showman:	Damn my eyes. What a fine-looking assemblage of young men.
	What a <u>sweet</u> little congregation of the flesh.

The kids look scared. They stare up at him. He steps into the middle of them, reaches out a long and almost clawed finger, and touches one of them on the chin.

Showman:	You look to me, yes indeed, you look to me like young gentlemen who would appreciate a little theatrical entertainment.
Jacob:	Uh. We don't <u>know</u> you, Mister.
Showman:	Ah, but I know <u>you,</u> Jacob Candleman. And <u>you,</u> Kyle Van Fleck. Would one of you desire to come and see the show?
	No?

Page 7

Showman:	I'll make it <u>easier</u>, I'll make it <u>lusher,</u> I'll make it a perfect <u>steal:</u> regard -

He reaches a hand into the pocket of his frock-coat, pulls out a ticket. It's a piece of printed, perforated paper, not a golden magic thingie. He thrusts it at one of the children. By now he's standing under a streetlight, almost as if he's standing in the spotlight.

Showman:	A ticket to tonight's entertainment.
Kyle:	So, what <u>is</u> it? Like some kind of <u>strip-show</u> or <u>something?</u>
Showman:	Nothing so <u>crass.</u>
	To even <u>attempt</u> to describe this panoply of peripatetic pleasures, this exhibition of extraordinary excitation and excess, would beggar the lips and leave me feebly mumbling.
	It's the <u>ultimate</u> sideshow. The only entertainment that gives you undiluted <u>wonder.</u>

He's moving among them, showing them the ticket, which appears and disappears from one hand to another, like a conjurer's coin.

Showman: Such a feast of marvels your eyes shall behold: such a terpsichorean array of sheer and unutterable delight.

Showman: Well, who's to be the lucky laddie?

Showman: What's the matter boys? You scared?

                Only one of you gets to come in, though. Don't all scream at once.

Page 8

Jacob: I got homework.

Kyle: My mom'll kill me if I'm late home.

Ben: You gotta be crazy.

Steven: I...

Kyle: Yeah, Steven?

Jacob: Ste-e-even's sca-a-ared.

Steven: I'm not scared.

Jacob: You wouldn't dare go in. Wuss.

Steven: I'm not a wuss.

Showman: No?

                Then I think we have found our volunteer.

Showman: Can I have a big hand for a young man filled with guts?

The Showman takes Steven by the shoulder, and walks him into the theatre lobby.

Steven: But-

Showman: No buts

Page 9

They are in the lobby, now. Decaying gilt, with a ticket office in one corner. There is a huge old victorian cash register. The room is hung with strands of spider webs. Part of it is completely covered by spiders webs, and, huge dark shadows move in the webs. The Showman brushes aside the webbing as he walks.

Showman: What do they call you, then, boy?

Steven: Steven.

Showman: That's a fine name. A good old name. It means a crown. Did you know that?

Steven: No, sir.

Showman: Come in, come in. We're new in town, but you'll have noticed that yourself.

                Now, if you're going to come in and see the show you'll need a program, won't you?

Steven: I don't know. I've never been to the theatre before.

Showman: Never? Oh, you poor deprived boy.

                Here. It's your ticket.

Steven takes the ticket. Looks at it doubtfully.

Steven: Will it cost me anything?

| Showman: | Cost? Of course not. It's free. Everything here's free. |

Page 10

| Steven: | Do I get popcorn? And a soda? |

| Showman: | This is the theatre, child. Not some cheap flickery what have you - *vitascope, kinematascope-* |

| Steven: | Movie? |

| Showman: | Movie! The very word. |

| Showman: | It's not something you chomp and guzzle your way through, munching heedlessly to the discomfort of the actors and your fellows in the audience. |

(Steven looks disappointed.)

Ah me, the disappointed visage of a little child. It rends my heart. It tears at my very ventricles.

I'm sure we can find you something to drink. What would you like? Human tears? Black wine? The waters of Lethe?

| Steven: | Just, like, a coke or something. |

The showman digs behind the counter, produces a dusty can of cola, strands of webbing attached to it.

| Showman: | Here, catch. |

There. It's free, too.

He presses a key on the old-fashioned cash register. NO SALE sign comes up.

| Steven: | Thank you. |

Page 11

(He's staring around, blankly.)

| Steven: | What is this place? |

| Showman: | This is where it gets good. It's the theatre of the real, boy. The theatre of blood. The greatest and grandest guignol. |

| Steven: | So it's like, a horror show? |

| Showman: | The aesthetic of gore? Far from it, boy. While I could certainly show you wolves and bats and bloodsuckers, we've all had to move with the times... |

He's got hold of Steven's shoulders, is propelling him toward the lobby.

| Showman: | Through there. I'll see you soon... |

Show the nice lady your ticket.

Page 12

We're at the entrance to the Theatre. It's a dark room - we can't see very much. Steven and the Showman: the showman with a paternal hand on Steve's shoulder, making sure he goes where the showman wants. And standing in the alcove, facing us, is The Red-haired Girl, who, up until this moment, we haven't named. Let's give her a slightly old-fashioned name. I've just rejected the perfect one (uh, Alice. Would have been perfect, but would have been confusing). How about Mercy? She's older than Steven (girls are always older than boys, whatever their ages), and she's been dead for at least 25 years, possibly more like 50 years. It's up to you, Michael - you get to pick the look, which means you get to, more or less date her. She can go back up to a couple of hundred years. She looks somewhere between 15 and 17, at a guess, and there's something dead sexual about her (she is, after all, His Temptation). She has a small armful of programmes. One arm and hand free.

| Mercy: | Hello. I'm Mercy. |

Can I see your ticket?

Steven: My, uh. Oh. Ticket? Sure.

Page 13

(He takes his ticket. Passes it to her. She looks at it. Then she looks at him, and smiles. She has a terrific smile.)

Mercy: That's fine. <u>Here.</u> You'll need to hang onto it.
                 Would you like a program?

Steven: I, uh. Yes. <u>Sure.</u> How much is it?

Mercy: It's free. <u>Everything</u> here's free.

Showman: What did I <u>tell</u> you? Now, give him the program, Mercy. The curtain's about to go
                 up.

Mercy: Here you are.

(He takes it.)

Steven: I... so, should I, uh. Where do I sit?

                 Um. Mercy.

Mercy: You go through there, and just find a seat. Sit anywhere.

                 There'll be a lot of empty seats.

                 To begin with, anyway.

                 It tends to fill up as the show goes on.

Showman: No more <u>yammering,</u> my little starlings. Steven - go through there. Find yourself
                 somewhere to sit.

                 Mercy. You and I need to get ready. The swish of the curtain awaits us. The <u>roar</u> of
                 the greasepaint, the <u>smell</u> of the crowd...

(He's let go of Steven, is propelling him through the alcove.)

Page 14-15

Okay. Now, a double page spread of the theatre interior. Michael, you've already designed this. You might be able to reuse some of your painting for Beth for this. But it's the theatre inside - we're looking from the back of the room. The curtain is down. Steven's small, walking around, looking for somewhere to sit down. There are an awful lot of empty seats. He's really impressed by this strange, dark, huge, awe-inspiring place. He's staring up at the stage.

Steven (small):   Wow.

Lettering draft up to here.

Page 16

Right. Now, the Showman walks on, in a spotlight. He looks pretty much exactly the same as he did before. The only real difference is that his make-up has been touched up; and I kind of imagine that someone just sewed a few spangles onto his raggedy coat and his top hat. They glint and glitter a little in the spotlight. And he says to the empty auditorium - empty save for Steven, anyway:

Showman: My Lords, Ladies and Gentlemen, honoured guests, dear friends...

                  Welcome, <u>all</u> of you, to *The Theatre of the Real.* Seeing you here is perfect bliss.
                  And knowing that you're going to watch the little lessons I've arranged - why, <u>that</u>
                  is a hellish ecstasy indeed.

                  You may be wondering why I called you here...

                  <u>Maestro?</u>

Page 17

There's an orchestra pit. We see a decrepit hand thumping down on a keyboard.

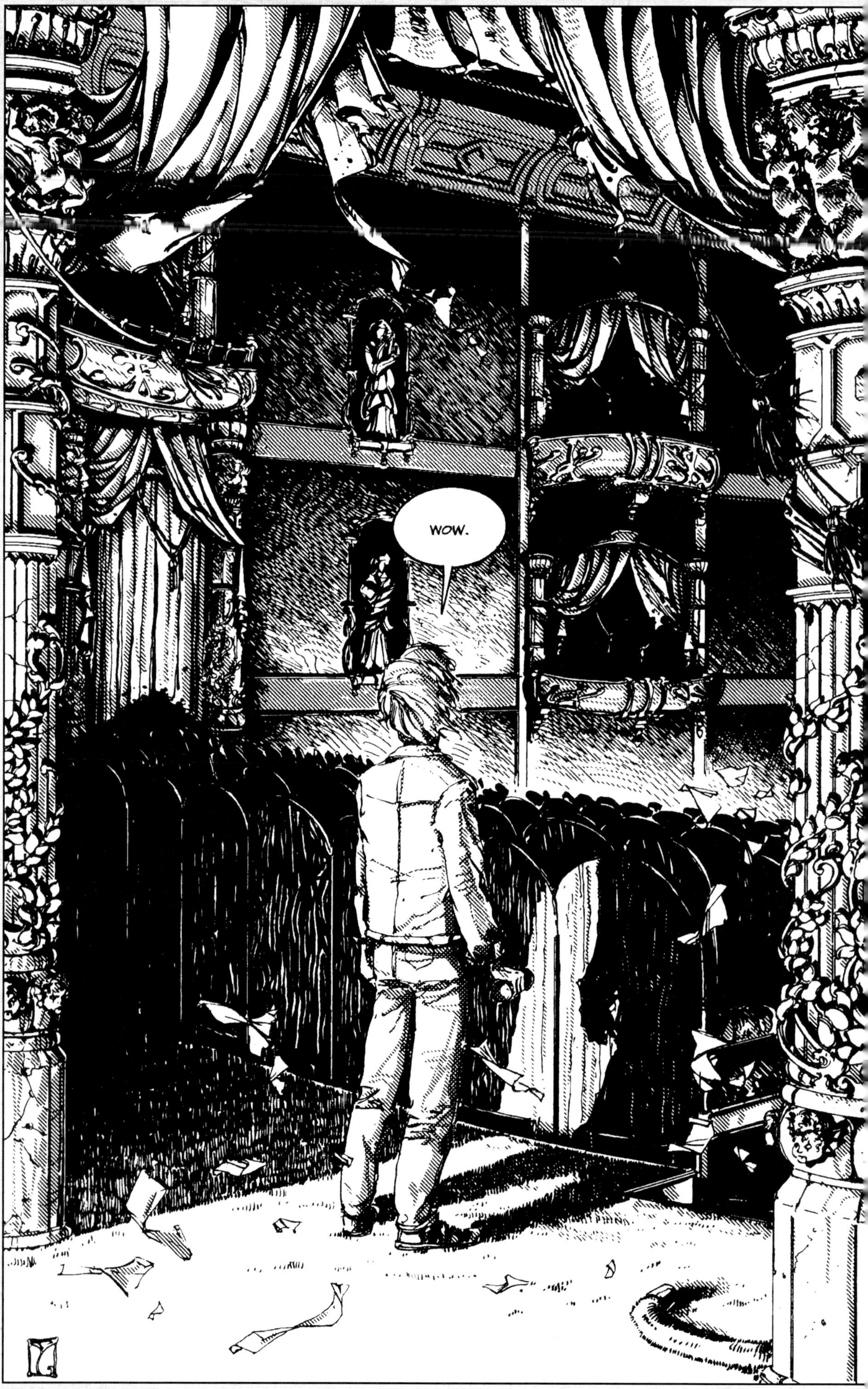
WOW.

final pages 14-15 inked art by Michael Zulli

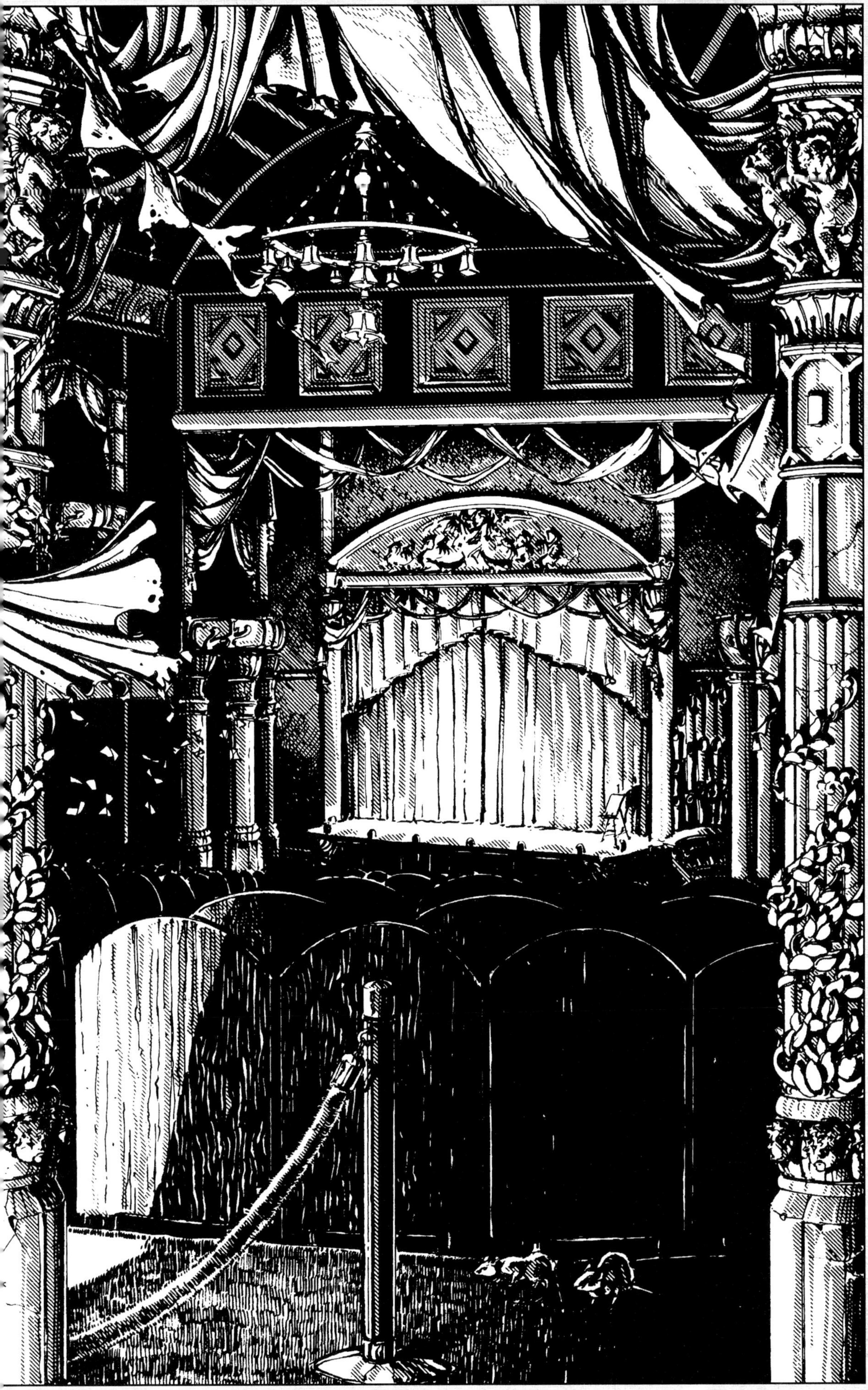

A carved stick with the gargoyle head is tossed in from the wings. He catches it with one outstretched hand, an old vaudevillian about to embark upon his favourite routine. He grins a delighted grin, waves his top hat. It's a routine that should be done with a straw boater and a short stick, not a decrepit top hat and huge arcane and slightly dubious wand.

He's not singing, but he's dancing while he's talking, in the spotlight.

Showman: This is the Theatre of the Real. It's the ultimate sideshow, the perfect escape from the workaday world.

            This is the Theatre of the Real. It's the only thing you're <u>ever</u> going to hear from anyone that isn't a lie.

            This is the Theatre of the Real. And it's going to tell you what it's <u>really</u> like, out there in the world of growing up and getting even.

            This the Theatre of the Real, Steven.

            <u>Curtain!</u>

The curtain rises.

Steven is watching in the audience. He's holding his can of soda.

On the stage is a painted backdrop. It shows a city scene, painted, not incredibly convincingly.

            Act One: The city. A long way from our little theatre. It's a bad place to be.

            Especially if you're on your own.
            If you're alone.

And now Steven's standing in the city. But it's no longer a painted backdrop. It's the real city. He's alone. It's late at night.

There's a garbage can near him. It rattles, and a hand comes out, followed by a body. The body's dead. FIsh-white, a little rotten. It's grinning a rictic grin. Its eyes bulge out. It has a tear-drop tattooed under one eye.

It looks like its been pushed through a window. It doesn't look anything like happy.

Word balloons with no tails:

            You're in a bad place, boy.

            All alone.

Page 18

Little Caesar: 'M a creature of the street and I ripped off all the money.

            Wuz kicked in the teeth shoved face-first through the window.

            Got a gangland name and a tear-drop-tattooed eye.

            They called me little Caesar in the brotherhood of crime.

Stephen: Don't <u>touch</u> me!

            Keep away from me. Please...

Another Zombie has come up behind Stephen. It has a hole in its head. It's grinning.

Zombie 2:   I know about the pain - dying in an alley with an air-conditioned brain. I know, it's for real, flatlined in an ambulance without a pulse to feel.

Page 19

Steven begins to run toward us, as Zombies start to sing to him. There's no shambling after him - they're all waiting in doorways, grinning out from garbage heaps, staring up at us from the sidewalk.

Basically, we're just trying to recreate the normal urban experience here, not do thriller. Everything's threatening, and everyone (by definition) is threatening. Go for a mix of sexes here,

Michael. And they're all smiling, as if they're starring in a broadway musical. They are all talking, one at a time. Steven's dashing and darting through the city.

Zombies: Hey blood brother

                   You're one of our own

                   You're sharp as a razor

                   You're hard as a stone

                   Hey Blood brother

                   You're bad to the bone

                   You're a natural killer

                   In a bad place alone

Steven: I'm not one of you. I'm not a killer. Get away from me.

A snaky hand - all skin, bone and tendons, no flesh, grabs his ankle. He looks down. Think of this as an underground comic, Michael. It's a dead junkie.

Smoky Joe: Hello Steven.

Page 20

Smoky Joe: They call me Smoky Joe. I'm as thin as a coroner's needle.

He pulls out a handful of something powdery from his pocket, holds it out proudly. His face is oozing - practically dissolving.

      I got a pocket full of rocks, and I shake like a cold chihuahua.

      I got a runny nose and a roadmap on my arm.

      I blew my gig horsing round the gallery with someone else's rig. I know, understand - I watched my body hauled off by the local garbageman...

The zombies are advancing. Now, think Busby Berkeley musicals, or the final sequence of ALL THAT JAZZ, where you get the musical stuff going on over his heart operation. Don't let this head off into self-parody, though. An almost skeletal Zombie comes from behind him, touches his face with one rotting finger.

A Zombie: This is what it's like, Steven. In the cities.

      It's a dangerous place out there.

The Zombie begins to pull lumps of rotting flesh off its body, like lumps of latex, which pull off with squishy sucking rubbery things, to reveal, as this dialogue progresses, the Showman, full dressed, underneath.

      It's not exactly friendly, is it? And it only gives you two solutions -

Page 21

A Zombie: Either you become their blood brother. Become one of them. Become part of the danger.

      Or you stay here.

      With me.

      In the theatre.

      And you never leave. And you never grow older. And there's no danger at all.

Now, between one panel and the next (maybe we closed in on his face and pulled back again) we're back on the stage, in the theatre again.

The Showman stands up on the stage. In on hand he's holding his cane. In the other hand he's holding a crude cardboard zombie-mask.

Showman: Doesn't that sound en<u>tic</u>ing?

Showman: Doesn't that sound <u>sweet?</u>

We cut to Steven. He's sitting in the audience, where he was sitting before. Now there are a few zombie figures behind him, maybe three or four dead children sitting in the whole theatre, spiders webs clinging to them.

Steven looks scared. He's sweating and his hair's rumpled.

Steven: What...

                What <u>was</u> that?

Showman: That was a bad place, Steven. It's waiting for you, somewhere.

                After all, you aren't planning on spending your whole <u>life</u> in this little town, are you?

Page 22

Steven: I... I think I should go <u>home</u> now.

He stands up, awkwardly.

The Showman is standing behind him now, as if he's transported magically.

The showman rests one gloved hand on Steven's shoulder. But he doesn't look at Steven. He's looking at the carved head of his stick.

Showman: Did you hear that? He thinks he should go home now...

The stick has a small, very rough lettering style.

Stick: **Hehh. Time to go home?**

Showman: Not <u>yet.</u> After all, the doors are locked at the start of the performance, and they won't be opened until the end.

                It's a long-standing policy of the house. Keeps things <u>interesting,</u> in case of <u>fire.</u>

Steven: Will you...

                Will you <u>really</u> let me go, when this is over?

The showman bends over so his face is on one side of Steven's. The stick-head rests on the other side of Steven's head. Steven's looking, scared, towards the Showman.

Showman: Why, Steven. We simply went to make sure you squeeze every <u>possible</u> oozing globule of pleasure from our little performance.

                We wouldn't want it cut off for you in its prime. Would we?

Stick: **Slice it.**

Showman: Do you want to know the future, Steven?

Page 23

STEVEN: Huh?

The Showman's up on the stage, now. Maybe he's sitting on the front of the stage. He moves from place to place in the theatre without necessarily visiting the places between.

Showman: The future. Not the <u>only</u> future.

                But the one that's waiting for you <u>here.</u> In the middle of nowhere.

A painted backdrop is coming down. It's got a map of america crudely painted on it.

                Happy America, Steven. It's all yours.

Let's see. Now we need someone to be you, Steven. Don't we?

The backdrop goes up. We're now looking at a bare stage with a couple of chairs on it. One of the chairs is empty. The other contains a zombie - a corpse - of a teenager. The showman starts talking into the stick, as it it's a microphone. We're in Montel Williams territory here. Or Donohue. One of them.

The Zombie's lettering style is slightly smudgy and grotty. There's little smudges of dirt in the balloons.

Showman:	So. Steven: you're five years older.
	The world is undoubtedly your lobster. And which wonderful far-flung corner of the world have you wound up in?
Zombie:	Here.
Showman:	And do you <u>like</u> it here?
Zombie:	No.
Showman:	And what are you doing with your, uh...
	(small) What do you call it? Oh yes -
(normal)	Your life?
Zombie:	Nothing.
Showman:	You don't have a job?
Zombie:	No job. No car.
	No money.
	No girl.
Showman:	Well, that's a <u>dreadful</u> state of affairs, isn't it? There must be something you can do to break this vicious circle. Why don't you hold up a Seven-Eleven?
Zombie:	No gun.

Page 24

Showman:	How about rock and roll? That's the traditional way of getting out and moving up.
Zombie:	No talent.
Showman:	And prostitution's out. Tch. These small towns...
	How about <u>suicide?</u>
Zombie:	No gun. No talent.

The showman pulls the thing's head off. The Zombie head comes off pretty easily, trailing a little bit of spinal column.

The Showman grins into its face. Then he rams a hand up inside it, wiggles his fingers through the eye-holes.

Showman:	You know, there just <u>aren't</u> many opportunities for a bright lad in this wonderful town, are there?
Zombie:	Uh-uh.
Showman:	Are you paying attention down there, Steven?
Steven:	Yeah.
Showman:	Do you see my point?

Steven: I think this is gross and - and dumb. I'm not him. <u>That's</u> not my future.

You're <u>sick.</u>

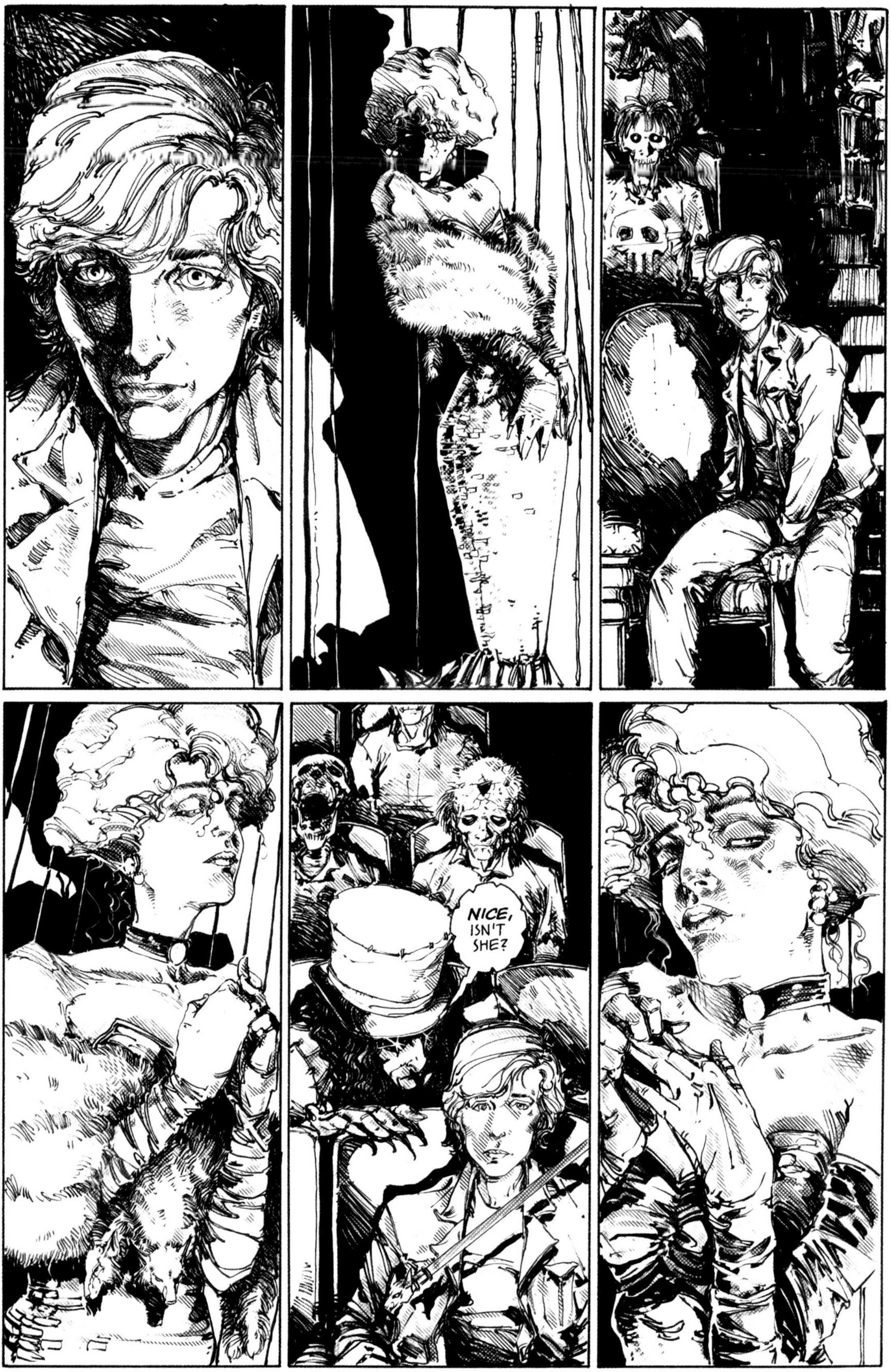
NICE, ISN'T SHE?
final page 26 inked art by Michael Zulli

Showman: Really?

The showman brings the head-on-his-hand up to the level of his head.

Showman (to head):   You are quite useless.

He turns to the headless zombie body.

Zombie head: Sorrrrry....

Showman: Get off my stage. And take this thing with you.

The headless body gets up. It takes the ripped-off head in its hands and shambles off and away.

Showman: <u>Curtain!</u>

              Come on, come on...

The Curtain comes down.

Steven stands up.

Steven: This is pa<u>thet</u>ic.

              I'm not staying here any longer.

Close up: The Showman grins, as does the head on the stick.

Long shot: Steven stands up to walk out.

He gets into the gangway between the seats. And then he stops. Turns, looks at the darkened stage. The showman is nowhere to be seen.

The stage is dark. But as she walks onto it, candles burst into flame.

It's Mercy. The girl we saw selling the tickets. Only now there's vaseline on the lens, well metaphorically there is, anyway. She's got lipgloss on, and she's wearing (and this will prove important) a backless dress. Maybe a fox-fur boa, with the head still on. Long evening gloves.

Steven (small):   Mercy?

She smiles at him.

Steven stops. Stares up at the stage. Then he sits down. We flip backwards and forwards from Mercy, standing on the stage, slowly, finger by finger pulling off a glove. We close in on her eyes, her lips, her silhouette.

Meanwhile, the showman has sat next to Steven, and, (while we cut backwards and forwards from Mercy, as she pulls off a glove a finger at a time,) is leaning over, whispering in his ear...

Showman: <u>Nice,</u> isn't she?

Showman: My <u>own</u> boyhood - if indeed such a thing existed - began, if I recall
              correctly, with a disdain for all things female, which slowly
              shaded, as the years went by, into an <u>obsession</u> with all things
              female.

              The realisation that there was <u>indeed</u> another branch of the human race, a softer,
              rounder, <u>lusher</u> breed, Eve to my Old Adam, tempting as a naked flame to my moth.

Showman: Among my friends I agreed that girls were to be <u>abhored,</u> that
              feminity was, on the whole, less welcome than <u>nose-picking.</u>

              But at home - in private - at night - perhaps...

Showman: I had begun to feel differently...

                    I had found my temptation.

Pages 30

Showman: And of course, young Mercy here is a perfect specimen of-

Steven: <u>Shut up. Just shut up.</u>
                Please.

Showman grins. (Michael - the way i imagine this, we break up the showman captions into relatively tiny bits: softer/ rounder/ lusher/ and so forth. Up to you, of course.)

She's beckoning him.

Steven gets up, walks to the stage. There's a packed audience of dead boys and girls now.

He reaches out.

The showman is grinning like a fox. The foxhead around Mercy's neck is grinning like the showman.

Mercy's reaching out one hand to him. Then she changes her mind.

Mercy (small):No. Please.

                Not <u>this</u> time. I can't.

Mercy (very small):Not again...

And she turns away from us.

We can see her back, nasty as any of the zombies - it's partly skinless and partly fleshless - we can see the spinal column, we can see skinless flesh. This is kind of yichhh.

Steven looks horrified.

Steven (small): Mercy?

Pages 31

He sits down on the stage.

Pull back. The Showman stands up. He's standing where Mercy was. She's gone.

Showman: Well, <u>there</u> we have it. That's enough for now. <u>Houselights!</u>

The lights come on. The dead children fade away as the lights come on.

It's just the Showman and Steven.

Showman: I see that I will have to speak <u>strongly</u> with young Mercy.

                Show's over, Steven.

                There will be one <u>more</u> segment to our performance, of course.

                Our <u>grand</u> <u>finale.</u>

                But not now.

                <u>Now</u>, you leave.

                But don't fret, child. I won't be far away...

Pages 32

(Editor's note: the original script file to book one was damaged, and the original page 32 was lost.)

ALICE COOPER: THE LAST TEMPTATION
Book Two Script by Neil Gaiman

Hi Michael,

not to mention hi to Todd, Alice, Toby, Shep, Brian, Mort and anyone else who might read this. Welcome back.

Now, we've done quite well with episode 1, all things considered. It looks stunning, and the character of the showman works just fine. Steven's not quite there yet, although I think he should be when we get to the end of this issue; his personality is more than a blank slate, but he hasn't had to do more than react so far.

This issue, all we need to do is a) get him home, b) give him a really good nightmare, c) get him to school, and ready to return to the Theatre, with some kind of understanding of what the threat is, with the old faustian deal up and running.

INSIDE FRONT COVER== Unholy War

Contains a 'Story so far' and a plug for the CD.

Plus the credits and such - all typeset

Page 1

It's evening- starting to get dark. It's maybe a few minutes later than the end of part one. Tim's running home, in the way that scared kids do. (I did, anyway.) He's really quite a lot more scared than he let on. So we see him running through a lower-middle class sort of residential area, although he's in small town america, so the houses are kind of interesting. Lots of them have hallowe'en junk - carved pumpkins on doorways, funny paper ghosts at windows. He's scared. He's still got his bag of school books. Same lettering style as the caps on the first pages of part 1.

Cap: His name is Steven. After school today he was taken to a theatre that doesn't exist.

Cap: At first he walked away from it.

cap: Then he began to hurry.

cap: Finally he began to run.

cap: To run as if all the powers of hell were close behind him.

cap: It's not impossible...

Page 2

He's on his own road.

cap: Steven knows that safety exists at home. If he gets home, he will be safe. In his room.

cap: A moment of fear. Perhaps when he gets there his home will be gone.

Right. Now he's reached his own home. And he walks up to the front door, slowing, catching his breath. Then he fumbles at the front door with his key.

cap: Or it will be filled with strangers, Or monsters. Or...

His front door opens. Standing in the door is his mother.

Steven: Hi Mom.

Mother: Steven? You're late.

Page 3

Steven walks in, drops his bag on the floor, sort of hangs up his coat, while talking.

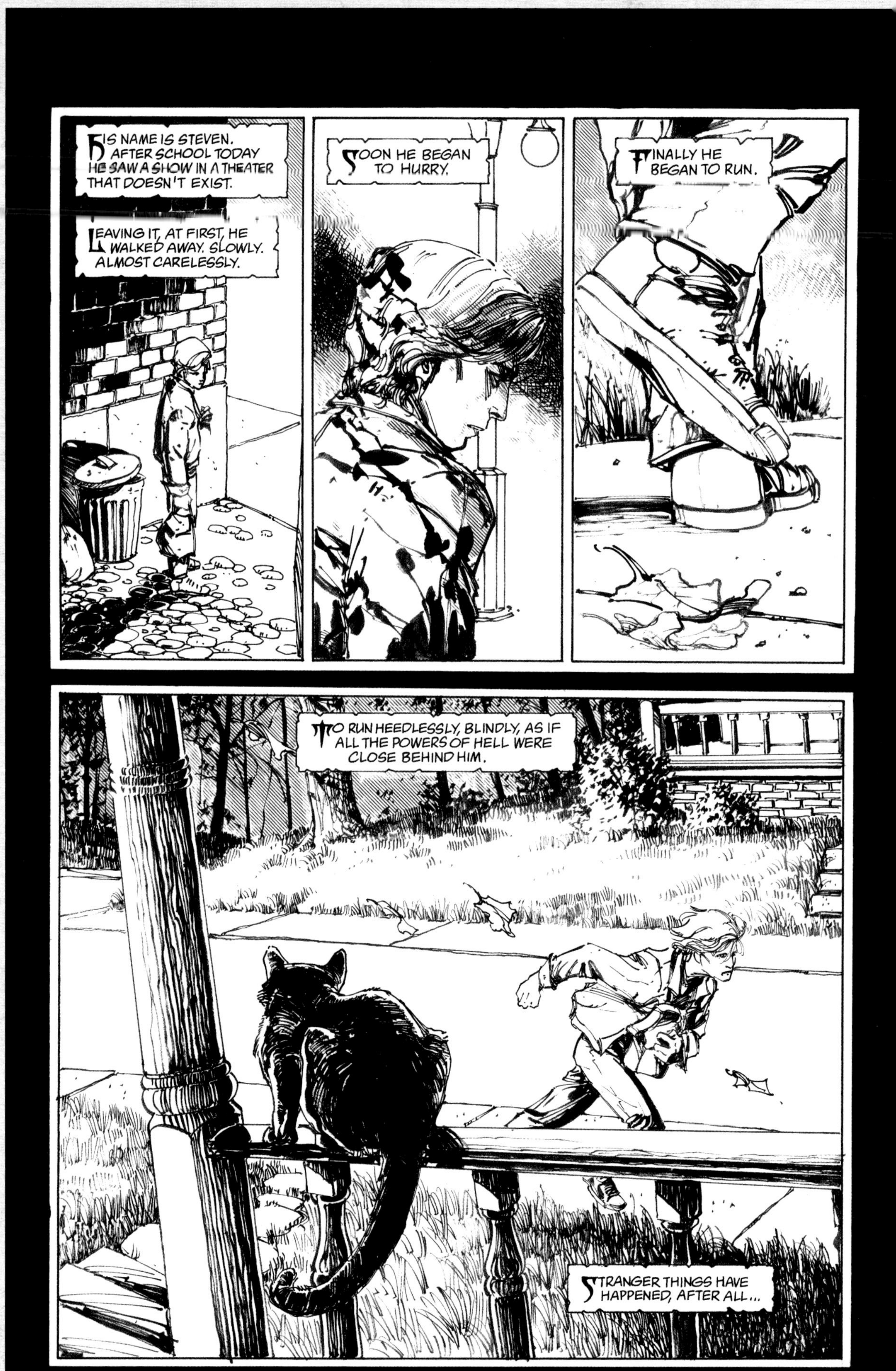
HIS NAME IS STEVEN. AFTER SCHOOL TODAY HE SAW A SHOW IN A THEATER THAT DOESN'T EXIST.
LEAVING IT, AT FIRST, HE WALKED AWAY. SLOWLY. ALMOST CARELESSLY.
SOON HE BEGAN TO HURRY.
FINALLY HE BEGAN TO RUN.
TO RUN HEEDLESSLY, BLINDLY, AS IF ALL THE POWERS OF HELL WERE CLOSE BEHIND HIM.
STRANGER THINGS HAVE HAPPENED, AFTER ALL...

final page 1 inked art by Michael Zulli

Steven:	Yeah.
Mother:	How was school, today?
Steven:	Mm.
Mother:	Stevie? Are you okay? Is everything all right? You look like you've seen a ghost.
Steven (small):	I'm fine.
Mother:	Dinner in five minutes.

Page 4

Now he goes into the family room. His father's sitting there. It should be pretty cosy. A nice log fire burning, maybe the father sitting reading the paper.

Steven sits down on the couch. His mother is bringing in a casserole dish of something hot, and putting it on the table.

Michael, make this all very cosy, very comfortable and warm and nice. It's a fairly good little nuclear family.

Mother:	Steven, are you and your friends going trick or treating tomorrow?
Steven:	I s'pose.

His father lowers the newspaper - it's a tabloid thing with a front page about torso murders or something.

Father:	I don't like the boy trick or treating, Pauline.
	You listen to me, Stevey, and don't you go biting into those apples, or just eating those candies. There are crazies out there. Put razorblades into apples. Poison candies. It's true.

Steven looks at him affectionately.

Steven:	It's not true, Dad. Mom told me it wasn't.
Father:	Huh?
Mother:	He's right, dear. It's an urban legend. There are no recorded cases of razored apples, or poisoned candies, except, some years ago, for a father who tried to kill his son with poison candy which he slipped into a trick or treat bag.

The father shrugs and grins.

Father:	Everyone's against me.
Mother:	You be quiet, Bill. Dinner's on the table.

Page 5

Right. Now everyone's at the table. It's lit by overhead light and firelight. They're eating.

Mom:	Stevie- take some of the lovely steamed broccoli.
Steven:	I don't like broccoli.
Father:	Nobody likes broccoli. Now, make your mother happy and take some of the lovely steamed broccoli.
Steven:	Uhhh.... Do either of you know anything about a theatre in this town?
Father:	There's the old drive-in on Highway 35...?
Steven:	No. Like an acting theatre. Up by the town hall.
Mother:	No.
Father:	Sure. When I was your age, someone said... it was years ago. Some guy who ran a theatre in town. I don't remember the details.

Something about him stealing children.

Steven: Really?

Page 6

Round about now, occasionally, while the conversation's going on, we look at the parent who isn't talking, and they look just a little Alicey around the eyes.

Mother: Bob, don't. He's pulling your leg, Stevie.

Father: I'm not. 'S'true. Are there any more potatoes?

Mother: Steven? You thought about your costume for tomorrow?

Steven: Nope. It's embarassing.

Mother: Ah, how they grow. It seems like only yesterday that I couldn't get you to take off your Pirate Costume.

Steven: Mommm...

Father: She's right. You even slept in it.

Steven: I figured maybe I'd do some monster make-up.

                 Look, I'm really tired. I'm going to get an early night.

Mother: You got a lot of homework?

Steven: I got some. Just reading stuff.

Mother: Are you okay?

Steven: Just tired.

Mother: Let me feel your forehead.

                 Well, you feel okay.

Steven: I'm fine. Just tired. G'night mom. Night Dad.

Page 7

He goes out into the hallway. He's halfway up the stairs, when his mom comes out, stands at the bottom of the stairs.

Mom: Oh - Steven?

Steven: Mom?

Now: we see Mom, and she's 'Alice'd' for real - the eyes are blackened, the mouth has lines on it. And the expression is a creepy sort of showman expression.

Mom: I never stole any children. It was a fair trade. Anyone who came with me wanted to come.

                 Just like you will.

Steven: Huh? Mom?

Mom: Pleasant dreams.

Page 8~ 9 (8)

Steven in his bedroom. We watch him stand there for a second, then rub his eyes between thumb and forefingers, as if he's starting to lose it. He's scared, but he's not really scared yet. He shakes his head.

Then a shot of him cleaning his teeth. He's got a little sink and a mirror on the wall.

He's reflected in the mirror. Establish the mirror well, Michael: this is where we're going to finish at the end.

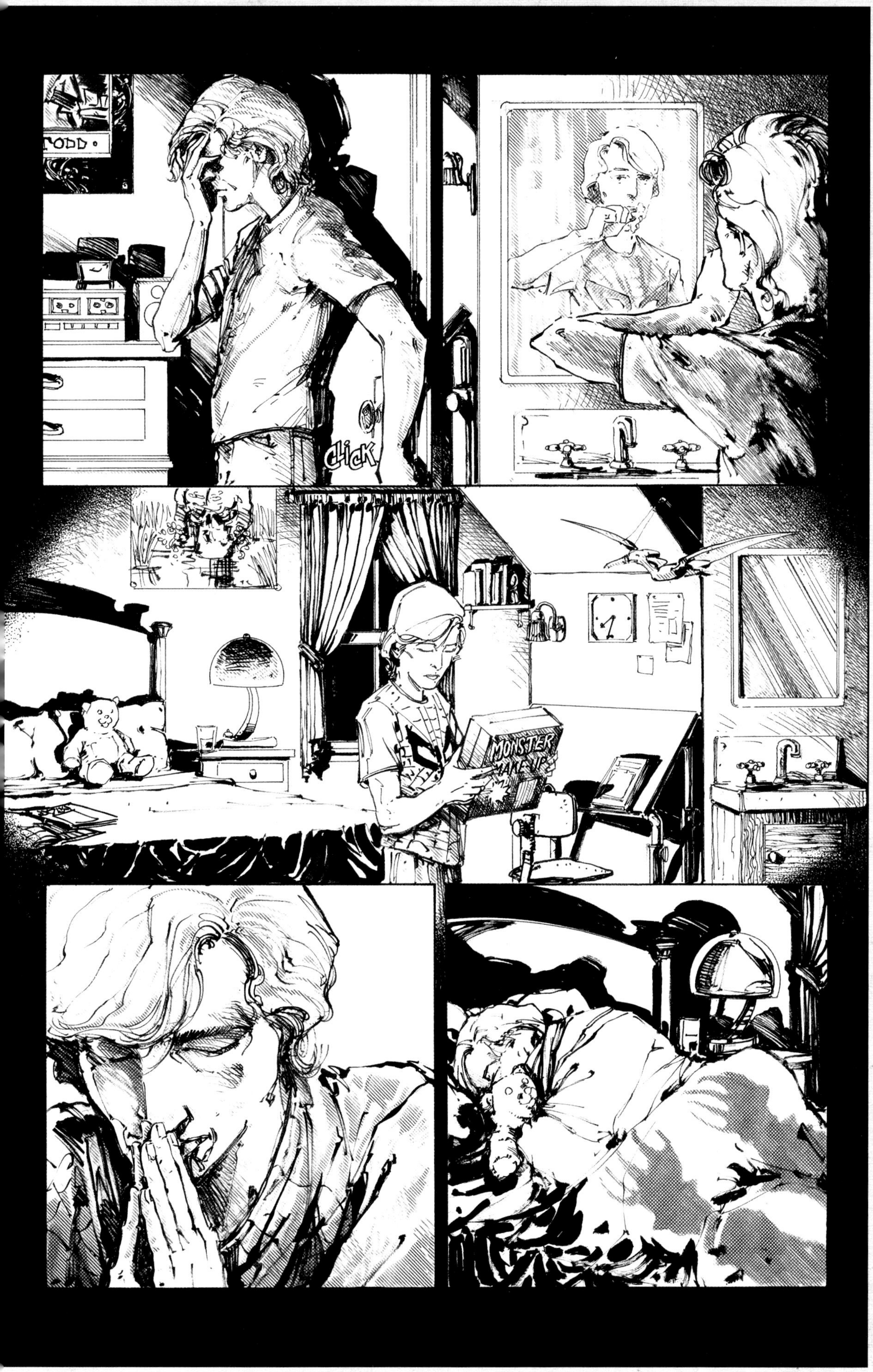
TODD
CLICK
MONSTER MAKE-UP

final page 8 inked art by Michael Zulli

His room is decorated with heavy metal posters, comics stuff (he's probably got a few marvel posters, a sweeny todd poster, and a Cerebus poster). He's got some books around, some CDs, some sports cards, a cd player. Still some toys.

Then we see him, in his pyjamas, looking at the MONSTER MAKE-UP KIT.

Then we see him kneeling by the bed, for a panel. (I think that's right. It feel right.)

Then he picks up a battered old Teddy Bear from the pillow, and hugs it tightly.

THEN HE'S ASLEEP.

Page 10/11 (Editor's note: see revised dream sequence script on page 145)

Michael, I want some knock-their-socks-off double page spreads. Actually they don't quite have to be double page spreads if you don't want to. You could play with panel-in-panel stuff. But basically we're looking at some strange, scary landscape, with huge, strange birds flying towards us. Part of it is kind of like the theatre - possibly we can see the pillars and the rats. There's smoke in the air - it's a little like a battlefield. Dead children. The sun and moon are in the sky.

showman cap: There's a legend

showman cap: There's a legend that the voice you hear

showman cap: In your dreams

showman cap: that the voice

showman cap: Is the voice of God

showman cap: And it tells you true things

Page 12/13

Over the page - the left-hand page is a full page splash that drips over to the right hand page. But we have panels on the right hand page. Now we're looking at the sun and moon in the sky - and they're eyes. The showman's eyes. The ragged birds are flying closer to us. There are corpses on the earth, reaching up boney and fleshless arms reaching up towards the sky. This should somehow be a huge Showman face. It's a complete nightmare place - a nightmare landscape of death and the aftermath of war or of destruction. Maybe we can see Mercy writhing in the mud.

showman cap: That's the legend, Steven

Then, running down the side of the right hand page, we get the showman, grinning at us. The landscape has coagulated into his face.

showman cap: But,

showman cap: as you can see,

showman cap: it's not entirely reliable.

He winks at us.

showman cap: Have a wonderful day...

Then darkness.

Page 14

I'm almost tempted to have the dream sequence go on another two pages; but I think we'll run this issue shorter than the last anyway, and bulk it out at the back with Neat Stuff. Some Alice hand-written lyrics, some photos, maybe a reprint of the marvel Age article, and a plug for the CD & tape. I'd say we're looking at 24-26 pages for this episode.

It's morning. We're looking at his house from outside.

Now we're inside. A shot of him in front of his mirror again.

We see him picking up his Monster make-up kit.

Now he's dressed, and downstairs. He's got his school bag. His mother and father are eating breakfast - his father's in shirtsleeves, his mother's obviously prepared to go off to work.

He stares at his mother and father. He's awkward.

Father: Steven? You havin' any breakfast?

Steven: Not really hungry.

Page 15 (22)

Mother: Well, then take an apple, in case you get hungry on the bus or something.

She tosses him an apple. He catches it. They're both completely normal. He turns away.

Mother (off):   Steven?

He turns.

Steven: Mm.

Mother: We do love you, darling. And we're both very proud of you.

Steven: Yeah. Thanks.

Now we're watching him walking him down the sidewalk to school. Then suddenly a hand touches his shoulder. He turns. A wolfman face leers at him.

The mask gets pulled down.

It's Jacob Candleman.

Jacob: Hey, Steven.

Steven: Hi Jake.

Jacob: Whaddaya think, huh? My Uncle got it for me in Hollywood. It's like a real movie mask. Probably this is the mask that they wore in all those movies.

Steven: You are so full of it, Jacob.

Page 16 (23)

Jacob: Oh yeah? So is your costume better than this, huh?

Steven: Maybe.

Jacob sticks out a leg, or pushes Steven, who sprawls onto the sidewalk.

Jacob: Have a nice trip? Hur hur hur...

Steven gets up. His jeans have a rip in the knee. He's skinned his knee.

He looks ahead of him. It's where the alley was and isn't any more.

Steven: Hey Jacob - look!

Jacob: What?

Steven: It's not there.

Jacob: What's not there?

Steven: The theatre. It's not there.

Jacob: You're weird.

Page 17 (24)

They get into the school. It's the school day: they put backpacks in their lockers.

The Pretty Girl Of his own Age - we'll call her nancy - looks down at Steven's ripped jeans.

Girl: Nice jeans, Steven.

Steven: Oh, uh thanks, uh, Nancy.

Girl: Aren't those ripped knees kind of out,though?

They file into their classroom. Teacher is a chubby, middle-aged woman. One of the kids has this huge costume - a giant carrot costume.

Teacher: Letitia. Why isn't that in your locker?

Letitia: I couldn't fit it in, Miss Robinson.

Teacher: Well, put it at the back of the classroom. Get it off your desk.

(Other kids sneer and grin).

Miss Robinson: We'll say the pledge, everyone.

Miss Robinson: I pledge allegiance to the flag of the...

Now, Miss Robinson walks over to Steven. She's still a chubby teacher. Only now she's got the Alice Cooper make-up on. She's being inhabited by the Showman, and she's talking only to Steven.

Miss Robinson: ...theatre of the real and to the darkness for which it stands.

                        One ancient underdog's invisible, with a litany of disgust for all.

Now she's Mrs Robinson again.

Mrs Robinson: Now, today, as you all know is Hallowe'en. I want to go over the Hallowe'en rules.

                        No costumes or masks are to put on until the two o'clock recess.

                        Now, does anyone have any news they wish to share with us?

Page 18 (25)

A girl puts up her hand.

Girl: Yes, I do, Miss Robinson.

                My gerbil had babies last night.

Miss Robinson: Oh, how sweet. How many little babies did she have?

Girl: I don't know. She ate them all afterwards.

Miss Robinson: ...Oh.

                        Okay. Reading books out, everyone.

The kids pull out copies of Bradbury's SOMETHING WICKED THIS WAY COMES.

Mis Robinson walks over to Steven. She's now the Showman Miss Robinson:

Miss Robinson: Now, Steven. Sleep well?

Steven: Can any of them see you?

Showman: They can only see Miss Robinson. They aren't candidates for stardom.

Steven: Like I am?

Showman: I told you the show wasn't over, yet. There's still the grand finale. And you're the star of that.

Steven: Who are you? Are you the Devil?

Miss Robinson is now Miss Robinson again.

Miss Robinson: No, Steven. I'm your teacher.

.....

140

CUT TO:

The gym. The kids are jumping up and down, doing 'jumping jacks'. A male teacher walks up and down the line, watching them. Steven's in the middle of the line.

Gym Teacher: Jacob, raise the arms higher...

                       ...Doug, c'mon, you're a human being, not a sack of flour,
                       ...Kyle, yeah, that's good...

Page 19 (26)

(And then he reaches out and touches Steven's chin with his forefinger, lifts his face up. The teacher has an Alice Face on too.)

Showman teacher: ... Steven, no, I'm not the Devil.

                       The devil is a huge concept. I am merely a humble showman.

                       I bring you little moments of pleasure to brighten your otherwise dreary
                       life.

                       Did you like the little show yesterday?

Steven: No. Not really.

Showman Teacher: Not really... so you don't want to see how it ends?

                       I thought perhaps you might.

The teacher's normal again.

Teacher: Okay. Now everyone on the floor for sit-ups...

.....

CUT TO:

Steven in line at the cafeteria. He holds out a plate and someone dumps something unsavoury onto it. He looks down at it, makes a face.

The lunch lady looks at him.

Lunch lady: Somethin' wrong with the macaroni?

Steven: I dunno. The way it looks. The way it tastes. The way it smells is pretty gross too,
                 now I come to think of it.

                 And it feels slimy to the touch. Is it meant to be like that?

The food lady is now Showman-made-up:

Showman-lunch-lady: Now you come to mention it, it does look like something vomited up
                       by a pig with a particularly nasty case of intestinal worms.

                       Have you thought about what I'm offering you?

Steven: I dunno. Is it something about my soul?

Page 20 (27)

He holds out his bowl for desert.

showman: I don't buy souls. I'm an impresario, not a costermonger. Your soul's health is your
                 own affair.

                 Jello?

Steven: Yeah. The jello's okay.

Showman: But there is a deal. And it's a good deal.

                 I want you to join the cast.

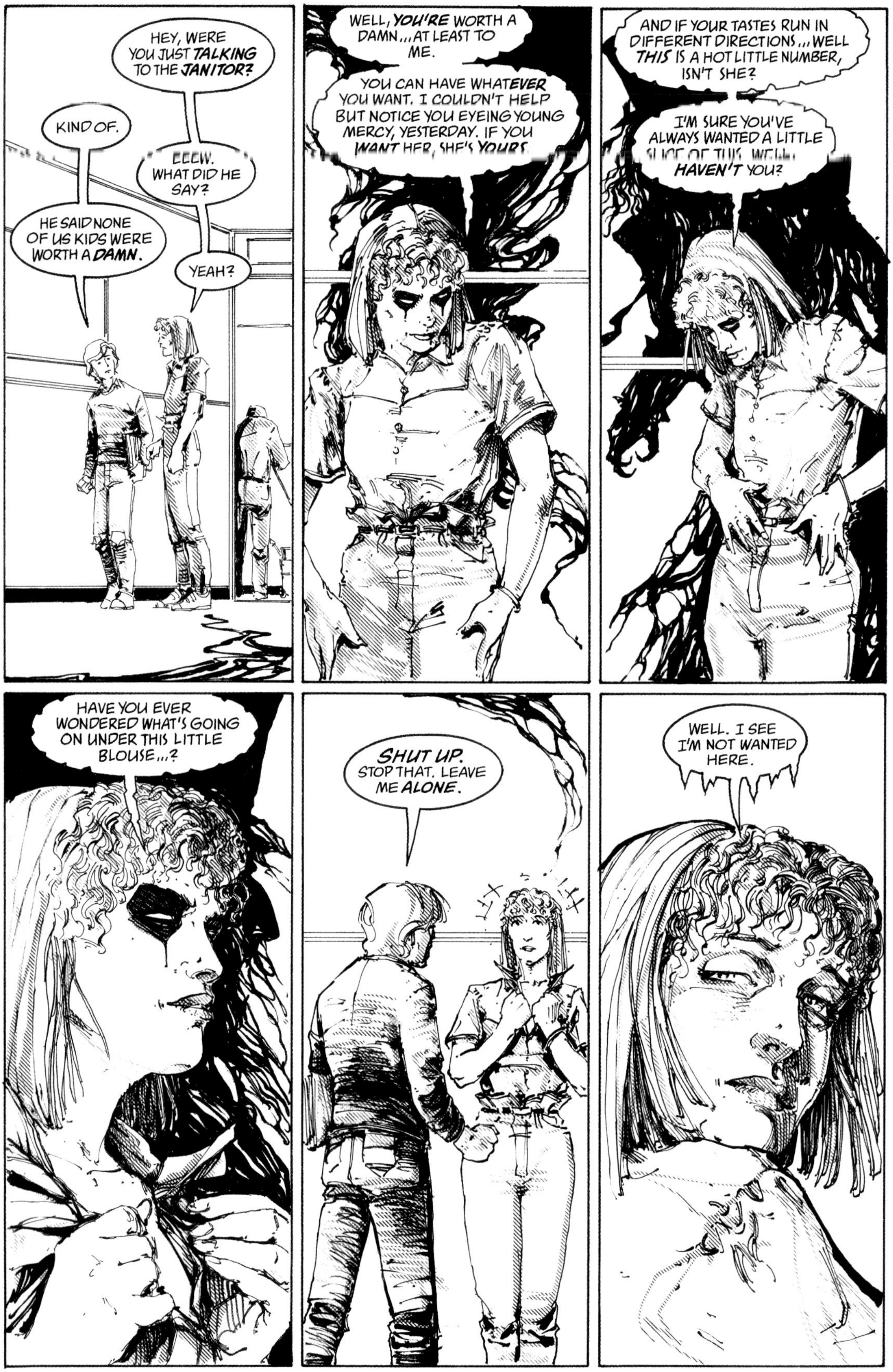
HEY, WERE YOU JUST TALKING TO THE JANITOR?
KIND OF.
EEEW. WHAT DID HE SAY?
HE SAID NONE OF US KIDS WERE WORTH A DAMN.
YEAH?
WELL, YOU'RE WORTH A DAMN... AT LEAST TO ME.
YOU CAN HAVE WHATEVER YOU WANT. I COULDN'T HELP BUT NOTICE YOU EYEING YOUNG MERCY, YESTERDAY. IF YOU WANT HER, SHE'S YOURS.
AND IF YOUR TASTES RUN IN DIFFERENT DIRECTIONS... WELL THIS IS A HOT LITTLE NUMBER, ISN'T SHE?
I'M SURE YOU'VE ALWAYS WANTED A LITTLE
HAVEN'T YOU?
HAVE YOU EVER WONDERED WHAT'S GOING ON UNDER THIS LITTLE BLOUSE...?
SHUT UP. STOP THAT. LEAVE ME ALONE.
WELL. I SEE I'M NOT WANTED HERE.

final page 29 inked art by Michael Zulli

CUT TO:

Steven, sitting eating his jello, a plate of macaroni sitting next to him, untouched.

A much bigger kid sits down next to him. Showman make-up:

Showman-kid: You've seen your future, Steven. It's a nothing place, an empty joke.

Steven: So?

Showman: So... I'm giving you the opportunity to change all that.

                 What - you ask me - am I offering you?

Steven: No, I didn't. I didn't ask you.

Showman: Nothing will hurt you ever again.

                 You'll never grow old.

The showman takes a mouthful of the macaroni and makes a face.

Showman: Tastes worse than it looks, eh? That's quite an achievement.

                 All you need to do is join the cast of my little theatre. The blood's just grease
                 paint. You do believe that, don't you?

Page 21 (28)

CUT TO:

*Steven in the corridor: the Janitor is leaning on his mop, talking to Steven with an Alice-showman
face.*

Janitor-alice: You can have whatever you want, Steven.

                 Your enemies will hang on the walls of your dress-
                 ing-room, writhing in unutterable pain...

*Now the Janitor is actually mopping the floor with his mop. Steven's standing out of the way. He's
holding an exercise book.*

Janitor-showman: Your friends will finally acknowledge that they were wrong about you -
                 always, entirely and ultimately wrong - that you were indeed as wise and
                 kind and generous and as worthy of their love and praise and adoration as
                 you thought you were.

Now - the Janitor as himself:

Janitor: Hey, you movin' your feet or what? You standin' where I'm washin'.

Steven: Sorry.

Janitor: You kids. None of you worth a damn.

Page 22 (29)

*Steven walks away down the corridor. The pretty girl, Nancy is in the corridor too. He's embarassed
around her. Awkward.*

Nancy: Hey, were you just talking to the janitor?

Steven: Kind of.

Nancy: Eeew. What did he say?

Steven: He said none of us kids were worth a damn.

Nancy: Yeah?

*And then Nancy's inhabited by the Showman. She stops by some lockers, or wherever she can stop
somewhere out of the way.*

143

Nacy-showman: Well, you're worth a damn... At least to me.
                       You can have whatever you want. I couldn't help but noticing you eyeing
                       young Mercy, yesterday. If you want her, she's yours.

The showman/Nancy looks down, runs his hands down the body.

                       And if your tastes run in different directions... Well this is a hot little
                       number, isn't she?

                       I'm sure you've always wanted a little slice of this. Well, haven't you?

Nancy makes as if to begin unbuttoning her shirt. The smile on her face is pure showman.

Nancy/showman: Have you ever wondered what's going on under this little blouse...?

Steven: Shut up. Stop that. Leave me alone.

*The showman leaves Nancy's body. She looks at Steven in the same way she'd look at something
unpleasant on the sole of her shoe.*

Nancy: Well. I see I'm not wanted here...

Page 23 (30)

Steven: Wait! Nancy, I didn't mean you. Oh... fudge!

*Right - now we see a load of kids milling about. They're all in costumes - there are young Draculas
and Frankenstiens, Little Mermaids, Wolverines, a Junior Sandman, the girl in the carrot costume,
ghosts and witches and Zully mutant turtles and so forths, and Jacob in his werewolf mask. We're in
the classroom.*

The teacher's around, trying to keep some kind of order - Mrs Robinson. Big Panel.

Mrs Robinson: Children - can I have some quiet, please? Please?

                       Now, we'll be lining up in the hallway - in twos - quietly - and we'll be
                       joined by the other classes. When the bell goes, we'll start the annual
                       school hallowe'en parade through the town.

                       John, don't do that. Lurene, give Roxanne back her teeth. Arnold, I don't
                       think X-men make those kind of noises, dear...

                       Are we all here?

The Werewolf - Jacob puts his hand up.

Jacob: I don't think Steven's back, yet.

Mrs Robinson: We'll give him another couple of minutes.

...

We're staring at Steven's MONSTER MAKE-UP KIT

*We're in the kiddie washrooms. Steven is staring into the mirror. He doesn't seem to know what to
do.*

He's just standing, staring.

*Suddenly the Showman is there: in the mirror. He's not in the real world, only in the mirror. He
looks very cool, very elegant.*

Showman: Can't decide who to be? Clowns are very popular. So are zombies.

Page 24 (31)

*The Steven in real life looks at the Showman (in the mirror) standing next to the Steven in the
mirror.*

It's like the Showman's finally getting to him.

Steven: What do you want from me? Why are you doing this to me?

Showman:	Come on back to the theatre, Steven.
	There's a grand finale.
	I'll explain it all. What the deal is.
Steven:	I don't trust you.
Showman:	So? It's like the Soda, boy. Like the theatrical display. It's free.
Steven:	Nothing's Free.
	And the theatre isn't even there any more.
Showman:	It'll be there at sunset.
Steven:	If I come back to the theatre, will you leave me alone?
Showman:	I give you my word as a gentleman and a showman.

Page 25 (32)

Then he grins, as if to indicate just what he thinks of his word. And he vanishes.

Steven: Yeah.

He reaches for the make-up kit, pulls out a stick of black make-up.

He looks at it.

And he runs the first thing of black under his eyes. Looks up:

He's wearing Alice make-up.

Steven: Okay. Now...

               Let's see how you like it.

Then, under the last panel:

To Be Concluded

Lettering draft.

Revised DREAM SEQUENCE, for Book 2.

Michael, I want some knock-their-socks-off double page spreads. Actually they don't quite have to be double page spreads if you don't want to. You could play with panel-in-panel stuff. But basically we're looking at some strange, scary landscape, with huge, strange birds flying towards us. Part of it is kind of like the theatre - possibly we can see the pillars and the rats. There's smoke in the air - it's a little like a battlefield. Dead children. The sun and moon are in the sky.

showman cap:	There's a legend
showman cap:	There's a legend that the voice you hear
showman cap:	In your dreams
showman cap:	that the voice
showman cap:	Is the voice of God
showman cap:	And it tells you true things

Over the page - the left-hand page is a full page splash that drips over to the right hand page. But we have panels on the right hand page. Now we're looking at the sun and moon in the sky - and they're eyes. The showman's eyes. The ragged birds are flying closer to us. There are corpses on the earth, reaching up boney and fleshless arms reaching up towards the sky. This should somehow be a huge Showman face. It's a complete nightmare place - a nightmare landscape of death and the aftermath of war or of destruction. Maybe we can see Mercy writhing in the mud.

showman cap: That's the legend, Steven

Then, running down the side of the right hand page, we get the showman, grinning down at us from his pillar. On other pillars we see things of horror and fear - Teddy bears of doom, rats, spiders...

showman cap: But,

showman cap: as you can see,

showman cap: it's not entirely reliable.

Showman: Have you ever baited a trap, boy? You need a different trap for every type of creature. And a different type of bait as well. A mouse trap catches mice. A bear trap catches bears. A Steven trap... well, what do you think that would look like, eh?

Steven: I don't know.

Showman: I do. I'd build it out of fear and lust, build it of wonder and awe, of blood and hope and terror. It would be such a strange little mechanism of desire and repulsion...

              And a little Steven would nuzzle its way in, hunting for the exit, sniffing the bait... sniff... sniff...

              and then,

              snap!

He picks up one of the little rats on the pillar, while he gives this explanation, then with the snap, he pulls its head off.

Steven: I'm dreaming, aren't I?

Showman: Of course.

The headless rat has fallen to the ground. It becomes Mercy. She reaches up to Steven...

Mercy: Don't let him do it. Please...

Showman: Pay no attention to her, Steven. Did I tell you that you'll be going crazy, tomorrow?

              Did I tell you I'm going to make you a star?

Steven's on his knees with Mercy. She's sinking into the mud...

Mercy: Please don't trust him...

Steven: I don't. He doesn't go out of his way to exactly make himself trustworthy, does he?

Showman: I can see that I'm going to have to deal with that young lady. I shall show no mercy: one must be cruel to be kind, after all. And I am famous for my kindness...

              Spare the knife, and spoil the child.

              In the best traps, of course, the quarry never realises it before it's much too late.

              Maybe it never realises it.

He winks at us.

showman cap: Have a wonderful day...

Then darkness.

One possibility might be a couple of inset panels top left, small, of Steven, in bed, opening his eyes, rolling over, going back to sleep again...

Steven's still asleep, still dreaming, on a blank plain.

Far above him is an angel, looking down on him.

Steven is a tiny figure, on this darkened place, far below the angel, a thing of beauty and wonder. We can almost hear the slow, majestic flapping of its wings.

Then it's morning, and Steven's awake.

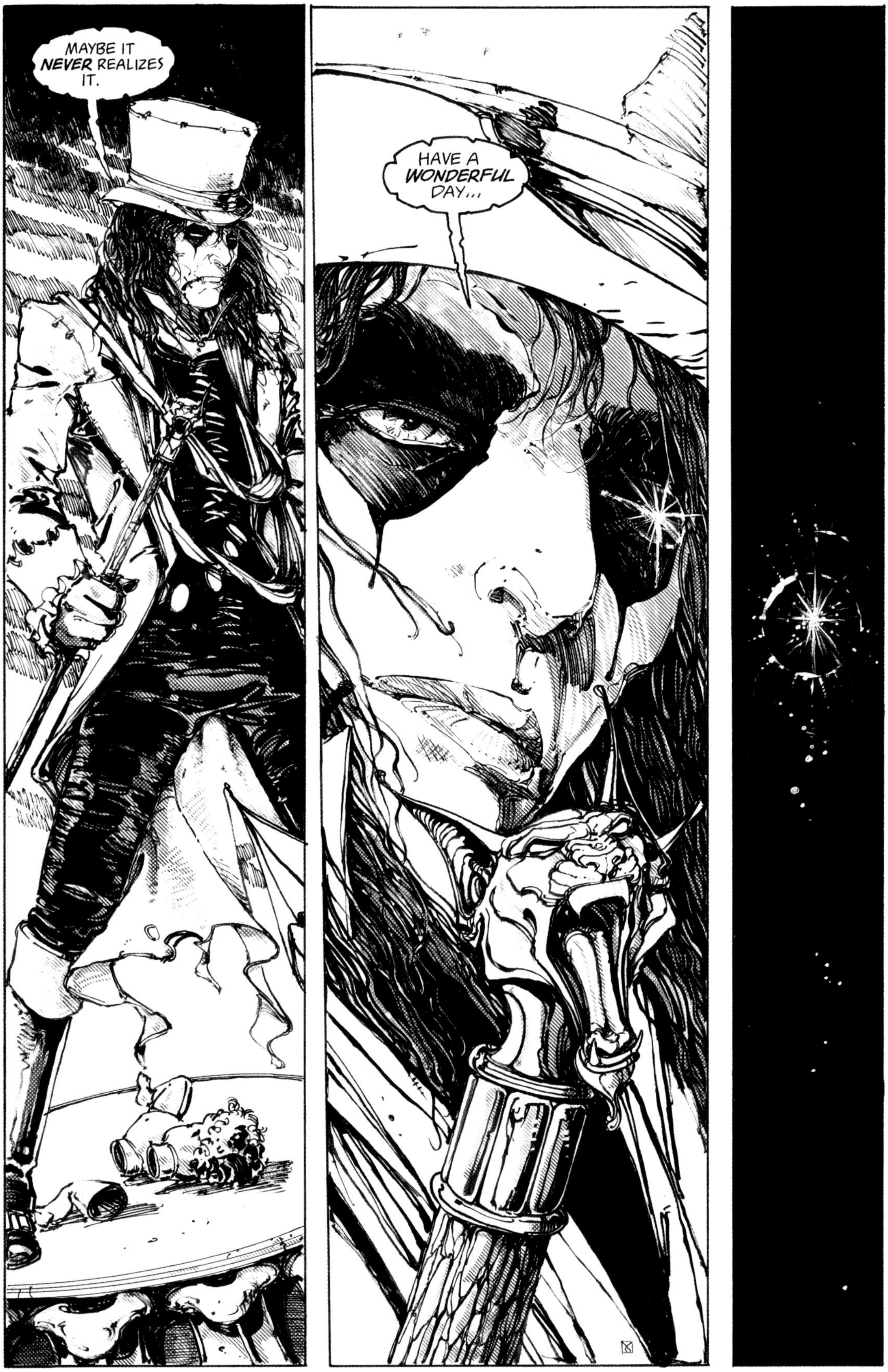
MAYBE IT NEVER REALIZES IT.
HAVE A WONDERFUL DAY...

final page 15 inked art by Michael Zulli

ALICE COOPER: THE LAST TEMPTATION
Book Three Script by Neil Gaiman

Hi Michael, Todd, Mort, and all at Alive,

Well, here we go with Alice 3. We're into what is very much the last act here.

I loved the shots of Alice as the showman in the It's me video. Really strange and sinister. He worked perfectly...

(Editor's note: this is an earlier draft than what was used for the final issue)

. . . .

Page 1

cap:	All Hallow's Eve. Hallowe'en.
cap:	The first day of the death of the year.
cap:	Folk-beliefs about this day go back forever.
cap:	On Hallowe'en, they say, the gates of hell swing wide, and the dead and the damned ride out from dusk until dawn.
cap:	On Hallowe'en, they say, the dark spews out all the nightmares, all the pain, all the death; and the hurt and the hate take shape and form. That's when they can hurt you - or so they say.
cap:	On Hallowe'en, children, and those who are at heart children, celebrate the year's end with coloured costumes, with masks and carven faces...

Page 2-3

cap:	His name is Steven, and he could be anyone. He could be you.
cap:	He's just old enough to find the school costumed Hallowe'en procession through the town streets faintly embarassing.
cap:	But that isn't why he works his way, quietly, to the back of the line.
cap:	That isn't why he waits until his teacher's attention is elsewhere to slip away.
cap:	There's a theatre that isn't there until sunset.
cap:	There's someone waiting for him in the theatre. Someone not very nice...
cap:	But first...

Page 4

Steven:	<u>Hello?</u> Is there anyody here?
Librarian:	I'm up here. And I'll thank you to keep your voice down in my library.
Steven:	I... I'm sorry. I've never <u>been</u> here before.
Librarian:	I'm sure you haven't.
	Might as well be the <u>morgue,</u> for all the attention people pay this library.

Page 5

Librarian:	What have you got on your <u>face,</u> young man? <u>War</u> <u>paint?</u>
Steven:	Monster Make-up.
Librarian:	And <u>why</u> do you have monster make-up on?
Steven:	It's Hallowe'en.
Librarian:	Hmph. Pagan stuff and nonsense.

Librarian:	Well, the children's books are back down the stairs and to your right. Don't bend any pages back, or eat any candy.
Steven:	I don't _want_ children's books.
Librarian:	_No?_ What _do_ you want?
Steven:	I'm not sure. A history of the town, if you've got one. I need to learn about some old theatre that used to be by the town hall.
Librarian:	Hmph. There's _no_ history of the town. Old Toby, he always _said_ he was going to write one, but he never did.
	You want to look at the local newspaper, I guess. We've got them on microfiche going back almost hundred and fifty years. They were taking up too much room. Becoming a _fire_ hazard. You ever use a microfiche reader?
Steven:	Uh, no.
Librarian:	I'll show you how to operate the contraption. Nothing _to_ it.

...

Page 6

Steven is sitting down at a microfiche reader. The librarian hands him the microfiche.

Librarian:	_Here._ Take good _care_ of them. Put them back in their holders as you finish them.
Steven:	Thanks.

Then we're looking at Steven, examining newspaper headlines, thrown up on the screen.

Steven caps:	Hallowe'en 1970. Missing child report...
	Hallowe'en 1965. Missing Child report...
	Hallowe'en 1960. Missing child report. There's also a report that two of the kids friends say they saw him go into an old theatre. The next day they denied saying anything of the kind...
	Missing child 1955...
	1950...
	1944... huh?

Page 7

Steven caps:	1940...
	1938... well... so it's not _exactly_ every five years...
	1935...
	and so on to - yup, here's 1900...
	they keep going back...
	A child who '_rose in the night in a fit of delirium and wandered away_'
	Here we go.
	31 October 1884...

Page 8

Newspaper captions - Todd, maybe these could be hand-lettered in a kind of newspapery font.

> _Townsfolk residing locally are living this day in terror of an incendiary who destroyed the Spaulding Memorial Theatre. The town's fire department is of the opinion that some crazy person is responsible for the destruction of the building._

> _Previously a mysterious individual had been severally observed in the vicinity of_

the selfsame theatre; and this person is thought to be identical with he who enticed from school Jack Rathke and his sister Hattie-May Rathke earlier this week. The children were hurried away in a closed carriage, which started off in a northerly direction. The chief of police, however, dismissed this as pure unfounded speculation.

The conflagration, which was scarcely prevented from destroying the newly-constructed town hall, is thought to be the work of a firebug with a mania to burn. Nothing of the theatre now remains.

Many human skeletons were found in the rubble. All of them appeared, to your reporter, to be less than fully grown.

Steven: Well.

Cut to Steven at the top of the stairs, talking to the Librarian. She's closing books and things.

Steven: Excuse me. Isn't there anything else on the theatre? On who built it, or anything like that?

Libraian: *Snf.* I'll have to see what we can find. But you'll have to come back tomorrow. We're closing now.

Steven: But I have to -

Page 9

Libraian: It'll keep till tomorrow, young man. It's closing time, now. Some of us have homes to go to.

Steven: Oh...

              Okay. I'm not sure I'll be here tomorrow.

              Well. 'Bye.

Now we watch him walk out.

He is standing at the bottom of the steps.

As he walks out of the door, rose petals fall.

He looks up. The rose petals are coming from a rose in a small vase on the upper floor, where the librarian lady is.

As he leaves, we move slightly over, and we see the corner of a wing from where the librarian was. Is the librarian an angel, watching over young Steven? Well, yes, probably. But we're being non-explicit.

(And no, I haven't forgotten about getting Steven something to burn the place down with. I've decided to do it another way...)

Page 10

Outside on the street: it's dusk.

Under the streetlights. Steven looks a lot more like the showman. He smears around one of the eyes...

The theatre's there. There are kids hanging around outside: as we approach, we can see they're very dead, and dressed in styles of dress that range over the century. Maybe one of them could be holding his head in his hands...

Dead boy: Hey. Stupid. What do you think you're doing back here again?

Page 11

Steven: Don't. Don't try and start anything.

Dead kid: Why you wearing the make-up, live boy?

Steven: Because I want to.

Another dead kid: You going to be joining us?

150

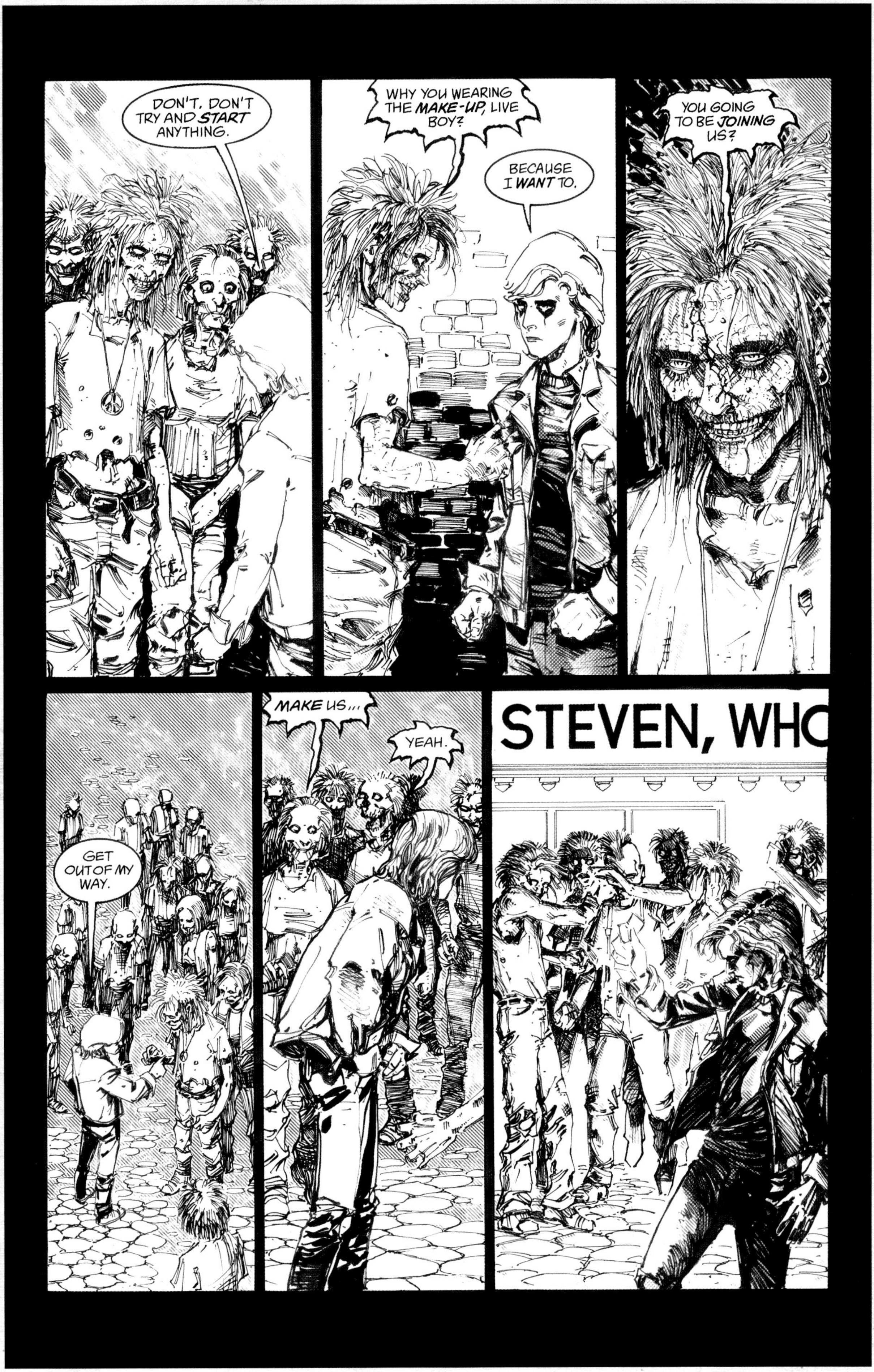
DON'T. DON'T TRY AND START ANYTHING.
WHY YOU WEARING THE MAKE-UP, LIVE BOY?
BECAUSE I WANT TO.
YOU GOING TO BE JOINING US?
GET OUT OF MY WAY.
MAKE US...
YEAH.
STEVEN, WHO

final page 11 inked art by Michael Zulli

Steven: Get out of my way.

Dead kid: <u>Make</u> us...

Dead kid 3:   Yeah.

(They're in his way now. Circling him. Barring his path.)

He puts his hand into his pocket. Pulls out the ticket. Reluctantly they step back and let him in.

. . . .

Page 12

Steven pushes his way through curtains. And finds himself standing up on the stage of the theatre.

The theatre is now quite huge. It's stranger, older, bigger than the earlier version that we saw.

Page 13

He's alone, for one moment, holding his ticket, looking dazed, with the spotlight on him.

Then the showman reaches out and takes the ticket from him.

Showman: <u>I'll</u> be taking that, I think.

              Well. I must com<u>mend</u> you on your <u>facial</u> decoration. It certainly shows the right
              idea.

              You returned. I take it you've decided to accept my offer?

Steven: You haven't told me what the <u>deal</u> is yet.

Showman: I haven't?

              No. I haven't.

*Now, play around with two things here, Michael. One of them is the audience ~ this audience of dead
boys and girls staring at Steven and the showman with dead eyes and with no eyes at all.*

And the other is the showman's control of reality.

Things that he's talking about manifest as he's talking.

Showman: I showed you <u>adulthood,</u> Steven. I <u>showed</u> you the world to come. You know that
              there's nothing to be gained from life.

              What I'm offering, Steven is so much <u>better</u> than life.

Steven: <u>What</u> are you offering?

Showman: Never grow old, Steven. Never decay. Never end.

              You can become part of the theatre of the real. When you've <u>become</u> the thing that
              <u>scares,</u> there's nothing to be scared of ever again...

Page 14~15

Steven seems tempted...

Steven: So... I wouldn't be scared of the monster under the bed if I was... hiding... under
              the bed... with him?

Showman: Or the movement in the shadows, when you're hiding in the shadows.

              You'd be <u>part</u> of every nightmare. Of <u>every</u> <u>fear.</u> In every town in the world.

              In return, I <u>only</u> want something <u>small.</u> Something teeeeeeeenytiny, you'd have no
              further use for....

Steven: Right. My soul.

Showman: Not at all. I want your <u>potential.</u> All you ever could have been... All you never

	will be...
	It's not anything you'd _ever_ use.
Steven:	So, let me see if I've got this straight.
	I never have to grow old by... never having anything to grow old _for?_
Showman:	How _very_ perspicacious of you. What a remarkable bright young man you are. With every golden syllable you utter I find myself further convinced of my utter rightness in choosing _you_ as this year's model...
	You remind me of _myself_ at your age... If ever I was your age...
Steven:	How long have you been _doing_ this?
	Getting kids to come to your theatre, and showing them your little scare shows? Buying their lives?
Showman:	Long enough.
	I'll take away the _uncertainty,_ Steven. I'll take away the _fear._ I'll take away the _boredom_ and the _pain._
	You want _more_ than _that?_

He's looking around, theatrically, shading his head, looking around the theatre. Possibly

Showman:	Where _is_ she? Where _is_ the little buttercup? Where is she _hiiiiiiiding?_
	In the _wings?_
	In the _flies?_
	In the _pit?_
	Under the _trap?_
	_No?_

He removes his hat. Reaches in and pulls out Mercy, by her hair. This obviously hurts her. he drops her on the stage, in front of Steven.

Page 16~17

Mercy:	Steven?

He reaches out a hand and helps her up. She cuddles up to him.

Steven:	If I _did_ stay here with you. Would you let her go?
Showman:	Now, _there's_ an interesting proposition, worthy indeed of a certain amount of negotiation.
Mercy:	Steven. You _can't._ You _mustn't._ _Really._
Steven:	I can.
Mercy:	But I don't have a life to go to. I don't have any existence outside of this place. I would have died a long time ago...
Showman:	Enough.
	You're offering a _swap?_ You stay, she goes?
Steven:	I'm not offering anything. I'm _asking._
Showman:	The further this goes, the more I suspect that I might have made it easier on myself, had I picked another Hallowe'en child...
	_No,_ I would _never_ permit her to leave. Mercy is part of the show.
	The show's the thing.

final pages 16-17 inked art by Michael Zulli

                    The show.

                    And the show <u>must</u> go on.

Page 18-19

Steven: No.

                    I don't want it. I don't want to be any part of your show.

                    I <u>know</u> that growing up is scary and weird. I know I don't have a lot of power. I know
                    that school's a bitch and real life probably won't be any better.

                    Except for not having to do homework, I suppose...

                    But I <u>want</u> to go out into life.

                    I want to make my <u>own</u> mistakes.

Showman: You want to grow <u>old,</u> and <u>die?</u>

Steven: Yes...

                    Yes, I suppose I <u>do.</u> If you put it like <u>that.</u>

Showman: Oh dear.

                    Oh, <u>dear</u> <u>dear</u> <u>dear</u>...

                    A minnow has slipped and slithered through my pale fingers. A fluttering butterfly
                    has fled from my flame.

                    Alas, and lackaday.

                    I weep bitter tears.

                    <u>Watch</u> me...

*He covers his face in his hands. Then he lowers his hands, we see he's grinning like a fox eating etc
etc.*

Showman: <u>There</u> now. My <u>heart</u> is <u>broken.</u> And, of course, you're free to go. I'm a man of my
                    word, after all.

Page 20-21

Showman: Find the way out, and you go free.

                    But if, of course, you <u>can't</u> find the way out, we'll certainly still adopt you here,
                    in the Theatre of the Real...

                    I bear no grudges.

Steven looks at him.

Steven: Come on, Mercy. Let's find the way out.

*We get a couple of shots now - just a page or part of one, not a whole wandering around sequence - of
him with Mercy, looking for a way out. Pushing against doors, curtains - but there's no longer a way
out, no longer an exit.*

Steven: Mercy? How <u>do</u> we get out?

Mercy: I <u>can't</u> get out, Steven. I told you. I'm part of the show.

Steven: Then how do <u>I</u> get out?

Mercy: I don't know, I'm sorry.
Steven: Look - <u>there's</u> a door. Let's try that one...

He pushes against the door. It opens. He's back on the stage...

Showman: And now, let's <u>hear</u> it for the newest, most vivacious member of our little
                    exhibition.

The crown in our jewel...

Steeeeeven.

So. Welcome to the cast...

Steven: There isn't any way out, is there?

Showman: Not that you've been able to find, boy. No.

Steven looks despondent. Then the penny slowly begins to drop...

Steven: This place doesn't exist, does it?

Page 22~23

Steven: It's just a ghost of a place. Somewhere that burned down a long time ago. Isn't that
              right?

Showman: of course not.

Steven: And if it burned down once... it can burn down again.

A moment's fear in the showman's eyes.

Showman: You're talking arrant nonsense, child.

Steven: No... No, I'm not.

Showman: And even there were the merest grainlet of truth in what you say, have you a tinder
              box on you? A lucifer?

Steven: No, I don't have any matches, or a lighter. But I don't need one. Do I?

              This isn't a real place.

              You'd need... a ghost-flame... to burn down a ghost house. A dream-flame....

close in on Steven's face. He's concentrating.

cap: He remembers a fire that burned in a fire-place, one snowy february long since gone.
              Remembers staring into it, watching a oaken log crumble into ash...

cap: He remembers passing his finger through a candle-flame; remembers a blue flame
              licking down the side of a burning newspaper, the acrid burning-paper smell; Steven
              remembers...

Showman: No!

We're in the theatre. It's burning down...

Flames everywhere. The audience begins to melt like waxen dummies.

*The showman grabs Steven - hauls him over. This is the first time the Showman has done anything
physical. He's angry - deeply angry.*

Showman: You little firebug-

              Someone's been talking to you. Someone's helping you. Admit it!

              You've hurt my theatre!

              You've burned my cast!

              It took me a hundred and fifty years to assemble those children.
              Now I'll have to start all over again...

....

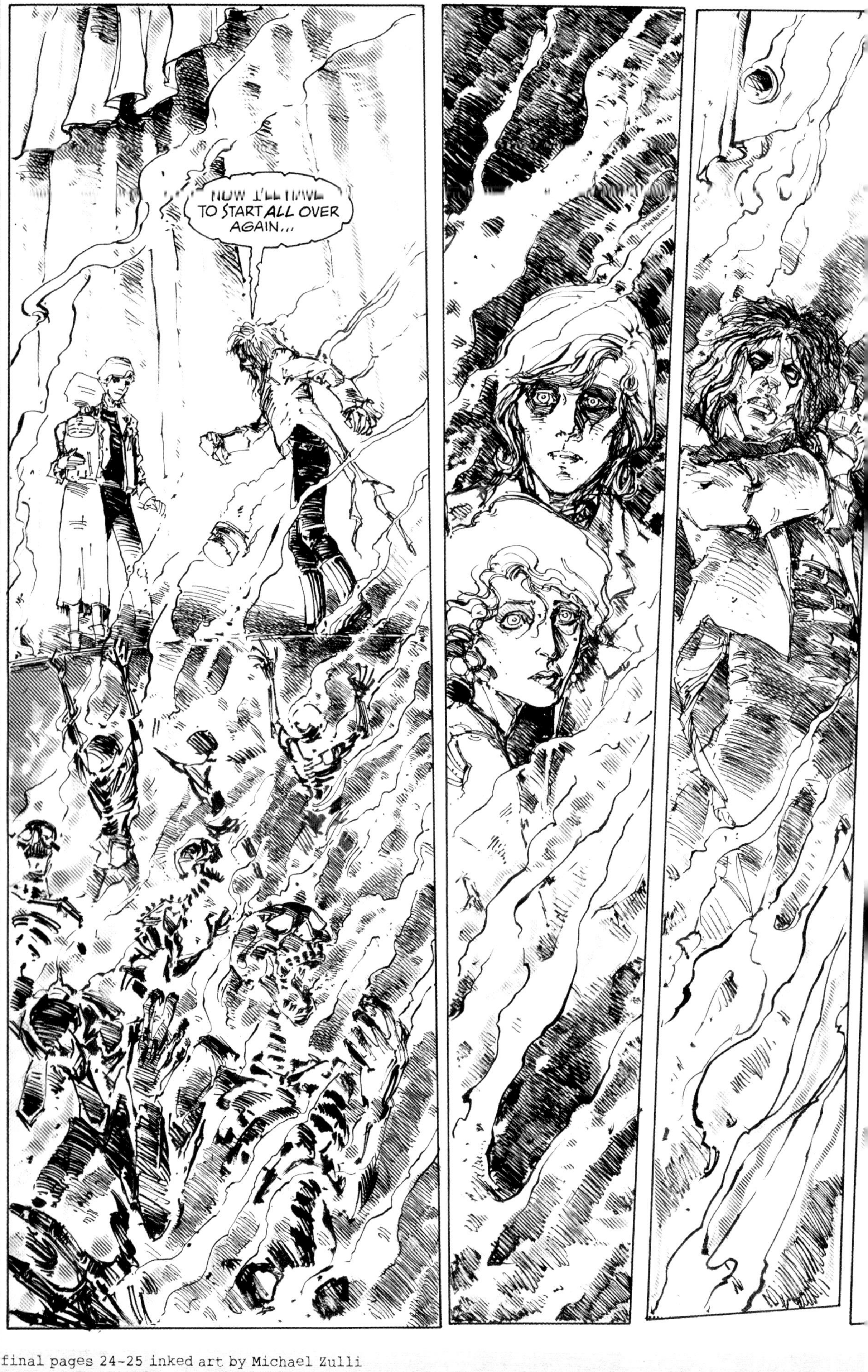
TO START ALL OVER AGAIN...

final pages 24-25 inked art by Michael Zulli

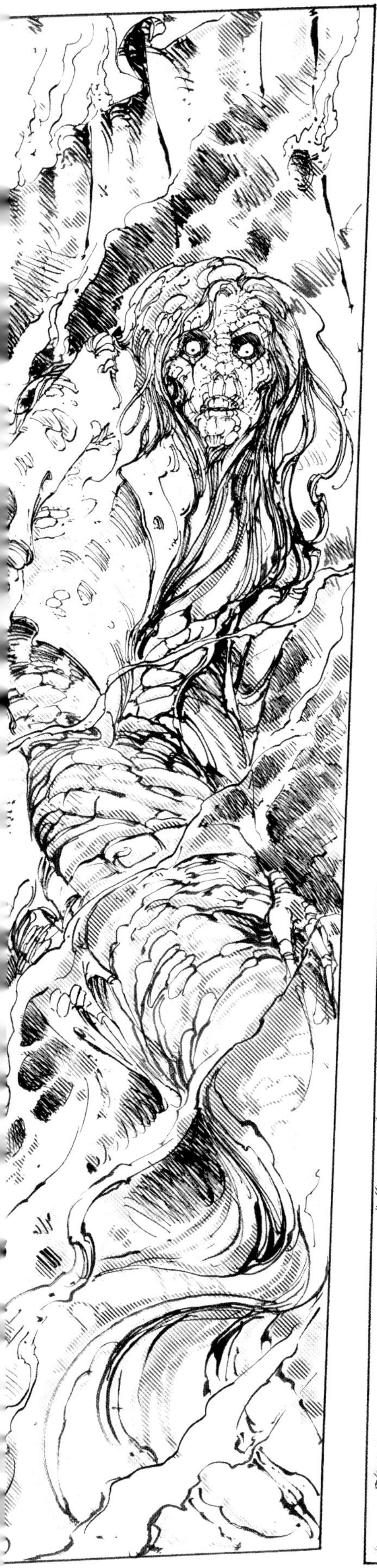

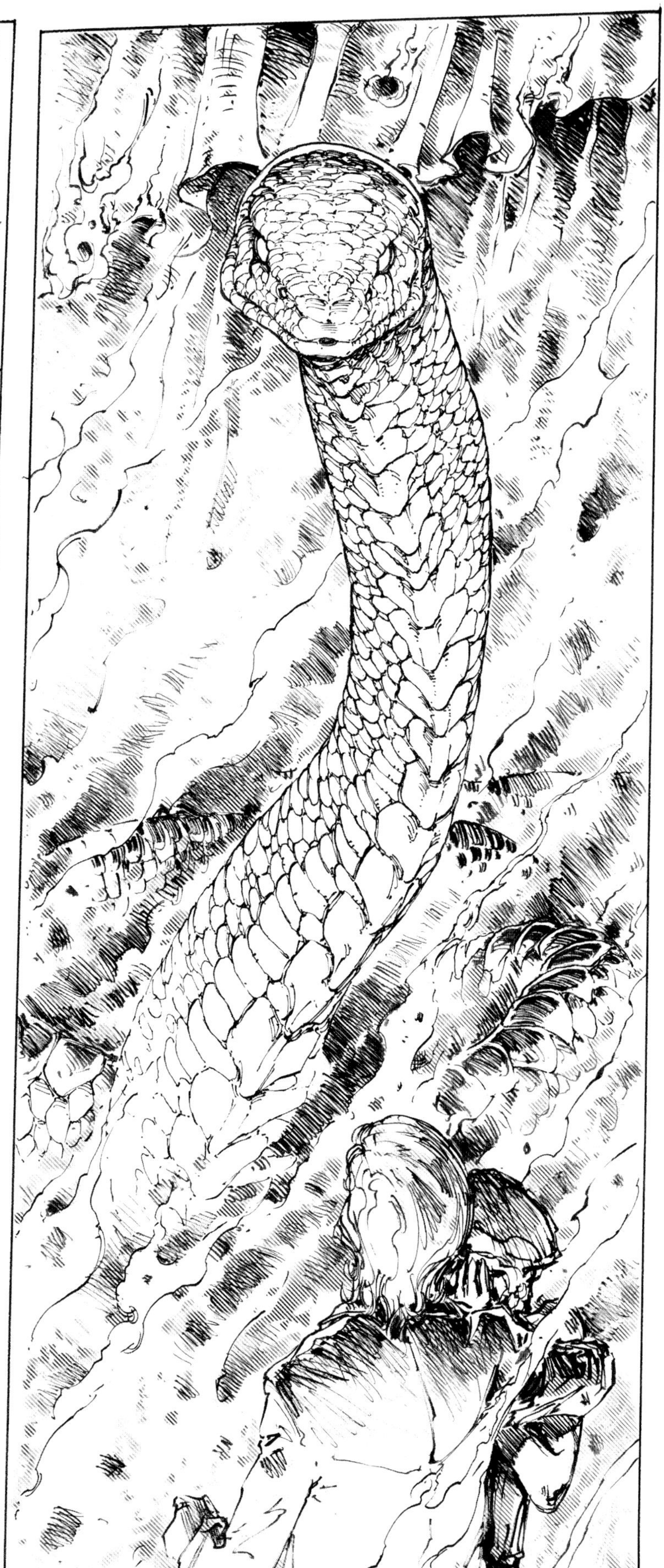

Page 24~25

The place is in flames, burning. The zombies are, if we can see them, burning skeletons, real messes.

The showman shifts and swirls.

There's no longer a Showman there. Now, in the middle of the flames, is an enormous snake, its body as thick as a huge oil-drum, rearing up high through the flames.

It lunges down at Steven. Steven is standing around in the flames, one arm around Mercy, who is also unharmed.

Page 26~27

Steven: You can't hurt me.

                <u>Can</u> you?

The lettering style here should play up the twisty S's of the showman style - exaggerate that utterly.

Showman-serpent: Ohh... I've already hurt you, sir Steven. Hurt you more seriously than you
                       know.

                       And now I'll hurt you again.

                       Little Mercy, your sweet little friend... she doesn't exist. She wasn't
                       even an actor. She was just a prop. A piece of scenery. A flat.

                       Something I made up.

Steven: You're lying. You're always lying.

Showman-serpent: oh, I'm the father of lies....

BLACK PANEL

Page 28

Steven and Mercy are standing on a vacant lot. The theatre is nothing more than twinkles.

Mercy: You were so brave.

Steven: I... I don't think so. I just did what I had to. That's not brave.

                He almost had me at the end, though. The stuff he was saying about you. About you not
                being real. I nearly believed him.

Page 29

Mercy: That <u>wasn't</u> a lie. Steven.

                I wasn't even a ghost. I'm sorry...

She's gone: where she was is the showman's animal-headed stick. It hisses at Steven, and slithers, snake-like, away, into the shadows.

Steven stands there for a moment. Then he puts his hands in his pocket and walks home.

A shot of his house at night. We could do this with Steven talking to his parents, or as captions over images of outside. Up to you - depends how you see it.

Dad: "How was hallowe'en?"

Steven: "Fine."

Mum: "Did you have fun, trick or treating?"

Steven: "I suppose."

Page 30

Mum: "Did you get anything really nice?"

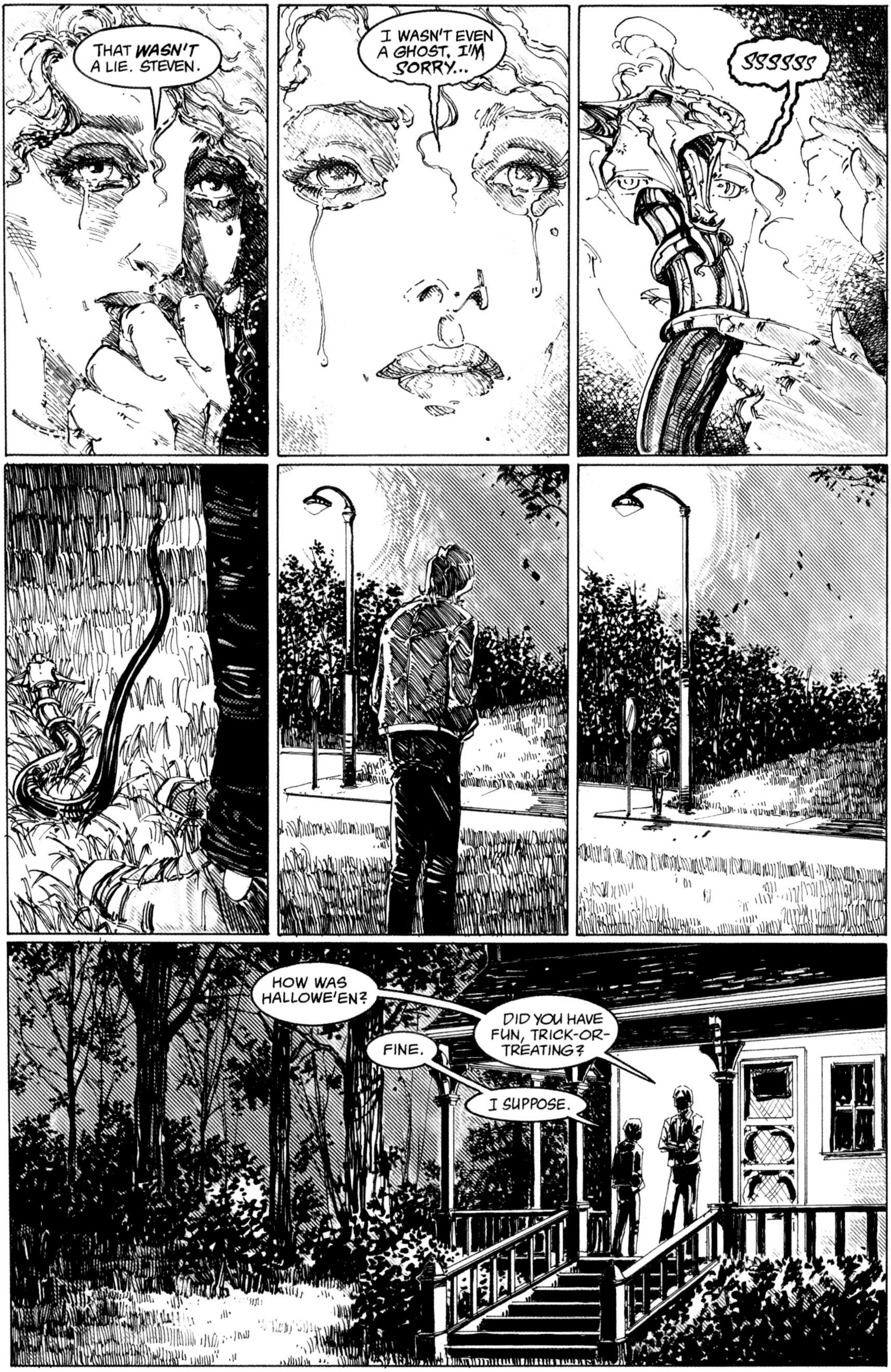
THAT WASN'T A LIE. STEVEN.
I WASN'T EVEN A GHOST. I'M SORRY...
SSSSSS
HOW WAS HALLOWE'EN?
DID YOU HAVE FUN, TRICK-OR-TREATING?
FINE.
I SUPPOSE.

final page 29 inked art by Michael Zulli

Steven:	"Not really."
Dad:	"So... if this isn't a dumb question, son... what were you tonight?"
Steven:	"I don't know... Maybe... an angel."
Dad:	"You don't look much like my idea of an angel."
	"Goodnight, Steven."

Steven goes up to his room. He looks in the mirror of the wardrobe

His reflection stares back, the grimy remnants of the showman makeup all over the eyes.

He washes his face, leaves a black pool in the basin.

Then he stares at himself for a beat.

Steven:	Goodnight Steven.
Steven:	Goodnight.

Page 31

He walks over to the bed. The light goes off. But his reflection remains in the mirror.

And as Steven's eyes close in sleep, the reflection shimmers and shifts.

Did Steven just fall asleep? We don't know.

The showman is looking out.

Showman:	There, boy.

Page 32

Showman:	And you took that hand in our little game; you won that battle, and turned that trick...
	Do you think it's over?
	It's never over.
Showman:	It doesn't matter where you travel. It doesn't matter where you go.
	I'll not forget you. I'm only a moment of reflection away.
	I'm older then you, boy. Older than you'll ever be. I'm the showman, and the show never truly ends. I can wait forever.
	And I will...

And then he turns his back on us, and walks away, into the distance, in the mirror....

as we-

END

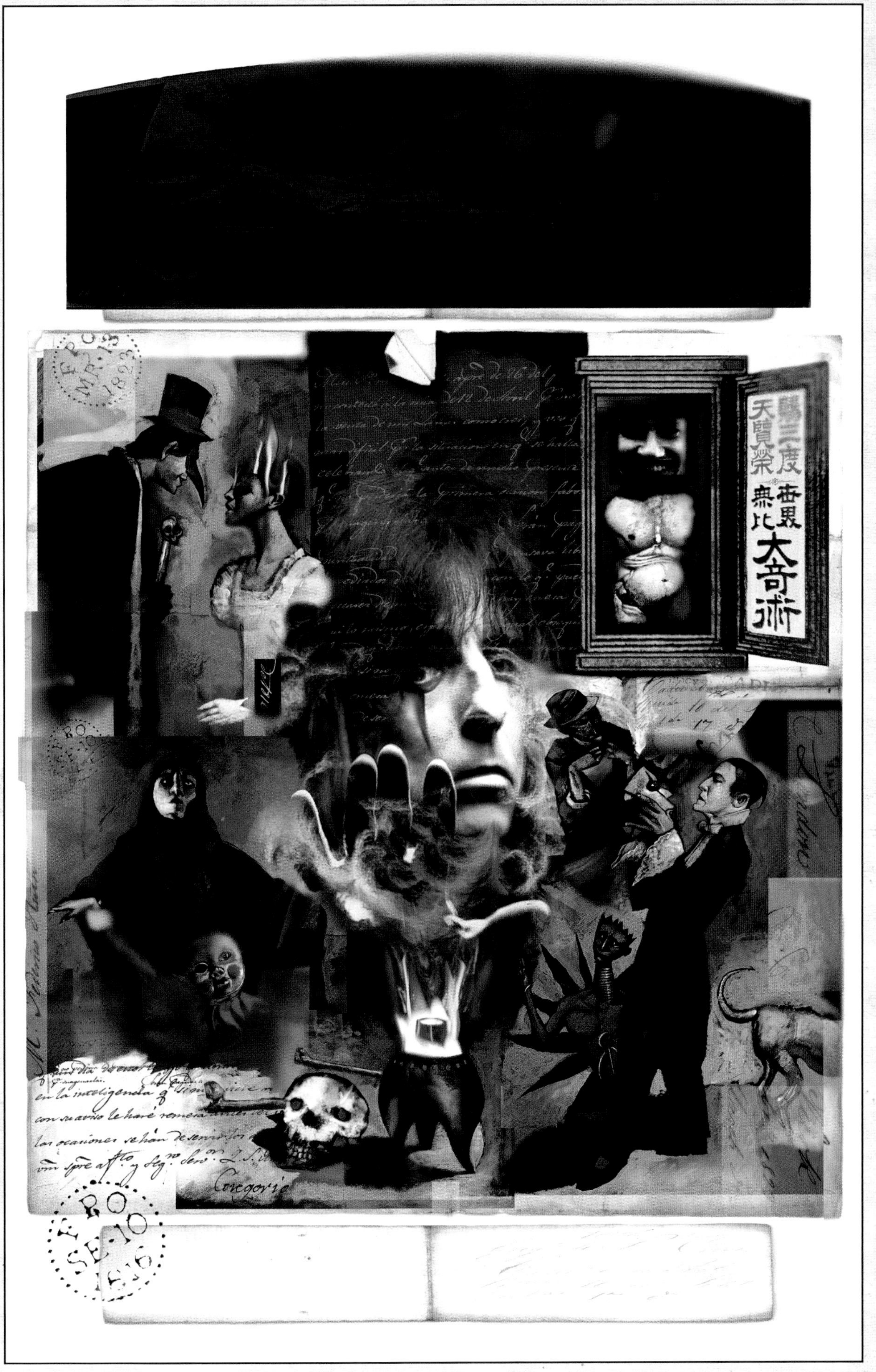
大奇術

ISSUE ONE

COVER ART BY DAVE McKEAN

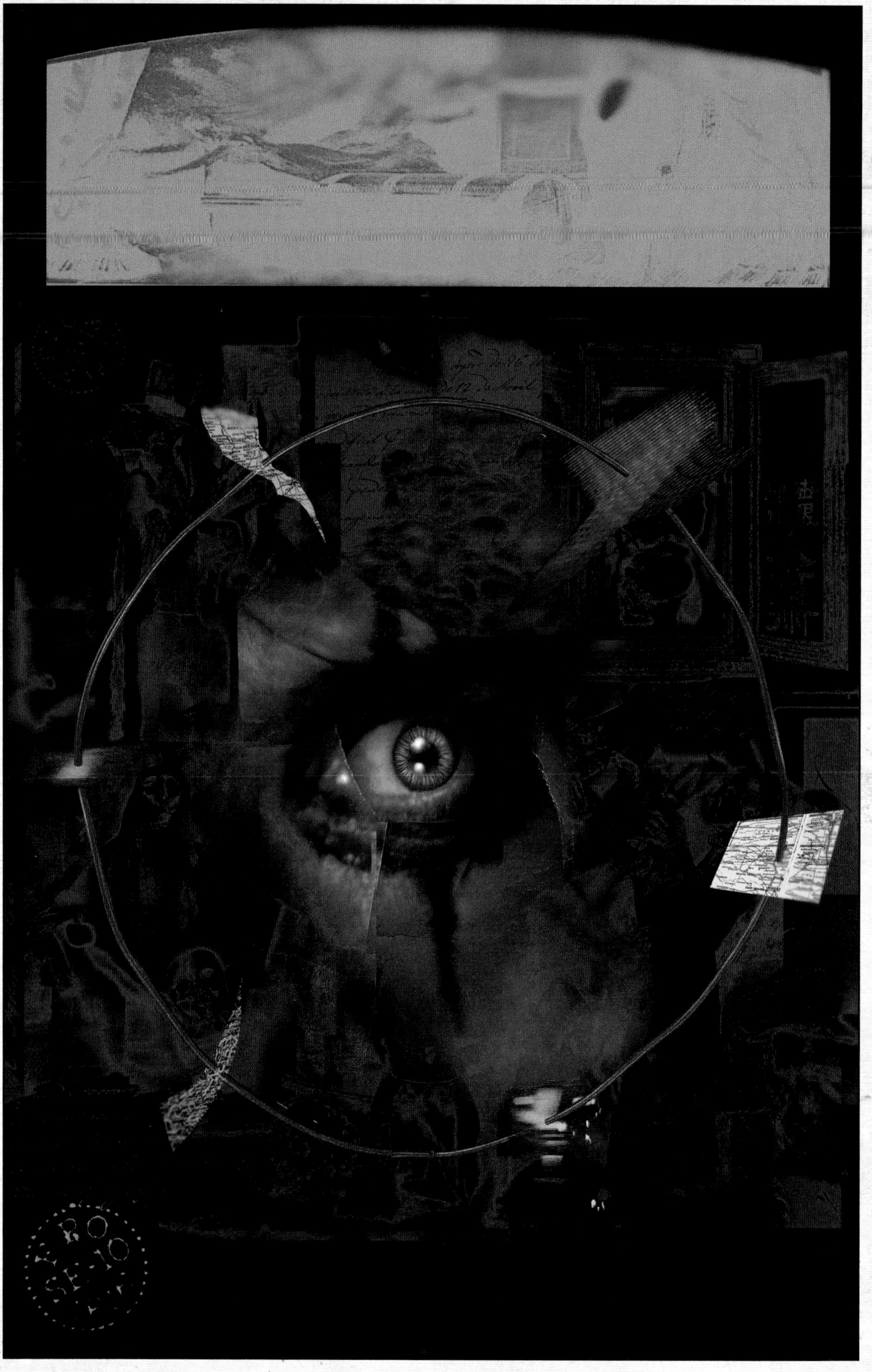

ISSUE ONE

ALTERNATE COVER ART BY DAVE McKEAN

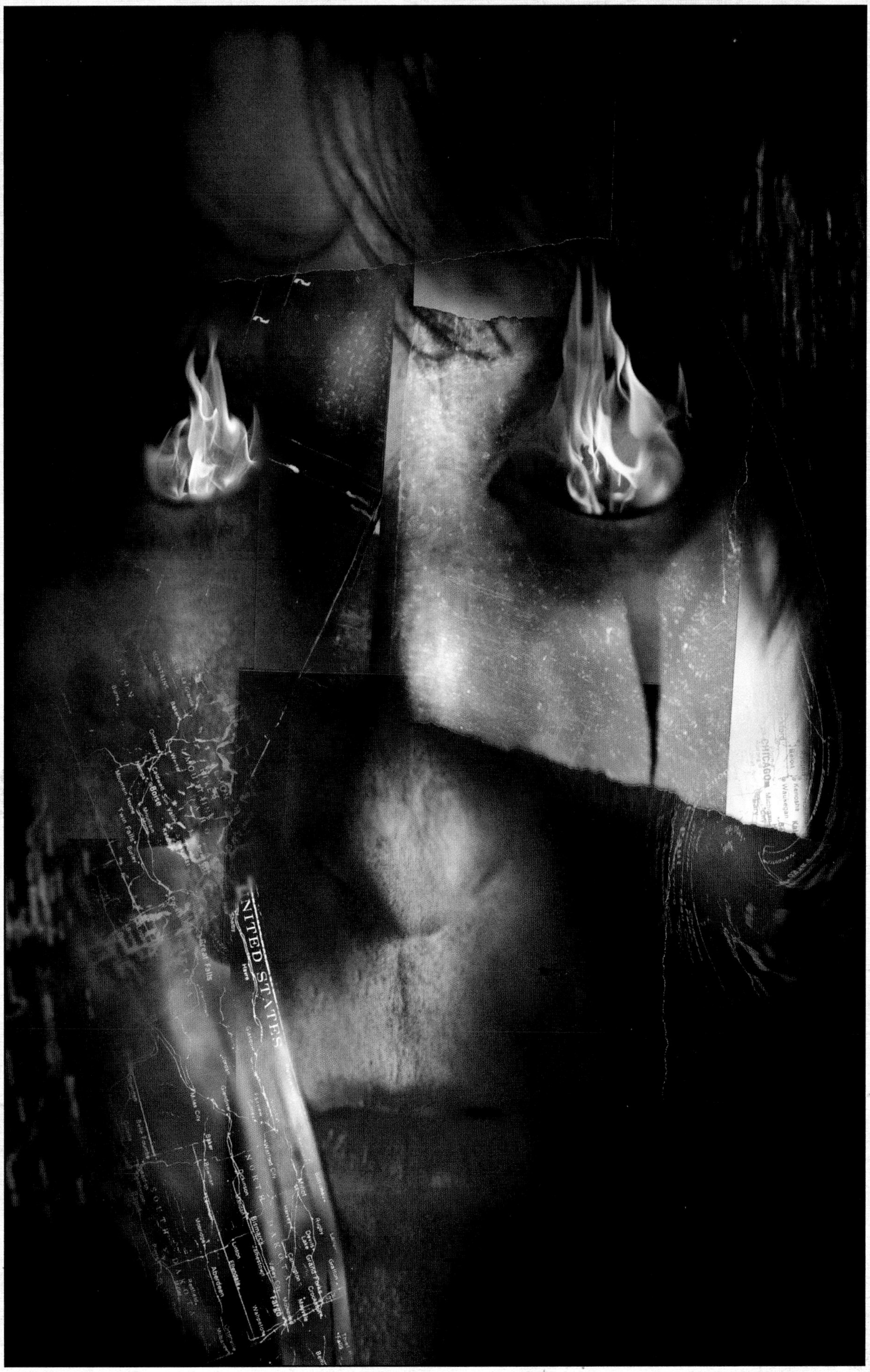

ISSUE TWO

COVER ART BY DAVE McKEAN

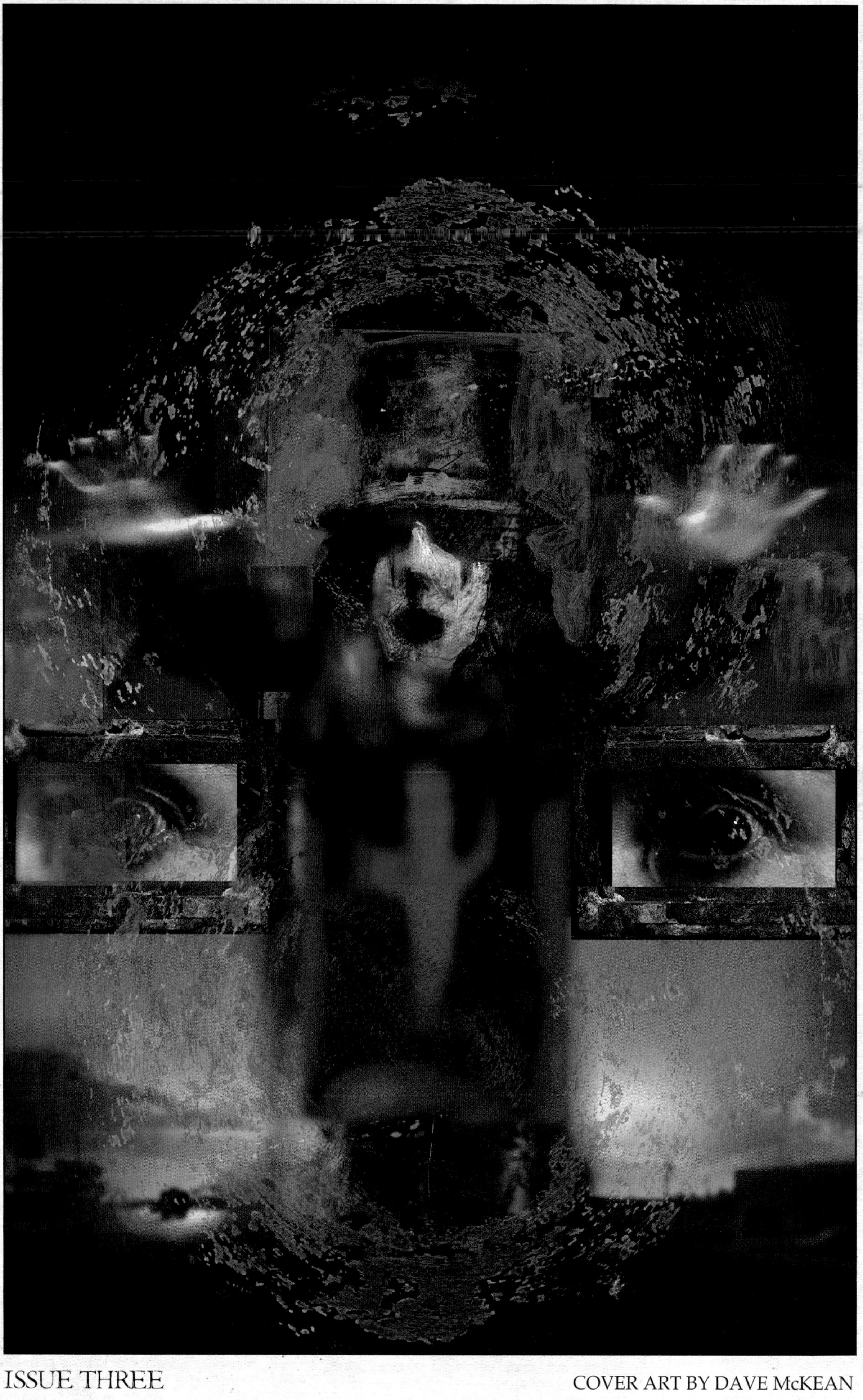

ISSUE THREE

COVER ART BY DAVE McKEAN

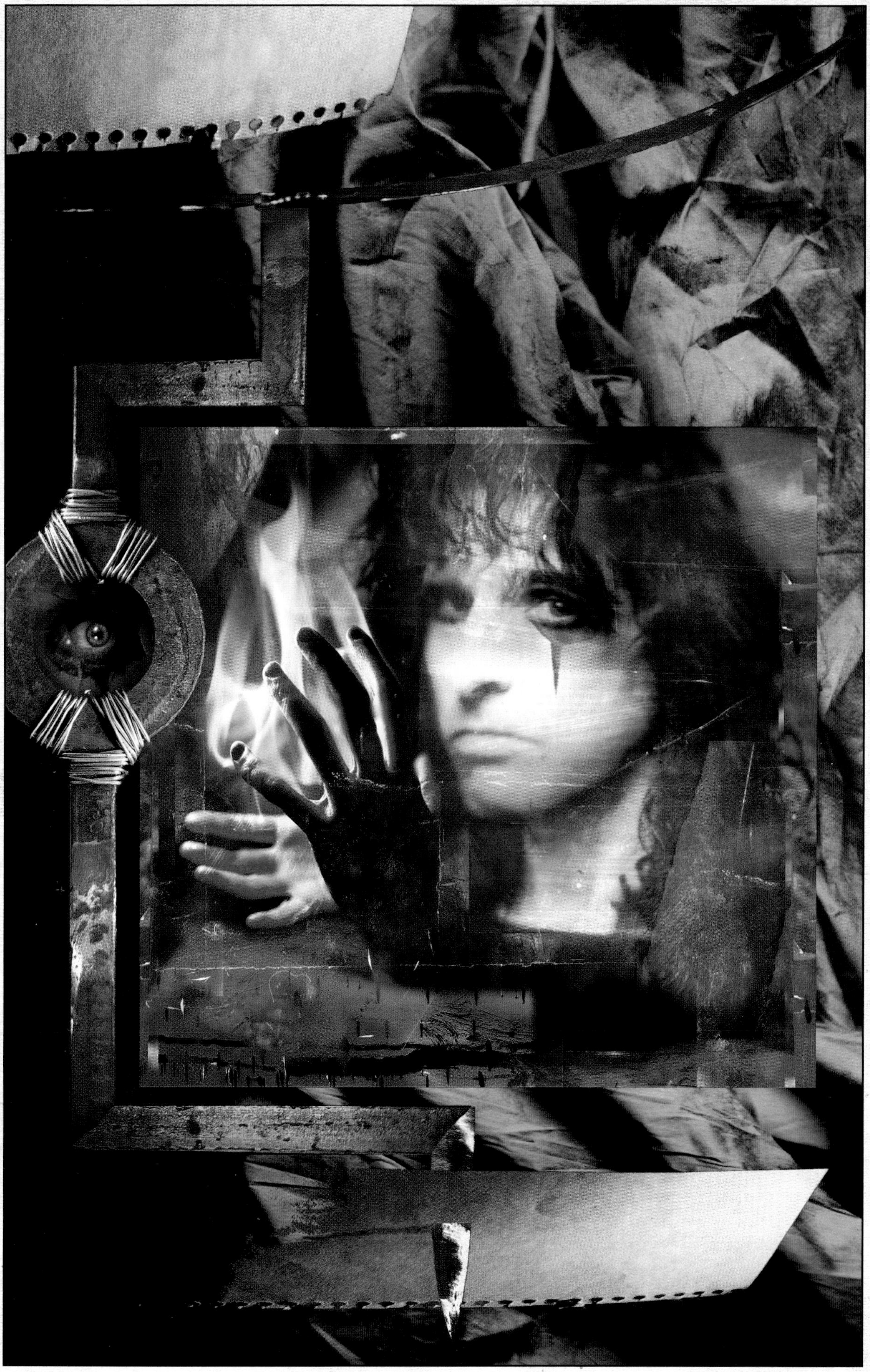

ORIGINAL COLLECTED EDITION

COVER ART BY DAVE McKEAN

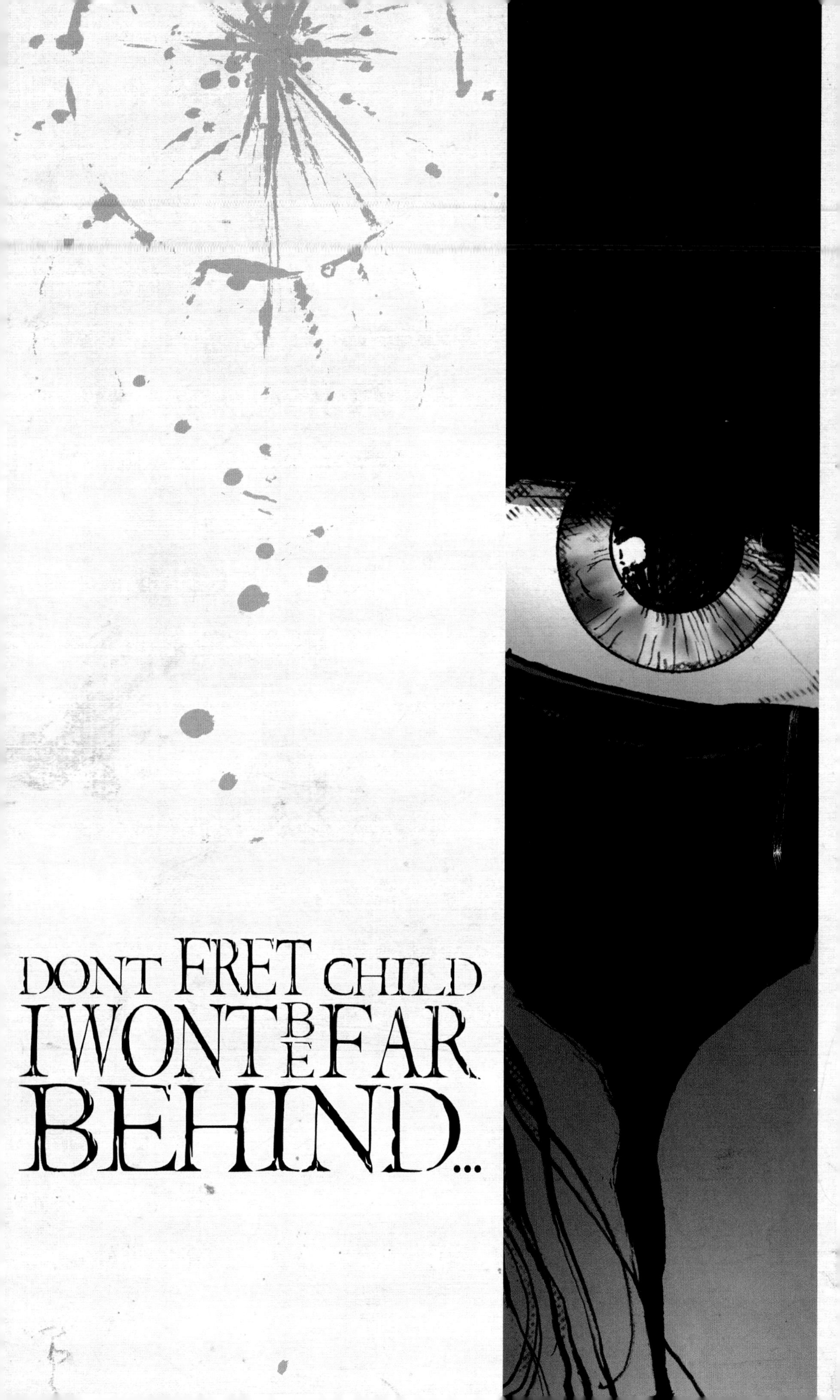
DONT FRET CHILD
I WONT BE FAR
BEHIND...

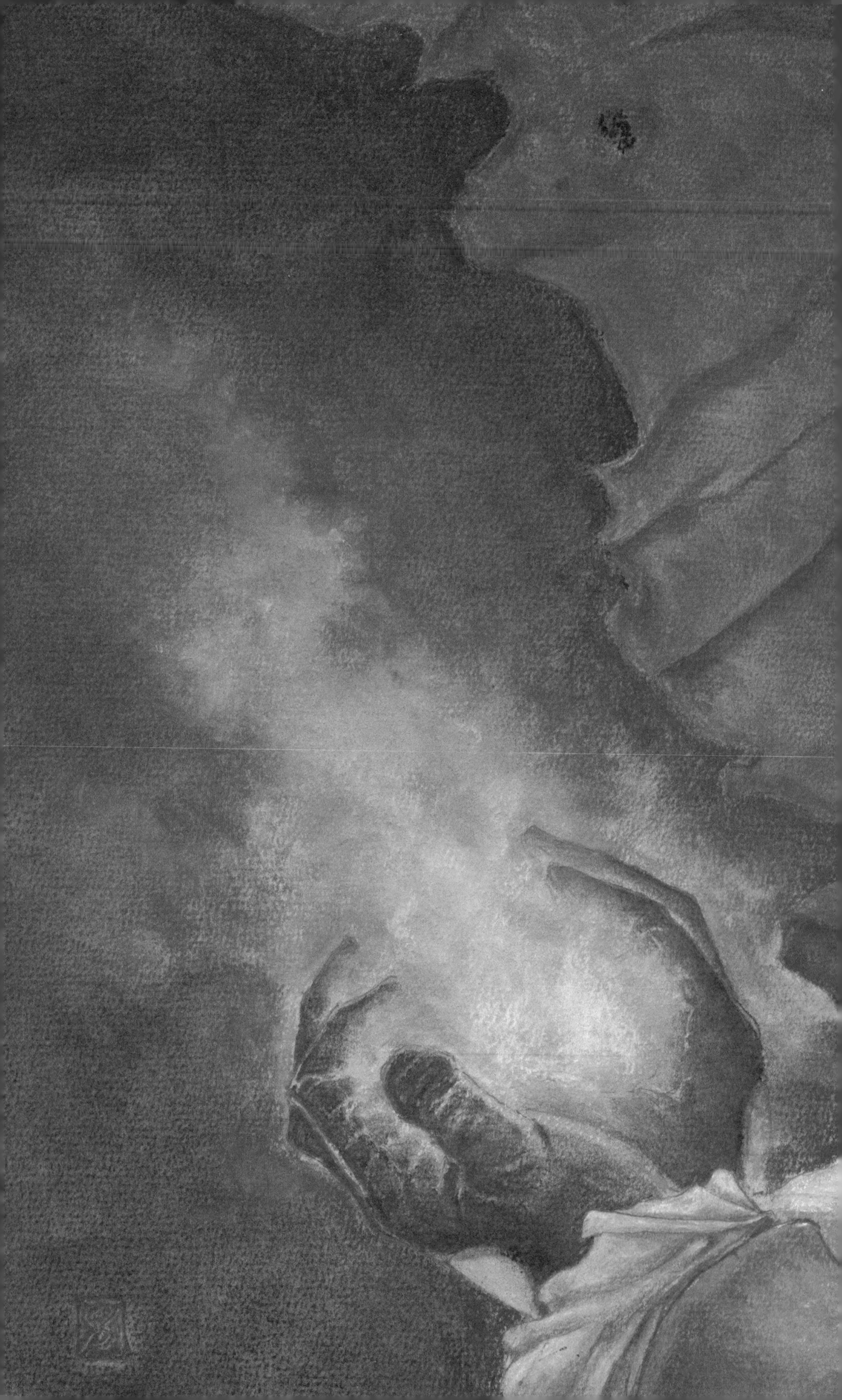